THREE ACTION-PACKED WESTERNS BY SPUR AWARD WINNER NELSON NYE IN ONE LOW-PRICED VOLUME!

GUNFIGHTER BRAND

"Talk is cheap, Sheriff," Blur Ankrom said. "You haven't got the guts to settle my account."

"Why you lousy, dry-gulchin' killer—"

Ankrom's posture did not change until the weapon came into sight. Then his hand went snapping down; like a cracking whip his gun sprang clear of leather.

Tensely, and with bulging eyes in a face gone white, the sheriff stared downward stupidly at the numbed fingers of his shaking hand. His gun was in the sand a good eight feet away, its mechanism jammed by Ankrom's lead.

"You was sayin', Sheriff—?"

BREED OF THE CHAPARRAL

"Come out of there, Tune," Safford yelled.

"Come get me!"

The man jerked up the gun and fired. Tune saw the flame leap from its muzzle. But the shot jarred off and rock dust dribbled down from the roof as Tune's lifted boot took the man in the throat and slammed him into his rising partner. Both men went down in a squirming heap and the squirmer, the bloody-faced man Tune had hit on the head, was too fight-drunk to leave it there and madly reached for the gun Skeet had dropped....

THE KID FROM LINCOLN COUNTY

The guy with the gun in my gut was the marshal. "May as well step along to my office."

I sucked in a fresh breath and went into the marshal's office, hearing him, behind me, advising the crowd to get on about its business.

He came in, slammed the door, parked a hip on the desk. He said, real quiet, "What's it going to be, Farris—reasonable or painful?"

I allowed I would do my best to cooperate.

"Smart boy," he said. "You can start by telling me why you killed him."

"Hell's fire," I said, "I ain't killed nobody."

The place got so quiet you could hear the clock. I had thought he was funning. He wasn't.

NELSON NYE

GUNFIGHTER BRAND/
BREED OF THE
CHAPARRAL/
THE KID FROM
LINCOLN COUNTY

LEISURE BOOKS ⬛ NEW YORK CITY

A LEISURE BOOK®

November 1992

Published by

Dorchester Publishing Co., Inc.
276 Fifth Avenue
New York, NY 10001

GUNFIGHTER BRAND

CHAPTER I

"BLUR" ANKROM

WHERE the trail crossed a high plateau and in the forward distance dipped down again across the desert's wastes the tall, lean rider on the gaunt buckskin halted his dusty animal and sat loosely in the saddle looking back. He scanned the burning backward way with eyes narrowed beneath his down-pulled hatbrim, but no single moving speck disturbed that rearward heat haze that hung like a pall low down against the earth.

This was not the first time that this bronzed rider had halted his mount for a cautious backward glance. Many times during the past few days he had done the same. Once or twice such probing looks had picked up solitary horsemen, but they had been traveling different courses and had held no interest for him.

As he lounged now, with one knee crooked loosely about the horn, his left hand went casually to his shirt pocket and extracted cigarette papers and a pack of Durham. The same left hand rolled a steady smoke and his tongue licked the tiny cylinder while his eyes still scanned the backtrail.

Presently with a shrug he lit the cigarette, broke the match in two and let it drop. Some of the cold intentness left his glance as he faced front once more and kneed the buckskin into forward movement.

He rode leisurely now for the sun was hot and such air as was stirring held a furnace-like quality not unmixed with dust. Yet he left his black neckerchief where it lay about his neck. Had anyone been present to suggest that he draw its folds up across his nose and mouth he would have laughed such suggestion to scorn. He was a desert man and used to dust.

Abraham Lincoln Ankrom he had been named by fond

5

parents in the hope that one day he might be great. But such distinction as had thus far come his way could not have been farther from their dreams. All up and down the twisting length of this Southwestern border country he had achieved fierce notoriety as "Blur" Ankrom—king of the corpsemakers.

He had found no pride in the distinction, nor had he sought it; it had come to fasten upon him octopus-like against his will and every effort. Men had deliberately brought him quarrels that they might lay claim to the eminence of having "downed Blur Ankrom." But their hands had been a little slow. . . .

The lines of his face etched perceptibly deeper as he thought of those drifting leather-slappers whose greedy lust for the reputation he did not want had taken them to hell on shutters. Gradually the realization was being forced upon him that nowhere could he hide himself from their breed or from the constant turmoil that, like some ghostly Nemesis, dogged his horse's steps.

He was grown weary of the fruitless attempts to find some peaceful haven where he might let down, for a moment, the walls of vigilance and relax. Such a place it seemed, for him, did not exist. Peso Pinto lay ahead and there, he told himself, he would stop tonight and give himself the rare treat of a night in bed beneath a roof.

To show himself thus openly in a town, even a place the modest size of Peso Pinto, would of course be dangerous. But danger, loneliness and himself had been constant companions during these last two years. And he was tired of his footless efforts to avoid trouble.

Hard white teeth gleamed coldly behind his parted lips as he recalled the sneering tones of those who held that the Old West was dead—a thing of the dimming past like gun-toting, rustlers and bison. His eyes, glancing downward, held a quizzical light. This cold blue gun with its shiny butt in the dark scuffed holster at his thigh looked anything but a relic of the past.

He crossed the sandy, stifling stretch of desert at a slow lope, passed the white-washed stone marker and urged his buckskin across that invisible line that separated himself from the State of Texas. His glance reached out across the land to where the blue ribbon of paved highway cleaved the arid distance and a twisted grin crossed his clean-shaved lips. Pro-

6

gress now had laid with its mainicured fingers a garish veneer of civilization across all this land, had erected brick buildings, had brought out here the automobile where horses once held sway and cattle once had roamed the unfenced miles. Progress, too, had flung its net of well-paved highways across the sand and lava.

Yet, underneath all this, as he well knew, lay the real Texas, primitive, turbulent, land of smouldering passions and ready trigger fingers. The longhorns may have gone and with them many an oldtime cowman, frontiersman, gambler; but those who had passed along had left behind them kinsmen, sons and daughters—folk whose memory was long and whose blood ran deep and red.

Old scars, old hatreds still remained and festered. None knew this better than Blur Ankrom whose father had been a frontier marshal. Old enmities, from the mere fact of being old, were not discarded here. More than the passing years were needed to wash the bitterness from the veins of dead men's sons.

The afternoon slouched along and the *plop-plop-plop* of the buckskin's hoofs made the only sound in the vast silence of this desert country. To the right of his trail, miles away across the shimmering haze of heat, a broad mountain range rose from the baking earth, one great upthrust peak towering high above its lesser companions. Ankrom knew this peak and from it checked his course.

Presently he could discern far off the sand-scoured adobes of Peso Pinto where they lay squat and solid against the yellow and green of rabbit brush. There he would spend the night. Perhaps, he mused, it would be well to drop his picket pin awhile. Here the danger of recognition, while always present, would not be so great. Word of him must long since have traveled here, yet never had he set foot inside this town, nor for several years had he come near this region. Who could say that this was not the haven of which he had been in search?

So thinking, he urged his mount along a little faster. He was not deceived by the apparent nearness of yon adobe structures. They yet lay many a mile ahead, for in this rarefied atmosphere things distant sixty miles seemed to the uninitiated but a long stone's throw away. This town, he thought, was about eight miles off. This morning had exhausted his

7

meagre supply of provisions and, though he realized that he would not reach his destination until the night was far advanced, he did not hurry his horse but only tightened up his belt.

After awhile he again looked rearward but as before no moving speck crossed his range of vision. He felt slightly more comfortable of mind. For if he had been followed he felt he would have observed some sign before now. Five days had he been upon the trail and not since the first day had he seen signs of any prusuit.

The sun, swinging low behind those distant mountains, was gilding their serrated crests and sending long blue shadows creeping out across the range when Ankrom's hand went toward the pair of felt-covered, metallic canteens that hung from the saddle horn. He had not tasted water since noon and did not taste it now. Into his hat went a portion of the precious liquid to wet the buckskin's muzzle. Ankrom loved this yellow horse; many times had the brute been tried and proved a friend in need.

Darkness came—the deep, dense darkness of the desert country. Presently came the stars and moon in turn to soften and make beautiful the night and bathe the plains in an argent glow and dapple them with cobalt shadows.

It was close to eleven o'clock when Ankrom reached Peso Pinto's northern fringe and beheld the electric lights of its old adobe structures close up ahead. Though he had eaten nothing since early morning he did not hurry even now. In this country a man in a hurry attracted instant attention and attention was one thing Ankrom did not wish.

He entered the town at a leisurely gait, tugged his hatbrim lower down across the alert blue eyes that were flicking probing glances into the shadows to left and right. Embarrassing situations confronted persons caught packing hardware inside town limits, he recalled. Pausing, he unpacked his slicker roll, took from it a coat which he donned and placed in it his gun belt and empty holster. The big gun he thrust into the waist band of his trousers in such a position that his open coat concealed it.

Sidelong glances disclosed to him that this end of town was not its best neighborhood. There were many saloons with beer and soft drink signs plastered on their dusty windows, and divers other places of even less repute. There were quite

8

a number of machines parked along this ill-lit street and here and there a cowpony dozing beside a post.

Unaccosted, Ankrom continued on his way until, passing a high false-fronted frame, he heard a woman's startled cry. The buckskin stopped of its own volition while Ankrom's tall lean form went tense. His narrowed eyes peered through the wavering shadows while he set the saddle moveless. A banjo tinkled from a place several doors removed. A burst of laughter came from the building across the street. Thoughtfully Ankrom dismounted, trailed his buckskin's reins.

That startled cry had seemed to come from close at hand from the false-fronted frame before which he stood. And yet this seemed unlikely for the place was dark and shuttered. He stooped down beside his horse as though inspecting the saddle's cinch.

Seconds passed and he finally straightened. He cursed himself for a fool; told himself this thing was none of his business. His proper course was to ride along. "Never trouble trouble till trouble trouble's you," he quoted softly, and was reaching for the horn with one foot lifting toward the near stirrup when the cry reached out again.

Slowly Ankrom set his foot down, the outthrust arm returned to his side. He turned then and stared deliberately at the wooden building. There was no movement among the shadows about its door. Boots came clumping toward him along the board walk; a burly man slouched past. Ankrom watched the fellow till he turned a distant corner and passed out of sight.

"Uncommon odd," he muttered and eyed the house again. He felt sure now that the cries he'd heard had come from there. The last one had been a sort of gasp. Slowly, not quite knowing just what he was going to do, Blur Ankrom started forward.

He was almost to the door when a scream sheared through the gloom. Thin and high it was and stopped abruptly as though a hand had roughly clamped across the mouth.

Ankrom hurled his body sideways. What warned him he did not know, yet even as he moved a gleaming thing of metal whizzed past three inches from his shoulder, embedded itself in the post beside his horse with a vibrating *chunk*.

Forward toward that door sprang Ankrom frantically.

From the smoky shadows about it flitted a dim-seen shape on silent feet and vanished in the gloom.

The muscles bulged like ropes along Ankrom's jaw as his shoulder struck the door and smashed it inward. His momentum flung him across the threshold reeling into a room dim-lit by a low-turned lamp that showed him three men crouched motionless before a wild-eyed girl who was lashed to a chair. By their clothes and evil faces he knew these for city thugs. A glowing branding iron was gripped in the outstretched hand of the nearest.

As Ankrom caught his balance that man snarled, "What the hell!" and let drive with the red hot iron straight at his head.

Ankrom ducked. When he came up the right hands of the thugs were behind them in hip pockets and were coming out weighted.

Ankrom had no choice. It was his life or theirs. One brown fist flashed beneath his coat and came out spitting flame in a steady stream. Deafening reverberations rocked the narrow room and snuffed the lamp, plunging the place in blackness through which cut lance-like jets of fire from belching weapons.

Something struck Ankrom's right shoulder heavily, smashed him backward and whirled him half around. From the tail of his eye he saw a black shape slide outward through the open doorway . . .

Cautiously the silence came creeping back.

For long moments, tensely alert, Ankrom crouched motionless in the gloom with leveled gun held ready. But nothing moved. Finally he struck a match.

One of those thugs lay slumped against a wall with open glazing eyes. Another was face down on the dusty floor with one arm outflung, the other doubled beneath him; his feet sprawled wide apart. The third had vanished.

The girl's eyes were upon him intently. There was some strange, unreadable emotion stirring in their depths. A dirty handkerchief had been tightly bound across her mouth; no doubt placed there after she had screamed. He moved toward her where she sat lashed to the chair and her eyes remained steadily on his face. There was a question in them now and a little frown between them.

He wished he could read her thoughts, but could not. An acrid stench of burning wood came to his nostrils and stopped

10

him in his tracks. Half turning he threw a glance across his shoulders. That branding iron—

A twisted grin cut his bronzed jowls angularly as the match in his fingers flickered out and the black shadows came crowding back. He struck a second, moved with it toward the lamp. A movement of the girl's head stopped him. She was shaking it negatively and a command was in her eyes.

He wheeled and went to her, took the gag from across her mouth. Her lips moved grotesquely but no distinguishable words came, only vague croaking sounds. Deep anger stirred within him for the renegades who had tied that filthy rag so tightly, and a wave of darkness crossed his tautened cheeks.

He passed behind the girl—she could not have been more than nineteen, he thought—and inspected the knots that held her fettered there. He snuffed the match, let it fall broken from his fingers. Then he hunkered down, working swiftly in the murky dark. Short seconds later the ropes fell away and she was free. Her voice came then huskily:

"That branding iron! Don't leave it—"

"I'll get it, ma'am," he said, and crossed to where a red glow marked its bite. He came back to her with it. "You been hurt?"

"I'm all right. Those . . . those men on the floor?"

"They won't bother you any more." There was no remorse in him for their passing. It had been his life or theirs and their fate had been justly earned. "Be a good idea if we got out of this. Two of them polecats got away. I reckon there's more where they come from. Can you walk, ma'am?"

"I think so. Will you strike another match, please?"

In him there was a strong admiration for her. She had a poise and serenity that struck a responding chord deep within him. He found himself wondering why she had screamed. That branding iron . . .

With a rasp a third match in his hand burned blue and yellow against the enshrouding gloom. Framed in chestnut curls her oval face was before him, leaping from the retreating shadows. Interest was strong in him and he studied her, found her good to look upon. Deep strength lay in her features and a latent storminess that made her personality intriguing. She was standing now and her tailored suit could not conceal the lovely lines of her slender figure. The charm of

11

her tugged at him, played havoc with his senses. Many women he had known—but none like her.

Her eyes lifted to his own, returned his scrutiny directly. "I'm glad you came. My name is Lee—Lee Trone."

"I was wonderin'. I'm Abe Streeter." he said it evenly. and no darkening cheek belied his words.

"You're a range man. Stranger?"

"Just driftin' through."

"Would you take a job?"

"Ranch work?"

"*On* a ranch."

"There's a difference?" he asked it softly.

"There may be—it depends."

"What on?"

She shrugged. Her eyes were on his fairly. In them he read something that stirred his blood, that hastened the beat of his pulses against his will.

She said, "This business here . . . there's a connection somewhere. My father runs the Rafter T. Cattle. High grade beef. It's sprouting wings . . ."

He snapped the match in two, flipped the pieces outward in a falling arc. He started her toward the doorway. Here it was, he was thinking; circumstance and that streak of rash impulsiveness in his nature were once again shoving him toward a quarrel of which he knew nothing. He sighed and yet his being quickened. He looked outward when they reached the doorway and saw the same old mocking stars agleam in the purple sky.

He was tired and there was a half desire inside him to mount his horse and ride away; to ride away before the sticky web of this new trouble enmeshed and snared him. He stopped by the doorway and silently handed this Lee Trone the branding iron she had told him not to leave behind. He noted its brand without consciously being aware of the fact.

He was ejecting the spent cartridges from his pistol, placing fresh ones in his emptied chambers. Her voice came to him with conviction:

"They won't be back. They'll have to report and get instructions."

His mind took in the import of her words but was busy with something else. "That branding iron," he said. "You know, they woudn't have dared to really use it. I been wonderin' why you screamed."

Though her reply was low, conviction fired her words and he could not doubt:

"I was afraid. And you're wrong. That iron was the reason I was lured here. It was to have been used on me."

The Old West had gone forever, eh? In the darkness Ankrom's grin was twisted. Some people had a lot to learn!

CHAPTER II

ABE STREETER TAKES A JOB

WE had better be cleanin' out," he said. "Those shots must have been heard."

Keeping to the shadows they moved toward the street, reached it. "This place has a reputation. Unsavory. Shots are common—dead men, too. I don't think you could drag the neighbors near here till the authorities have come and gone. They may be watching, though."

"How did you get here?"

"I have a car. Have you decided to take that job I offered you? The pay will be one hundred and fifty dollars payable regularly once a month."

Ankroms lips pursed in a soundless whistle. "You tryin' to buy a manager?"

Her voice came frankly, shearing straight to the point with the directness of a man's. "I'm trying to buy loyalty."

"Does it come that high?"

"I haven't found any yet." There was no irony in her answer, only a slow wistfulness.

His blue eyes, cold and alert beneath his hatbrim, were questing the shadows about them. Against his will her words had moved him.

"You don't know a thing about me, Miss Trone—"

"Abe, will you take this job?"

The soft melody of her voice touched him strangely, stirred unsuspected longings. It disturbed the cold deliberation of his

13

thoughts and caused his blood to leap. It brought a strong appeal to that streak of rash impulsiveness that had ever been his direct undoing. "Yes," he said. "I'll take it."

He found her hand in his. A moment only it lay there, warm and pulsing. But that moment was one he could long remember. She said:

"You have a horse?"

He nodded. "The bucksikn."

A glow of appreciation lit her eyes. "You'll not be wanting a lift, then. I'll see you at the ranch tomorrow. The Rafter T—twenty miles due west. You'll find it. We'll be expecting you by supper." With a smile then she turned and left him, walking rapidly down the ill-lit street.

He watched her until she stopped and entered a long, rakish touring car. He heard the door slam shut. Then he turned to the buckskin, his mind a maze of interested speculation, his vigilance temporarily relaxed.

"Just a moment, friend," a voice beside him said. "I'd like a word with you."

A rough-looking man with a star on his vest stood anchored at Ankrom's stirrup. An arc light, affixed high up on the post, shed glaring light down on them; showed Ankrom there was a cruel twist to this man's mouth. He read harsh purpose in the fellow's narrowed glance.

"You better come along with me."

"Yeah? Who are you? An' where do you think we're goin'?" Ankrom drawled.

The man with the star grinned meaningly. "I'm marshal of this town, buddy. We're goin' to take a look inside that house," he added, and his left hand flapped an explanatory flip toward the house Ankrom had just left.

"Supposin' I don't want to?"

"I ain't supposin'. You'll go, buddy, whether you want to or not. An' don't get tough—I've handled hard guys before. D'you hear them shots?"

Ankrom nodded.

"See who fired 'em?"

"I saw a fellow go dashin' out of there a few minutes ago."

"Who was he?"

"If I could tell you that I'd make my livin' tellin' fortunes," Ankrom grinned.

"Yeah? Well, you may be makin' your livin' busting

14

little ones from big ones before I get done with you. You packing' a gun?"

"You don't see any, do you?"

"Listen, you— I've had enough of your gab." The marshal flared, cheeks darkening. "You got a gun or ain't you? Talk straight.."

There was open mockery in Ankrom's glance.

The marshal's left hand brushed aside his flowery vest, his right went beneath it. Blue windswept ice glinted in his eyes.

Ankrom said, "Yeah— I got a gun," and saw the marshal's reaching hand grow still. There was a cool maliciousness in Ankrom's voice, hard white teeth gleamed coldly behind his parted lips: "You want to see it?"

"Huh?" The marshal started. "No, I don't want to see it —not yet. Come along. We're goin' to look round inside that house an' see what all that shootin' was for."

"No we're not. You may be, but *I* got different notions. I'll be sayin' 'Adios'."

"Not by a damned sight!" the marshal snarled, and the hand inside his vest pushed deeper. Ankrom knew that in another second there would be gunplay if he let matters take their natural course. And he had had enough of shooting for one night. He half turned, as though to mount his horse, whirled in a blurring arc that landed a smashing left to the marshal's jaw. Beneath that battering blow the marshal's head rocked back, his body followed, struck the post behind and slid down it heavily to lie grotesquely motionless in the dusty gutter.

Ankrom's left foot came up and he reached for the saddle horn, grasped it. Yet even as his fingers closed about it and his horse got into motion with a forward lunge a bullet whistled past his head, the gun-bark slamming echoes back and forth across the street. Before the buckskin had taken seven rocketing strides with its pounding hoofs, guns were spitting leaden death from all directions, save dead ahead.

A machine gun's raucous song went *rat-a-tat-tat-tat-tating* in wild refrain, cleaving through and above the sounds of lesser voices. Lead sang periously close as Ankrom put a row of parked machines between himself and the crouching forms that swarmed like bees behind him. One swift backward look across his shoulder disclosed the marshal struggling up. He

15

was on his knees and rising higher when, with a sudden shriek, he flattened in his tracks.

Toward the second floors of the wooden structures fringing this street Ankrom's eyes were drawn by the rattle and bang of upflung windows as, for a moment, the machine-gunner's weapon went dry. Parted red curtains framed women's pale faces from half a dozen houses. One, a little nearer than the rest, leaned out across the sill with frantically beckoning hand:

"Up here, cowboy! Quick!" she cried, and Ankrom saw that she had beautiful yellow hair that shone like a golden halo around her outthrust head in the radiance of some unseen light behind her. But that was all that Ankrom saw, save a fleeting glimpse of piquant features in the vague oval that was her face. Then he was gone, tearing down the road at breakneck speed while shouts and curses and crashing guns made hideous the night behind.

Ankrom's progress westward was leisurely. He doubted much that any town lay between Peso Pinto in this direction and his objective, the Rafter T. Nor was he wrong. The country, where not entirely sand and cactus, was semi-arid desert country; habitations were few and far between.

The following morning he stopped at a small-spread ranch and breakfasted. There was plenty to eat; a fortunate circumstance, for he was ravenously hungry. Smoking, he and the rancher sat awhile at the table after they had finished, and the rancher's son sat with them, sucking on a corncob pipe that was loaded with an evil-smelling mixture.

"Seem to me," Ankrom said casually, "a fella named Trone owns a spread around here somewhere—Rafter T, ain't it?"

The rancher and his son exchanged furtive glances. "Trone? Well, yeah. There is a Trone around here some place. Friend of his?"

"Don't even know him. Heard his name mentioned a couple times. In the cattle business, ain't he?"

The rancher's son spoke around his pipe and his tone was surly: "You seem to know all about him."

Ankrom shrugged his shoulders, smoked awhile in silence. An atmosphere of suspicion seemed to have settled upon this room. He could feel it like an air current pressing insistently

16

against him. But no awareness of the fact was permitted to show upon his face.

"Any outfits round here that could use an extra hand?"

"What kind of a hand?" The rancher's eyes were on him and there was a cold intentness in them.

Ankrom drawled, "What kind of a hand usually rides for a brand?"

"You ain't no common puncher."

Ankrom let the statement lay. Suspicion and unfriendliness rolled across the interval and heavily lapped against him. These men were taking him apart with their thoughts, probing him, weighing him bit by bit. He swept cool smoke gustily into his lungs, expelled it in blue spirals from his nostrils. His eyes were watchful, mocking.

"You ain't no drifter, neither." The rancher's glance said, "What are you doing in this country?" But he did not put it into words.

Ankrom's features were immobile; cold as sculptured marble they gave nothing of his thoughts away. Plainly Trone and the Rafter T as subjects for conversation were tabu. "No," he said, "I'm not a drifter. I'm a man that works at his trade. You don't know of any outfits that are hirin', eh?"

"Not your kind of man."

Ankrom sat motionless a moment and the room took on a chill. Then he crushed his cigarette upon his plate and with a short laugh rose to his feet.

"You might try that Rafter T you mentioned!"

The spitefulness of the tone drew Ankrom's eyes to the gangling youth across the table. "Yeah," he said. "I think I will."

For long hours after leaving the place Ankrom rode at a comfortable jog across the undulating range, seeing neither other riders nor other habitations. In the distance to right and left blue mountains shimmered in the heat haze. The silence of this vast country was like a brooding threat.

There was at times a gnawing sadness in him that in this land he was not to find that haven of refuge which he sought. That he was not to find it was an obvious fact, he told himself, for already he had become embroiled in the trouble which menaced the Rafter T. By his act last night in delivering Lee Trone from the hands of those who would have harmed her, he had definitely placed himself in the position of being an

17

enemy to the power aligned against her family. Unless he rode forthwith from the country he would be dragged steadily deeper into the quagmire of turmoil which he sensed ahead. There was no side stepping this business—nor would he attempt to. He had passed his word.

The sun was swinging low behind the western peaks in a valley spread below him, Ankrom obtained his first glimpse of the Rafter T.

Timbered ridges pushed up around this valley in such way that cold winter winds would be forced to pass it by. The sun's long slanting rays struck gleaming sparkles of silvery light from the rippled surface of a stream that cleaved its gurgling way behind a group of old log buildings. From where he sat his saddle Ankrom could pick out the ranch house easily. It was the only building boasting a veranda and before it was parked a long, low rakish touring car—the car Lee Trone had entered in Peso Pinto the night before.

Ankrom sent the buckskin down the trail. As he neared the buildings the talk and laughter of a group of loafing punchers by the bunk house fell away. He could feel their eyes upon him, intently probing. He swung down before the ranch house porch.

A man broke from the group beside the bunk house, came striding forward purposefully. Ankrom, watching him come, saw that he was a tight-lipped, bottle-nosed man whose bowed legs were encased in scarred black bat-wing chaps. His was a burly figure, solid and strong and hard. He was close to forty, Ankrom judged. There was an arrogance in his stride and a something in his manner that bespoke a wicked temper.

"You lookin' for somebody?"

"This the Rafter T?"

"You got any business on it?"

"You got a special reason for askin'?"

"I'm the fella that runs this outfit. I'm not doin' any hirin' so you can just climb back on that nag an' be on your way."

The blue of Ankrom's eyes beat hard against him. "I've got a job already," the drawling softness of Ankrom's words reached out and snapped dull color to the range boss' cheeks, lit a gleam of flame in the range boss' eyes.

"What you doin' round here, then? 'D you bring a message of some kind—"

Ankrom cut in, looking the man steadily between the eyes: "I got a message for you. Abe Streeter's on your payroll. Go write his name in the book."

The thin lips of the range boss parted. Then, as though his mind had changed, he shut them tightly without speaking. He folded his thick arms deliberately across his heavy chest, looked Ankrom up and down while the red flame in his eyes took shape and brightened.

Ankrom without a word swung into his saddle. He kneed the buckskin toward the group of watching punchers beside the bunkhouse. A grin twitched across one man's face and vanished. Ankrom heard the range boss' voice break raggedly across the silence: "Where the bloody hell you goin'?" But he gave no sign that he had heard, nor did he answer.

When he reached the bunk house he dismounted and trailed the buckskin's reins. No man spoke while he took his blanket roll and slicker from behind the cantle. But when he started toward the bunk house door the harsh clump of running boots beat out behind him.

His left foot was lifted to cross the threshold when a heavy hand clamped viselike upon his shoulder, jerked him viciously around. He dropped the blanket roll and slicker. The range boss' ruddy face was within three inches of his own.

"Damn you! I said I—"

"I'm not deaf," Ankrom's modulated drawl cut off the other's flow; Ankrom's chill blue eyes were upon him with malicious interest. "I heard what you said the first time. Mebbe you don't understand American—*I* said *I*'d been hired already."

"You—you—" The range boss swore a lurid oath that brought admiring glances from his men. "You get to hell on outa here!"

Ankrom's body sagged a little at the knees, his upper body settled slightly forward. He stood like this and stared, arms hanging strangely at his sides. The long fingers of his hands were a little flexed. "You figgerin' to put me out?"

There was a noticeable shifting of the group behind the burly man. He looked around and scowled. His smouldering glance snapped back to Ankrom. His voice was thick: "Who hired you?"

"That's somethin' you can talk over with ol' man Trone," Ankrom said and, picking up his things, passed on inside.

CHAPTER III

COMPLICATIONS

HARDLY had the men of the Rafter T concluded their supper and started fishing in their pockets for the "makings" that a shadow darkened the mess shack's doorway. Mose Hackett, the range boss, stood there swinging his smouldering glance about the room. It stopped abruptly when it reached Ankrom and through it there flickered swiftly some unreadable emotion.

The range boss growled, "Streeter, the Ol' Man wants to see you up at the house. Right away." Without waiting for a reply, he turned upon his heel and passed from view, heading toward his private shanty across the yard.

Ankrom could feel the eyes of his companions upon him. His face was inscrutable as he rose leisurely from his place, pulled the last lungful of smoke from his cigarette and ground the butt into a dish. Still without speaking he passed through the open doorway and out into the thickening gloom of early night.

When he reached the ranch house a vague slim shape was there awaiting him among the shadows of the veranda. He sensed that it was the girl, Lee Trone. Her voice reached out to him softly: "You came, then, after all."

"I reckon I did, ma'am."

"Did you have any trouble on the way . . . ?"

"What kind of trouble did you think I might be havin', ma'am?"

There was silence for a moment, then she said, "Dad will be waiting for you in his office. It is the first room off the right of the hall. I—I have told him that you are the friend of some friends of ours in Arizona; that I happened to run

20

across you in town last night and offered you a job. Good night."

She stepped past him and entered the touring car. A second later Ankrom heard the soft sleek purring of the motor, the blended meshing of the gears. Twin beams of brilliant light cut gleaming parallel paths across the deepening night. With the crunch of gravel the car moved smoothly off across the yard.

Ankrom turned then and entered the house. Upon the first door to the right of the hall the entrance gave upon he knocked. "Come in," a gruff voice bade and Ankrom entered an electrically-lighted room and shut the door behind him.

His eyes went at once to the room's sole occupant, a man whom he judged to be well above sixty, who rose from behind a desk placed a little to the left of the door. This man Ankrom knew at a glance for the girl's father. Pinched of cheek he was, and firm of lip. His dark features held the weather-bitten appearance of having been much in the windy open. His was a big-boned frame—big, but gaunt with the leanness of a man too familiar with a horse's back. He thrust a wrinkled brown hand across the unmarred surface of the desk and Ankrom gripped it.

"Son," Trone said, "I'm glad to know you. Streeter's the name? Abe Streeter? Well, I'm glad to know any friend of Colonel Struthers. How is the Colonel? Been some time since I've seen the boss of the XOT."

"He's making out," Ankrom said.

"Lee tells me she ran across you in town last night."

"Well, we met. She invited me out. Said you could use another hand." A whimsical light appeared far back in Ankrom's eyes. "I'm kind of at loose ends right now an' a job of work would suit me fine."

"Glad to have you with us—" Trone broke off to stare past Ankrom's head. "What is it, Hackett?"

Ankrom had heard the opening of the door, but had not turned. He did so now and saw the burly range boss standing in the doorway. Hackett did not look at him. "I was figurin' to see you about that load of—"

"If you reckon on talking business with me," Trone cut in, "come back later."

"Well—" Now Hackett's eyes turned full upon Ankrom and there was cold hostility in them. "I was figurin' on ridin' out to the southeast line camp in a few minutes."

21

"We'll talk business later then," Trone's voice held a note of gruff finality.

The foreman nodded curtly, strode heavily away. But in that look he'd flashed at Ankrom there had been a definite threat. There was a strong vanity in the man; he would not forget that scene before the bunkhouse. He would bide his time until an opportunity came that would enable him to even up the score for the loss of caste inflicted on him by Ankrom before his men.

Ankrom found Old Man Trone studying him shrewdly. "What's up between you an' Hackett, son?"

"Hackett? . . . Oh, you mean that fella? Shucks, I don't even know the gent."

But Trone was not fooled, Ankrom saw, by this evasion. "Hackett's an odd man," the rancher said in a musing sort of way. "Good cow man; knows his business. But he's a man that takes a deal of pleasure out of giving orders. When he gives one, he usually aims to see that it's obeyed. Likewise, he knows a thing or two about guns. He's a man most folks try to get along with."

Ankrom grinned. "I know my place," he said. "I don't know a whole lot about guns, but I reckon I could find the trigger if I had to."

"Well, sit down, son. Visitors are too scarce around this range not to be treated with proper respect."

So Ankrom pulled up a chair and tilted it back against the wall. A hour sped by while they talked about cattle, horses, range conditions and this and that.

"Guess I better be gettin' on back to the bunk house. 'Twouldn't do for the boys to be gettin' the idea I was too familiar. I—" he broke off as he heard the purr of a motor in the yard outside. It was cut off swiftly with a squeal of breaks, a car door slammed and high heels tapped across the veranda. The door opened and Lee Trone came into the room. There was a letter in her hand.

"Dad," she said with sparkling eyes, "Colonel Struthers and Betty are on their way to Dallas. They're going to stop off with us for a week or ten days and visit!"

Trone looked at Ankrom and a pleased grin crossed his grizzled lips. "Say, now! that sure is fine!"

To Ankrom the prospect appeared anything but fine. Why

22

had this Lee Trone felt it incumbent on herself to tell her father that Ankrom, or "Streeter" as she knew him, was an old friend of these old friends of theirs? Why, indeed, had she even deemed it necessary to tell him anything save that he was a hand looking for a riding job? Certainly, she seemed not to have mentioned their adventure last night in Peso Pinto.

But that wasn't the only odd thing about this business, he told himself. The whole layout was odd! Why should those city thugs have lured her to that disreputable neighborhood? Why were they attempting to run a brand on her? Or weren't they? Why did the Rafter T's neighbors regard this spread and its owner as bad subjects for conversation with strangers? Was there some sort of a range war building up?

It would not surprise him a great deal, he thought. Things and people Western were not as tame and humdrum as some folks would like to believe!

He looked up and found Lee Trone's glance upon him. The laughter now had left her eyes and in its stead he saw a tiny cloud. As plainly as though she had spoken the fact aloud, he realized that she was now tardily recalling the lie in which she had involved him with these prospective guests. He felt a little thrill of malicious satisfaction stir him as he saw how the possibilities of the situation were coming home to her.

He said good night to her father and with a nod to her passed down the hall. She caught up with him among the shadows of the veranda and placed a hand upon his arm.

"Abe What will I do? Those people are coming here tomorrow!"

"Didn't you think they might when you told your Dad I was a friend of theirs?"

"Of course not! I had no idea they were coming." She bit her lip in vexation. "This is not going to be exactly comfortable for any of us."

"I expect not. I shouldn't wonder but we'll manage to live through it, though." The derisive mockery in his voice was plain. "Why didn't you tell your Dad about that affair in Peso Pinto? Lies are dangerous things—especially when they come flocking home to roost."

"But I never dreamed . . . I couldn't have told Dad about that business in town. You don't understand— He has troubles enough of his own without my bringing him any of mine."

"Well," he said roughly, "I might be able to understand bet-

23

ter if you gave me a hint or two as to what this is all about. You can't expect me to be much help while I'm goin' it blind."

He could see the vague, pale outline of her face among the shadows and knew that she was trying to read his expression; knew, too, that she could not. Had it been broad daylight now she still would have been unable to come by the sight of his features to any definite conclusion, for his face was wrapped in a mask of cold inscrutability.

"You—you don't understand," she began when he cut in.

"You said that before. We're wastin' time. I'll say good night to you ma'am."

Her grip tightened on his arm and stopped him. "I'll trust you, Abe," her voice came huskily. "Let's get in the car. You can drive it into the stable. We can talk there without anyone seeing us."

He helped her into the machine, climbed in behind the wheel. The motor thrummed to life and he shoved in the clutch, meshed the gears and they rolled bumpily into the stable. He shut off the motor and doused the lights. "Well?" he said, a perverse mood upon him. "Let's hear the yarn."

Her breath was indrawn sharply. He felt a twinge of conscience. "I'm sorry—"

But she cut him off: "I know—you think I'm a little liar! Go on and say it!"

He could not see her face in this darkness, but he knew by the tenseness of her posture that she was mad—mad at herself for the position into which she had lied them both, and mad at him for taunting her. He changed the subject slightly:

"Are these troubles of your Dad's connected with the ranch?"

"I think so."

"Don't you know?"

"I'm not sure. He never confides in me . . . These last few months he's become very reticent. He's grown moody. It's—it's so difficult to explain; it's nothing you can put your finger on, but there's a feeling about this place that never used to be here. It's like sitting atop a volcano and waiting for it to erupt."

A thoughtful silence fell between them. "Perhaps," Ankrom suggested, "it's money matters that's botherin' him. This has been a tough year most places, water holes dryin' up, springs

24

peterin' out an' grass burned to a crisp. You've got better water here than your neighbors, I expect. They might let their resentment spur 'em into somethin' that would end in powder-smoke. No tellin' what a fella'll do when he sees his cow-brutes droppin' like flies an' them that can still stand upright lookin' like starvation week in hell. Maybe your Dad's sort of anticipatin' what might start to pop round here 'f we don't get some rain dang soon."

"I don't think that is it," she said slowly. "It might aggravate the trouble, like this rustling that's been going on—we seem to be losing more than anyone else. But Dad's been acting odd for months. This rustling is something new around here. One night the boys notice a little tad of critters in a certain spot —say twenty or thirty prime beeves. Next morning these critters have disappeared—vanished. Hackett says there's not a sign to show where they went or how. It's uncanny!"

"And you think maybe this Hackett gent might be sort of . . . on the make?"

"I—I don't know what to think, Abe. It seems so fantastic to connect him up with this rustling or with this other thing that's been bothering Dad. Hackett's been with us over two years. Dad swears by him—and at him, sometimes. He has been trying all sorts of things in an effort to trap these cattle thieves. Don't you think perhaps you're letting your personal feelings toward Hackett warp your judgment of the man. After all, you don't really know him. You two seem to have taken a violent dislike to each other on sight. I was watching that scene before the bunk house this evening. I couldn't catch much of the conversation. What was it about? What started it?"

"Well, I expect maybe there wasn't any start to it, ma'am. We just sort of fell out before we'd had time to get acquainted any. Hackett sort of made it plain he wasn't aimin' to hire any help. He was mad mainly I reckon because I didn't pay much attention to him. He's the sort of gent that has to have attention, if you get what I mean. He wasn't built for the background."

"Well," Lee decided, "he certainly wasn't cut out to be a cow thief, either. He's much too smart—"

Ankrom chuckled. "Smart, ma'am? Shucks, I'd say he was not so much smart as foxy. Foxy. Cunning. I'd say he even had a heavy leanin' toward the coyote side."

He could feel her eyes upon him; they seemed to be tugging at him, probing to turn his innermost thoughts to light. There was earnest conviction in her low voice when she spoke:

"Mose Hackett is no fourflusher. If he's bad, which I don't believe for a minute, then he's a curly wolf. He's not the 'yes-man' type."

"Neither is a coyote," Ankrom countered. "He's a believer in the motto; 'Them as fights an' runs away, will live to fight another day'. Now let's talk about somethin' else. As a conversational topic, Brother Hackett grows extremely odious."

He was aware that in the darkness her eyes still remained upon his face; he realized his slip almost as soon as he made it and so was not surprised to hear her say:

"Where did you learn to sling words around like that?"

He answered carelessly, "I wasted a number of years at a university once." and was relieved that she let it go like that and did not press him further. Several moments passed, then he put a question to her that caused her breath to be indrawn sharply:

"What makes you connect what happened in Peso Pinto last night with these troubles of your father's? What makes you think someone might be trying to strike at him through you?"

"Who said that's what I think?"

"But you do, don't you?"

After dragging seconds she said "Yes" slowly. Then, "You don't miss much, do you?"

"Can't afford to," he answered simply. "In my business a man has to stay awake." His voice went grim and just a little bitter, "It's the price a gun man pays for continued existence."

"But you're not a gun man . . ."

"Some people have called me one. I can recall a number of occasions—"

"Those people were fools with no perception!" she almost snapped the opinion forth, so indignant did she seem. The beating of Blur Ankrom's heart stepped up terrifically.

"Lee—" he dropped the arm that had lain across the seat-back down upon her shoulders in the earnestness of what he was about to say. "Lee—"

But he felt the sudden stiffening of her supple form beneath that arm and the words he had been about to launch were scattered. The moment was lost and in the darkness a cynical

26

curve twisted the line of his tightened lips. It was just as well, he thought, that he had not said those things that had been in his mind. He *was* a gun man, and a gun man had no right to speak of personal things to a decent woman. He removed the offending arm as though it had been burnt.

A rush of words came breathless to her lips and in his mood their tone was lost upon him. "I think I'd better go."

He heard the door beside her open; the seat squeaked slightly as she rose. Dimly, a blacker blot against the stable murk, he watched her leave. When she had gone, the bitter mood clamped more firmly down upon him than ever had been its habit in the past. Her passing left the gulf between them plain. He'd been a fool to ever think . . .

With a sneer he stepped from the car, strode purposefully toward the oblong of lighter space that marked the door. As he stepped through it a figure lounging there grew straight and blocked his path; he read a definite menace in its rigid tenseness.

"Hold on, you."

Recognition cocked Ankrom's muscles; that voice belonged to Hackett!

CHAPTER IV

"Shake Hands with Colonel Struthers"

"HACKETT!"

Ankrom's face, limned as though in a spotlight by the downstreaming radiance of an argent moon, despite the suddenness and unexpectedness of this encounter reflected no surprise nor showed the faintest tinge of fear. That Hackett was primed for trouble he knew well, for he recognized certain signs to which he was accustomed in men who packed him quarrels. He stiffened a little, but that was all.

A red flame was flickering in Mose Hackett's deep-set eyes, his upper body was bent slightly forward from the waist

27

and his right hand hovered clawlike above the pistol at his hip. An ugly snarl twitched his lips apart:

"Yeah—Hackett!"

"Got something on your mind?"

"You're damn well right I have. There ain't no man in Texas can run on me the way you done this afternoon and get away with it. Go on—shuck your iron, you imitation bad man!"

"The place an' time to stage this melodrama was before the bunk house this afternoon. I'm not heeled now an' you know it." Ankrom eyed the burly range boss coldly. "Thought you told Trone you were leavin' for the southeast line camp."

"What I told Trone ain't none of your business. An' if you ain't heeled that's your tough luck." A wicked jubilation added fuel to the flame in Hackett's eyes. "By Gawd, I'm gonna work you over till your own mother won't even know you!"

With the words he started forward, jerking the heavy pistol from his holster, a cold grin on his twisted lips.

Ankrom's jaws closed grimly and the muscles bunched along them, relaxing suddenly. Ankrom's soft laugh mocked the range boss' threat. It caused Mose Hackett to draw up swiftly and peer at him through narrowed lids, suspiciously.

Ankrom did not move as Hackett thrust his gun in leather and balled his horny fists. He made no movement but his eyes took on a dread look of bitter wrath; a wrath surcharged with confidence in his ability to meet and check any deviltry Hackett might see fit to set afoot. The range boss, looking into them, should have taken warning. Instead, he came forward in a cursing rush, his fists cleaving air with whistling strokes as Ankrom backed away.

Then suddenly Ankrom stopped—stopped short in his tracks and struck. That lashing fist took Hackett flush upon the jaw and checked all forward movement. His body kind of sagged and he took an uncertain backward step or two. Then Ankrom's fist lashed home again. Hackett reeled back against the stable heavily. A moment he paused spread-eagled there, then slumped inertly to the dusty ground.

Ankrom stood where he was and waited. He wanted this settled now.

A minute passed in dragging silence. Ankrom knew the men inside the bunkhouse had got wind of the affair and guessed that they were watching. But he did not turn; all his faculties

28

were concentrated on that inert, huddled mass that was Mose Hackett. The man might be really out, or he might be playing 'possum. Long experience had taught Blur Ankrom to take no chances that were avoidable.

Another minute passed. Hackett stirred and groaned. His eyes came open and looked dull, uncomprehending. Finally he got to his feet, staggering a little. He was a strong man, inured to danger, hard as the stones of the Sierra Tinaja Pinta. Obviously he had never known a pulse of fear till now. But as his eyes encountered Ankrom where he stood in the moonlight as cold and motionless as some man of bronze, Mose Hackett's knees shook visibly, his eyes went wide and he drew air into his cramped lungs in noisy gasps.

There fell a silence; strained, awkward, portentous. Ankrom broke it. "Well?"

There was an accusing glare in the range boss' eyes. "You —you hit me."

Ankrom's glance filled with a smiling hardness. "I sure did. Twice! You wanting to make somethin' out of it?"

"No damn man can do that to me—you're fired!" He licked his battered lips, cleared his throat and said again, less certainly: "You're fired."

Ankrom laughed. "I told you this afternoon that Abe Streeter's on your payroll. He's goin' to stay on it till it suits him to drift along. Now look—" Ankrom's leisured tones grew soft and earnest; "When I see a tarantula I usually aim to let it alone. But when a tarantula jumps at me I squash it. Do you understand?"

"Damn you!" Hackett snarled, and his right hand dropped in swift descent to his holstered weapon. There it paused, fingers clamped about its butt. Ankrom had not moved an inch. His face was colorless and seemed to Hackett hard as a granite crag. A moment ago Hackett had had notions—vicious ones. He would have shot down this apparently unarmed interloper swiftly as he could get his gun from leather. But now, something stayed his hand. The will to murder had been written on his face, but now it was ashen, twitching. There had been wild courage in his heart, but now it was gone, dissolved by the icy sweat that clammed his brow. He stood there rigid, leaning slightly forward, paralysed. He could not have drawn that gun his fingers grasped for all the wealth in El Paso. Cold fear held him in an iron grip.

29

Yet the punchers, silently watching, saw nothing menacing in Ankrom's attitude; to them his pose was the acme of studied carlessness. Neither did they think his voice had been noteworthy for the promise of impending destruction. But they could not see his eyes, and it was into Ankrom's eyes that Hackett stared. They swam with a wanton light that defied and taunted, that challenged Hackett to draw that gun his fingers clasped.

It was sheer bluff; Hackett knew it. Yet he paused to wonder—and was lost. He *was* lost, and knew it. One tiny upward pressure on that gun and death would grab him. Hackett shivered and raised his hands.

Bare contempt lay in the cold grin parting Ankrom's lips. "All right, Hackett," he drawled. "You can take your hands down. Now that we understand each other I reckon we'll get along. You better be gettin' on to that line camp 'less you're figuring to spend the night there."

Some measure of courage had returned to the range boss while Ankrom talked. He wondered now what could have caused him ever to refrain from drawing his pistol and sending this salty drifter on to drier pastures. With the wonder came resentment that he had been bluffed before his men again. As he lowered his arms an ugly light sprang into his narrowed eyes.

"Don't crow, hombre. You ain't heard the last of this," he snarled and, swinging round he shoved his way through the group of grave-faced punchers, made his way to the pole corral to get his horse. As he jerked the rope from his saddle Ankrom's laugh, deep and throaty, rang discordantly in his reddened ears.

The following morning dawned bright and hot. At eight o'clock the sun had long since climbed from bed and was slowly mounting the heavens, a ball of fire against the white glare of desert sky. Side by side on the front seat of the Rafter T's rakish touring car, Lee Trone and the new hand were speeding across the sandy miles to where El Paso lay beyond the Hueco Mountains.

Ankrom drove with both hands, staring straight ahead across the wheel. His smooth cheeks showed close contact with a razor, his clothes were neatly brushed and his high-heeled cowboy boots shone like polished bottle glass. Yet his lips were firmly pressed in lines of cool indifference. His greeting of the girl beside him had been courteous but brief. Thereafter, for the past two hours, he had spoken not at all. He was cold and politely uncommunicative.

Lee's chic attire fit snug and trim her willowy figure; her foolish little hat was very smart but offered a minimum of protection from the sun's hot stare. Her soft profile with its gentle curves appeared a little stiff just now and her back was straight and rigid against the leather of the seat. She was accustomed to having men look at her—more; look at her with longing. This Streeter's cold reserve of manner was annoying, to say the very least.

She studied him with covert curiosity. His profile was strongly masculine; there was a bold sweep to his nose that matched well, she thought, the forward jut of his rugged chin. As she watched him the impressions formed at their first meeting, that turbulent scene in Peso Pinto two nights past, were strengthened. Despite certain indications of bitterness and cynicism which she discerned, she found him vital, colorful, intriguing.

Great strength of character, she felt, was expressed in his bronzed, clean-shaven countenance. Not merely experience nor age was registered there, but a mighty inward strength, unbounded confidence, strong mental viewpoint.

She could not guess his thoughts for he wore an inscrutability of feature that, she reflected, would defy the stoutest probing. He seemed to live aloof from other folk in a world that was obviously his own. In this man, self-sufficiency, she thought darkly, was carried to an odious extreme. When she had more time, she resolved, she would take a deal of pleasure in proving to him, and to her own satisfaction, that there were other cacti in the desert.

His overpowering strength of character, she believed, would prevent him from being too-easily aroused. But she found herself curious to know what he might be like once those barriers of reserve were swept aside. Yes, certainly she must get to know him better. Undoubtedly there was much more to him than at first glance appeared upon the surface; several times she had sensed a vein of bitterness deep within him that excited curiosity. Enigmas were her forte, and she was determined to probe this one to the depths.

"You're not overly conversational this morning," she observed. "Cat got your tongue?"

"Nope."

"Feeling kind of low?" she asked, nettled that he had not turned his head nor even cast a fleeting, sidelong glance at her.

"No lower'n usual, I reckon."

He still stared straight ahead. For a time she left him staring, her head upturned in pique. He did not *have* to talk to her, of course. She thought it likely she could survive *without* his conversation. But as the miles sped by with only the vibrant purring of the smoothly-running motor making sound in the vast stillness, curiosity overcame resentment and she spoke again.

"When I left you last night," she hoped her voice sounded firm and even as she intended, "I noticed Hackett lounging by the stable door. It looked like Hackett. You haven't had any further trouble with him, I hope?"

"No, ma'am. No trouble at all."

"You've seen him, though?"

"I expect we sort of nodded to each other, ma'am."

Had she caught a vein of sarcasm in his voice? Had she really observed a tiny glint in the eye that, nearest her, Streeter kept conscientiously upon the road? Lee wondered. She determined to have a talk with one of the men when they got back. If this reticent fellow were keeping something from her, she wanted to know it—and likewise what it was.

"You don't like Mose Hackett very well, do you?"

"Oh, Mose is all right, if a fellow knows how to handle him."

"Do you consider yourself that sort of fellow?" she prodded.

"I reckon. I've met his type before." Lee, watching him, thought that he had been about to say more. If so, he had abruptly changed his mind, for no further words came from him. Spurred by irritation, she asked icily:

"Are you taciturn by nature, Mr. Streeter? Or is this reticence intended to show dislike?"

"Neither," he said with eyes still on the road. "I just can't see the sense in wasting gas."

She stared at him indignantly. "Wasting gas!"

The angry impatience in her voice brought a sharp look from him. "I mean," he said, staring back upon the curving road where it wound up through the foothills of the Huecos, "that I can't see much use indulgin' in small talk when there's weighty problems occupyin' my attention."

"Indeed?"

"Yeah. F'r instance, I'm wonderin' a heap what kind of habla you're figurin' to throw tryin' to get around my bein' an old friend of folks I've never laid eyes on? These Struthers people, if they've any sense at all, are goin' to smell one dark nigger in your personal woodpile!"

"That is *my* problem."

"It sure is—but you don't seem to be givin' it much attention. What *are* you aimin' to tell 'em?"

"More lies, probably!"

"Likely enough," he agreed, and chuckled.

Lee felt her fists clenching. Hot color flamed her cheeks. It served her right, she thought. She had had no business talking to him—a common hand! All that talk of loyalty . . . The fellow was a boor whether he'd gone to college or not, just another uncouth savage of the saddle—a self-centered drifter with neither manners nor perception!

While Lee Trone went off to meet her friends, and to take them somewhere for luncheon, Blur Ankrom took himself to a small restaurant on a side street labeled "GREASY SPOON" and put some grub under his own belt. It made him feel a little less sardonic and resentful of the girl's hurried departure before his meeting with Mose Hackett. It was, therefore, in a fairly cheerful frame of mind, considering the imminent prospect of more trouble that lay before him, that he returned to the car, climbed in behind the wheel and gave himself up to speculation concerning the appearance, habits and characters of those old friends of his—the Struthers'.

Colonel Struthers, in all probability, would be a stuffed shirt, he mused—a pompous old belligerent with horsey notions and little depth. The thought brought a faintly malicious grin to Ankrom's wide lips. Should the Colonel be such a character, Lee Trone would find her work cut out attempting to shore the lie with which, to her father, she had described one Abe Streeter an old friend of Struthers'.

Despite the fact that Ankrom considered himself unworthy of the girl's attentions, considered any further intimacy between them a thing most emphatically barred by any and every standard of decency, the lure exerted by her magnetic personality had uncovered unsuspected longings deep within him that he was powerless to combat. These latent longings made him a little resentful of the abruptness with which they had parted in the stable the night before.

A man whose every emotion had long been controlled by an iron will, he could not understand his feeling toward this girl who had come so precipitously into his life two nights before. That he was drawn to her tremendously he realized, and the knowledge irritated him, made short his temper. He strove to fight against the charm and pull of her. There could never be anything between them; to push their acquaintance deeper could only mean sorrow and heartbreak for one or both. This frame of mind had been the cause of his reticence during the drive this morning, mainly.

There was another cause, of course, contributing. He had headed for this country in an effort to leave his past behind him, to lose himself in obscurity—to live as other men had the right and freedom to live. But already the promise of further turmoil was driving black thought clouds across the horizon of his mind. Nowhere, it seemed, could he find the peace he craved. Where his reputation failed to follow, he found himself embroiled in new difficulties; new patterns of trouble enmeshed his steps. So he had always found it in the past. Even here it was becoming so.

His father, a frontier marshal, until checked in mid-career by dry-gulch lead, had in his time made many enemies, some of whom survived him. One of these, two years ago, had found occasion to slur the marshal's memory. With gunsmoke young Ankrom had purged the insult. That incident had started Ankrom on the trail of No-Return.

In many ways it had been a luck shot with which he had downed "Storm" Drean that day. The man had been a former rustler, a man whose "draw" was speedy as a striking snake. He had that day got in first shot, yet only Ankrom had lived to tell about it, for Ankrom's fire had been more accurate. Since that day a constant flood of trouble had forced the marshal's son to become a past master in the art of draw-and-shoot; had forced him also from the trodden trails in very self-defence. For even now, as in the olden days, there were some men hunting trouble for the doubtful pleasure of enhancing evil reputations. "Glory-hunters" some folk called them, though Ankrom named them different.

Because of these things that lay behind him, yet were ever catching up, Ankrom long since had resolved to live his life

34

alone. The life of a gun man's wife was in his opinion no fit lot for any woman. There should be no place for sentiment in Ankrom's mind; the dictates of his heart should be discounted.

But though he had made these decisions firmly, and lived up to them as well, never before had he encountered anyone remotely like Lee Trone. Her beauty was vital, of mind as well as body he felt sure, and the charm of her tugged at his senses mightily. Despite the shortness of their acquaintance he could recall her every feature vividly; indeed, her vision was before him brightly during all his waking hours. He could not get her out of mind.

Voices drove in upon his consciousness and he looked up with an ironing-out of face. There came Lee now, and with her a man and girl. The girl got but a glance from him; it was the man that drew his eyes.

Well-dressed this fellow was, and big and dark and handsome. Around forty-eight in years. There was laughter in his close-set eyes, sardonic, mocking laughter, though his lips were grave and closed.

Lee said, "Colonel Struthers, this is Abe Streeter, the friend I told you of. Abe, shake hands with Colonel Struthers."

"Howdy." Ankrom nodded, and guessed the gods were chuckling. For the owner of that hand stretched out to his was the cousin of Storm Drean!

CHAPTER V

GUESTS FOR THE RAFTER T

ANKROM read amusement into the faint smile with which the fellow said, "Glad to meet up with you—Streeter."

"You're going to find I don't improve with age, or time— Struthers." Ankrom said it coldly and, reaching back across the seat, pulled open one of the car's rear doors for them all to enter. In Lee's green eyes that were fixed puzzledly upon him he read wonder and speculation and knew that she had not missed entirely the significance of those low-spoken words.

But when she spoke there was no hint of her thought in her voice: "This is the Colonel's daughter, Betty," she said.

For the first time Ankrom let his glance play over this girl. She was little and pretty and golden. Her bare head in the down-slanting rays of the past-noon sun was a tousled mass of fine-spun gold. Her smiling eyes were vividly blue in the piquant oval of her face, and seemed holding forth to him a glowing promise even while they challenged. She thrust toward him almost timidly her hand, as though fearful lest his own much larger one might crush her tiny, well-manicured fingers. She smiled adorably when he released it.

"Pleased to know you, ma'am," Ankrom said and, dropping her hand, turned back to stare across the wheel as the girls climbed in. The Colonel got in last. When settled, he said "Let's go, fellow."

Ankrom pressed down on the starter and roared the motor into life. He let the clutch in gently and sent the long low car sleekly forward into the line of traffic gliding past.

"By way of Peso Pinto, Abe," Lee called, and Ankrom nodded.

Once clear of the town Ankrom opened up the motor and sent the rakish car forward in a moan of contented purring. Scant were the scraps of conversation reaching him from the back seat; gossip about the range, fragments of speculation concerning the time which might elapse before the eventual and long-hoped-for termination of the present drought. Waterholes were going dry that never before had done so.

But Ankrom felt no interest in their talk. His mind was busy with things which meant more to him than a general lack of water and the condition of other people's thirty steers. This situation in which he found himself was not at all to his liking and had been complicated enough before Lee had told her father that crazy lie. But now, with the supposed Struthers proving to be a vengeful cousin of the man whose death had placed Blur Ankrom's youthful feet on the trail to gunhawk glory, immediate prospects for that hoped-for peaceful oblivion looked dark indeed.

Why had Kelton Drean come here masquerading as Colonel Struthers, as an old friend of these Trones? Not because he'd guessed that here at last he would find Ankrom. No— that veiled pleasure and sardonic gleam of amusement in his

36

glance on seeing Ankrom disproved at once that theory. Why, then, had he come?

It bothered Ankrom, put a black frown between his forward staring eyes. The girl who here was posing as his daughter also bothered Ankrom. Who was this glowing, golden creature introduced by Lee as "Betty?" Not Drean's daughter —legitimate or otherwise. Was this girl the real Colonel's daughter? "But no," he thought, "She would never lend herself to this deception."

Where then did she fit into this ominous web of conspiracy that was spinning tight about the Rafter T? Was she merely an accomplice of Drean's—a gracious backdrop placed to improve and make seem more valid his portraiture of Colonel Struthers? Or was she more—Drean's wife or—

Behind the wheel Ankrom's lean-muscled form went tense, his hands clutched the hard-rubber circle tightly. It had come to him in that flashing instant that he had seen this girl before. It was she with her golden hair that had leaned from between the red drapes of that second-story window in Peso Pinto the other night and cried "Up here, cowboy! Quick!"

For long seconds as the winding road flashed past, Ankrom's mind was a whirl of wild conjecture, then as the rush of blood receded from his brain he forced himself to think more coolly. Drean, he reasoned, had not come here unprepared. He must have known that the real Struthers had not been seen by Trone for many years, else he would not have dared this impersonation. That he had now committed himself to the role, showed that he had every intention of bluffing it out.

Why? What was he expecting to get out of it? Ankrom knew the Drean breed pretty well, both from experience and reputation. He knew that a Drean would never risk his neck without there was money, and good money, to be forth-coming for accomplishment. The man, he reasoned, must be working under orders. Whose?

Blur Ankrom was a deeply puzzled and apprehensive young man as he sent the rakish car across the spinning miles toward Peso Pinto. And it was not for himself, just now, or for his own future that he felt apprehensive—it was for Lee Trone and the gaunt old man who rodded the Rafter T.

For any possible danger this mystery might hold for himself, Blur Ankrom was not concerned. Even his object in coming to this country was momentarily thrust into the back-

37

ground of his mind by the intriguing nature of current events and a sudden interest and absorption in the riddle set up by them.

That Drean would give away the Streeter masquerade, he did not believe. The man could not afford to—yet. Nor could he immediately afford to bring his quarrel with Ankrom into the open, Ankrom thought. The chances were that Drean would bide his time, would wait until this sinister business that was bringing him to the Rafter T was finished before calling Ankrom to account for the killing of rustler cousin Storm.

Was there some connection between Lee Trone's adventure in Peso Pinto and the sudden arrival of this spurious Colonel? To Ankrom it seemed likely that there was, but its nature he could not surmise. One thing only seemed certain—there was trouble, bad trouble, ahead for Old Man Trone and all who sided him!

Before the Stockmen's bank in Peso Pinto, at Lee's wind-whipped order, Ankrom shoved down a booted foot upon the brake pedal and brought the long low car to a squealing stop. A solid-looking man with a great wide forehead lounged dreamily against one of the twin pillars guarding the bank's entrance. He did not raise his head, but his sleepy lids, rolling slowly up, disclosed smoke-gray eyes whose glance brushed past Lee as she stepped upon the walk and came to rest unblinkingly upon Blur Ankrom.

Ankrom returned the gaze with interest. He saw that the lounger was dressed in range clothes which he guessed to be of expensive make. These clothes, he saw, were well-filled, in fact were billowed out, by the heavy-muscled figure of their wearer. The man's cream-colored Stetson was shoved far back from the great wide forehead, disclosing a rebellious tangle of curly black hair.

Abruptly the man's head came up, the gray eyes slid nearer. A great brown paw came up and removed his hat while across the boldness of his heavy features flashed a smile. Ankrom's gaze, slightly shifting, saw that Lee Trone had come abreast the fellow.

The man bowed with a gallant flourish. "Gosh," he said, "but it's good to see you, gal. Where you been keepin' yourself?"

"Out of your way," she answered coolly, and Ankrom saw that there lay no warmth in the directness of the look she gave him.

But the big man's white-toothed grin no whit abated. A whimsical humor lay in the fleeting twist of his eyes to Ankrom. Then back they flashed to the girl and the man behind the wheel saw a joshing twinkle flood their depths. "Shucks," came the lazy drawl, "that ain't no friendly way to talk."

"I wasn't trying to be friendly."

Ankrom saw the big man shove free of the pillar in such a way that his bulk presented a barrier between the girl and the door. "Lee, some folks are givin' an old-time dance on the twelfth. What say we take it in? Been a long time since you an' I have shaken a hoof together."

There was a dry sarcasm in Lee's reply that was not wasted on Blur Ankrom: "It will be a long time before we do again—if ever. Let me pass now, Tom. I wish to go inside."

"Why, shucks, I thought you'd stopped to talk with me," he said, and made no move from where he stood. "Seems like you're awful cool today. An' this is the first time I've seen you since you got back. We used to be good friends. What's the matter? Did that dude college put big notions in your head?"

"Times have changed, that's all—people, too," she answered; "my going away to college has had nothing to do with it. You're not the man I used to know, Tom; you've changed. A strange unrest seems to have settled on this range. It's got into the people, made them different. Old friends I've known for years no longer speak. Things—"

"What's all that got to do with you and me?"

"Your father and my father were never friends—"

"But that don't have to make enemies out of you an' me."

"I'm not so sure. My loyalty lies with my father. Things that you and I once found possible are so no longer. I don't think we had better meet again."

Ankrom could not see Lee's face; her back was to him now. But he could see the big man's features well; could see a look of resentment stir the gray smoke of those sleepy-lidded eyes. "I reckon," the big man said, "someone has been spreadin' a pack of lies about me."

The man's lips had hardly moved yet Ankrom plainly heard the words. Lee's voice came to him now; it seemed a little thick with feeling:

39

"I'm not so sure that they were lies. There was bad blood between your Dad and mine for many years, I've heard. Can you assure me that all this time you have not brooded on Ed Ratchford's death? Can you assure me—can you tell me *honestly*—that you've never had ideas of vengeance?"

Ratchford's sleepy lids masked all feeling from his glance. "I didn't think," he said, "you'd ever doubt me, Lee. It's hard to see . . ." Ankrom heard his voice trail off. He stood there, hat in hand, his chin sunk down upon his chest, darkly brooding. Abruptly he looked up and his eyes went straight to Lee's.

"This—this talk that's goin' round. The best way to put an end to it an' stop these malicious, wagging tongues, Lee, is for you an' me to be seen together." His lips rolled back in a flashing smile that showed his hard white teeth. "We better go to that dance."

"I can't," Lee said quietly. "It would be disloyal to my father—you mustn't ask it, Tom." Ankrom saw a tremor shake her slim straight body, then her chin came up. "Will you please let me by."

Ratchford stepped aside and watched her vanish inside the bank's interior. When his eyes swung round there was in them still the look with which he'd watched her go. Then they swept the occupants of the car and a new light flickered in their smoky depths as they came to rest again on Ankrom's grave, inscrutable features. He came striding forward and in the musclar roll of his shoulders Ankrom read discriminating belligerence. He stopped three feet away, looking Ankrom over coldly.

"Who're you? I don't seem to recall seein' your face round here before? Stranger?"

Ankrom's glance was calm. "I don't recall that askin' personal questions ever got to be a habit in the cattle country. New fad?"

Ratchford's sleepy lids rolled lower; the smoky eyes stared back unblinking. It seemed plain that he was not used to being addressed in just this manner. Yet there was no resentment in his stare, just heightening interest. He suddenly grinand shoved out his hand. "My name's Ratchford. I run the Straddle Bug brand."

Ankrom seized by some perverse impulse he could not himself have put in words, ignored the ranchers' hand. Looking straight into those smoky eyes he said. "I'm Streeter. Now I've answered your question, Ratchford, do you know of any reason why this palaver should be dragged out any further?"

Ratchford's wide forehead puckered roughly above the heavy brows that topped his eyes. The eyes themselves clung to Ankroms' sober face and the light of interest in them deepened. He thrust his hands deep down in his trousers pockets. Teetering on his boot-heels a slow grin crossed his lips.

"Glad to know you, Streeter. Wish we had a few more proddy pelicans like you around this country. Land needs 'em. Can't see no sense in you an' me not hittin' it off, though. How'd you like a good job?"

"I got a job."

"I said a *good* one."

"I got a good one. What's wrong with workin' for the Rafter T?"

Ratchford shrugged. "Nothin'—if you're huntin' a quick grave."

"What's the meanin' of that? I never was good on riddles."

"No riddle. You heard what Miss Trone said to me, I reckon. Well, it's true that there's a lotta loose tongues begun to wag. Don't know where the thing got started, but there's a rumor loose that I'm out to bust the Rafter T; out to even up with Old Man Trone for the death of my Dad. It all happened years ago. In his younger days, Lee's ol' man was one of the graspin'est, hardest, fightin'est old cocks on this whole damn range. He made it awful hard on my ol' man, who was runnin' sheep then. Fact is, Trone put my ol' man outa business. Some folks has got the notion I'm figurin' to square things up. Nothin' to it of course, but there you are," he shrugged. "Folks will talk."

"What's all this got to do with me working for the Rafter T?"

"Just this," Ratchford said. "Somebody *is* out to bust that outfit."

"An' figgerin' to make you play the goat, eh?"

"That's about the size of it," Ratchford admitted.

"Why don't you do something about it? Haven't you got any suspicions who's back of it all?"

"I got suspicions, yes," Ratchford answered slowly. "But suspicions don't mean a thing. I got to have proof." Sardonic glints appeared in his smoky eyes as he added, "You see, Streeter, I'm the sheriff of this here county."

41

Lee Trone came from the bank talking earnestly with a man. His clear cut features held that hint of underlying bronze acquired only by years beneath a broiling sun. He was, Ankrom decided, a man of striking and unusual appearance. A good six feet in his shiny black boots he stood, and carried himself like a Spanish Don. His thick, bushy eyebrows appeared facile at expression; black side burns, long and curling, together with the black pencil-line mustache, gave his smiling face a sharp touch of the Mephistophelean. His hat, out of courtesy to his companion, was in his left hand; his right waved a thin brown cigarette in airy gestures. He had a thick mop of gray at either temple but added to the fierce vitality of his long, dark countenance.

Ankrom saw Ratchford exchange brief nods with this man. The girl, Lee Trone, broke off their conversation and turned to indicate her guests. "Mr. Claydell," she said. "I'd like to make you acquainted with our friends the Struthers. Colonel Struthers and Betty. Betty is the Colonel's daughter. Folks, this is Mr. Claydell, a neighboring rancher.

As Ankrom watched the spurious Colonel's genial nod he wondered why the sheriff had not been introduced to the Rafter T's guests. Evidently Lee considered Ratchford now with distinct hostility, though their words evidenced that once their relations had been more cordial.

Ankrom, covertly studying the faces of this group, saw strange, unreasonable light fleet through Lee Trone's green eyes as, momentarily, their gaze rested upon the piquant face of the golden Betty. The latter was speaking, saying some commonplace thing to Claydell in lilting accents. The rancher's deep voice came back as upon his long dark countenance there flashed an admiring grin:

"I certainly can think of no acquaintance I'd rather make than yours, little lady," his eyes were bold as he looked up from a gallant bow. "Are you going to stay at the Rafter T?"

"Harry—that's Dad—and I are going to Dallas. We'll stop off with the Trones for a few days though. Dad and Mr. Trone are old friends. We haven't seen them in years; I'd practically forgotten how they looked. I can see already that I'm going to love it here."

"I can see that you are, too," Claydell chuckled, leveling a meaning look into the girl's sparkling blue eyes. A tinkle of mirth came forth of her lips as answer; to Ankrom the sound was like silvern chimes.

"Mr. Claydell, with you around I'm sure I shall."

Ankrom scowled and looked at Lee. But Lee was studying the Colonel's face. She turned as Claydell addressed her. "Tell your Dad I'll be seeing him tonight, Lee."

She nodded. Ankrom saw a hint of deeper color brush the cheeks of Sheriff Ratchford. "Believe I'll stop out at the Rafter T tonight myself," Ratchford said. "Mind giving me a lift?"

Lee did not answer, nor did she look the sheriff's way. "Let's get going," the Colonel said. "I'm anxious to see old Trone again—"

"When was it you saw him last, Colonel?" Lee cut in.

"Let's see—ten years ago last May, 'f I remember right."

"Ten years is a long time. Probably you wouldn't recognize him if you met him on the street."

The Colonel grinned. "I'd recognize him any place this side of hell, ma'am." He looked down at the golden blonde. "We been intendin' to visit the old Rafter T for dang near a year, ain't we, honey?"

Betty smiled with understanding. "For months Father's talked of nothing but Old Man Trone and the Rafter T," she backed him up.

Ratchford's smoke-gray glance crossed Lee's, arrested it. His voice was sober, "Will you give me a lift to the ranch, Lee?"

Lee faced him directly now. Her jade-green eyes were cold. "I don't believe the Rafter T's hospitality could include you, Mr. Ratchford. I'd stay away if I were you."

He took the insult calmly; his faint smile never wavered. "I'll take the chance," he said, and climbed into the front with Ankrom.

CHAPTER VI

PROMISCUOUS SHOOTING

THE sun was sinking low behind the western timbered ridges when Ankrom sent the car down the valley trail, out across the yard with its long blue shadows and braked it to a halt before the ranch house.

Ratchford was told to make himself at home—in the bunk house. "Streeter will show you an empty bunk if you're planning to stay all night," Lee said coolly after Ankrom had unloaded his passengers before the broad veranda.

Faintly, almost regretfully it seemed, a crooked little smile parted Ratchford's lips as he watched her walk into the house after Betty and the Colonel. He sighed when she disappeared and sank back in his seat. He scowled, seeing Ankrom's glance upon him. "If a polecat," he said bitterly, "happened to wander into a meetin' of the Old Ladies Sewin' Circle he wouldn't be a damn bit less popular than I am here."

"You didn't have to come," Ankrom said and, shoving in the gear, sent the long touring car across the yard and into the stable. Cutting off the motor he climbed out. He heard the sheriff walking behind him as he left the stable. As he crossed toward the bunk house the sheriff strode abreast.

"You don't think so, eh? Well, you're dead wrong. Somethin's crowdin' up for a bust, you mark my words. This range is gettin' ready to tear loose, Mister, an' when it does, all hell ain't gonna stop it! Look—you don't see no man lazin' round that bunk house, do you? 'Course you don't. Do you savvy why there ain't none around here now with grub time just about to strike?"

"I expect Hackett's got them out on the range some place," Ankrom answered. "Nothin' unusual in that, I reckon."

"Well, you reckon wrong. Mose Hackett's been keepin' his men hangin' round this ranch like he was scared they'd catch small pox if they stirred outside the yard. But they ain't here now. There's something—"

Ankrom cut in: "Any sheep interests located round here?"

Ratchford gave him a sharp look from beneath his sleepy lids. "Boone Heffle, a half-witted old coot, has a little band of a coupla thousand back in the hills."

"Any rustlers' fraternity workin' this range?"

A deep crease cut the sheriff's forehead angularly. His flinty, smoke-colored eyes stared intently at his questioner. "Trone claims he's been losin' a little beef. That's what I came out here for—want to see him about it. What's this stuff pointin' up?"

"Your guess is as good as mine. I was just sort of wondering what sort of trouble you had in mind."

"It'll be gunsmoke trouble—you can bet on that."

Ankrom was inclined to agree, but he did not say so. Instead he asked, "an' you can't do nothing to stop it?"

"That offer," said Ratchford, pointedly, "is still open."

"An' the answer's still the same. I got a job."

"I figure you won't have—long."

"I expect you haven't considered all the factors," Ankrom's soft chuckle filled a silence. "Even if you have, and the Rafter T goes down, I imagine we can make the scrap right interestin' while it lasts."

A snorting sound issued from the flaring nostrils of the sheriff's squat nose. His eyes traveled up and down Ankrom's lithe, lean-muscled figure, resting longest at that wrinkled spot on the right leg of his faded blue jeans where, when on the range, his scabbarded pistol customarily hung. "Let me tell you something, pilgrim: there's a fella lined up against this spread that wouldn't even be afraid to cross guns with Blur Ankrom, that Arizona Smokeroo what's reputed to be hell on wheels an' thirteen claps of thunder. I don't reckon you'd cotton to goin' up against a gent like that, would you?"

"What kind of handle does this fella wear?"

The sheriff grinned. "He's a Mex breed. Goes under the name of Bandera."

"Bandera, eh?" Ankrom's eyes were speculative. "Is the front end of that 'Chato?"

"Chato Bandera is the gent I'm gassin' about," Ratchford admitted. "Know him?"

"Seems to me I've heard of him some place or other," Ankrom shrugged.

"Listen," Ratchford said. "Listen. The Rafter T, case you ain't posted on the subject, started as a nester spread. Big outfits like my Dad's hated their guts. They tried to put Trone out of business once or twice, before my time that was, but they didn't get very far. They weren't organized an' Trone had some hard characters workin' for him, fellas that would liefer shoot than eat.

"After a while our outfit, Claydell's Swingin' J an' Corson's Double Circle got together an' doped it out that they'd have to throw in together an' all pounce on Trone simultaneous if they was goin' to clean him out. Well, they tried it. I was a kid then an' didn't have no part in it. But it was some fracas, let me tell you, an' when it was over there was Trone still sittin' pretty like before it started. That little scrimmage busted Corson flat. He sold out to Trone an' cut his stick.

" 'Bout that time my ol' man got the idee that the only way to get Trone right was to bring in sheep. He brought 'em—but it lost him Claydell's support. Claydell figured it out that Trone was jest a little tougher than we was an' turned his coat. He threw in with the Rafter T. One mornin' Ed Ratchford found his sheep piled up in the bottom of a canyon. He come home an' brooded for three-four days an' finally went out an' shot himself."

"Where did this Boone Heffle jasper come into the picture?" Ankrom asked.

"He came in when my ol' man imported them sheep. He brought Heffle in as foreman."

"An' Heffle lasted it out." Ankrom studied Ratchford thoughtfully. "Was Heffle the only one of that crowd that stayed on after the war died out?"

"I guess so. Most of the others that weren't planted pulled up stakes an' hit for other parts. But—" and the sheriff's tone went grim, "there ain't nothing holdin' 'em from coming back now. An' there's a hell of a lot of strangers drifted into this country in the last few months. You ain't the only one by a long shot!"

After supper, Ankrom sat outside the bunk house smoking. Two of the Rafter T punchers, who had been fence-riding during the day, had come in just before the meal and now sat sprawled alongside Ankrom, as did the sheriff who, so far, had held no conversation with Old Man Trone.

"Wonder where the boys been workin' today," Ankrom slid the words casually into the easy silence that had shrouded the

46

smokers for some while. "Looks like they might be figuring to spend the night."

"Don't let nothin' surprise you round this dang place," one of the cowboys muttered. "All kinds of queer things been happenin' round here the las' few months. Hackett's been keepin' us close to the home ranch most of the time. He's been sorta on aidge, if you're askin' me."

"He's been missin' cattle, too," his pardner chipped in significantly. "Leastways, he says he has. Told the Ol' Man we've lost close onto three hundred head in the las' eight weeks. I heard him."

Ankrom shot a sidelong glance at the sheriff and found Ratchford's eyes upon him meaningly. It was as though the sheriff were saying "I told you so." Only he didn't put the thing in words.

He glanced casually toward the cowboys. Both of them were watching Ratchford expectantly. But Ratchford now was staring off toward the distant peaks beyond and above the timbered ridges hemming in this valley. There was a faraway look in his eyes and his beefy face showed no emotion, nor even interest in their remarks.

Dusk was rapidly darkening the evening sky. In a little while it would be dark. The solacing quiet of the open lands lay across this Texas country, calming the spirit and making man and his works seem puny, insignificant things.

Ankrom threw away his burned-down cigarette and yawned. "You boys goin' to the dance in Peso Pinto?"

"Might—if they hev good likker."

His pardner grunted, "I don't like that damn town. Too crowded an' a heap too partial tuh dudes. I get in a fight ever' time I get within gunshot of the place!"

Ratchford's lips moved faintly, sardonically, in the deepening gloom. One of the punchers said, "Either of you two gents wanta sit in on a game of stud?"

Ankrom shook his head. Ratchford said, "Not me, fella. I've played cards with you before."

The cowboy sighed. "It's hell hevin' a repitation like I got. How about you, Chuck? Wanta play casino?"

"I might play awhile if yuh play by Captain Hoyle's rules. 'f yuh start subtractin' though, I'm quittin' sudden."

The two men got up and tramped inside. A moment later Ankrom heard the scraping of a match. A flicker of light came through the window; grew steady and brightened. He heard the men dragging chairs up to the table and, a little later, the flap of cards against its top.

"Funny Trone never wired any of these buildings but the ranch house an' stable."

"Yeah. Where does he get his juice?" Ankrom asked, to help along the conversation.

"He sent to El Paso for a generator an' some other doohickies couple years back. Said he might's well keep up to date. I reckon it was Lee put the idee in his head. He'd jest about cut his neck off for that girl—an' she for him." Ratchford sighed. "They're pretty close, them two."

"Seen Trone yet?" Ankrom asked, although aware the other had not.

"No," the sheriff answered slowly. "Reckon it's about time I sauntered over to the house an' had my talk. I been sorta hopin' them dude friends of his would drift off to bed. I'd prefer to see the Ol' Man alone."

"You'll have a long wait if you're waitin' for *them* to go to bed. City folks have a way of sittin' up all night. They go to bed with the owls," Ankrom said. "Do you think there's anythin' in this rustling talk?"

Ratchford rasped his chin. "Don't seem to be any other outfits losin' critters. They might be keepin' it to themselves, of course. Again, there might really be some stealin' going on an' Trone be the only gent that's gettin' hit." With a grunt he surged to his feet, stood peering down at Ankrom where he sat with his back against the bunk house. "You heard what that puncher said."

The muted sound of muffled voices came to Ankrom from the card players. Now that Ratchford was standing, radiance from the lamp inside illumined the beefy face beneath his hat. Weariness was written there; in the creases of the heavy jowls, in the maze of criss-crossed lines about the long, sleepy-lidded eyes. His gaze was melancholy, brooding. "You see, it all ties up with that damn gab that's going round 'bout me bein' out to break the Rafter T," he growled with bitter feeling.

"Well, there would seem to be some substance for the rumor," Ankrom murmured gently.

The sheriff stiffened. "Yeah—that's why I'd like to get my hands round the neck of the gent that's backin' it. Because my ol' man an' Trone burnt gunpowder years ago folks are willin' to swaller any kind of hog-wash that tends to picture me looking for revenge. Damn 'em! I believe in lettin' sleepin' dogs sleep!"

Ankrom watched the sheriff strike out across the yard to where twinkling lights revealed the uncurtained windows of the ranch house, where it abutted the broad veranda. As he watched Ratchford's broad back, etched sharp and black against those distant lights, conflicting thoughts struggled to adjust themselves upon the backdrop of his mind.

There was much about this sheriff he did not understand, he told himself. A vital, magnetic figure, there was yet something about him, some latent, smouldering force, some indefinable sense of evil, that made a man hesitate to trust him far or to put great credence in his words.

Just why this was so Ankrom could not say. But the feeling lingered. He could not shake it. Some way, big and magnetic as he was, Tom Ratchford measured short in Ankrom's estimation.

He wondered if Ratchford had been trying to talk him into something, if Ratchford in springing Bandera's name had hoped to take him by surprise. How much did this sheriff suspect? How much did he know? Did he really connect Abe Streeter with the Arizona smookeroo, Blur Ankrom? Or was he—?

"Shucks," Ankrom muttered. "looks like I'm tryin' to develop a case of nerves."

Then he chuckled softly as he recalled the sheriff's statement that Bandera was lined up against the Trones. That would mean that Bandera either was in the country now or would shortly be coming in. It had been well over a year since that one night when his and Bandera's trails had crossed. In old Nogales it had happened. He remembered the circumstances well. He had taken malicious pleasure that night in upsetting a little deal the Mexican had been striving to bring off—a deal involving a woman. An amusing case of 'biter-bit' he'd made it, leaving Bandera a seething bundle of impotent fury, swearing revenge by every saint in the calendar.

With another chuckle Ankrom rose to his feet, lounged against the shadowed wall while he fished the makings from his pocket and rolled a cigarette. He would have a final smoke, he told himself and go hunt his bunk. His left hand rolled the quirley while his right sought the band of his hat, procured a match and struck it. The bursting orange flame illumined his

49

hard bronzed face and brought out the clean sharp angles of it.

Even as the match burst into flame, another flame licked out from the deep shadows beneath an ancient pepper tree thirty yards away. The cigarette ripped from Ankrom's mouth, so close had been the miss. A report smashed loudly on the stillness, flattened out across the yard, beat caroming up against the buildings. And on its heels another, even as Ankrom whirled, his hand streaking to the waistband of his trousers. A blur of motion stirred the shadows beneath yon fluid foliage some thing dropped heavily in the dust.

With gun held ready in his hand Ankrom sprinted forward. He jerked to a stop before the tree as a vague white figure snapped up from the ground to confront him with a little gasp. It was the figure of a girl.

"Who—who are you?"

"Abe Streeter, ma'am. Was that you doing that shooting?"

"No—yes! No! No, of course not!"

Despite the agitation in her low voice Ankrom recognized that this was not Lee Trone. Therefore, he reasoned, it must be the golden-haired creature posing as Betty Struthers. What was she doing here? What was that thing glinting in her hand. Ankrom leaned suddenly closer and saw that it was a pistol; he saw also that with her other hand the girl was holding something that looked like folded papers.

"What are you doing here?" he whispered fiercely. "What have you got in your hands?"

She drew back away from him. The hand with the papers disappeared inside the neckline of her dress and came out empty. His ears told him that people were running toward them; his eyes, as he swung them briefly from the girl, told him that the people would soon locate them and be upon them hurling questions. This girl could not be questioned now. He could hear her teeth chattering though the night was warm.

"Duck out of this," he said. "I'll see you later."

She seemed, as well as he could judge in this cursed darkness, to be peering at him strangely. Then suddenly she turned and ran.

A man came pounding up, grabbed Ankrom by the arm. "What's goin' on?" he growled. "What was all that shootin'?" Before Ankrom could frame an answer, this man turned his head bellowed across his shoulder: "Get a lantern, somebody! We got to have a light here!"

Ankrom saw one of the running figures whirl and retrace its steps. The others came on and grouped themselves about Ankrom and the burly man who held him. A hand felt down his wrist and closed upon the barrel of his gun. "I'll take this," the heavy voice said. Ankrom, recognizing now the sheriff in the man who held him, gave up his gun.

"Speak up, you. Let's hear your name."

Ankrom said. "Abe Streeter."

He felt the sheriff's grip relax. "Oh. . . . Well, who in hell was you shootin' at?"

"I wasn't. Somebody else was doing that shooting, Ratchford."

Ratchford showed impatience. "Is the fella's name a secret?"

"Reckon so—leastways, he didn't leave me any card."

"Where was you standin'?"

"By the bunk house," Ankrom said. "I was lightin' a cigarette. That shot came along an' snicked it right out of my mouth."

"Kinda close, eh?"

"Well, I don't know. The fellow might have been aimin' to have some fun with me. I mean he might have done it on purpose—"

"Ain't no one round could shoot that good," Ratchford grunted. "Excepting maybe . . . Claydell. An' Claydell hasn't got here yet. Prob'ly changed his mind an' decided to postpone his visit till tomorrow," he cleared his throat. "This where you figured them shots came from?"

"One, anyway. First one, I think. I ain't sure about the second. When that cigarette went skallyhootin' I whirled an' saw a blur among the shadows here under this tree an' came pelting over. Hadn't had chance to make out anything when up come you an' these others."

A bobbing light showed Ankrom a man running toward them with a lantern. Ratchford took the lantern from him and with his left hand he held it high above his head. In the sand a short three feet away a dark shape lay huddled motionless.

51

CHAPTER VII

A GUN STRIKES HARD

"GOOD LORD!" choked a voice— a girl's voice "It's Colonel Struthers!"

It was; Ankrom had known it instantly.

"Hold this lantern, somebody," Ratchford growled, and thrust it into Ankrom's hands. The sheriff then dropped to his knees beside Kelton Drean's limp form. Ankrom, watching Ratchford sniff and paw and probe, was reminded of the antics of a swollen monkey. But there was nothing monkeylike about Ratchford when he got abruptly to his feet; his smoky eyes grabbed Ankrom's squarely and they were opaque and hard.

"Pretty quick," he said, "we're all going to saunter over to the house an' go inside an' stay there until daylight. Meantime, I don't want to catch anyone trampin' round over by that bunk house. This Struthers dude is dead."

A heavy sigh reached Ankrom's ears. It came from a man beside him. Looking up Ankrom saw that the man was Trone. The rancher's face looked haggard; his hands were clamped so tightly about his belt that their wrinkles were not discernible and their knuckles stood out like gleaming lumps of chalk.

Then Ankrom saw Lee Trone. Betty stood beside her. Lee's face he thought a trifle pale but her eyes were bright with interest—a little horror was in them, too. Betty's eyes were like burnt holes in a white counterpane; just now the rouge upon her cheeks gave her face a ghastly appearance, Ankrom thought. He guessed she had just now joined the group. As he watched her lips sprang wide apart in a lifting scream:

"Daddy—Oh, God! it's *Daddy*!" there were tears and laughter in her voice, and the laugh ran thin with hysteria. She swayed and Ankrom sprang to catch her; he scooped her up in his arms and strode angrily toward the house. Behind him came Ratchford's voice: "Trone, you an' the others better go along, too. I'll be with you in a minute."

Lengthening his step to hold his lead, Ankrom gritted fiercely, "You little fool!"

They were close to the ranch house now and light from the unshaded windows showed Betty's eyes come swiftly open. "Don't scold me—please. I had to see you. I've got to talk with you alone right away—"

"We'll get no chance now," Ankrom cut in gruffly. "That sheriff's nobody's damn clown. He made sure this wasn't no bluff by sendin' them others with us. What did you want to talk to me about?"

She got a hand inside the neckline of her dress. When it came out it held a gun. As Ankrom carried her into the house and laid her on a sofa, she held the gun out to him anxiously. "Quick—take it! You'll have to get rid of it for me. I—"

"Did you shoot Drean?"

"I had to. He wouldn't have missed you the second time." Her eyes grew large again, filled with apprehension. "Quick—put it out of sight! The others are coming!"

They were. Ankrom heard their steps upon the veranda. Hastily he thrust the weapon—a short-barreled .32—inside the waistband of his trousers, out of sight beneath his coat. And none too soon.

Lee Trone came into the room, her father and the others behind her. Ankrom lifted a hand to push back his hat and found his forehead moist. "Gosh," he said. "She keeled right over, didn't she?"

Lee looked oddly at the girl with the closed eyes who lay so limply on the sofa. "I'll get some water," she said, and crossing the room, passed out an inner door.

"Poor kid," Old Man Trone heaved a sigh. "Pretty tough on her, havin' her father shot down like that." The two punchers stood behind him, looking on with obvious interest, hats in hand, mouths partly open.

Ankrom saw that Trone's glance, resting upon him, held a gleam of something he could not define. Clearing his throat Trone said, "Did I understand you to tell the sheriff someone took a shot at you, Streeter?"

"Someone shot a cigarette out of my mouth, yeah."

"Pretty good shooting for night work, don't you think?"

"Depends. I was lightin' the cigarette. I'd say I made a pretty fair target."

"Do you think the same man fired both shots—the one at you and the one that downed the Colonel?"

"Kind of hard to say," Ankrom evaded, and felt relieved when the sheriff came striding into the room. Lee came, too, bringing a towel and a basin of water. She passed Ankrom without a look and, bending above the sofa, began bathing Betty's forehead. "She looks awfully white," Lee said.

Ratchford flung the girls a disinterested glance, cleared his throat and looked at Old Man Trone. "Sit down, boys," he growled, the words smacking more of a command than of an invitation. "We'll be here quite some spell an' I reckon we might as well be comfortable. Be at least four hours till daylight an' I make it nearer five."

For a moment it seemed to Ankrom that Old Man Trone was about to explode. Veins swelled in his neck and forehead before he got himself in hand. Then he said vibrantly: "It's been a long time since a Ratchford gave an order on the Rafter T. 'Stead of making your authority felt you'd be doing more good if you got after that killer! Seems to me you could track him pretty fair by lantern light. Leastways it would be a damned sight better than standin' around here waitin' for daylight while he gets farther an' farther away!"

"My ol' man didn't bring me up to trail skunks in the dark," Ratchford's lazy drawl chucked back. His smoky eyes were on the gaunt old man unblinkingly. "Besides, I ain't at all sure it'll be wastin' time if we sit around here for a spell."

Lee Trone looked up from the sofa. "What do you mean?"

"To my notion the killer of the Struthers dude is in this room," he said, and his lips tightened up formidably.

A startled light flashed into Trone's old eyes that made Blur Ankrom wonder. He saw the rancher's body brace itself as for a blow. Trone's voice was a bit unsteady, his cheeks looked a little gray. "In this room," he said mechanically. "In this room?"

"Yeah—" the sheriff's lips drooped dangerously; "right damn now!"

In the silence following Ratchford's portentous words someone's breath came raspingly. To Ankrom the temperature seemed to have dropped visibly in this room in the last half

54

second. This cold silence cocked his muscles, set his teeth on edge. The air seemed to be tightening up, strangling these people who stood about like so many carven statues. Across the uncanny stillness stole the low, vibrant purring of an automobile motor. Louder and louder it grew, swelling to a wild crescendo that suddenly ceased in the yard outside to the squeal of brakes. Gravel crunched, bootheels thudded across the veranda and a man stepped through the open door.

It was Claydell, and his smiling lips grew suddenly stiff as his narrowing eyes took in the scene before him. His glance darted to the sheriff.

"What's wrong, Ratchford?"

There was antagonism, cold and smoky, in the sheriff's eyes. "The Struthers dude got in the way of a blue whistler," he said softly. "Claydell, let's see your gun."

A flush snapped into the heavy bronze of Claydell's dark cheeks. "Ratchford," twin streams of smoke splayed from Claydell's nostrils as he threw his cigarette into the yard outside. "Ratchford," he repeated. "You have a nasty mind—one of the nastiest it has ever been my misfortune to encounter. Just what's the reason for that demand?"

"A man's been murdered here an' I'm in the process of checking up." Ratchford's words were slow and measured. "Murder is a nasty thing. Claydell, an' it won't surprise me if it take a nasty mind to solve it. Let's see that gun."

"Why, you damned fool—I wasn't even here!"

"Can you prove it?"

Ankrom saw that Claydell's lips appeared about to frame a sharp retort, then abruptly clamped down tight. This man, Ankrom thought, is more dangerous than Ratchford; he's a fellow that can keep his thoughts to himself. "He's a gent that knows when to talk an' when to keep his mouth shut." He looked at the rancher more carefully. He looked at Trone, too, and for the first time realized that Lee's father had been drinking. There was that bleary look about the eyes, and the hand that Trone had propped against the wall was shaking. Ankrom remembered the startled expression he had seen in the old man's eyes a moment before. What thoughts were running throught Trone's mind?

Ankrom glanced toward the sofa and saw that Betty now was sitting up; that Lee had straightened and was eying the sheriff with distinct hostility. He looked again at Ratchford;

55

Ratchford's eyes were on Claydell and their smoky depths were stirring.

"Can you prove you wasn't here?"

"I'm not so sure that I can." Claydell finally said. "I've been driving for several hours. I've been to El Paso since I saw you this afternoon—"

Ratchford cut in, Can you prove *that?* Who did you talk with?"

"None of your damned business." Claydell tossed the words out coldly.

Ankrom tried to read some expression from his face, but it was work in vain. Claydell had the ability, the iron will, to mask his thoughts; there was no more expression on his dark countenance than there would have been on the face of a bust chopped from wood with a dull axe.

Ankrom looked at Ratchford. There was a sneer on the sheriff's heavy lips. "I'll take that gun then. You can have it back when I get the murderer."

Claydell reached inside his coat and took from someplace a .38 Police Positive. He held it out toward Ratchford. Ratchford grinned with mockery. "You can put in on the floor, brother. I wasn't born yesterday."

If Claydell felt resentful he hid it well. Ankrom watched him bend forward and lay the gun before the sheriff's booted feet. Ratchford shoved the weapon under the table with the toe of his boot. "I'll look it over later," he said.

"So Struthers has been killed and you don't know who killed him, eh?" Claydell spoke.

"When you came in I had just finished saying that it was my notion that Struthers' killer was in this room. I still think so. Your comin' ain't changed my mind a bit."

"You always were a regular Indian for holding a grudge," Claydell murmured. "I reckon it runs in the family. Your old man was that way, too."

A dark flush spread across the sheriff's face. "You damn' malignin' polecat! I've a notion to—"

"I've a notion to go to bed." Ankrom yawned, cutting Ratchford off in mid-sentence. "I'll be around; if you want me for anything you can find me in the bunk house."

"Take one step out of this room by Gawd, an' I'll put you under arrest!" Ratchford growled. "You or anyone else! There's been a killing here tonight an' I aim to find out the

56

whys an' wherefores of it—an' furthermore, who done it!"

A brooding hush closed in upon the room as the sheriff ceased speaking. Ankrom saw that the people about the sheriff even as himself, glanced covertly at one another. There was something sinister, something evil in this malignant waiting hush. Each man studied his companions with narrowed suspicious eyes. Ankrom saw that the girls did likewise. Only Trone kept his eyes off the others. *His* glance was fixed upon the sheriff and in it Ankrom saw a dread.

"Streeter," the sheriff's voice broke in upon his thoughts, "I'd like for you to give the same spiel to these folks you gave me awhile ago when we found Struther's body."

"Why, I was standin' by the bunk house lookin' at the stars an' watchin' the play of the moonlight through the foliage of the trees," Ankrom said, thoughtfully. "I remember rollin' a cigarette an' had just struck a match to light it when a gun went off an' a slug took the smoke right out of my mouth. I whirled, dragging at my gun, not knowing what was up. The shot had come from a little to one side, I guessed— from under that big pepper tree. Before I could get my gun out I heard another shot—"

"Did you see the gunflash?" Ratchford asked.

"I think I saw the first one. I couldn't see the second." Ankrom paused, then said, "As I looked toward the tree I saw a blur of movement among the shadows. I ran forward with my gun held ready. I had just got there when you came up behind me. One of the punchers brought a lantern and we saw Struther's body lyin' in the sand."

Ratchford drew a blue-barreled .45 from his belt and held it out. "Is this your gun?" he asked.

Ankrom nodded. "You ought to know—you took it out of my hand."

Claydell laughed. "That wouldn't mean anything to a suspicious devil like Ratchford," he grinned "Ratchford's old man came from Missouri."

Ratchford's big-boned frame went tense, his hand half dropping to the bone-handled weapon sheathed upon his thigh. Then a sneer crossed the heavy lips and he chuckled maliciously deep down in his great thick throat. "Have your fun, Claydell. Have your fun," he drawled. Turning toward the girls he said, "I sure am sorry about all this, Miss Struthers. Wouldn't have had it happen for the world. Just one of those

57

things, I guess, that only God knows the reasons for. I'll do all I can to bring the killer of your father to the end of his rope. You can count on it."

Betty eyed him silently, her dark eyes round and moist-looking. A fold of her dress lay clenched between her hands; so shocked by this tragedy did she seem as to be unaware that her grip of the fabric pulled it slightly above a pair of bare and dimpled knees.

But Ankrom saw, and so did Claydell, Ankrom told himself. He watched Claydell cross to where she sat upon the sofa and pat her shoulder sympathetically. "You can count on my help, too, Miss Struthers." Ankrom heard him say. "You can count on me to the limit."

"The altruist," jeered Ratchford, sneering.

"Thank you," Claydell said, and bowed. "By the way, Sheriff—among the collection of guns you've been making, I suppose you've got Struthers'? Mind if I see it?"

"Struthers did not carry a gun, so far as I can learn. What made you think he had one? Were you an' him ol' friends? Like him an' Streeter, here?"

Ankrom stared alertly at the sheriff; he did not like the tone in which the sheriff had delivered those last few words—those words linking himself and Struthers. But Ratchford was not looking at him; he was staring sardonically at Claydell and waiting for an answer.

"An old friend?" repeated Claydell. "Hardly that, Tom. I had only met the Colonel this afternoon. There was something fine about him though, I thought," he smiled. "A great nobility of mind—a thing seldom found in the characters of gamblers."

Ratchford's heavy lips were white, so closely did he press them. In the smoky eyes behind those sleepy lids Ankrom saw that clouds of caution gathered. Then Ankrom's glance passed swiftly to Old Man Trone to see how he was taking Claydell's ironic words and the revelation of Kelton Drean's actual calling; a revelation which, if Trone believed it, must have shown him that this Struthers was an imposter.

Trone's face held an odd expression. The dread which Ankrom had before noticed in his eyes was more pronounced, more evident. His gaunt form seemed to be shrinking before Ankrom's eyes. But he was sober, now; cold sober, Ankrom saw.

Ratchford was leaning a little forward. There was a dangerous droop to the corners of his mouth as he eyed the dark-faced Claydell. "Just what," he asked portentously, "did you mean by that last crack?"

Claydell raised his bushy eyebrows, shrugged. "Wasn't it evident?" he said.

Betty's voice crossed the silence recklessly: "My father was not a gambler!"

Claydell's brows shot upward far. He looked surprised. "I did not say he was, Miss Struthers. Perhaps you misunderstood me in your overwrought condition. I am sure you would be better off in bed, young lady," he smiled. "this affair tonight must have proved an awful shock to you."

Ankrom could not be sure, but he believed that in the rancher's last words he had caught a touch of sarcasm. But a glance a Claydell's suave dark face was enough to convince him that he had not. A kindly sympathy was registered there.

"Do you think I could sleep after what has happened?" she flared.

"Sleep? Well, perhaps not. But merely lying down would likely rest you."

I guess she can manage to sit up with us till daylight," Ratchford's voice reached roughly out. "She ain't so bad shook up as all that. She was around when the Colonel crossed the line. She may have seen something. When she gets a little stronger I'm goin' to question her, and until I do I aim to see she stays where she can't be got at."

"Still the suspicious soul," Claydell made a clucking sound with his tongue. "You'd be suspicious of your own grandmother, Ratchford. What makes you think she might have seen something, if I'm allowed to ask?"

"I," said the sheriff heavily, "saw a woman duck out from under that tree as I came up—the pepper tree where we found Struthers' body."

Once again that electric silence that Ankrom had felt before stole down across the room. Its very intensity seemed to presage something monstrous. To Ankrom, experienced in the feel and shadings of trouble, there lay a definite threat in the stillness of this place. He shifted his feet uneasily, moved to place his back against a wall.

And then it happened—

Some heavy object struck the floor with a metalic *clank*.

59

Every eye in that old room seemed to focus at Ankrom's feet. Ankrom had no need to send a glance questing downward to reveal the cause of the accusing looks he read in those staring eyes—he knew. He had felt that cold metallic thing go slithering down his leg; the gun that a scant half hour ago Betty had tremblingly forced upon him.

In plain sight that weapon lay upon the floor!

CHAPTER VIII

RATCHFORD SCORES

IN plain sight, blue and cold and grim it lay.

The stillness of the place before had been nothing to the monstrous quiet now wrapped about this motionless group; the very air was breathless. The impact of surprise had frozen them all to a rigid tenseness—an absolute lack of movement that would have been comical under any other condition, but that here wrote DANGER in flaming caps across the horizon of Ankrom's mind. He could almost taste the acridness of gun smoke. He thought the pounding of his heart must surely shake him.

"Well!" the sheriff drawled at last. "Well! what parlor trick is this, Streeter?"

Ankrom grinned with a feline mirthlessness that showed the hard whiteness of his teeth. "Shucks," he said, "I feel right down ashamed to call that weaklin' mine."

"I shouldn't wonder." With heavy irony Ratchford stooped to pick the weapon up. Yet even as his fingers spread to grip it, Ankrom covered the pistol with his foot.

Grimly Ratchford straightened. His burly shoulders slouched a trifle forward; the head on his squat thick neck came forward, too—came forward vulturelike until his heavy features were within ten inches of Ankrom's own. Unblinking, the smoky eyes stared balefully.

His words were low, spaced wide apart: "Where did you get that gun?"

Across Ankrom's mind came the vision of the girl from Peso

Pinto rising from the crumpled form of Kelton Drean with one hand holding papers, a pistol in the other. *This* pistol!

He eyed it warily. Had the spurious Struthers' life been snuffed with this?

He let his glance rest hard upon the sheriff's. "By your tone," he told him "a man would figure it was a crime to own more'n one gun in Texas."

"Never mind airin' your opinions. I want to know where you got this gun."

"I don't know that it's any of your business, Ratchford."

"I'm makin' it my business."

"Boot Hill is filled with fellas that had that habit—"

"Damn you!" Ratchford swore. "You answer my question an' answer it quick or by Gawd I'll slap the bracelets on you an' take you in for this killin'!"

"What evidence you got that I downed Struthers? Law says you got to have evidence before you can arrest a man for a thing like this."

"Yeah? Well, that law don't cover you. The law ain't made for driftin' saddle tramps that go round stirrin' up trouble. Talk, fella—talk, or by Gawd I'll take you in!"

There was a sinister leer on the sheriff's face; his tone rang flat with menace.

Blur Ankrom stood there the blue of his eyes like tempered steel, the lean wind-scoured cheeks drawn taut. Conflicting emotion stabbing through him as he listened to the sheriff's voice.

Trouble he told himself, was like his shadow, ever dogging his steps. He could not escape it—wherever he turned his eyes, there lay trouble waiting. To move amid scenes of turmoil seemed to be his portion. There was no escape . . . save Death.

Very well, then; he was through trying. He would give these trouble-bringers what their bringing asked for. He would give them all the trouble they wanted from here on out; he would hurl it in their teeth, he would smash them down with it. He would bury them of it in some desolate, unmarked grave!

As the sheriff's voice stopped Ankrom's right hand shrank into a rock-hard fist. He took a forward stride as the sheriff stepped back a pace and stood. His eyes held Ratchford like a grip; they were palely blue like glinting ice, they were baffling, mocking, hateful. "What was it you wanted, Ratchford?"

Caution clouded the sheriff's watchful glance. "I want to know where that gun came from."

"From the waistband of my trousers."

"Where'd you get it?"

As Ankrom was about to make answer, from the tail of his eye he caught a warning gesture. Just a tiny movement of a hand it was; a girl's hand—Lee's. Then she was not completely indifferent to him: the thought crossed his mind like light. Evidently she realized, as did he himself, that Ratchford was out to find a goat and meant to find one before he left this room.

But Lee's cautioning gesture no longer held the force it might have held this morning. Temper was stirring the steely depths of Ankrom's eyes; anger at his turbulent lot was tightening his muscles. He knew by the chilling feel of this room that suspicion was levelling against him. . . .

Stooping swiftly he came up with the gun his foot had covered; came up so suddenly the sheriff had no time to guess his purpose before the pistol's muzzle held him in grim focus as Ankrom backed to the wall beside the outer door.

"It didn't come from no dead man's hand, if that's what you're insinuatin'," Ankrom drawled. "If you're aimin' to find a goat for this night's work, Ratchford, you better pick on someone else."

"Any man can talk behind a gun," the sheriff sneered.

With a blur of motion the pistol left Ankrom's hand and no man saw where he had sheathed it. Hard white teeth gleamed coldly behind his parted lips. He stood there lounging easily, brown hands at sides, a cold humor glinting in his eyes. His attitude was a challenge to big Tom Ratchford, yet Ratchford did not move.

Ankrom said, "What caliber gun did the Colonel use, Miss Struthers?"

"Why . . . a thirty-two, I believe."

"The pistol I just picked up was a thirty-two. It came off the ground near Struthers' body. One shell has been exploded. Do you know Ratchford, what caliber slug it was that killed the Colonel?"

"A forty-five," the sheriff's voice came back. "I cut it out."

A moment's pause, and then: "Like the gun I took out of your hand a while ago."

"Did you?" Ankrom said.

The sheriff shrugged. His sleepy lids concealed the expression in his eyes. "All right, then," he said, "like the forty-five you gave up at my request a while ago— if it makes you feel any better to have it put that way."

"It does. No man ever took a gun away from me yet, Ratchford—"

"Hard hombre, eh? I've seen your type of salty drifter before—the kind that hires out its guns to the highest bidder. *Who hired you to gun the Colonel?*"

Ankrom's soft laugh mocked the silence. "I didn't gun him. I told you that before. Now let me ask you one: How'd you know the slug that downed him was a forty-five? Mightn't it have been a forty-four?"

"Listen," Ratchford said testily. "I've fooled around guns long enough to recognize whether a chunk of lead was thrown from a forty-four or a forty-five, no matter how badly it happens to be battered. There's a diff'rence in the weight. Besides, this slug was pretty smooth. It was like the ones your gun—the one you gave me—shoots."

"That doesn't mean anything," Ankrom said. "You've got a forty-five yourself. It's slung in that shoulder holster under your coat. Mr Trone may be packin' one, to, for all I know. Claydell here, produced a thirty-eight at your insistence but he may likewise have a forty-five cached about him someplace. I don't see any guns on these two cowboys, but if I was to judge them by the rest of you I'd say they was each packin' a forty-five, at least. For a country that's shucked its irons—"

"Never mind the sarcasm," Ratchford broke in roughly. He turned toward the two girls: "Miss Struthers, *where were you* when your ol' man was shot?"

The unexpectedness of the question, together with the ominous emphasis placed upon it by the lawman, brought a startled breath from Lee Trone. Her eyes flicked wide and darkened. Instinctively they sought Ankrom's. He gave her a reassuring quirk of the lips and turned his glance on Betty.

The sheriff's courtroom procedure elicited no sign of dismay from her. The girl from Peso Pinto seemed marvelously recovered from her distress of a little while ago. Her powers for recuperation were something to whistle about, one might have said. But not Ankrom; she had given him a sample of her acting when he'd carried her into this house. She had her wits about her every minute of the time, he reflected sardonically. "A girl that has all the answers," he summed her up.

When she spoke her voice held just that amount of throaty huskiness, genuine grief for her father's death might have caused. Her eyes were round and sparkly:

"I—I—Let me see," a white hand went to her forehead, rumpling the golden curls; a tiny pucker grew between her thoughtful eyes. "I had just stepped out the door there. Father had asked me to meet him out beneath that pepper tree; he said he had something private which he wished to talk with me about. . . ." She bit her lip; her thoughts seemed concentrated far away. "I'm trying to recollect—it seems to me I had just stepped out the door and crossed the veranda. I was leaning against one of those funny posts looking up at the stars—"

"Come, come, Miss Struthers," the sheriff exclaimed impatiently. "I asked you where you were when you heard the shots. I'm not interested in the history of your movements from the time you finished supper."

Upon the big sheriff the girl from Peso Pinto turned wide blue eyes in which there shone the hurt expression of a child who has been unjustly reproved. "But Mr. Ratchford, that is what I am trying to tell you. I had stepped out on the veranda and was leaning against one of the posts looking up into the purple heavens when I heard two sharp reports—"

"Then you did not see the gun flashes?" the sheriff growled irritably. "You couldn't say from which direction the reports came?"

The girl shook her head perplexedly. "I'm afraid not. You see, I was looking—"

"Yeah—I know where you were lookin'," Ratchford cut her off. "You told me that before." He swung round upon Lee Trone; "Lee," his eyes were on hers probingly "what were you doing under the pepper tree when Colonel Struthers got shot?"

Lee Trone's red lips curled scornfully. "I'll bite," she said. "What was I?"

Ratchford scowled while a dull color swept into his cheeks. "You're talking to the sheriff of this county now. I expect a civil answer."

64

"Very well," she answered, "I was not under the pepper tree when that man was killed."

"Where were you?"

"I was walking toward it from the rear of the bunk house." Ankrom saw suspicion in the sheriff's glance. "Why?"

"It was warm inside and I wanted to get some air."

"Why did you happen to pick that pepper tree to head for?"

"I wanted to be alone. The shadows were dark out there and I didn't think anyone would see me."

There were puzzled corrugations on the sheriff's wide forehead. "I have often felt like bein' alone, myself," he said. "But I can't see why you would want to be alone when old friends you hadn't seen for years had just arrived."

"I felt strange toward them. Somehow I couldn't accept them as old friends," Lee said simply. "I could not help feeling that they were strangers—and they were, you know." Her glance went to the girl who called herself Betty Struthers. "Why did you and that man practice this imposture on us?" she asked curiously.

A tear fell slowly from one moist blue eye as the girl from Peso Pinto faced her hostess. "Miss Trone—You'll never forgive us I know but we knew the real Colonel and his daughter. He had often told us of the Rafter T. I have always wanted to spend a summer on a ranch. Finally I persuaded father to impersonate—" She broke off and, turning her head away, put a handkerchief to her eyes.

Ankrom wondered if this were the truth. He felt strongly inclined to doubt it, for he knew the man she called her father was Kelton Drean, and so far as he had ever heard, Kelton Drean had no daughter. Too, he recalled the place where first he'd seen this girl. No, he decided, this yarn was a lie. But the girl was a clever actress—she knew every cue in the piece.

He saw the sheriff looking at her closely, saw the sudden tautening of Ratchford's rocklike figure. "Isn't this bogus Colonel *Kelton Drean*, the Tombstone gambler?"

The golden head drooped lower "Thought so!" the sheriff grunted. "Drean," he told the others, "is that tinhorn that made a lot of brags about someday gettin' that shootin' fool, Blur Ankrom. Seems like Ankrom gunned this Drean's cousin coupla years back, an' the gambler swore he'd never rest till he evened the account."

"What's all that got to do with us?" Trone asked, pulling himself together. He was still pale, Ankrom saw, but the fit of shaking had gone out of him, and the glance he focused on big Tom Ratchford was one of patent hostility.

"Mebbe nothing," the sheriff answered. "then again it might have a whole heap to do with you. It all depends. . . ." He broke off to frown at Claydell who was grinning.

"He means," Claydell chuckled "that one way of explainin' Drean's presence on your ranch in any guise—"

"Button your lip, damn you!" Ratchford snarled.

The dark-faced rancher returned the sheriff's frowning glare with bland surprise. "was I about to give state secrets away?" he asked politely.

"Some day," Ratchford's voice was deeply vibrant, "You're goin' to push me too far, Claydell. When that time comes you better have your holster greased."

"You remind me of a spoiled boy. When you can't have your own complete way you sulk and pout. It's about time, Ratchford, you grew up."

Before Ratchford could frame a fitting reply, Claydell went on to air his mind:

"You may be the sheriff of this county, unfortunately, but that don't come anywhere near givin' you a corner on the conversation. Any time I feel the urge to break forth in speech, neither you nor all your sheepherdin' deputies are going to hold me back. This here's a warning, Ratchford. You watch your step!"

While the sheriff stood spluttering with purple face, Claydell bowed to the others regretfully and took his leave, permitting his revolver to lay upon the floor where Ratchford's boot had earlier shoved it. Perhaps, Ankrom thought, he had forgotten the weapon. At any rate, he left without it, and a few minutes later the soft thrum of his purring motor faded on the distant night.

Ankrom's abrupt laugh broke the silence Claydell's departure had left.

"What the hell you laughin' at?" Ratchford snarled.

"Laughin' at the way that fella curled you up an' left you gaspin'," Ankrom chuckled.

"Oh, you are, are you? Well, you keep right on laughin' then while you got the chance. When you're all through I'll

66

have a few things to say that'll give you an opportunity to laugh on the other side of your mug!"

"Hop to it, then. It's long past my bedtime an' nothin' makes me so dang ornery as missin' my beauty sleep—"

"You knew," growled Old Man Trone, cutting sharply into Ankrom's sentence "that that fellow impersonating Colonel Struthers was a damned fake, sir! Why didn't you expose him?"

Ankrom's face grew sober as he gazed into the stern, accusing eyes of Lee's father. "I was waitin'," he answered, "to see how far the skunk carried it."

He saw Lee's glance travel past him to the girl from Peso Pinto, whose head was still averted. "I think his brain was addled by a pretty face," Lee said.

Hot color flowed through Ankrom's cheeks. "Perhaps it was," he told her quietly. "But you needn't worry about it happenin' again." With a curt bow he turned on his heel and went striding toward the door.

Ratchford's voice came leaping after him: "C'm'ere! You tryin' to slide out on me like that? By Gawd you better stick around!"

Ankrom, looking back across his shoulder, saw that Ratchford's hand was at his hip. He grinned coldly at the sheriff. "I expect that's your way of advisin' me to linger in this country. Well, don't fret yourself into no lather; I'll stay, all right. I guess you ain't used to my kind, brother. I belong to a breed that sticks to the last damned gasp."

"All right, Curly Wolf," the sheriff jibed. "You listen close now. You saw me prove that this Struthers dude was really Kelton Drean, the gambler. Drean's been spendin' a heap of time in the las' two years chasin' after one Blur Ankrom. This Ankrom killed Drean's cousin in a gun fight. Now it seems to me it would put you in a awkward spot, seein' as how Drean was killed here tonight, was I to prove that your real name's Blur Ankrum. That's somethin' for you to be mullin' over while you're gettin' that beauty sleep you mentioned!"

CHAPTER IX

WHERE MOSE LEFT OFF

WITH the sheriff's ominous words still coursing through his mind, Ankrom sat on the edge of his bunk several minutes later, bent double in the task of pulling off his boots. But suddenly his jackknife form went tense and his fingers ceased all operations. From the hard rock slope leading down from the great ridge hemming the valley rang a wild rataplan of hoofbeats.

For one breathless second he sat there listening while sinews of dread strained at his thought. Then with a bound he was on his feet and moving toward the open door with long swift strides that made his spurs ring thinly in that hoofshaken, moonlit silence.

In the shadow outside the doorway he halted to gaze keen-eyed across the night. But no moving thing met his roving stare along the trail leading down from the darkness of the timbered ridge. That land lay desolate and empty, devoid of life.

With hurried quiet he moved to the rear of the bunk house. What he saw stilled the breath in his throat, inured as he was to danger.

A forward-bent rider with flogging arm and flapping legs was tearing madly down that treacherous rear pitch from the valley's rim. Ankrom's eyes glinted narrow as he watched that crazy course. It seemed impossible to him that horse and rider at that fearful headlong pace should reach the valley's floor alive. Yet, thrilling, he saw them make it and marveled at their skill.

His being quickened as the reckless saddle-slicker drove his rocketing mount across the stream, sending the boggy slime along its edges flying beneath the bite of quirt and spur.

Between the buildings and straight across the yard they tore, the horse breaking to a stop in an obscuring cloud of dust as Ankrom rounded the far corner of the bunk house.

He heard the rider hit dirt, saw him go lurching toward the ranch house's broad veranda at a staggering run, stiff-legged from long contact with the saddle.

Ankrom saw the ranch house door burst open; saw dark figures come spilling out across the porch like red ants from a burning log. They were silhouetted black against the front room's lighted windows so that by their shapes he could guess at their identities. He heard the sheriff's low curse and Old Man Trone's excited voice hurling questions at the running man.

The runner stopped, stood swaying before the ranch house steps as he fought for breath. There was a sob in the words that finally came: *"Rustlers!* Gawd, boss—they've got that beef we had on the northwest range!"

Ankrom saw Trone's gaunt form shrink back as from a blow; saw a trembling hand come up to brush across his forehead. Trone's question came husky from a thickened throat: "Wiped clean . . . ?"

"Clean as a hound's tooth!" the puncher blurted. "Them rustlin' polecats was on us boys before we could get from our blankets—blowed Charlie's lamp plumb out! Slammed Ed outen the saddle s' quick he never knowed what hit 'im! I riz up emptyin' my iron fast as I could work the trigger; grabbed Ed's horse as it come larrupin' by, I been slickin' leather ever since—figgered you'd wanta know right quick."

"Where'd they head for?" bellowed Ratchford.

"I didn't do no lingerin' on that lan' scape! 'F you wanta know, I'd suggest you fork a bronc right out there, Mister."

"Where'n Hell was Hackett?" Trone demanded, spurred by sudden surge of anger at his loss.

"Couldn't say, boss. Haven't seen 'im fer a week."

Ankrom stepped forward from the shadows. "Didn't he go to your south-east line camp last night?" he asked. And at Trone's dispirited nod: "He hasn't showed here since?"

Trone shook his head and again his hand brushed across his eyes as though to shut away unpleasant pictures. "It's been this way right along," he muttered slowly. "Hackett's always somewhere else when these rustlers strike. I can't understand this thing. It's got me fightin' my hat."

"Must be a leak some place," Ankrom suggested thoughtfully.

"Leak!" Trone thundered bitterly. "Leak! Hell—they know

69

every move we make!" He glared resentfully toward Ratchford, "If the law was worth a damn—"

"That's enough of that brand of lingo," Ratchford growled. "I ain't no damn mind-reader!" He turned to the puncher grimly. "You say two of the Rafter T men were downed?"

"I ain't sure whether they cashed in Ed's chips or not. But they sure blowed Charlie's lamp out! An' last I seen of Ed he was sprawled out on his face an' not doin' any movin'." He looked toward Trone. "We goin' to stand round here gassin' all night?"

"I guess the sheriff here will take charge," Trone answered wearily.

"Not now I won't," Ratchford growled. "Right now I got all I can tend to runnin' down this murder business. You'll have to take care of it yourself, Trone."

To Ankrom it seemed that Trone was about to make some violent retort. His gaunt frame straightened stiffly. But then he shrugged. "Streeter, take the boys an' see what you can do," he said and, turning, went back inside the house.

Ankrom wheeled, went striding toward the corral. "Rattle your hocks fellas, an' let's get moving," was his only remark.

"An' be damn sure you come back when you're finished!" the sheriff growled. But Ankrom paid no heed. Swerving aside he strode with that slow sure grace of movement that marked all his motions, to a saddle-hung fence and got his rope. The two punchers who had passed the early evening playing cards did likewise. They were followed by the man who had brought the unwelcome news.

Ankrom strode inside the corral building a loop in his rope. The horses broke and circled, piling up against the pole enclosure's farther side. His buckskin saw him coming and dropped its head. Ankrom waited. When the buckskin's neck came up again the rope snaked out and dropped its loop for a ringer. Ankrom led the horse outside and swiftly saddled it. Leaving it then with trailing reins he went to the bunk house and left the corral to the punchers.

When he emerged several moments later a dark scuffed belt and holster sagged heavily about his waist. His silver spurs rang thinly in the early morning coolness as he crossed to where three mounted men awaited him beside the saddled buckskin. He climbed aboard and threw his glance against the man from the northwest line camp.

"Lead off," he said, "and don't wear these horses out. We may need 'em later on."

When Ankrom returned to the Rafter T's home ranch it was almost noon and the sun struck hotly down from overhead. After caring for his buckskin, Ankron strode stiffly to the ranch house and, without knocking, quietly entered Trone's office. The old man looked up from his brooding with a scowl.

"Back, eh? What did you find out?"

"You got any idea where these rustled cattle been goin'?" Ankrom countered.

Trone's scowl grew blackly deeper. "No," he said, and crossed his arms.

"Do you know how they've been got away with?"

"No, I don't know that, either."

"Don't you ever take a pasear out around your range?"

Trone regarded Ankrom coldly, hard-held temper plainly visible behind the pupils of his faded eyes. "I gave you a chore this morning—but I don't recollect givin' you any authority to—"

Ankrom checked him with a curt gesture. "This isn't the time for that," he drawled. Thrusting his hands deep down in his trousers pockets he took a turn or two about the room. When he next faced Trone his eyes were hard and cold. "You've got a polecat on your payroll. Mebbe two or three."

Trone stared back in silence, waiting.

Ankrom said, "This polecat I mentioned is passin' the word to these rustlers. He tells 'em when it's safe to make a haul an' likewise where to make it."

"You got proof of this?"

"Hasn't Hackett been reportin' that you're losin' cattle?" At Trone's nod Ankrom shrugged. "I'd say it was evident then. As your range boss, it is up to Hackett to stop this stealin'. Evidently he can't stop it. There's only one reason, as I see it, why Hackett can't stop your losses with the men at his disposal. Someone of these men on your payroll is tipping the rustlers off, telling 'em where Hackett and the men will be at a time when a bunch of your critters are loosely guarded someplace else."

"Cripes," Trone said sarcastically. "You ought to be a detective, Streeter."

71

Ankrom grinned coldly. "Then you've known that much right along, eh? How come you don't know then how your cattle are bein' stolen?"

"They're bein' run off into the badlands, into the lava beds or across that big salt flat. Trail peters out in them places an' we can't—"

"Do you know why the trail peters out?" Ankrom interrupted.

"Sure. It peters out in the badlands because steers don't leave much trail on lava. An' who the hell could trail steers across a loose salt flat with the kind of winds we have in Texas?" Trone growled. "You got any more bright remarks?"

"Yeah—one or two. You, or your foreman, has jumped to the wrong conclusion."

"What do you mean?"

"Those rustled cattle of yours have never been driven more than a hundred yards into the badlands or out onto that salt flat."

"You're crazy!" Trone snapped testily.

"Your cattle," Ankrom went on imperturbably, "have been taken off this range in trucks."

For the space of two seconds there was dead silence, then—

"What the hell you been smokin'?" Trone demanded.

"I'm talkin' facts, Trone. An' I can prove 'em. I've got those three men of yours trailin' tire marks right this minute. They've got orders to find out where those tracks are headin' for an' then to come back here an' report. Mebbe when they return you'll know a little more about what's been happenin' to your cattle."

Dawning belief was struggling against the suspicion and incredulity in Trone's faded eyes. Ankrom hooked his thumbs in his gun belt and waited for the rancher to speak.

"By Gawd," Trone said at last, "it *could* be done."

"It's being done. They've been rustlin' steers by truck in Colorado for the last coupla years. Swoop down on a herd of a dark night an' in the mornin' the cattle are clear out of the state. Your cattle are goin' that way, too. Either by truck alone, or by truck an' train."

"How come Alkali didn't see no truck then?" Trone asked, still fighting against belief.

"If by 'Alkali' you mean that puncher that fanned in here

72

with the news, he did," Ankrom stated flatly. "He also tells me one of the other boys mentioned something about tire tracks crossin' the trail of one of your herds several months ago—one of your rustled bunches, I'm talking about. Alkali says Hackett fired the man the same day he made the crack about seein' those tire marks. Does that mean anything to you?"

Trone's seamed face went red. "Are you tryin' to tell me Hackett's crooked?"

"I'm lettin' Hackett's actions answer that," Ankrom said. "He's comin' now."

Mose Hackett, followed by three punchers who had just ridden in with him, dismounted at the pole corral. Hackett was relegating the job of unsaddling his mount to one of the punchers when Ankrom and Trone came up.

"Never mind unsaddling that pony," Ankrom said. "Mr. Hackett isn't staying long."

Hackett swung round with a hard stare. "Huh? Who the hell are you to be sayin' what I'm gonna do or not gonna do? Who the hell gave you any authority around here?"

"I'm the new range boss," Ankrom told him levelly. "You can come up to the office an' get your time. We've got no use for double-crossin' polecats on the Rafter T. Those men of yours can come along an' get their time, too. We won't be needin' 'em any longer."

The three men mentioned turned startled glances upon Ankrom, then looked at Hackett enquiringly. Hackett's face was livid as he ripped out a lurid oath. His burly figure slid into a crouch and his right hand hung poised and talon-like above the bone-handled gun protruding from his holster. His lips writhed venomously in a bloated face.

But Ankrom's soft laugh mocked. "Better wash that war paint off, sonny. You're dealin' with a man now; a man that's got your measure."

Hackett's hand stopped where it hung a short four inches above the handle of his pistol. His lips still twitched spasmodically; his mien evidencing the stormy passions that tore at him. Yet no words left his mouth.

"If you're tryin' to have a fit," Ankrom said, "you better have it someplace else."

No man smiled at Ankrom's taunting words. Something they read in Ankrom's wind-whipped face seemed suddenly to have cast a chill over all these men about him. No man knew him personally; none knew his reputation. To them he was merely Streeter, a drifting cowhand whom Trone in his generosity had taken on. Yet into his manner now they must have read a cold intentness—some hint of coming violence that froze them in their tracks.

Hackett's belligerence, even as on a former occasion, seem to be draining from him. The rouge-like spot of color staining either graying cheek spoke, as did his suddenly twitching fingers, of a morale that was rapidly cracking under the bleak stare of Akrom's eyes. He licked his lips. Twice he cleared his throat before the stumbling words came out:

"What . . . what's wrong?"

"Hackett," said Ankrom, "when a man finds a sidewinder in his blankets there's only two things he can do—drive it out or kill it."

"Why—why, what do you mean?"

"You can write your own ticket."

"You're makin' it pretty boggy. Can't you ride that trail again?"

"I said you can write your ticket the way you like. I'm leavin' it up to you to say what I ought to do with the rustlin' snake I've cornered."

Hackett started like a man smashed unexpectedly across the mouth. The burning spots washed out of his cheeks. His voice was hoarse, "Rustling . . . Wh—what you mean?"

"I'm calling you the sidewinder that's been tipping off the rustler fraternity to the best time an' place to strike the Rafter T. *You* are the leak' them rustlers been dependin' on, Hackett," Ankrom's drawl grew low and cold, "You're not a snake—*you're a dirty stinkin' skunk!*"

Hackett's eyes bulged wide and the ghastly pallor of his face betrayed his fear. He threw his glance about him with the desperation of a trapped rat. But always it came back to Ankrom's face as though it dared not leave for long that mocking countenance.

Hackett's three companions, now equally pale, began to edge away from his proximity. Their arms went above their heads in token of the peacefulness of their intentions. Hackett cursed them roundly with every obscene word in his vocabulary until his glance crossed Ankrom's once again. His blustery voice fell away like a reed before a Norther's blast.

74

Hardly conscious of the fact, he joined the backing movement.

"Exit *'los bravos'*," Ankrom jeered. "Four coyotes in eagle feathers!"

For some reason a shudder shook Old Man Trone's gaunt frame. Perhaps it was the timbre of Ankrom's voice; again, it may have been the wanton savagery of that malicious glance accompanying the words.

Slowly Hackett backed away. He moved cautiously so as not to precipitate the threatened action. He moved haltingly, foot by feeling foot. At last he felt his horse behind him and sent his left hand questing upward for the horn. He seemed afraid to take his eyes from his accuser; the very expression of his bloated face revealed with what degree of accuracy he read the blazing fires of wrath, destruction and contempt that lay behind the frigid serenity of Ankrom's countenance.

Ankrom's voice reached out with cold authority:

"Get off this ranch an' don't come back. That goes for all four of you. From now on the Rafter T is going to take open season on skunks and other varmints. Get goin', hombres," he said, and with a jeering laugh turned on his heel.

A malignant scowl creased Hackett's ugly features. His poised right hand swooped downward like a striking hawk and got his gun. Ankrom's turning body did not stop but whirled clear round with the speed of light. The satanic up-curve of his tautened lips held an evident malice.

The end came swiftly. Too late Hackett saw the leveled gun in Ankrom's hand. His own was halfway out when Ankrom's roared—just once. Hackett seemed to bend forward to meet that leaping spurt of flame. For a moment then, as though seen through the lens of a slow-motion camera, he hung poised in an awkward bow. His knees gave way abruptly and spilled him forward to the sand. He did not move again.

"*Geez!*" the exclamation burst from one of Hackett's men.

Cold fire smouldered now in Ankrom's gaze. "Anyone achin' to take up where Mose left off?"

Hastily the men denied their interest.

"Fork your broncs then an' keep on travelin'," Ankrom advised. "An'," he added softly, "be right careful our trails don't cross again."

75

CHAPTER X

SHOCK

IN THE days immediately following Ankrom's killing of the crooked range boss, the placid surface of rangeland life at the Rafter T flowed smoothly on with no least ripple created by untoward event. To be sure, Trone's beef had apparently vanished from the face of the earth; the three men Ankrom had set trailing the marks left by the tracks in the sand of this semi-arid range had returned that very night, sheepishly confessing the rustlers had eluded them. The tracks, these men claimed, has "just plumb petered out!"

Sheriff Ratchford had left the ranch before Ankrom's set-to with Hackett, and had not been back since, though he had told Trone upon leaving that he would soon be back to wind up the matter of Kelton Drean's mysterious killing. One of the Rafter T hands reported having seen the sheriff one night in Peso Pinto roaring drunk.

"He was makin' some powerful tall brags," the hand —'Windy' Jones—told Ankrom confidentially.

"That was the rot-gut talkin', I shouldn't wonder."

"I dunno. But Ratchford, he's a lot smarter than most folks gives him credit for," Windy mused soberly. "He was drunk, I'll concede you that. But he was sure doin' some awful plain talkin'. 'Allowed as how he's a-goin' to cinch that tinhorn's killin' onto that Arizona gun-slick, Ankrom. I ain't acquainted with the gent, but from what I've heard about him, I'd sing low was I Tom Ratchford." He looked at Ankrom speculatively.

Ankrom grinned. "By that remark, I judge you think he's got some sort of evidence against this Ankrom jasper."

The puncher rasped his jaw. "Well, if he ain't he's sure gettin' uncommon careless. I don't think he cottons to you, Streeter."

"I expect there ain't much chance of us gettin' on huggin' terms," Ankrom said, and closed the subject. But he did considerable thinking about Windy Jones' remarks in the days that followed. He felt certain the sheriff knew about his gunning of Hackett, for he'd sent Alkali in to report the man's death the following day. The coroner and one of Ratchford's deputies had come out, asked a few questions and taken the body back to town. Nothing further had been said about the affair, but Ankrom had a feeling that the incident was no more closed than was the business of Drean's death. Ratchford, he decided, was merely biding his time.

But with what object? Ankrom shook his head; he could not guess.

Nor could he guess why, or under what circumstances the girl calling herself Betty Struthers continued her visit with the Trones. Following her inquisition by the sheriff, Ankrom had expected her to pack her bags. She still remained on the Rafter T however and often sought him out when he spent a night at the home ranch.

Lee Trone, on the contrary, avoided him like she might a plague, and took pains to show him that the avoidance was deliberate. She had not spoken to him since the day of Hackett's exposure and resultant death.

Not that he cared, he told himself. The less they saw of each other the better it would be for both of them. He could not risk many close contacts with a girl of Lee's tremendous personal magnetism. He could not afford, he admonished himself for the hundredth time, to fall in love. He was a gun man—notorious. That the fact was not entirely his fault made no difference to the issue. To a man of his adventurous breed the better things in life must needs be barred. That, at least, was Ankrom's way of looking at it.

Nevertheless, her attitude toward him hurt, and more keenly than he would admit. Often when riding across the range her vision would come between his eyes and distant things. Thought of her was ever in his mind, and this further widening of the breach in their original relation made his position here intolerable. Gradually a grim resolve was forming: he would go to her when this Struthers business was settled and ask her to release him from his word that he might go his way—that he might cross the valley rim for a final time and never more return.

Some such thoughts were in his mind one afternoon when, traversing the miles between the southeast line camp and the

77

home ranch, he rounded a bend in the dry wash he was following and came abruptly face to face with another rider —the golden girl of Peso Pinto.

If he was surprised by this unexpected meeting, she appeared equally so. But Ankrom, having witnessed previous samples of her excellent acting, would have been willing to bet his last *centavo* that she had somehow deliberately engineered this encounter.

He regarded her quizzically. "Haven't we met some place before? Paris . . . Berlin . . . London? Or was it Bombay where we sat on the terrace eating bananas?"

She laughed at his nonsense—a merry tinkle of sound. Her yellow curls were tousled by the wind, for she persisted— against all advice—in wearing her hat looped by its chin-strap on the back of her neck. Yet he had to admit that she made a most enticing picture as she lounged easily in her saddle atop the big blue horse.

That horse, he reflected, was the pride of Old Man Trone. "I'm surprised that you're riding Smoky," he said. "Better watch out one of the boys don't pass the word to Trone."

"Why, that's all right. He told me I could ride the blue."

"He did!"

She laughed. "I have a way with horses," she confided. "Men, too—some of them, anyway."

He thought he read a challenge in her eyes, and nodded. "I'm not amazed," he answered drily. "By the way, how does it happen that you're still staying on at the ranch?"

"I'm suffered on Ratchford's orders. He forbade my leaving until after the solving of the mystery surrounding the death of Kelton Drean."

"Then you admit the Colonel's real name was not Struthers."

"Sure—why not? They could find that out easily by a little investigation. I don't think I'd want them to look into things too closely."

"Why not?"

She regarded him thoughtfully, but finally shook her yellow curls. "No . . . I don't believe I will answer that . . . now. Perhaps when all this—" she spread her hands expressively, "is past I may. It will depend."

But he did not grab at the bait she dangled with that last

sentence. He said, "What were you doing in that house in Peso Pinto?"

Her blue eyes clouded and for a moment she did not speak. Then—

"I worked there," she answered simply. "I did not think that you'd remember . . ."

"I don't often forget a face."

She bent forward in her saddle, impulsively leaned toward him. "You don't like me, do you? It is because you saw me first in . . . in there?"

"If I don't appear to like you," Ankrom evaded, "it is because of the manner of your introduction to this ranch. A contemptible imposture. I'm surprised that a girl of your perceptions would lend herself to such a thing."

A strange light had come into her eyes, he thought. They looked somehow darker, deeper, larger. When she spoke her words were low and vibrant, as though great feeling lay behind them.

"If there was deception in the way I came to the Trones it was only in my association to Drean. It happens I lent myself to his plan when he approached me only because it seemed to offer the only possible escape from my environment—my only means of withdrawing from a hateful past. Do you think I liked my lot? Do you believe I *wanted* to live that way?" she demanded fiercely. "Do you think I would not have stooped to *anything* that offered me the chance of turning that hateful leaf?"

In that moment of arousement, in that moment while stormy passions had her in their grip and she was fighting to defend her action, Ankrom thought her almost beautiful. His glance must have reflected the thought, for her face went white and she turned her horse abruptly. "I'm going back to the ranch," the words seemed husky as her mount leaped forward to the spur.

They rode possibly half a mile in silence. The pace was fast at first but gradually slowed. Then Ankrom put a question. "Do you know what Drean was up to?"

"In coming out here, you mean?"

"Yes. I'm trying to get at his purpose. I don't think he'd have come unless he saw money in the scheme. It appears to me that he was not acting on his own—that he was

79

following the orders of some man who's stayed in the background."

"Why do you think that?"

"That's hard to explain. Queer things are goin' on in this country; things that have got me fightin' my hat. Some man has been sharpening up his knife for Old Man Trone. That night you called to me in Peso Pinto, a bunch of thugs had lured Miss Lee to an empty house. I busted in as they were threatening her with a red-hot branding iron. Sort of spectacular, isn't it?"

"But of course they were going to use it," she smiled. "Yes—quite melodramatic in this humdrum day and age."

Ankrom's lips quirked. "It ain't so damned humdrum as a lot of people seem to think. Another thing about this business," he went on after a moment's reflection. "Trone has been losing cattle. Rustlers have been workin' his range in a wholesale way. An' I'm here to state those boys are experts. They're ridin' Trone beef out of this country in trucks—an' they're getting away with it. There's head work back of that. Drean was crafty in his way but he never had the brains for that. Drean, I shouldn't wonder, was just a two-bit pawn in a big-shot game."

"You're thinking," she said, "that Drean wouldn't have been interested in cattle. Well, perhaps the man you think was behind Drean isn't interested in cattle, either." Ankrom looked at her sharply. "Maybe not," he finally said. "Anyway, he's not puttin' all his eggs in the same basket. He's getting at Trone from all angles. The stolen cattle were all prime beef. First time I ever heard of rustlers bein' so finicky —or lucky. Well, they've stripped his range of salable stuff. That means that unless he's got money in the bank—"

"He has," she cut in swiftly. "The bank at Peso Pinto. Drean told me he had. Does that help any?"

"Can't say. It might help Trone, if he's got enough. Probably depends on things I know no more about than you—"

"Would you care to know more about me?" she cut in, urging the blue up closer.

Ankrom felt heat come into his cheeks. "We're discussin' Trone, right now."

The blue lunged ahead beneath her sudden drive of spurs. Remorse for his rudeness came to Ankrom as he urged the buckskins after. He did not wish to hurt this blue-eyed Roxana needlessly. Already, he guessed, she'd suffered enough at the hands of fate. But love must have no place in his life; and if love could have had a place, that love would have belonged to Lee. Why did this golden-haired girl persist in intruding the personal equation into their conversations?

Urging his horse alongside the running blue he was about to make his peace-talk when her voice came at him evenly: "Please go on. You've got my curiosity aroused."

Relieved, Ankrom said, "Well, here's another angle. Trone's name is tabu among his neighbors. There could only be one reason for that, since it ain't at all likely that the whole country has a mad on at him."

Betty laughed in soft exuberance. "I'll be interlocutor. What's the one reason?"

"The reason is these people are onto the fact that someone's got his knife out for Trone, an' they don't want to get mixed up in any feuds."

"Sounds fairly reasonable."

"It is reasonable. These neighbors of Trone's are mostly men with families to think of. They can't afford to get involved in a range war—another man's bread might come too high." Ankrom's voice became reflective, confidential: "The way things are shapin' up right now, I would hate to bet that even the Rafter T will go to war."

"Then there is a silver lining to this cloud?"

"If there is, I haven't seen it," Ankrom grunted. "What I mean is that it looks like Trone's opposition isn't aiming to leave him any weapons to fight with—an' darn few men. Look: counting myself, Trone has exactly four men on his payroll. You can't stage much of a war with four men against God knows how many."

"I thought the Rafter T was large, as ranches go today."

"It is. It's the largest cattle spread in this state." Ankrom looked at her curiously. "What's that got to do with it?"

"Why, I thought large ranches hired lots of men. If Trone needs more men why doesn't he hire them? He's got money—"

"What you don't know about ranches," Ankrom broke in, "If you'll pardon my frankness, would fill three or four extra-large books. Listen; we don't know how much money. Trone has in the bank. The chances are he hasn't any to spare. The last coupla years the stock market has been damn bad. This year we've had drought from the word go. Under such conditions it takes a lot of dinero to swing this ranching game; not to mention the amount of money that goes into puncher pay.

"*But*—an' here's the catch, no matter how much coin Trone's got tucked away—this man that's out to smash the Rafter T has fixed it so that Trone can't hire any men. No one will work for him; no outsider, I mean. The word's been passed around. I tell you, some right powerful gent is after the Ol' Man's scalp, an' between you an' me, it won't surprise me if he gets it!"

"I hate a quitter!"

"Quitter? What're you talkin' about?"

"You're lying down, or planning to, aren't you? If you're not, then you ought to sue your voice for libel."

"Whether I look ahead and figure the chances are better than sixty-forty that Rafter T gets smashed, or not, has nothing to do with where I stand. When I set out to back a thing, I back it all the way." He gave her a sharp look. "Kindly remember, though, that I'm just one puncher—not an army."

"You might hand somebody that line an' get away with it," she grinned, "but little Goldie's been around."

It was Ankrom's turn to bend forward. Amusement was written on the oval face of the girl from Peso Pinto, but there was no amusement in the dark glance Ankrom fixed upon her. "Ride that trail again," he said, "and take it slow an' easy like. Mebbe I'm a little dense."

"I guess maybe you are, at that."

"What are you getting at now?" he scowled.

"Lee Trone."

"What about her?"

"Listen," she came back at him, "I may not know more than a hoot or two about ranches, but brother, when it comes to women, you don't know a thing!"

"I won't argue that," said Ankrom; "I never claimed to know much about them."

"Well, you sure don't."

Their horses, taking advantage of their riders' interest in one another, had stopped and now were nibbling contentedly at a straggly bush that grew from the pebble-and-sand floor of the dry wash. The golden girl leaned forward, facing Ankrom earnestly. "What you need, Friend Abe, is someone to wise you up on a little female psychology."

82

"Some women," she went on swiftly, "would go through hell for the man they love; they'd get down on their knees an' crawl through flame for him, thanking God for the chance. And right now I'm not talking of your blue-ribbon thoroughbreds like Lee Trone who decorate drawing rooms and swanky teas with fine lines of flippant patter! I'm speaking of the *real* women—the kind that don't mind working. Women who've never had much to make life worth living—ordinary women; gangsters' molls, racketeers' wives, coppers' wives, cigarette girls, shop girls; *common women*. Girls like me! They wouldn't give a damn what their husbands were, what their men did—if they loved them."

The passion went out of her voice and she went on more quietly:

"Do you think the Lee Trones of this world would ever marry a gun man? That's what she called you—a *'gun man'!*" Her voice grew hard, scornful. "She told me she saw you kill Hackett. She said you 'egged him on'; turned your back so he would reach for his gun, and when he did you turned and shot him. She said if it wasn't that they needed you here so badly now, she would have made her father run you off the ranch just as you ran those others off!" There was bitterness in her blazing eyes, "That's the kind of a person your Fine-Lady-Lee is! She hired you for your gun because she was afraid that this 'someone' you've been talking about would 'get' her old man. And while you risk your life providing protection for that drunken has-been, she despises and loathes you for the very prowess that caused her to hire you!"

The impact of her searing denunciation left Ankrom rigid. Then—

"Let's go," he said, and jogged the buckskin into motion. But where it carried him he did not see. He had not known what it felt like to be really cold, till now. His legs and arms, his head, his body seemed lumps of frozen lead. His heart was a ball of ice.

CHAPTER XI

The Wedge Drives Deep

FOR a man to be sure that a thing is so, is one matter; for a man to be sure that a thing is so and then be forced to listen to some woman's corroboration of that unpleasant fact is quite another. In the peaceful days that followed the golden girl's revelation, Ankrom rode the range with bitter thoughts and sombre countenance; rode in solitude and frowning silence. His glance took on a colder inscrutability, his lips a more grimly sardonic twist. As foreman of the Rafter T he got the ranch work done to impeccable perfection, but his manner of getting it done soon warped the playful disposition of his men and left them saturnine and curt as he was himself.

As Alkali one day put it to Windy Jones, "Ridin' for this cold-jawed, rifle-eyed Streeter wolf is sure gonna sap every drop o' the milk of human kindness from my system, Windy, ef I keep it up much longer. 'F it wasn't for Miz Lee, by cripes, I'd tell that dang slave driver a thing or two an' pull my picket pin an' drift."

"I expect you'd pull yore picket pin, all right," Jones grinned. "But if you went to handin' Streeter any gas I don't reckon you'd do a heap o' driftin'—leastways, not on this mortal coil!"

If Ankrom realized his growing unpopularity with the men, he must have cared not, for he gave it no attention nor modified his treatment. As much as possible he kept away from them, taking many long rides into the surrounding country, engraving deeply upon his mind the topography of this country Visits to the home ranch were made no more frequently than absolute necessity demanded, and then were brief.

Two searing, wayward emotions over which he could gain no control swayed his being by night and by day, driving him ever deeper into an embittered reticence that was broken only by sardonic comment which, at times, bordered on the vitriolic. These emotions were hurt and anger. He was hurt by the knowledge that to Lee Trone he was in much the same category as a bonnet—a thing of use to be discarded when its use was ended. His anger had been roused by a number of things, but chiefly by the discovery that Lee's reported opinion of her "hired hand" could so effectively throw him out of stride—could so swiftly warp his nature.

To be sure, he had repeatedly reflected, her opinion of him was at heart an estimate deserved. It was practically his own estimate of himself as given to her *by himself* that first night of his arrival when they'd sat in the touring car together in the darkness of the stable.

At *that* time, however, she had rejected that estimate; had protested vehemently against it, and he—blind fool—had believed that protestation sincere. Somehow he had expected better at her hands than this; he had taken pride in thinking that the only barrier to a more intimate relationship between them was the barrier raised by himself. That Struthers dame was right; what he knew about women were better left unmentioned.

He could quit the ranch of course; he could throw his job in old Trone's face and go his way regardless. That is, he could do so had he not passed his word to see this unknown business through to its final end—but he *had* passed his word! In Ankrom's code the oral acceptance of a commission was binding as the strongest contract; his given word was a thing by which he had always abided, come what might, and bitter as the realization was he must abide by it now.

It was early afternoon one day about a fortnight after his illuminating conversation with Betty, that Ankrom came riding in to the home ranch to find Lee Trone watching his approach from the shady coolness of the broad veranda. She stood leaning against a post, her shapely brown fingers tracing out the deep-cut initials carved in its surface by forgotten knives in years long past.

He tried to deny the hunger in his soul and told himself he would not glance toward her again; to do so would be too much like emulating a scolded dog who, by its abashed antics, seeks to insinuate itself once more in the good graces of its master. He would never be like that—not with her. Let his cold indifference show her that far from being master (or mistress, more correctly speaking), he regarded her merely as the Old Man's capricious daughter.

Her voice came across the interval softly—calling him. To his surprise he found his horse moving toward her where she leaned against the veranda post. With a muttered oath he swung the buckskin's head around and rode him in the opposite direction, dismounting stiffly by the pole corral.

Later he was eating a cold snack the cook had grumblingly got together with more speed than care of flavor when a shadow darkened the cook shack door and looking up, Ankrom found Lee Trone's green eyes upon him oddly. In grim silence he continued eating. Let her stand there like a fool if she had no message for him; he'd be damned if he'd speak first!

Against his will her cool voice reached across the interval and brought him reluctantly to his feet: "Your education in manners, Abe, seems to have been neglected."

Resentfully he doffed his battered hat. The sunlight streaming in the open doorway struck across his rumpled sandy hair and burnished it like copper. He stood there stiffly by the table and his cold unwavering glance held no faintest sign of friendship.

"What do you want—?"

"Quoth the bear," she mocked. "I wanted to see you, Abe, but I didn't know you'd be eating. I called to you when you rode in, but I guess you didn't hear me."

He held himself grimly silent, trying to eye her down. But it proved wasted effort; her glance was steady as his own and gradually took on something of its belligerency.

"Well?" he finally said. "If you got somethin' on your mind, go ahead an' air it."

"There's an unpleasant change come over you in the last few days that's neither appreciated nor necessary. If you don't like it here, you're free to leave when the notion strikes you," she told him coolly. 'If you're in a hurry you can come up to the house and get your time right now."

Surprise showed fleetingly in Ankrom's glance. Then his bronzed features resumed their former cold inscrutability.

"When I make a bargain I keep it. If you feel like releasing me from my word, go ahead. But I'm telling you right now that I ain't goin' to be got rid of that easy. I'm not gettin' out of this till the Ol' 'man sends me walkin'

86

down the road. Like I told your tough sheriff, I'm a gent that sticks to the last damn gasp!"

"You seem to have a pretty good opinion of yourself," she said with curling lip; then asked, "Have you found out yet who's in charge of the rustling activities on this range?"

"No, I haven't yet—but I will."

"It must be nice to have such confidence as yours."

"Confidence, ma'am, is part of a gun man's stock in trade." He saw that he had scored. The tiny smile slipped off her lips.

"I could name a number of less desirable things which seem to be a part of yours," she retorted frostily.

"Yes, ma'am, I expect you could," he said and, to occupy his restless hands, began twirling his dusty hat. It surprised him to find that all Lee Trone's old allure was still in evidence; still retained its power to move him against his will. Just being near her like this, he found, did things to him; accelerated his pulse; made his stormy heart miss beats, and caused his blood to flow more hotly.

He resented her power to sway him. He felt shamed to realize that he could still feel interest in a girl whose expressed opinion of him was steeped in cold contempt. What kind of a man was he? he wondered bewilderedly. Did Lee Trone affect all men so?

His livening glance, playing across her, took in her belted overalls and woolen shirt, yet did not see them. He was conscious only that these rough clothes could not conceal the willowy grace of her slender body, could not detract from the spirited poise of her lifted head.

He said, "If the talk-fest if over, I'll get on with my eatin'."

The green eyes raked him furiously. The next moment she was gone.

He tried to finish his meal but could not. Lee Trone's visit had left him a deal too agitated. Contemplation of the doorway left him moody. It loomed desolate and empty—useless now that she was no longer framed by its dimensions. It brought home to him more forcefully than ever the subtle magnetism of her. Even the sunlight, where it spilled in golden pools across the floor, seemed dim and cold now that she was gone.

With a muttered oath Ankrom got irritably to his feet and quit the place. He strode across the yellow sand to the bunk house, entered wearily and flung himself down upon his bunk. But plainly sleep was not for him. As he lay there his mind, filled with its many pictures, mocked him. For every picture was a vision of Lee Trone.

He was amazed to learn how effectively his memory had grasped each changing expression of her mobile countenance, each poise of her slender figure, each graceful move and gesture. He recalled especially well the tempting curve of her parted lips, and the vision struck him hard.

Savagely he snapped his cigarette through the open door. He heard a little gasp and saw a shadow cross the opening. Like a flash he was off the bunk and on his feet, his right hand gripping a leveled pistol. With a sheepish grunt he slipped the weapon back in leather and tossed his hat upon his bunk. The girl from Peso Pinto stood eyeing him gravely from the door.

"May I come in?"

"I reckon," he said ungraciously, "there ain't no one going to stop you."

"You and I," she answered smiling, "have a lot in common. We are both what might be termed 'adventurers.' We're both blunt, possess very little tact, and seldom use what little we have. Right now you're in a vicious mood. I am, too. I get into a vicious mood every time I come in contact with you."

He must have shown interest, he reflected, for she approached, stood staring at him searchingly, her lips a little parted, her blue eyes big and wide. "Why don't you like me?" she asked him suddenly. "We ought to be friends. Why can't we get along?"

"I'm not good enough for you—I'm not good enough for any woman. I'd ought to be made to wear a sign 'GUN MAN—DANGEROUS; STEER CLEAR' so that folks in passing would not be contaminated. They've got me pegged as a bad one; a killer. I can't deny it for I have killed men. That they were people the world is better off without makes no difference in the fact. There is no place for a woman in the career of a man like me."

"You're bitter," she said softly. "Some woman has hurt you . . . I can see it in your eyes. Whoever she is, she ought to be boiled in lard. Not good enough? What do you mean, 'not good enough'? In every man's life there is a place for a woman. For the right one," she amended swiftly.

88

"Don't you remember what I told you the other day? For a man—a real man like you—there are lots of women who would go through hell, and be glad of the chance. What difference if you have had to kill a few tough hombres in your time? That has nothing to do with the relations between a man and a woman. How could it have? Women live for love, Abe, and they want strong men to love them."

A silence fell between them, an uncomfortable silence to Ankrom. He could find no words to answer this girl. Why couldn't he transfer the interest he gave Lee Trone to this golden creature before him? To this glowing, golden girl whose warm nature shone from her passionate eyes?

Affection, he thought, cannot be transferred at will. He stiffened to a sudden realization. *He was in love with Lee Trone;* in love—God save the mark—with a girl who felt toward him nothing save loathing and cold contempt!

His cheeks went white. God, what a fool he was! Ankrom, the man who had always prided himself on having his emotions under control. In love with a girl who would not have him, and loved by a girl he did not want!

He brought his thoughts up sharply. Betty was speaking again; what had she been saying? He cleared his throat, hoped his voice would not betray him. "What was that?"

"Why don't you like me?" she repeated, coming closer.

"Did I ever say I didn't?"

"Not in so many words, perhaps. But actions, Abe, speak loudest. There is an air about you—I can *feel* that you don't like me. What have I ever done to you that you should feel this way about me?" She came to him swiftly, placed a hand upon his shoulder, her blue eyes searching his face a little fearfully.

He did not draw away—innate courtesy would not permit him to offend her. He said slowly, "Let me ask you a question, Betty; why did you shoot Drean?"

"Because he would have shot you," she answered huskily. "He missed the first time, but he would not have missed again."

"Would it have made so much difference to you—?"

"Of course," she broke into his question hurriedly. "I told you a woman will go through hell for the man she loves." Her arms went about him hungrily; there was a sob in her pleading voice: "Tell me that you see some good in me; that

89

I'm not all bad, Abe. Tell me that you love me just a little . . ."

Somehow at that moment Ankrom's eyes were drawn toward the door. He went stiff and cold. Lee Trone stood in the opening, her red lips parted in a curling smile.

"Yes, tell her, Abe, by all means. Don't let me spoil your fun."

She was gone before Ankrom found his voice.

CHAPTER XII

"To String a Fence"

A DISTINCT product of his early environment which no amount of polishing could erase, Blur Ankrom was at heart an adventurer. Frequently hot-tempered to the point of recklessness, he was an idealist yet, withal, a man of turbulence. Born with the crash of gunfire in his ears he had swiftly, at a tender age, became inured to danger.

Deprived of his mother while still in swaddling clothes, he had been raised to the best of a father's ability whose time was largely spent amid scenes of wildest violence, and whose reputation had been founded not so much on personal integrity as on his swift and expert manupulation of a brace of Frontier .44s.

Marshal Ankrom had insisted that young Abe get an education that he might not, by circumstances, be forced into punching someone else's cattle at forty per and found. So, to please his father, Abe had gone away to college and studied engineering. In the vacation following on the heels of his junior year, young Ankrom had returned to Tombstone to find the former marshal dead and buried of a treacherous bullet through the back. Incensed at the scurvy fate that would permit such a thing to happen, he had parted ways with conducted education then and there. The following year had witnessed his killing of Storm Drean and had placed his booted feet upon the smoky trail of violence followed by his father. Yet no blow received by him in the adventurous, troublous years that followed had struck one half so deep as the shocking impact of that moment when, with Betty's arms about his neck, he had looked up to find Lee Trone standing just inside the open bunk house door!

That moment caused a constriction of the muscles of his stomach, caused a curling of the hair at the back of his rigid neck and almost stopped the beating of his heart. In that crisis he could find no voice with which to answer the scornful mockery of Lee Trone's stinging words. And then she was gone . . . and he had offered no defense.

There was a flinty brittleness in Ankrom's glance as he removed the girl's arms from about his body. Not even the despairing twist of her parted lips or the stricken look in her wide blue eyes held the power to move him now. He was like some soulless thing hewn out of iron and his tight-lipped inscrutable face seemed cold and hard as a granite crag.

He clamped his hat upon his head and strode toward the blinding spot of light that marked the door's dimensions. But in its radiance the girl from Peso Pinto caught him, whirled him around.

"Wait!" she cried. "You can't go like that! Is there nothing you can say to me? No tiniest ray of—"

There he stopped her with his eyes. "I'm afraid not," he said, and his voice was bleak.

"You're hard! Bitter!" She reached out to put her hand again upon his shoulder, but his eyes warned her and she dropped the hand impotently to her side. "There . . . there is information I could give you if only you'd treat me a little kinder . . ."

"I don't," Ankrom told her flatly, "buy information in that manner."

He turned to depart but she would not have it thus. The hunger in her would not let him go like this. She clutched him desperately, frantically. "Wait—I'll tell you anyway!"

Looking down into that golden, passion-racked face up-turned to his, Ankrom wondered why it was she felt so drawn to him—even as he himself felt drawn to Lee. In this thought he was struck again by the futility of human hopes and plans, with the utter uselessness of human strivings. A little of the harshness left his features. "Well?"

"This feud of Trone's—you've been trying to see the pur-pose back of it." She swallowed uneasily, wet her lips; her hands twisted nervously at a fold of her dress.

91

"Yes. Do you know?" Ankrom asked, not bothering to see who the horseman was he could hear in the yard outside.

"I—I'm afraid," her voice was thick.

"Afraid?" Ankrom stared. "What are you afraid of?"

"This whole thing."

Ankrom scowled half turned to leave. "Let it go, then." A mirthless grin flashed across his lips. "I'll be findin' out directly anyway, I shouldn't wonder."

"You'll not find it out in time. Wait, I'll tell you. There are plans afoot to lay tracks across this ranch."

"Tracks? What are you talking about?"

"A railroad—from Amarillo to El Paso!"

"A *what!*" Ankrom swore and saw the girl's face go deathly white. She took a faltering, backward step and one hand came up before her face as though to fend off a blow. Ankrom spun and saw behind him, framed against the light, a heavy rocklike form. There could be no mistaking that great hunched figure—it belonged to big Tom Ratchford.

Ankrom drawled, "Howdy, Sheriff. You ought to go in for sleuthing."

A knowing grin bulged Ratchford's beefy face. His long, smoky eyes passed from man to girl and the leering grin grew wider. "Say! I'm sure some sorry to come bustin' in on a pair of love-birds this way, Streeter. I'll amble over to the house an' wait till you get through."

"You needn't bother." A blush stained Ankrom's cheeks. "You've jumped to false conclusions. We were just having a little talk."

"Oh, sure. Just havin' a little talk. No harm in that. When a gent is talkin' to a lady, though, he can do without an audience. I'll go over to the house. Come over when you're through."

"I'm through now. What did you want? Did you come out to the ranch to see me?"

"Well, yeah, I did. Wanted to put you next to somethin', but it'll keep a spell I shouldn't wonder."

"Won't have to," Ankrom said. "Go ahead an' spill it."

"Well," Ratchford led him off a few paces. Through the bunk house door he led, and out into the cool shade beneath the pepper tree's drooping foliage. "I think I've got a line on the fella what's after ol' man Trone. Figgered you'd want to know."

"Why me? You're the sheriff. I ain't got nothing to do with it."

"You're workin' for him, ain't you?"

"For Trone—yeah."

"Then I'd say it concerned you, too."

"Have it your way," Ankrom shrugged. "Who is the gent?"

"You wouldn't guess, I'll bet." Ratchford chuckled, but there was no mirth visible in the smoky eyes he fastened on Ankrom's face. "The fella's name is Claydell."

"The rancher?" Ankrom laughed. "You must be drinkin' a poor brand of whisky!"

Ratchford's smoky glance grew dark. "This is cold turkey, Streeter. Claydell's the one who's out to smash the Rafter."

"What for? What's he stand to gain from a stunt like that?"

"There's a railroad going to cross this ranch—"

"*Railroad!* Where'd you get that crazy notion?"

"It ain't crazy—leastways, Claydell doesn't think it is. He's figurin' strong on that road goin' through here. Anyhow, that's why he's after this spread."

"How'd you get wise?"

Ratchford's lips curled in a slow grin. "I've got my ear to the ground." A glint of inner mirth came into the long dark eyes. "I hear a lot of things a fella wouldn't think." He was very expressive with his burly shoulders. A bland humor slid into his glance: "The other day, for instance, an ancient history fell into my hands."

"Yeah?"

"Yeah—you ought to see it. Make your eyes bug out."

Ankrom's cold look swept the sheriff's mocking features. "Anything personal in that remark?"

Ratchford assumed surprise. "How could there be?"

"Let it ride," Ankrom said, then musingly: "So you think Claydell's the dog with the brass collar. You think there's a railroad goin' through from Amarillo to El Paso, an' that it's going to cross this ranch and that Claydell knows it and wants this property to hold the railroad up . . ." He sighed, shook his head. " 'Fraid there wouldn't be enough money in it to tempt a fellow like Claydell. I expect mebbe you've missed your guess, Sheriff."

"Missed hell! I know what I'm talkin' about. It'll be worth a cool two hundred grand for that road to lay track through here!"

Ankrom's cold glance beat against him speculatively. A blur of motion off to one side caught at his attention. It was Betty walking hurriedly toward the house. He turned his glance back on the sheriff and caught the tag end of a scowl being ironed from the beefy cheeks. "What are you figuring to do about it?"

"Do? Hell, man, there ain't nothin' that I *can* do—yet. I've got to wait till Claydell comes out into the open. He's a slick one; he'll be right careful not to tip his hand."

"Must have tipped it some already. You got onto him."

"I got onto him, yeah. But from another angle. Claydell ain't tipped nothin' an' likely won't. Trone's due to have his hair lifted."

Ankrom's brows raised slightly. There had been a strong conviction in Ratchford's words. "If you think that, why don't you do something? Ain't that what you're packing that star for?"

"Listen," Ratchford said. "A sheriff can't act until a crime's been committed. When Claydell grabs this ranch I'll have him, an' believe me, I'll see that he gets the limit! I'm bettin' he's the damn back-biter that's spreadin' these yarns about me bein' out to even up with Trone!"

"What have you done about that Drean killing? Found the fellow that fired the shot yet?"

The sheriff's heavy lips curled grimly. "I won't have to go very far to put my hand on *him!*"

"That's interesting," Ankrom said. "I never did cotton to sort of hombres that start their smokin' when a fellow isn't lookin'. When you're ready to go after him, let me know. I'd like to lend a hand."

Ratchford's eyes stared back unblinking. "I'll see that you're around."

"By the way," said Amkrom casually after a moment's silence. "Have you heard any more about that Bandera gent you was telling me about?"

Ratchford nodded with what seemed to Ankrom an odd reluctance. A dull glow crept into the eyes which his sleepy lids did not quite mask. "Yeah. He's not only arrived, Streeter, but he's bedded down snug as an old houn' dog with Claydell."

Ankrom's muscles stiffened, but no expression reached his wooden face. If this were true it would account in part for Ratchford's thinking Claydell the power behind the things that were happening here. In fact, reflected Ankrom grimly, if this were true it might well be that the sheriff was *right* in thinking Claydell the man who was out to smash the Rafter. And if Claydell *was* the man, it was high time something was done to put a halt to his activities; it was time steps were taken to bring him into the open. Plainly here was something to think about!

"What did you say gave you the idea Claydell is figuring on a railroad coming through here?"

Ratchford grinned. "I didn't say. But I don't mind tellin' you I got at a couple of his men—higher-ups. He's not only figuring on a road comin' through here, but aims to build a town not half a mile outside this valley. His idea is that a railroad will make it boom. He plans to have a bank, two or three good-sized saloons, ten or twelve stores, corrals and shipping pens, chutes and squeeze. With a town like that taking his orders he'll be good as a king in this section. He's got vision an' a hell of a lot of nerve. He'll smash Trone flatter'n a pancake—he's got to have this ranch."

"You tell it good."

"By Gawd, I'm tellin' you the truth!"

"What's he want the valley for?"

"I never said he did. I said he was after the ranch, an' I mean entire."

"Yeah. He'll be wantin' this valley though, as much if not more than any other part."

Ratchford's heavy features wrinkled in a scowl; there was perplexity in his glance. "Why?"

It was Ankrom's turn to smile. "Because if Claydell's aimin' to build a town when—and if —the railroad builds through this ranch, he'll be smart enough to see that this valley here will control one hell of a big section of this range."

"How do you figger that?"

Ankrom's teeth flashed wider. "Water!" he said it coldly.

The sheriff put a hand to his forehead and sent a roving glance out over the valley from rim to distant rim. There was a strange light in his smoky eyes when he turned them back on Ankrom. "You're right," he admitted softly. "I hadn't thought of that."

Ankrom, looking toward the house, saw Old Man Trone and Lee come out upon the veranda. Trone beckoned him curtly. Ankrom left the sheriff beneath the pepper tree and strode out into the smash of burning sunlight that filled the sandy yard. He saw Lee wave and knew the gesture was for Ratchford and saw her coming toward him. They passed in the center of the yard. Ankrom would have attempted to make some explanation of the scene she had witnessed in the bunk house, but she passed him with lifted head and eyes that were filled with scorn.

A feeling of bitter resentment welled up within him; not at Lee, but at the scurvy tricks of fate. At Ratchford, too, for he was remembering now that Ratchford and Lee had once been intimate. As he strode the remaining distance to the veranda, a passionate hatred of Tom Ratchford slowly but inexorably tightened its grip on Ankrom. He wished that it were Ratchford instead of Claydell who was out to smash the Rafter; a wicked desire was surging through him to cross guns with the burly sheriff. Nothing, he felt, would give him so much pleasure as sight of that heavy figure pitching forward in the dust!

He paused at the veranda steps, looking up at Trone expectantly. "You wanted me?"

"I did," Trone's voice was curt. "What have you done about finding them rustlers?"

"Nothing I can do, now. They've got your beef and they've vanished. I told you how they were working. There's nothing more that I can do unless they strike again."

"Well you can't be hangin' around the home ranch wasting your time. When I hire a man I expect him to keep busy. I want results."

Ankrom stared at Trone in silence. Trone's eyes finally shifted; twin spots of color appeared in his cheeks. "When a man hires me he *gets* results. Any time you don't like my style you know what you can do. An' if you got any notions about handin' me my time, why I'll tell you right now I'll be damned well pleased to get off this lousy range."

Trone stepped back a pace before the suppressed fury that he read in Ankrom's look. "Why—why, no. I wasn't figuring on handing you your time," he stammered. "This rustling has got me rattled. I reckon mebbe I spoke a bit hasty-like, Streeter, Forget it, will you?"

Before Ankrom could answer the sudden pound of galloping hoofs rang out from the valley rim. He turned and his eyes flashed upward quickly, raking that ragged edge. They caught a horse man driving a staggering bronc. Like a madman the roweling rider drove his pony down the treacherous pitch to the valley floor, and out across that floor on a reeling line for the building clustered at its center.

"Good God, what now?" Trone's husky voice growled wearily. "Don't the fool know better than to ride a horse like that in this dam blistering heat?"

Ankrom's glance stayed with the oncoming horse and rider; the horse's hoofs struck our more floundering with every nearing yard, and forty yards away it dropped. The rider lit on sprinting legs and kept on coming. He reached the veranda panting. Hot wrath blazed from his eyes.

Trone grabbed the puncher by the shoulders; shook him. "What in blazes," he hissed, "has happened now?"

The man gulped panting, striving to catch his breath. He looked appealingly to Ankrom.

"Take your time," Ankrom told him.

Trone glared, but held his temper somehow.

Ankrom studied the bow-legged rider with probing glance. The man was known upon the payroll as 'Ring-Legs' —so far as Ankrom knew, he had no other name, and if he had he did not use it. He was a bald-headed fellow with big buck teeth and squinty eyes. Just now those eyes were wide and filled with anger. Ankrom had assigned him to the southeast line camp with orders to keep his glance upon the cattle ranging there. Plainly something had gone amiss or the man would not be here; equally plain was the fact that this was no ordinary trouble, or the man would not have come in the manner in which he had.

"Cripes!" said the man, still breathing fast. "I wasn't sure I'd make it!"

"What's happened?" Trone demanded, and licked his lips.

"Plenty! There was surveyors all up an' down our tank this morning. They was peerin' through them little teleyscopes they carries an' wavin' their hands an' all. I asked 'em what was the big idea, but all they'd say was that they was county surveyors follerin' orders."

While the man paused for breath Ankrom glanced at Trone. The rancher's face looked gray and drawn; evidently he had reached some ominous conclusion Ankrom looked back at Ring-Legs.

97

Ring-Legs said. "Them fellas cleared out a little 'fore noon. 'Bout two o'clock a bunch of gents drove up in a coupla wagons an' began unloadin' wire an' posts. I says, 'This has gone about far enough! What do you polecats think you're doing?'"

"Go on," said Ankrom coldly. "Let's have both barrels an' get it over."

"They said there's been a mistake in boundary lines. That tank don't belong to us. Boone Heffle has give 'em orders to string a fence!"

CHAPTER XIII

"FEET FIRST!"

A BRITTLE stillness trod the heels of Ring-Legs' words; a brooding hush made ponderous by the heavy desperation of men's thoughts.

With face gone grim and bleak of eye Ankrom wrestled with his problems, balancing them against his conscience and his code. Insistently one solid truth thumped through his pulses: This thing was bad—*and would be worse!* Unless he left this country forthwith he could see no thinnest possibility of escaping the thickening pattern of trouble now bidding fair to strangle the House of Trone. Whether ancient animosities, jealousy of water rights, or a railroad and the prospect of a future town lay behind this turbulent web, he had no means of knowing. But of one thing he was certain: things were speeding up and Trone needed him—a powdersmoke showdown could not longer be far away. These men against Trone were wary, dangerous, and their next move might well be directed at himself.

He looked at Trone and saw the old man lift a shaking bottle to his lips. When the bottle was empty Trone hurled it from him with a muttered oath. Ankrom's lips curled a little then. This old hellion, he thought, is trying to bolster up his shattered nerve with whisky.

Trone glared at Ring-Legs wildly. "Say that again."

"Them fellas," the puncher growled, "say there's been a

98

mistake in boundary lines. They claim we been hoggin' too much land. They say that tank ain't on our land at all. They been given orders to string a fence that'll keep our cattle away from it. An' Boone Heffle give 'em the orders."

"Boone Heffle!" Trone whispered the name and licked his lips. His courage seemed to be ebbing swiftly, Ankrom thought.

Ring-Legs' wrathful words cut across his thoughts: "You made a mistake lettin' that sheepman live. When you was fightin' Ratchford an' them others years ago you oughta tromped the bunch of 'em underground—partic'lar Heffle!"

"But Heffle was on my side," Trone protested faintly. "Why should he be strikin' at me now after all these years?"

"The Heffles of this world ain't on nobody's side but the man that's payin' the highest!" the bowlegged puncher snarled. "Ain't you never yet learned not to trust no blasted sheepman? Gawd, you sure been slippin,' boss! It's plainer'n sin at the crossroads that this Heffle snake's been bought!"

The clump of hurried boots in sand turned Ankrom's glance. He saw Ratchford and Lee Trone come running toward them, lured on no doubt by the spectacular manner of Ring-Legs' arrival.

When they came up Ratchford shoved his burly frame to the front, grasped the puncher by the shoulder and whirled him around. "What's up?"

"Boone Heffle's jumped the tank an' cabin at our south-west line camp!"

Ratchford released his grip and swung on Trone. "Jumped your tank, has he? Well, I'm here to say he hasn't. The tank an' cabin at your southwest line ain't on your ground, an' you know it. You've been squattin' on that government land for twenty years—but that don't make it yours!"

Trone opened his mouth, but Ratchford's voice came first: "Let's see your patent to that land."

Ankrom saw the last vestige of color was from Trone's gray cheeks; his gaunt form seemed to shrink under the impact of the lawman's heavy words. But not Ring-Legs' "Spreadin' it thick won't buy yuh nothin'," he jeered. "You jest watch how long Heffle stays there, Mister—"

"He'll stay there as long as he damn well pleases!" Ratchford's heavy voice rode through the puncher's words like a knife through cheese. "I'm the law around these parts an' I say Boone Heffle's in the right. I've looked his title up an' it's good as gold. You pull any rough stuff out there an' you smack square up against the law!"

"Says you!" Trone sneered, making an obvious effort to pull himself together. But he was not the man he had been twenty years ago—not the man who had torn this range from the loosening grasp of its former owners. Yet for a fleeting moment he tried to make these men believe he was. "Says you!" he sneered again.

"You heard me!"

Ankrom drawled, "What you figurin' to do about this, Trone?"

"Do? By Gawd, Streeter, you go down there an' run them water pirates off!"

Ankrom tapped his gun suggestively. Trone nodded.

But Ratchford caught the significance. " 'F he does, this country'll be too dam' hot to hold him!"

All the worry, all the agony and doubts and strivings for peace of two long years in Ankrom's life were swept aside in the tumultuous surge of his mounting hatred for this ponderous, blustering sheriff. Ratchford's heavy arrogance: the part he once had played in Lee Trone's life and now had bade fair to play again: the sinister magnetism of his overbearing personality—all were as fuel to the fiercening flame of Ankrom's definite enmity. There still was about this business much he did not grasp, but one thing he saw with vivid clarity—too long by far had the hand at the helm of Rafter T been idle. Action swift and violent was an immediate necessity if Trone's dominance of this range were not to end!

What parts of this trouble he did not understand there was now no time to analyze. *Now* was the place for decisive action, and Ratchford's deep-growled threat was the final straw to Ankrom's caution.

A grin swept his taut face coldly; a devil's temper leered from his pale blue eyes. "Sort of anticipatin', ain't you, Ratchford? I'd say offhand you were right smart of an optimist countin' chicks before they've hatched." His glance ran up and down the sheriff's rocklike form contemptuously. "You can't run a sandy like that on us."

"Sandy, eh? You think I'm bluffin'?" Ratchford thrust a long step forward, bringing his beefy, stubbled face within short inches of Ankrom's own. "By Gawd, you bother Heffle

100

or Heffle's men an' I'll have a posse at that waterhole inside twelve hours!"

Ankrom gave no ground; he stood hipshot, serene, contemptuous. "That'll be just eight hours too late," he said, and his glance on Ratchford swam with mockery, derision.

The sheriff's face went purple, bloating poisonously with vicious rage: "It may be too late to do Boone Heffle any good, but it'll leave ample time to settle *your* account!"

"Talk is cheap. You haven't got the guts to settle my account."

"Haven't got the— Why you lousy, dry-gulchin' killer—"

That was far as Ratchford got. Ankrom's fist smashed hard against the sheriff's lips with a force that sent him sprawling in the dust. He got up with slobbering oaths, his beefy hand tugging at the shoulder-holstered pistol beneath his coat.

Ankrom's posture did not change until the weapon came in sight. Then his hand went snapping down, like a cracking whip his gun sprang clear of leather; spat!

Tensely, and with bulging eyes in a face gone white, Tom Ratchford stared downward stupidly at the numbed fingers of his shaking hand. His gun was in the sand a good eight feet away, its mechanism jammed by Ankrom's lead.

Malicious joy whipped up in Ankrom as he sheathed his smoking pistol. He backed off a little from the group, the better to encompass it. There was a delicious thrill in making Tom Ratchford appear for once ridiculous. But Ankrom's anger still was riding high; his cold blue glance shone bleak.

"You was sayin', Sheriff—?"

Ratchford's heavy lids drooped down across his eyes, but not before Ankrom had seen the new caution flooding their smoky depths. The big man's color came back in a whelming wave. The words he spoke came out through lips that were set in vengeful lines:

"You take this trick, Streeter—but some other gent'll be draggin' in the next," he gritted harshly. " 'F you ain't fannin' dust inside two hours I'll see that you're strung up for the killin' of Kelton Drean!"

Ankrom's soft laugh mocked the sheriff's threat. "I'll be fannin' dust, all right. Fannin' it towards the southwest line camp an' that bunch of thievin' sheepmen. Next time you try throwin' down on a man you better have your gun in hand an' make sure he isn't lookin'."

101

Spinning around on his heel Ankrom set off toward the pole corrals.

Lee Trone called, "Abe!"

Ankrom continued on his way without sign of having heard.

Looking down upon the Rafter T's southwest line camp, and upon the desert and semi-arid range that hemmed it in, stands a great lone butte known as Eagle Point. As Ankrom, afork his buckskin, laboriously climbed its rock-stream slope, his mind was occupied with many and divers thoughts—chief among them many concerning Ratchford.

He was sure the sheriff would be a long time forgetting his recent humiliation. He counted heavily on Ratchford wasting no time before attempting to even up the score, for about the sheriff he had recognized a vanity that would permit the man no peace so long as men might laugh at mention of the episode. In only one way could the sheriff curb such laughter —by rubbing the insult out in blood!

Well, let him try. Ankrom wanted him to try. Action was what Trone needed now to shake him from his frightened lethargy or indifferent apathy. And Ankrom deemed it wholly likely that his blow to the sheriff's chin would soon produce all the action they could handle—not to mention the manner in which Ratchford's pistol had left his hand!

His mind turned to the line of gab the sheriff had handed out while they'd stood beneath the pepper tree. A smoke screen, he thought sardonically. The thing was too glib and pat; it hung together much too nicely, he felt, to be the truth. Yet Ankrom was not cocksure enough to discount the story entirely—that yarn about Claydell had not been woven from whole cloth.

There was truth in it some place. The question was where?

Some railroad, Ankrom believed, must actually be planning to build a road from Amarillo to El Paso; this much was a thing too readily verified or disproved for the sheriff to find worthwhile the risk of a lie. It was even possible, he reflected broodingly, that someone was planning to build a town but a short distance from Trone's valley. His engineering years at college had shown him that the damming of the valley could easily be made to prove a blessing to a vast expanse of country were the project controlled by scrupulous men. In the hands of a man like Claydell, such a project would undoubtedly

102

prove a curse. But he did not believe there could be sufficient material profit in the venture, or in the combined ventures even, to attract or tempt the dark, suave owner of the Swinging J.

The tall saturnine Claydell might well be a rascal, Ankrom admitted to himself. Yet he could not see the man in the character painted for him by the burly sheriff. Claydell was, in Ankrom's opinion, much too big a man to fit that guise.

As his buckskin labored up the tortuous slope, the mutations of Ankrom's galloping thoughts turned as ever to the girl—Lee Trone. He could not get her out of mind. But whereas his visions of her formerly had been pleasant, the ones his memory now evoked held devilish power to wound. He kept seeing her as she had stood in the open bunk house door when Betty's clinging arms were round his neck; he kept visioning her with that look of mingled hurt, reproach, resentment in her eyes and her red lips curled in scorn. "Yes, tell her, Abe, by all means." she had said. "Don't let me spoil your fun."

Ankrom groaned aloud; those words still held their pristine power to sear. Though the afternoon was hot, cold sweat came out upon his forehead. He should, he reminded himself bitterly, be glad she felt toward him as she did. There was no place in a gun-man's life for a decent woman, and with these new barriers raised between himself and Lee there seemed no longer any danger of their ever becoming intimate. But he found this unconsoling; he wanted Lee Trone, he realized now—wanted her as he had never before wanted anything in life!

And between them now lay a bar as strong as Fate.

The buckskin topped the crest of Eagle Point and Ankrom's deviling thoughts were scattered on the instant. Down below him lay the Rafter T's southwest line camp, and about it there was presented a scene of great activity. A man stood in the cabin doorway watching five or six others busily stringing wire to a long row of heavy posts that completely circled the great water tank and cabin.

In the depths of Ankrom's narrowed glance there was a stirring as smoke is stirred by sudden draft. One ungloved hand gripped hard upon the pommel so that its knuckles stood out white. Whether this land down yonder belonged to Trone or not, one fact stood clear above all doubt in Ankrom's mind. Trone's long rule upon this range was being challenged; unless the challengers were met and battered down, Trone's hold would be forever broken!

With a soft-voiced oath Ankrom sank his spurs and the gallant buckskin lunged forward down the treacherous slide in a fine appearance of wild abandon; indeed at such a pace that one false step or a rolling stone must spell disaster irrevocable.

Yet so intent upon their work were the men about the cabin that for some moments Ankrom's hurried approach went unnoted. Only when the uneven pound of hoofs and the rising rattle of rolling rubble set off by that precipitous descent beat loud by increasing nearness, did one of the wire-stringers glance up from his task to send a fretful look toward the distant butte. Ankrom saw the man drop his pliers on the instant saw his lips spread widely in a shout he could not hear, and dash for the cabin as the man in the doorway ducked within, to reappear a moment later with a border rifle in the crook of an arm.

But Ankrom did not slow his pace by a fraction; rather he urged the buckskin to further effort, ringing forth an added burst of speed lest those men should fire before he could close the distance separating himself from the disputed cabin and water.

Ankrom was outnumbered by at least five men, and knew it. But the reckless mood induced by his smouldering anger against Ratchford, Fate and himself would not permit him to take cognizance of odds. Passion flung its red glow across those lean, taut cheeks as he saw the last of the fence-stringers sprinting frantically toward what they judged to be the scene of coming action—the weather-beaten old cabin built years ago by Rafter T. And the eyes staring out above those tautened cheeks held a glint that was bleak as sun on wind-swept ice.

Straight up to the cabin he swept, and the ground-hitched mounts of these staring men shied nervously as, grim-lipped, he flung the reins across the buckskin's head and slid lightly from the saddle to stand hipshot, loosely, his vacuous glance taking in the situation with a glacial calm.

These men silently flanking the cabin stood moveless, tense and wary. They were picturesque in their rangeland garb, but they were neither cowboys nor sheepmen; Ankrom recognized this at once.

Tall, lean and sinewy men were these, some sallow of countenance, others bronzed by many suns. Yet about them

104

all in their wide-brimmed hats was a look of cold efficiency as, across the sudden hush, they returned his stare enigmatically, their features wooden.

Ankrom saw in that first glance that within swift reach behind them a row of rifles stood against the cabin wall, and that each was hooked by its thumb to the cartridge belt that sagged from each motionless waist.

Flashing across this group Ankrom's gaze rested momentarily upon the man in the cabin doorway. He was tall, lean, rawboned, with a lantern jaw and close-set eyes in a pockmarked face. A cud of tobacco bulged one beard-stubbled cheek and a tangle of grayish hair hung down across a corrugated forehead whose most prominent feature was the knife-scar that ran slantwise above one eye.

Ankrom's voice broke the quiet with a truculent snap, "Who's roddin' this crew?"

The man in the doorway shifted the rifle crooked in his arm. "Me," he said, and spat.

"An' who are you?"

"Boone Heffle—if it's any of yore damn' business."

"I'm makin' it my business," drawled Ankrom softly. "What are you doin' on the Rafter T?"

The man's squinty eyes showed a rush of temper. "I'm drivin' posts an' stringin' wire—an' I'm not on the blasted Rafter! Anyone'd think that go-to-hell outfit owned the earth to hear 'em talk!"

"They own this cabin an' waterhole," Ankrom said, "an' they're givin' you just three minutes to make yourselves scarce." There was a drive to his voice that made them stiffen. "An' them that haven't felt when that time is up will be carried off later—*feet first!*"

CHAPTER XIV

AT THE WATERHOLE

WHEN Ankrom, heading for the corrals, ignored Lee's call, her face went white. But only for a moment. Then a flood of crimson to her cheeks gave indication of her feelings. One gloved hand clenched tight on the quirt that was looped to her wrist by a leathern thong. It almost seemed as though she was of a mind to use it as she took two swift steps after the new man's retreating figure. But she stopped abruptly, underlip caught between her teeth.

With an unfathomable light in her strange green eyes she stood abstractedly beside Tom Ratchford and her father. She could hear their voices in a sunken monotone, but she paid them no attention. Idly she watched Ring-Legs follow Ankrom to the pole corrals, shake out his rope and send its loop snaking across the head of a bay whose long, slim legs seemed built for speed. Plainly Ring-Legs had notions of tailing the new foreman back to the disputed water.

When Ankrom sent his buckskin out across the yard and into the trail leading to the valley's rim, Lee snapped from her mood and turned to speak to her father. But Trone, followed by the burly sheriff, was at that moment disappearing through the ranch house door. A sudden resolve shone from Lee's green eyes as Ring-Legs stepped into the saddle he'd geared to the long-legged bay. She raised a hand and beckoned.

Reluctantly the puncher turned his mount in her direction. When he stopped the bay beside her and sat looking down with a nervous scowl, Lee said:

"Just leave him here, Ring-Legs. Thanks for saddling him."

"Huh?" the puncher's jaw dropped open. "Mind ridin' that trail again, ma'am?"

"I said you can leave the bay here—get out of the saddle."

"I was figgerin' on followin' Streeter—" he began, but she stopped him with a gesture.

"Then you'll have to saddle another horse. I'm in a hurry an' this one's handy."

"But, ma'am," Ring-Legs protested, red of face, "you can't ride in them duds!"

Lee glanced down at the light blue frock that sheathed her slender form.

"Can't I?" her green eyes snapped. "You'd be surprised at what I can do once my mind's made up. Get down, now; I want that horse."

Ring-Legs dismounted sullenly. "It ain't right, ma'am," he muttered. "Your Dad wouldn't think a heap of it was he to know."

106

"You'd better see that he don't find out, then." Taking the reins from his hand, she added, "You'd better look the other way now; you might be shocked."

With face brick red the bowlegged puncher turned clear around. The next moment Lee was in the saddle, smoothing down her skirt. She had no time to change her clothes if she intended to be at that southwest line camp when Abe Streeter faced the sheepmen. She brought her quirt down hard and the bay broke into a run.

Through the hot afternoon she rode with only the steady flogging beat of the bay's drumming hoofs for company. From time to time in the distance she caught glimpses of the rider she was following, but not once did he look around.

When she reached the crest of Eagle Point, her downflung glance saw that Streeter was standing before the cabin and that a line of men stood facing him. He seemed to be talking to a man who lounged in the doorway, a rifle held in the crook of an arm, but she could not catch his words. Impatiently, yet cautiously, she urged the bay into the trail leading down the slope.

If she was seen, the men gave no evidence of the fact; their expressionless eyes seemed glued to Streeter's face. He couldn't see her for his back was turned toward her. Drawing near, in what seemed to her to be a sinister silence, she kneed the bay to one side of the clearing before the cabin, to a place where she could see all faces and easily hear any spoken words. As she settled herself to watch, in her interest forgetful of the length of leg she was exposing to these men's gaze should they care to look, she heard Streeter's voice cross the silence recklessly:

"They own this cabin an' waterhole an' they're givin' you just three minutes to make yourselves scarce. An' them that haven't left when that time is up will be carried off later—*feet first!*"

Dark folds of silence fell again about the cabin in the clearing. Boone Heffle's close-set eyes took on a burning glitter. He spat abruptly; said—

"Who the hell might you be? 'Pears to me you're mighty free with your orders."

"I'm Streeter—foreman of the Rafter."

"Yeah? When'd Mose Hackett quit?"

107

"He didn't quit—he had his lamp blown out. I'm some surprised your boss ain't put you wise."

"Dead! Mose Hackett?" Heffle's angular jaw sagged in amazement. It closed swiftly with a harsh snap. "What d'ye mean '*boss*'?"

"I am referrin' to the gent that gives you orders—like the order you got to jump this camp."

"Orders? Hell, no man gives *me* orders, Mister—you included. I do jest as I please, an' when I damn' well feel like it!"

"Then you'd better start feelin' like clearin' out," Ankrom's drawl was soft and wicked, "cause you've only got two minutes left if you're aimin' to leave under your own steam."

A cold chill got into Lee Trone's spine as she looked from Boone Heffle's burning black orbs to the steely depths of Ankrom's blue ones. Ankrom's lips were compressed to an inexorable line and his face was grim and rigid.

Boone Heffle suddenly laughed—a fluting wail of sound. "I don't scare worth a damn," he said, and his tobacco-stained fangs showed between the leering curl of his lips. "Unleash your wolf an' let him bark."

No other person within Lee's vision smiled with him. It seemed that what they saw in the eyes of the Rafter foreman left a cramp in their facial muscles. One or two shifted their feet uneasily, cast longing glances toward their horses. Suddenly slipping, Boone Heffle's smile revealed the scowl that lay beneath it.

From a distance the muffled pound of shod hoofs beat softly across the quiet. Lee, hearing them, thought of Ring-Legs and guessed it must be him.

Boone Heffle heard them, too, and a deeper flame burned through his dusky glance. He settled his rawboned length more easily against the doorframe. "Well," he sneered, "what you waitin' for?"

"I'm waitin' for the rest of that three minutes to slide past," Ankrom said, and Lee saw that a sardonic grin spilled across his lips as he added: "But that needn't hold the rest of you gents back—any time you feel the need for action just jerk a pistol loose."

"You brash fool!" Heffle's beard-stubbled cheeks blazed red.

108

"Nothin' but my pers'nal hatred of violence holds me back from lettin' these boys give you what you're needin'!"

Lee saw a horseman top the crest of Eagle Point, pause an instant to take in the scene below, then cautiously urge his pony down the trail toward the cabin. As he drew nearer she caught her breath. This man was not Ring-Legs—he was a total stranger to her!

While Ankrom drew a watch from his pocket Lee's eyes stayed on the coming horseman. He was much closer now; near enough for her to make out his features plainly. He was clad in a tight-fitting jacket of bright velvet and a pair of bat-wing chaps over trousers of green corduroy. The chaps looked scarred and old from long usage, but their studdings of turquoise and silver told her of their former worth. Upon his head was a huge, bell-crowned sombrero.

But it was not at his trappings that Lee was gazing; her glance was fastened upon his face. Dark and swarthy it was, and handsome despite the tight, thin-lipped mouth and the dark little eyes that flashed with cunning.

She watched him approach and slide down from the saddle not twenty paces back of Ankrom, who gave no appearance of knowing the man was behind him. A Mexican, obviously, Lee decided, and saw him glance with upward arching brows at Heffie. Boone Heffie's amber-stained mouth spread wide in a vicious grin.

"Them three minutes up yet, Mister?"

"Gettin' nervous?" Ankrom countered. " 'F you are, just haul your hoglegs an' get this thing to goin'."

"You make me so bull-headed mad, by cripes, if I wa'n't so cussed filled with the milk o' human kindness I'd take you up on that an' start a-smokin'!"

"Don't let me hold you back," Ankrom said with a grin that showed his hard white teeth.

Lee wanted to shake him, to shout—anything to awaken him to awareness of the stalking Mexican behind his back. Why didn't he look around? The man in the big sombrero was catfooting closer with each passing second, his dark face wreathed in a pussycat leer of anticipation. She opened her mouth to call, but no words came. Cold fear strangled the cry in her throat as the advancing Mexican, a cruel glitter in his little eyes, drew the heavy pistol sagging his brass-studded holster.

She tried desperately to blot out the coming horror by shutting her eyes. But as the warning cry had died within her lips, so now her nerves refused their function. She could not move a muscle, such strength had the terror gripping her.

With unheard steps she watched the Mexican creep up behind Ankrom; creep up to a point so near that by merely reaching out his hand the man could have touched him. She saw the gun-weighted hand go slowly up and back and there, as the breath caught in her throat, it stopped.

It seemed to Lee, white-faced and tense, that something must have palsied the Mexican's muscles. From the tail of her eyes she noted the blackening scowl that warped Boone Heffler's features as the Mexican's gun-filled, upraised hand began to tremble, slowly began to sag. And with the sight she suddenly found her voice.

"Abe! *Abe!*" she cried. "Behind you—*QUICK!*"

Ankrom did not whirl or even turn. Swift as light two smooth, long sideward paces took him out of the Mexican's reach; placed the man within his vision and held the others likewise.

She saw his smile freeze them all to a tense rigidity; heard his drawling voice dropping flat cold words of amusement across the frightened hush:

"Why, howdy, Chato Bandera. I'm quite some pleased to see you. Were you figurin' to wave that gun at me?"

"Blur Ankrom!"

They were like a wail, those words that fell from the Mexican's twisted mouth. The eyes in his livid face were like two fat burnt holes in a linen sheet. A tremor shook the slender form from his polished boots to his bell-sombreroed head as, beneath the impact of Ankrom's mocking glance, he went backward a few uncertain steps. "Before God." he cried, "I deed not know eet was you, *Señor!*"

CHAPTER XV

Some Gunplay and a Threat

BLUR ANKROM!

Bandera's words seared into Lee Trone's consciousness with the scorch of a branding iron. They left her weak and feeling very feminine and helpless; they drove the color from her cheeks and snapped constricting fingers of ice about her heart. Her mind was a churning, reeling chaos of turbulent emotion. *Blur Ankrom*—those words explained a lot of things about the man she had known as Streeter!

"Before God I deed not know eet was you, *Señor!*" Bandera's ingratiating whine brought Lee abruptly to a new and clearer understanding of this drama being enacted before the cabin and the possibilities therein embodied.

In a sullen silence whose feeling of strain seemed almost to the snapping point, in a metallic hush that sent cold chills up Lee Trone's back, she saw Bandera lower his shaking hand— saw the glint of sun-splashed steel as his loosened grip released the pistol and it slithered back in leather.

From mouth held open by sagging jaw she saw a trickle of amber trace a course down Heffle's stubbled chin. Heffle's men were like a row of handcarved figures, their faces blank as so much rock; not even their eyes released a movement as they stared with glassy fascination at Rafter's foreman.

Such was the shocking power of Ankrom's name.

His long lean-muscled body, as he stood there lounging easily in hipshot slouch, gave an impression of vast reserves of strength and confidence. His cold unwavering glance rode heavily across those staring faces, broke loose a glint of saturnine amusement as it came to rest on the sweat-bathed features of the swarthy Mexican. "I reckon not," he said.

Boone Heffle's lantern jaw came up with a snap. Lee heard it plainly. Behind that shock of dangling hair his forehead was creased and frowning; the knife-scar stood out whitely against the dull brick red of his stubbled face. The tenseness of his

111

posture, each rigid angle of his rawboned body showed the lust to murder that was in him. Yet with every advantage on his side he dared not draw—dared not squeeze the rifle's trigger.

As the mere fact of Ankrom's identity had proved sufficient to cow the Mexican killer, so now the sardonic amusement and cold confidence to be read in Ankrom's pose appeared to spill the sheepman's nerve.

Ankrom looked at him and Lee could feel the laughter in his eyes. Abruptly he laughed aloud. The bold mockery of the sound drove Heffle back a pace. Ankrom's voice reached out and stopped him. Heffle glared in mingled fear and hatred as his tongue licked burning lips.

Lee shuddered. She wished she had not come.

Watching the group with vacuous gaze Ankrom said, "Who bought your gun, Bandera?"

"But no one, señor." Bandera shrugged and spread his hands. "My gun she's no for sale, amigo. I have queet that business—seguro si."

He wiped cold beads of moisture from his face, backed a few more steps away, awkwardly, fearfully, as though expectant that each step would be his last. "Madre de Dios, senior—eet ees true!" he cried with breaking voice.

Ankrom jeered, "The guise of reformed and repentant bad man fits you well, Bandera. I could almost find it in my heart to believe you—if I didn't know what a black-bellied snake you really are. Throw that gun in the water!"

With glassy eyes, like one in a trance Bandera mechanically lifted the heavy pistol from his holster, drew back his arm for the toss. Perforce Ankrom's eyes must remain upon him. Lee recognized the danger even as the sheepman realized that here was his longed-for chance. As the Mexican's weapon struck the water with a splash, Boone Heffle's rifle leaped to his shoulder—his finger curled against the trigger.

Yet fast as the sheepman was, Blur Ankrom's move was swiftest. His eye must have caught the tag-end of Heffle's upward sweep with the rifle. Even as the shot cracked out, the Rafter foreman dropped and whirled. Red flame licked outward from his hip. Heffle clutched at his chest and went reeling backward out of sight within the cabin. Lee heard him fall and a wave of nausea washed the color from her cheeks, yet she could not drag her eyes from the cold fury of Ankrom's features.

"Come on, you back-shootin' polecats! If it's fight you're honin' for I'll give you a fracas to remember!"

Several of those hard-eyed men before the cabin had gotten their guns a hand. A rifle cracked and hurled a whistling streak above him. Ankrom fired from the hip and grinned maliciously as the rifleman staggered backward, pawing at his middle. With a side leap another of Heffle's gun-slicks got himself a weapon and whipped it up. It spat—and so did Ankrom's! Lee saw sand jump at Ankrom's feet, spill down across his boots. She saw Ankrom's lead smash the luckless pistol-bender back and down—saw him drop to hands and knees and sway there coughing while the blue pall of powdersmoke overhead trembled to the rolling echoes.

There was not a tinge of nausea in Lee's system now. She was filled with a wild surge of exultation; pride and elation had snapped glowing spots of color to her cheeks and the blood was pounding through her arteries at a heady gait. The thought came to her that she should fear this man, that she should shudder to the things he'd done. But she didn't—she was glad and proud this man was Rafter's foreman!

Smoke hung thick about his crouching figure. Each flare of his belching pistol illumined the hard white teeth behind his grinning lips.

Abruptly the fight was over—killed as swift as was its birth. Heffle's men dropped weapons as though they burnt their palms; thrust shaking hands in hurry above their heads. As he straightened, Lee saw that there was blood on Ankrom's neck where a close-placed slug had torn the lobe from his ear. He seemed unconscious of the wound.

The ironic gleam had left his glance; now his eyes held a steely glitter as he drove his words across the thinning echoes:

"If you skunks have got enough, back away from them guns! If you're wantin' more, reach for one of them rifles an' I'll give you all you can handle!"

Angry, sullen, cursing—but cautiously—the men before the cabin moved away from their weapons, stood clear of the rifles placed against the cabin wall. There was a hint of smooth coordination of mind and muscle in the springy noiseless step with which Ankrom placed himself between those men and their discarded guns.

113

"This," he told them curtly, "is Rafter property. From here on out trespassers will be shot on sight. Now pick up your carrion an' make dust."

Character! Lee decided that was what his face expressed; not age. Not so much hardness nor experience as inner strength, mental viewpoint and an indomitable will. His was a nature to ride through obstacles like so much dust. His was a courage that would take no stock in odds. Suddenly she found a new reason to be glad they'd met that night in Peso Pinto; glad that he was fighting Rafter's battle.

When the men were ready to go, one man looking down from the saddle said, "We won't be forgettin' thees, senor!" Lee recognized the Mexican, Bandera.

Ankrom laughed. "Save your breath to blow your beans," he advised, and tipped his hat derisively.

When the men had gone Ankrom turned and saw Lee Trone. He had known all the time that she was there; he had sensed her presence instantly—it was too powerfully magnetic to remain unfelt for long. Even the waning sunlight had seemed somehow brighter when she came. Knowing that she was watching had given him the nerve to face those overpowering odds, had endowed him with the fighting courage to beat those border gun men down and make them crawl away like a pack of whipped curs. But she must never realize this; the fact must remain permanently locked within his mind.

So it was that when he faced her now at last his face was smooth with an unruffled calm that was almost cold. "Get it over with," he said.

"Get what over with?"

As usual when tense circumstances did not cause him to lapse into the rangeland idiom of his early youth, Ankrom's English was reasonably good. But his tone was mocking, like the tone he'd used on Bandera:

"The remarks you've been saving up since that affair you miscontrued in the bunk house—the analysis of my character you've hit upon from observation of my conduct."

"Your conduct," she answered coolly, "is your own affair." And now her green eyes flashed. "But had you mentioned manners, I'd tell you frankly they're deplorable."

He doffed his hat in a mocking bow. Lee Trone, he felt, not

114

only regarded him as a philandering liar, but as a man who readily unshucked his irons for pay. That she had some justification for such thoughts, made no difference—she had jumped to conclusions. Hadn't Betty's words proved this amply when the golden girl had passed on to him that day the condemnation she had heard from Lee's own lips?

He doubted that there was now any chance of Lee Trone and himself becoming intimate; that which she had seen this noon in the bunk house and this gun fracas she had just now witnessed must certainly have put an end to whatever chance there might have been. He was satisfied to have it so, he told himself, now that the initial hurt of her satyric words had slightly eased. She did things to him—her personality was too alluring. There was no place in her warped life for her, or any other woman. He was not afraid of becoming too interested in any other woman. She was the one he must guard against! Very well; he would put her beyond the reach of this soft streak he had uncovered in himself!

So he doffed his hat in a mocking bow. "Since we're just a couple of redheads trying to be pleasant," he drawled, "I'd admire to remind you that we're not on a college campus here. This is the West—a place where men ain't never got accustomed to . . ." He let his voice trail off, but made his meaning clear by the mockery with which he eyed the patch of bare leg visible where the saddle drew her skirt above her stocking.

He showed amusement when a deep flush swept up her throat, incarnadined her cheeks. He laughed at the anger blazing her jade-green eyes as she jerked the silk down with a savagery that tore it.

He was still grinning when she spoke:

"God knows why I should have steeped my hands in blood to save you from that lying tinhorn!"

Like a sum sponged from a schoolboy's slate, Ankrom's smile wiped off. He closed the distance between them by one long stride. "What's that?"

"God knows that I should have let that Drean snake kill you—the world would have been a finer place!"

Ankrom's thoughts were crazy—steeped my hands in blood' . . . 'should have let that Drean snake kill you.' He did not hear the beat of approaching hoofs. He was staring at her blankly.

"What are you talkin' about?" He crossed to her horse with rapid strides. "What's this you're sayin' about Drean?"

He reached for the bridle but her loaded quirt struck down his hand; slashed him hard across the face.

"Don't touch me! Get away!" Her voice was thick with suppressed emotion. "*I* killed Kelton Drean!"

With a sob she whirled her horse and was gone.

She had killed Kelton Drean! The impact of that revelation struck Ankrom far harder than her whip had done. The significance of her act was suddenly all too plain—she had shot Drean to save his life because she loved him! Under any other circumstance she would have shouted a warning; but she hadn't risked that chance. His life had meant too much.

Ankrom's back was bathed in sweat. He—blind fool—had dealt her love its final blow! The clearing reeled before his eyes. He had deliberately hurled a taunting innuendo at her which could never be forgiven!

Betty's version of Lee's opinion of him flashed across Ankrom's whirling mind. Recalled also were the golden girl's words regarding the killing of the pseudo Struthers. *She had lied!* He knew it now; what a fool he'd been not to have realized it before!

And Lee's biting words as she'd stood in that bunk house door and seen Betty's clinging, calculating arms around him came also flooding back, borne on the tide of his penitence. The result of jealousy those words had been, and jealousy, he reflected somberly, was but an attribute of love—a decided desire for exclusive possession.

It was very plain to Ankrom now that Lee had loved him. Her love—if not her trust of him—had withstood that bunk house scene and her very real fear for his safety had brought her after him to this cabin in such vigorous hurry she had found no time to swap her dress for more suitable riding gear. *And he had taunted her with the fact!*

He groaned aloud. Truly his trail was strewn with ashes!

"A damn pity," he snarled, "my mouth wasn't stopped with dust!"

"My Gawd!" gasped a voice behind him. "What's happened to the water-gobblers? Where they gone?"

"I sent 'em packing." Ankrom, after recognizing the newcomer for Ring-Legs, fell back in his pool of gloom.

116

"Gosh, what happened to yore ear, boss?"

Ankrom put a hand uncertainly to his head. "The other one," Ring-Legs advised. Ankrom took the suggestion; grimaced. His hand came away wet and sticky. "I dunno," he said indifferently. "I expect I must've got hit.' His mind was busy with more uncomfortable, more important things.

Ring-Legs shoved back his hat, ran a puzzled hand across his shiny dome as he looked about the clearing regretfully, "I don't reckon them coyotes could 'a' left peaceably," he mused aloud, eyeing Ankrom hopefully. " 'D anyone get bad hurt?"

"I expect I hit two-three of 'em." Ankrom was not interested.

"Was Heffle here?"

No response.

"I bet he was hoppin' mad if he was—"

Roused at last by the puncher's continued questions and speculations, Ankrom broke in roughly. "His hoppin' days are over. Next trespasser you catch on Rafter property you've got my permission to shoot. I'll be responsible. Get on back to the—" Ankrom broke off abruptly; said:

"Never mind. Stay here an' see that nobody jumps this water. You got plenty of ammunition?"

Open-mouthed, Ring-Legs bobbed his head.

Ankrom strode to the buckskin, pulled himself aboard. Looking down from the saddle he growled: "Remember what I told you now. Shoot the first damn trespasser you see. If you got any palaverin' to do, do it after you've knocked him off his bronc!"

Ring-Legs swallowed noisily. The Adams apple in his skinny neck bounced up and down like a rubber ball. "Wh—where you figgerin' to head for?"

"I'm going to have a talk with Claydell," Ankrom said, and fed his buckskin steel.

Claydell's ranch house was a rambling, single story affair with a thick sod roof and adobe walls that were tinted pink. A man seated alongside the bunk house looked up with a surly stare as Ankrom rode into the yard. Ankrom dismounted before the ranch house porch, dropped the buckskin's reins and strode within.

He found himself in a long broad room that was neat and clean. Its tall walls were adorned with trophies, an Indian blanket or two, a mounted Antelope head, a rack of rifles and a large Indian calendar bearing the oval seal of the Santa Fe.

117

Back of a heavy desk beside a window Claydell was rising to his feet, an expression of polite wonder on his dark and lean-carved face.

"Let's see," he said. "You're—"

"I'm Ankrom—foreman of the Rafter."

Claydell was regarding him curiously. "Ankrom? Seems to me you're the chap who made Tom Ratchford back down over to the Trone place that night the pseudo Struthers man was killed. Seems like I recollect your name was Streeter . . ."

Ankrom grinned coldly. "Your mem'ry's good, Claydell. However, I didn't ride way over here to enter into a discussion of names. I hear you're interested in railroads."

"Railroads?" Claydell's face was blank.

"A particular railroad, then."

Claydell's eyes narrowed, then took on a puzzled light.

"I'm afraid I don't quite get you," he said, at last. "I'm not interested in any railroad. Whatever gave you that notion? Were you hoping to sell me some stock, or something?"

Ankrom said, "Are you interested in acquiring the Rafter?"

"Not especially. I made Trone an offer once, several years ago. He didn't want to sell, he said."

Ankrom's white teeth gleamed coldly behind his parted lips. There was a drive to his voice that made the rancher stiffen: "Didn't want to sell, eh?"

"What are you driving at?" Claydell snapped.

"You wanted the Rafter because you had learned that a big road was planning to lay track from Amarillo to El Paso and would have to cross that land. You offered to buy, but Trone wouldn't sell. So you set out to smash him—to put him out of business so you could steal the property from Trone's daughter, for a fraction of its worth. You hired a bunch of saddle bums to rustle Rafter beef. You bought Mose Hackett to help that deal along."

Claydell's yellow eyes were widening; the look of bewilderment they first had held was giving way to startled incredulity—to anger.

Ankrom hurled charges at him like bullets from a pistol. "You weren't making headway fast enough. You were afraid news of the railroad would be leaking out. So you bought Heffle, the sheepman, body and soul an' sicked him onto the water at Rafter's southwest line camp. To hold that

118

water in case Rafter kicked up you gave Heffle a bunch of gun-slicks an' you brought Bandera, the Mex killer, in to strengthen Heffle's hand."

There were loop-holes in Ankrom's accusations—plenty of them. And he knew it. But what he was after was a reaction; he wanted to see how Claydell would take it.

And he saw!

CHAPTER XVI

THE POWER OF WORDS

CLAYDELL'S bushy eyebrows drew sharply down above his yellow stare. The six-foot figure in his shiny black boots drew stiffly erect, as would the figure of an insulted Spanish Don. The fierce vitality of his long dark face was not lessened by a fraction as he eyed Ankrom coldly in a lofty silence.

"Is this meant to be a joke?" he asked, and dropped his hands casually into his jacket pockets.

Ankrom watched those hands intently until finally they came forth with cigarette papers and a pinch of dark tobacco. He held moveless while Claydell rolled a smoke and lit it. Then he said:

"Does it sound like a joke to you?"

"It sounds to me like the raving of a crazy man," Claydell said contemptuously. "Do you think I'd be fool enough to do such things for the sake of a paltry railroad right-of-way? Use your head!"

"I'm usin' it. Want to hear the rest?"

"If it will give you any relief to elaborate further, by all means spin ahead."

Ankrom nodded. "The railroad right-of-way is not the only thing you're after. You would indeed be a fool to risk so much for that. But that ain't all. You plan to build a town alongside the proposed tracks about half a mile from the valley housing Trone's home ranch. Your ultimate object is to dam Trone's Valley in an attempt to boom Rafter land to the bunch of homeseekers the railroad is going to entice in for you!"

119

"So!" Claydell expelled a cloud of smoke from his nostrils. "A likely yarn," he jeered, "whose only difficulty is in getting people round here to swallow it. I think that's where you're going to run up against a snag, Mister." A calculating gleam shone momentarily from the yellow eyes. "Mind telling me where you gathered all these notions? Did Ratchford unload them on you?"

"Why Ratchford?" Ankrom countered. "what's he got to do with it?"

"That's something I'd give a deal to know." Claydell inhaled deeply, held silent for some time while he regarded Ankrom through the smoke with speculative eyes.

"I'll tell you something," he said at last with the air of one about to reveal a secret. Tony Ratchford's got it in for me. He'd like nothing better than to catch me mixed up on the wrong side of trouble. You see the point?"

"What point?"

Claydell took a restless turn about the room. When he stopped he faced Ankrom squarely. "Ratchford gave you all these notions to focus your interest on me."

"Why should he want to do that?"

"How do I know? I told you he didn't like me. He's been laying for me for years. The Ratchfords are a breed who don't forget—"

"Don't forget what?" Ankrom cut in swiftly.

Claydell snorted. "Don't forget anything! Years ago there was a sort of range war in this valley. The ranchers here were trying to keep out nesters, squatters, homesteaders. They succeeded till Old Man Trone came in. He was a hell-bender in his day, and he brought a tough crowd with him. We couldn't budge 'em. I'm a sensible man, I hope. I saw the way things were going. I was losing money hand over fist. The fight was at a deadlock. I recognized that Trone would never be licked." He paused to search Ankrom's face with his yellow eyes, then said:

"I threw in with Trone."

"An' come out on the winnin' side, eh?" There was a scornful curl to Ankrom's lips as he put the sneering question.

Claydell took the insult calmly; neither by glance nor word did he show resentment.

"Yes," he said, "Trone and I won out. Old Ratchford— —Tom's father—tried to break us by bringing in sheep. He

120

was the one that got broke—him and three-four others. But he took the biggest loss. Not long after the thing was finished he went out back of the house one day an' blew his brains out. Do you understand now why Ratchford's got it in for me?"

Ankrom made no reply for several moments. Scanning a number of things in his mind he finally asked:

"What happened to Ratchford's sheep?"

"They were found one morning at the bottom of a canyon."

"Slick. Who had been in charge of 'em?"

"Sheepman named Boone Heffle. A surly devil an' still in the country, by the way."

"Not any longer he isn't," Ankrom said, and watched Claydell's face intently. "I killed him this afternoon."

Claydell showed surprise; a little interest even. But not more than anyone else would have shown under the circumstances. "Is that so?" He drew a lungful of smoke and puffed it out. "Why?"

"He was trying to jump the water at Rafter's southwest line camp. I mentioned it before."

"So you did," Claydell nodded reflectively. "I take it then the Rafter still controls that water. If you need any more men to hold it, let me know. I've aided Trone too long to let him down now. I'd—" He broke off abruptly, snapped his fingers.

"Say!" he exclaimed with more than usual enthusiasm. "I believe you've about solved it!"

"What are you talking about?"

"Those sheep! Heffle would never take it on himself to try jumping Rafter's water." He appeared to be in the grip of a powerful thought as he added. "A man who can be bought once can be bought again—an outfit that'll use sheep once will sure as hell try 'em out again!"

Ankrom felt a surge of anger. "You mean—"

"Ratchford. Tom Ratchford, the sheriff, is the man you're looking for!"

Ankrom, as he sent the buckskin leisurely across the darkening range toward the Rafter T, was not entirely convinced. Like his own accusations of Claydell, the rancher's case against Ratchford had a number of loopholes. Not that what he had said seemed unconvincing—on the contrary. But there were a lot of things Claydell had not mentioned.

Both the sheriff and the boss of the Swinging J undoubtedly

121

hated each other's guts, as the saying went. But whether the reasons given by Claydell were the correct ones, Ankrom could not decide. So far as he knew for certain, it was quite possible that neither the sheriff nor Claydell were behind these things which were happening to Rafter. Each, in their enmity, would naturally suspect the other.

Ankrom's thoughts shifted momentarily to Betty Struthers, as the girl from Peso Pinto called herself. It was plain to him now that her words to him concerning Lee and concerning the killing of Kelton Drean were deliberate lies. She had been seeking to prejudice him in her favor; to drive, if she could not lure, him away from Lee.

He recalled now Ratchford's statement that Drean had been killed by a slug from a .45 caliber pistol. The one the golden girl had forced upon him had been a short-barreled .32. How could he have missed the significance of this these many days? Why the girl had said herself under the sheriff's questioning that Drean used a .32—she had forced upon Ankrom Drean's own gun!

He laughed shortly. "An artful baggage if I ever saw one—she'd ought to have taken up the stage!"

Deliberately he avoided thoughts of Lee, though her vision flashed before his tired eyes repeatedly. Bitterly he forced his mind to other subjects, for he could not bear to recall his treatment of her.

It was nearly time for the moon to rise when he reached the Rafter T. He stripped the gear from his buckskin, rubbed the moistness from the animal's coat. Turning the horse into the big corral he hung his saddle on the fence and went striding toward the lighted window that marked Trone's office in the house.

Trone looked up from some papers with a scowl as Ankrom entered, closing the door behind him. Ankrom saw that the gaunt old man had been drinking, for there was a bottle almost empty beside his elbow and his eyes were red and surly.

"Well," Trone grunted. "What happened at the waterhole? What's the matter with your ear? Did you drive them bums off?"

This was not quite the reception Ankrom had been expecting. He squared his shoulders. "Isn't Lee here?"

"Of course she's here!" the old man grunted testily. "What's

122

that got to do with what I asked you? What's the matter with your ear?"

"A bullet nipped it."

"Did you have a corpse an' cartridge occasion at the camp?" Trone's bleary eyes showed sudden interest. "What happened to the other fellow?"

"There was a little shootin'," Ankrom admitted. "What other fellow are you talkin' about?"

"The fellow that knocked that slice from your ear."

"I didn't see. I was kinda busy about that particular time."

"Well, *what happened?*" Trone growled. "For God's sake, say somethin'! Do I have to get a rope an' drag it from you?"

"I shot up two or three gents an' the rest cleared out."

Trone swore. "You tell it like a teaparty! Is that all you got to say? Wasn't Heffle there? If he was I'm bettin' strong there was some action!"

"He was there." Ankrom's drawl was bitter. "His light was the first I blowed."

Trone's glance flashed excitement. A grin curled his leathery lips. "Good! Now you're talkin'. I'd have give a year of my life to have seen that! The damn double-crosser! I'm glad you cashed his chips. What else happened?"

"Nothing much worth mentioning. I wounded a couple other birds. The rest threw down their guns. I warned them off the Rafter an' told 'em the next one caught would be shot on sight."

"Nothin' much happened, eh? You're one hell of a sight too modest!"

"I'm not proud of this afternoon's work. Do you think I like to have folks pointin' me out on the street an' sayin' 'There goes that killer, Ankrom'?"

Ankrom stiffened abruptly. Trone's stare was strangely intent; the bleary eyes were focused coldly on his face. "Ankrom?" he said. "I thought your name was Streeter."

Ankrom laughed mirthlessly. "It doesn't matter—you'd be hearin' it anyhow before long. I'm Ankrom, all right. One of them gun-slicks with Heffle's outfit recognized me—fellow named Bandera, a Mex renegade. I guess you'll be wantin' to pay me off."

"So you're Ankrom. I've heard a lot about you." Trone thrust his hand across the desk. "I'm glad to meet up with

123

you. Why the hell didn't you tell me who you were at the start?"

Ankrom took the old man's hand dazedly. "You—you mean you're figurin' to keep me on anyway?"

"Why not?"

"But my reputation, man? You can't employ a gun man like me openly!"

"Can't? The hell I can't! I employ whom I please—when I can get 'em. I wish I had six more of you!"

A sudden thought struck Ankrom now. His lips curled sardonically. "I see. You're hirin' me for my guns," he said. "That's why you ain't sore about—"

"'Course I'm hirin' you for your guns!" Trone snorted. "You got the biggest reputation of any man in this part of the country. In my position your name's worth more to me than twenty guns an' the men to man 'em! I'm raisin' your pay—"

Ankrom stopped him with his eyes. "You're doin' nothing of the kind. If I stay on here I take the same pay I been gettin'. Foreman's pay. I'm not hirin' out my guns."

"What!" Trone barked. "Say that again!" he surged to his feet with an angry scowl. "You ain't *what?*"

"I ain't hirin' out my guns." Hard white teeth shone from behind his parted lips. "I'm no leather-slapper an' don't want to give any man cause to call me one. Oh, I know," he held up his hand to silence Trone, "that plenty of names have been hung on me—but no man can say I've earned 'em. But don't let that bother you," he said sardonically. "When I eat a man's salt I earn my keep!"

Trone sat down and his scowl ironed out. "Well, if you're damned fool enough to take all that risk for reg'lar pay, I'm sure I ain't the man to beller. Have you got any line on who's back of this business yet?"

"The sheriff claims it's Claydell."

Trone laughed crazily. "Where'd he get that damn-fool notion?"

"He says there's a railroad plannin' to lay tracks from Amarillo to El Paso; they'll have to cross the Rafter. Claydell, accordin' to Ratchford, aims to build a town outside this valley someplace an' persuade the railroad to bring him in homeseekers—"

"Ratchford belongs in an asylum!" Trone snapped. "Who

124

the hell'd want to locate in this damned desert? An' who ever heard of a railroad bein'—"

Ankrom held up his hand. "Did you ever stop to think that this valley could be dammed? The resulting irrigation project would supply water for one whale of a jag of land. Think it over."

Some of the color washed from the old man's cheeks. Ankrom let his remarks sink in, then said:

"Claydell blames this trouble onto Ratchford."

Trones eyes brightened; he sat straight up in his chair. "Now you're talkin'!" he said with conviction. "Ratchford's the man, all right. That breed would nurse a grudge till hell froze over!"

Ankrom's soft laugh mocked the old man's interest. "That suits you right down to the ground, don't it? Well, it would suit me, too. I don't like Tom Ratchford none whatever, but —like you—this thing's got me fightin' my hat. I can't tell up from down about it."

"Well, I never knew a Ratchford yet that was any good," Trone said, and spat. "This one thinks he's the greatest lawgiver since Moses!"

"Don't judge him light. He's a pacer, mebbe, but he's a hard-tie man. The trouble is, I think Claydell's lettin' his antagonism for Tom run away with him. I could easy do that myself."

"What's Claydell say? Didn't he offer any reasons?"

"None you could put your finger on. He said that a man who can be bought once can be bought again—meanin' Heffle, of course. Well, you evidently bought Heffle away from Ratchford's ol' man in that war you had here back awhile. It seems to be Claydell's notion Tom Ratchfold bought him back. Another thing he said was that an outfit who'll use sheep once will try 'em out again—he aimed that slam at the sheriff. But things like that are only opinions. They don't amount to much when you're sifting evidence."

The old, worried light had returned again to the old man's glance. He seemed tired and weak to Ankrom as he sat huddled in his chair. Of what was he thinking? If one were to judge by his posture and expression, his thoughts were the antithesis of pleasant.

Ankrom sighed. This business would have been far bad enough if a rugged, dominant man were boss of Rafter. But

125

with this gaunt old relic rodding the spread with a whisky bottle in one hand and a sense of failure filling the other, he felt that the end was but around the corner.

In Ankrom's mind one thing stood out above all others in this moment. The force against the Rafter was contemptuous of its owner! Were Trone the fire-fighter he apparently once had been, no man would dared have raised his hand against this ranch.

Plain to Ankrom also was the fact that if this spread were to be saved for Lee, Ankrom himself would have to be the man to save it. He could place no trust in Trone.

He resolved a sudden course of action. The golden girl knew something: somehow he must get it out of her. "Where's that imitation Struthers dame?" he asked.

"That yellow-haired hussy?" Trone poured himself a neat two fingers of the bottle's content. "Tom Ratchford took her back to town with him—said he had some questions he wanted to ask her about that gambler's death."

A cold wave rushed over Ankrom; a recollection clicked home in his mind. With cheeks drawn taut he yanked the door open, plunged down the hall and out across the broad veranda. He dashed for the corrals at his fastest pace.

CHAPTER XVII

JAIL INTERLUDE

MOUNTED on a bigboned strawberry roan Ankrom crossed the moonlit, shadow-hollowed range. He let the big horse have its head and it ran with a will. He did not check its rocketing run until but a few miles outside of Peso Pinto; then he drew it slowly down. When he entered town the big animal was moving at an easy jog trot.

Through a series of back streets he approached the brick building whose ivy-covered walls housed the sheriff's office. One or two open touring cars were drawn up at the curb across the street, their tonneaus being rapidly filled by men carrying rifles, and from whose vests the glint of metal was reflected by the street lamps. Directly before Ratchford's office a group of soft-voiced horsemen were collecting.

Ankrom swung from the roan nearby and ignoring these signs of unaccustomed activity, strode within. His cold glance raked the office from beneath his low-drawn hat-brim. Three or four men were conversing here, but as Ratchford's burly form was not among them they held no interest for him and he passed on down a hall that led to the cells.

If the golden girl was in town this, he felt, was where he would find her.

A frail old man with a bunch of keys at his belt sat on a stool at the end of the passage. He rose as Ankrom approached, peered near-sightedly at him through a pair of horn-rimmed spectacles. Ankrom saw the watery-eyes take in his belted gun; the range dust that powdered his clothing. Evidently the man mistook him for some unknown lawman, for he asked with that ingratiating tone used by jailors to their higher-ups:

"Yes, sir?"

"I want," said Ankrom curtly, "to speak with a prisoner the sheriff brought in. A girl with golden hair. You probably know the one I mean—she used to be in one of the brothels down the street."

"Yes. You mean Miss Betty."

"That's the one. Lead the way. I'm a little pressed for time."

"I shouldn't wonder, sir," the jailor said, as he clumped flat-footedly down one of the rows of iron-barred corridors. "The posse will be leaving any minute." They rounded a corner. "Here you are, sir—Number Eighteen."

Ankrom waited till the fellow walked away, then approached the bars. The golden girl's frail figure was slumped dejectedly on the tiny cot within. She did not look up but sat there drearily regarding the floor. There were deep, dark circles under the eyes concealed by her lower lids. For a moment Ankrom felt a trace of pity. She looked so frail and all alone.

"Miss Struthers—"

She looked up wildly at sound of his voice; came surging to her feet and grasped the bars. "You!" she said, and Ankrom caught a note of hope leaping upward through the word. "I didn't think you'd come!" She pressed her face against the bars, reached a hand through eagerly to grasp his own. "God bless you, Abe," she whispered huskily. "I didn't think you cared."

Ankrom held her hand uncomfortably. She was placing him in a false light yet he dared not disillusion her. So much depended on what she might have to tell him. Hating himself for the part circumstances were forcing him to play, he patted her cold hand reassuringly. She had information which he needed; he could not risk its loss.

"There, there," he said. "I came as soon as I learned you'd been brought to town. What was Ratchford's idea in bringing you here?"

"He overheard what I told you about the railroad. He was furious. I thought for a while he was going to kill me—he took me away as soon as you left."

"Did he question you about Drean's killing?"

"That was just a stall."

"How?"

"He wanted to get me away from the ranch. He had to give the Trones some kind of an excuse."

"Yes, but—"

She broke in hurriedly, her eyes pleading and a warmer color in her cheeks. "I told you I shot Drean. I didn't realize— But Ratchford knew."

"Knew what?" Ankrom demanded impatiently. "What did Ratchford know?"

"He knew that you were the one who killed Drean. He told me tonight on the way to town."

Ankrom shot a quick glance over his shoulder toward the office. No danger yet. Those men out there were still talking. "When I found you bent over Drean that night, what were you taking from his pockets?"

Her eyes flew wide open. "Didn't you know? Haven't you guessed?"

"I saw you take some papers and a gun—Drean's gun?"

"Yes, I took it from the sand where it fell when we went down." She flushed.

Ankrom guessed she was thinking of how she had forced that gun upon him later, making him think it was the murder gun. He patted her hand again, feeling mightily like a Judas.

"That's all right," he said. "What was in the papers? Why

128

were they so important you risked detection to remove them when you must have heard us running toward you?"

"I didn't want them found in Drean's pockets—they would have given everything away if the wrong person had gotten hold of them."

"Why?" A wicked restlessness was creeping upon him. He looked toward the office again and saw the men going out. "Why would they have given things away?"

"Ratchford's name was on them—they were I.O.U.s he'd given Drean."

With crystal clarity things stood out abruptly in Ankrom's mind. Drean and this girl had been Ratchford's tools!

"Did you ever hear Ratchford speak of a man named Hackett—Mose Hackett?"

She nodded eagerly. "He had charge of the rustlers who were plundering Trone's ranch. You mean Rafter's foreman, don't you? The man you shot?"

Ankrom's cheeks drew taut and glistened. That recollection which had sent him hurrying to town had been a lucky one; the suspicion it had engendered had been well-founded.

Trone's remark that Ratchford had taken the girl to town for questioning had been the thing to drop that peg in place. For with the rancher's words Ankrom had recalled the sheriff's reaction to the statement he had made this noon. To his pointing out that a man who would go to so much trouble to smash the Rafter would scarcely be likely to be satisfied with so small a reward as the price of a railroad's right-of-way and the chance to build a boom town when by damming Trone's Valley he could control a veritable kingdom, Ratchford had said: "You're right. I hadn't thought of that."

Yet even with the recollection Ankrom had been afraid to trust his judgment. He had felt he might be swayed by his own antagonism and hatred of the man. But he'd been right. Claydell's guess had hit the nail!

"What were you and Drean impersonating Struthers for?" he asked.

"As a means of getting on the ranch."

"But why?"

"I can't tell you that. It was one of the reasons why I wanted Drean's papers so badly; I thought Ratchford might have given him written instructions. I wanted a hold on him. But he hadn't. Those papers were only I.O.U.'s."

129

Ankrom felt a leaping exultation. Claydell's guess was right; Ratchford was the man!

Ankrom dropped the warming hand that lay in his. The girl's eyes jumped to his face in quick alarm.

"What is it?" her voice came huskily as he stepped backward from the cell. He caught himself; his part was not played out. There was one more thing he wished to know. "Wait," he said, and stepping close up to the bars asked softly:

"How did you get tangled up in this? Why did Drean pick *you* out to play the roll of Struthers' daughter?"

"Drean didn't," she said, and grimaced. "It was Ratchford."

"Ratchford?"

She nodded reluctantly. "I had known him for almost two years. It was because of him I ran away from home and let Dad die of a broken heart. I've never forgiven myself. But I was young and inexperienced, easily impressed. He was so big and strong and handsome." Her lips curled bitterly.

"I'm not trying to find excuses for myself; I'm just telling you how it was. He said he loved me. He'd been telling me what an important man he was out here; a big rancher; a man with a future; a man who might even one day be governor! I imagined myself in love with him. Of course I wasn't —I see that now. I was in love with the pictures he painted in his flights of fancy. I was a fool, but one night I ran off with him. He brought me here.

"It didn't last long; it took about a week for the glamour to wear away. When I saw the husk of him showing through I was sick. But I had some pride; I asked him to marry me. He laughed and told me I'd better clear out; said he'd already picked out the woman he fancied for a wife—a girl with brains, he said, not some damn backwoods hick!

I tried to get work but he fixed it so I couldn't. No one would hire me; he'd passed the word. He wanted me out of the country. But I was determined to stay. To keep from starving I found employment in that house from which I waved to you that night we first saw each other when those thugs were trying to gun you down."

Though her cheeks wore a mantle of shame her eyes clung bravely to his face. She seemed to feel he'd understand.

He did, and it made him feel lower in his own estimation than the belly of the lowest snake. Yet he had done nothing

130

to place himself in this position. If she had built her hopes on a premise that was false, could that be charged to him? He had not said he loved her; he'd done nothing to imply it—unless his gesture in patting her hand could be so construed. It was, he told himself, the fact of his *being* here that had brought her hopes to their present peak; she must feel he would not have come unless he cared!

He realized with a start that his face must in some measure have given him away, for abruptly she pressed close against the bars. "Don't! Don't take it so hard, Abe," her voice came softly as her hand touched tenderly his tautened cheek. "I never loved him. I didn't, really—not as I love you."

Cold sweat bathed Ankrom's forehead; he felt he could stand no more. He was on the point of rushing blindly from the jail when—

"So when Ratchford came to . . . to that place where I was . . . where I was staying, and asked if I would help a man impersonate my father, I told him yes. I believed the time had come when I had it in my power to give Ratchford back his taste of hell. Drean I had never seen until Ratchford took me to the hotel and introduced him as the man who was to play my father—"

She broke off as Ankrom, with a sudden oath, thrust close against the bars.

"*Father?* That's the second time you've used that word. Who are you?"

"Betty Struthers."

"I mean really!"

"Betty Struthers was the name my mother gave me."

Ankrom's stare did not take in the shadow on the floor. He was marveling at the pranks of Fate. He was still marveling when a grim voice behind him snarled:

"All right, *Streeter!* Git up them hands! I'm arrestin' you for the murder of Kelton Drean!"

A laugh left the golden girl's crimsoned lips, and it was not pleasant. He read the mockery in her jeering eyes and an icy numbness swept through his veins.

"Here, Blur Ankrom, is where you reap the price of a woman scorned!"

The corridor rang to her taunting words.

Tricked! The thought roared through Ankrom's mind as he stood there stiff and moveless. Staring into the golden girl's

131

taunting features he was seeing the grim irony of the qualms which so lately had assailed him. A bitter laugh spilled shortly from his lips. What a fool he'd been to be taken in by the glibness of her tongue and the cleverness of her acting when already he'd had samples of both. Like a sleek, plump fly he'd walked jauntily into her web and now was caught there fast!

With her words still ringing in his ears he could not but realize the neat simplicity of the trap in which he had been snared. Ratchford had feared he was getting too close to the truth of things. The girl, angered by his indifference to her passion, had been ripe for Ratchford's use. They'd pulled it slick!

Flame coalesced in Ankrom's glance. For one mad whirling moment the wild chaotic blood of anger surged to his brain and threatened to unthrone his reason. The desire to strangle this treacherous jezebel before him grew almost beyond his power to control. Drawing heavily upon his reserves of strength and will power he fought the impulse down—yet not before, pale-faced and suddenly trembling, Betty Struthers had backed away.

Lips twisting in a crooked smile, Ankrom whirled to find a gun jammed hard against his stomach and Ratchford's gloating face within short inches of his own.

"Go ahead," the sheriff jeered. "Grab onto your irons an' I'll get it over quick! I can't see as it'll matter much to you one way or the other. If a blue whistler don't mow you down, within the hour you'll be stretchin' hemp!"

Ankrom's glance flashed past the sheriff's head toward the office in the front. He felt certain Ratchford and himself, with the possible exception of the jailor whom he could not see, where the only men in the building.

His glance came back to the sheriff's mocking features, lingered on the big teeth showing in a tigerish smirk. Ratchford thought he had him dead to rights. Ankrom prepared to give that confidence a jolt.

"Too bad you can't cut it, Ratchford," he said. "But you're a little late gettin' started. Claydell an' his men are on their way to town right now—must be nearly here by this time."

"So you've swung over to him, have you?" Ratchford scowled. "Well, let 'em come. I've got sixteen deputies in the streets outside with orders to shoot the minute Claydell shows. I'm copperin' *all* the bets, Mister, so if there's any prayin' on your mind you better get it done."

"Got your Mex killer outside, too?"

Ratchford grunted an oath, but no reply.

"Look," said Ankrom softly, "what proof you got that I'm the one who shot Drean?"

"Miss Struthers seen you; she'll swear to it."

"What if she won't?"

"Don't matter. I've got her statement down on paper an' signed."

"You hear that?" Ankrom said for the girl's benefit. "You're in the same boat I am. He'll bump you off soon's he settles with me. You've played your part; your use is over."

The girl said nothing. Ratchford snarled, "Shut your trap or I'll shut it for you!"

Ankrom grinned. "What you waitin' for? Go ahead an' shoot."

"I'll shoot when I get ready," Ratchford growled. "This thing ain't over yet."

Ankrom regarded the sheriff's beefy countenance with speculative eyes. What was the meaning of those words? Ankrom was neatly trapped; what else had the sheriff planned?

He raked his mind to seek an answer. He tried putting himself in Ratchford's place; tried imagining himself with Ratchford's personal ambition, lack of moral scruples and ruthless drive for power.

The sheriff's first move at this time would, he felt, be the removal or suppression of Rafter's foreman—a man whom the sheriff would feel was dangerous to his plans. He wanted to smash Trone's power, to usurp Trone's possessions. Already he had gone a long way in undermining the old man's nerve; Trone had taken to whisky to bolster his failing courage.

What, he wondered, would hurt Trone most? His answer came with a blinding flash that made him cure himself with silent intensity that he had not foreseen this move!

With a crawling of the hair at the base of his skull Ankrom realized what the sheriff's next move must be; saw only too clearly what Ratchford had meant by that surly 'This thing ain't over yet!' The most effective way of smashing Trone would be the destruction of Lee—it would prove the crowning blow to the old man's series of misfortunes!

He recalled that an attempt to get at Trone through Lee had once been made already. Only Ankrom's own interference that night in Peso Pinto had caused the sheriff's plans to

133

miscarry. He remembered that glowing iron with its Straddle Bug brand; he recalled the burly figure slouching past him on the street before that house and he knew that Ratchford was waiting for Lee now!

CHAPTER XVIII

GRIM ULTIMATUM

ANKROM stared at Ratchford's heavy features with new understanding; at the curly black hair spilling down across his forehead from under his shoved-back Stetson; at the long smoky eyes peering out from beneath his sleepy lids; at the stubborn jut of his beefy jaw and his great bulging-muscled form and realized that nothing save Death would ever stop Tom Ratchford from carrying out his plans. His was a one-track mind and it was obsessed by the greed for power.

The sheriff, seeing Ankrom's eyes upon him, chuckled deep down in his throat. "Got 'em over?"

"What?"

"Them prayers you was fixin' to say."

Rage issued from Ankrom in a savage snarl of breath. "Damn you, Ratchford! You can't cut this thing!"

"Can't cut what?"

"What you've got in mind for Lee."

"So you've guessed it's her we're waitin' for, eh? Well, you're right about that; it is. She'd ought to be here now. I had things set for eleven o'clock."

"You locoed fool," Ankrom spat the words contemptuously. "The hand of every honest man in this country will be raised against you if you harm that girl!"

"You're wrong about that," Ratchford assured him with a lazy grin. "Not a one will dare say 'boo!' I've got this range eatin' out of my trousers pocket, Mister. Folks around here'll do what I tell 'em an' like it."

He looked at Ankrom amusedly. "Besides," he added, "I'm not figurin' to harm Lee Trone. I've got better sense than that. I'm gonna get the same results by marryin' her."

134

Ankrom laughed, and the sound brought a scowl to Ratchford's face.

"What's so funny?"

"The picture of you as Lee's adoring bride-groom. Why, she wouldn't wipe her feet on you!"

"That's all right," Ratchford's teeth showed in a jeering smirk. "She wouldn't wipe her feet on you, neither. But she'll marry me to save your life or I'll have you shot before her face—and in the end I'll get her anyway!"

Ankrom, looking deep into those smoky, mocking eyes, had an uneasy feeling that this was no vain boast. Loathing him as she now must, it would yet be like Lee to sacrifice herself for him, he reflected bitterly. On the other hand, if she refused he believed that Ratchford would be fully capable of carrying out his threat. The man had gone too far to be balked on the eve of victory.

Another thought struck Ankrom—struck with jarring force. Once Ratchford wedded the girl, there was nothing to stop him from putting Ankrom out of the way; there was always the *Ley del Fuego!* Escaping prisoners were shot as sighted.

A devil's temper was stirring in Ankrom; a savage desire to get his hands on Ratchford and bruise and batter. It was a desire born of the cumulative hate engendered in him by this burly sheriff; a desire born of desperation.

But somehow he kept his head; held the turbulent, mounting fury under control. He forced his lips apart in a grin of mockery. "Very slick, Ratchford; plenty slick," he drawled. "But you're forgetting one factor—a weighty one that's goin' to break your string."

"Yeah?"

"You know it."

"What am I forgettin'?" Ratchford growled.

"You're leavin' Claydell out of your calculations."

"You're the one that's forgettin'," Ratchford grinned. "That posse out in the street's got orders to shoot Claydell on sight."

"How're you figuring to get away with that?" asked Ankrom, playing for time in which to find a loop-hole in the other's defense.

A deep chuckle of joy left the sheriff's mouth. "Claydell," he said, "is the gent that's out to smash the Rafter. An' by Gawd I got the proof at last—I've found out what he's after!"

135

Ankrom's mind spun round in a dizzy whirl; these plots and counterplots were enough to unseat a man's belief in the fundamental decency of human intercourse. Was it possible that *both* Ratchford and the boss of Swinging J were out to break the Rafter? That both were working toward a common goal but driven on by different motives?

With the weight of evidence against the sheriff this seemed impossible, and yet—

He knew that Drean and this girl in the cell behind him had been accomplices of Ratchford. That much had pretty well been demonstrated. Of Hackett and Heffle and Bandera he was not so certain. True, the girl had *said* that Hackett was a tool of the sheriff's in charge of rustling operations put in motion to drain the Rafter's resources. And Claydell had implied that Heffle was a tool of Ratchford's. But he had seen that Betty had a habit of weaving much fiction with her facts, and if Claydell was in this too he would naturally swing all blame toward Ratchford.

It might well be, Ankrom suddenly realized, that Claydell and the sheriff were pitted against each other—both determined to gain possession of the Rafter. If this were so, and it now seemed possible that it was, Bandera and Heffle and Hackett might have been leagued with the boss of Swinging J. And Bandera was still very much alive and no mean factor in a fight, even if he had backed down this morning!

With a raucus squeal of brakes a car was stopped before the sheriff's office. Ankrom heard the hurried pound of booted feet come tearing toward them down the corridor. He looked at Ratchford; the sheriff was watching him with head cocked to one side in a listening attitude, his smoky eyes opaque and hard.

A man came round the angle of the steel-barred aisle. It was one of the Rafter punchers, Windy. But for a moment he stood in panting silence. He looked from the sheriff's leveled gun to Ankrom wonderingly. Ankrom noted that the puncher was unarmed apparently, which was as it should be since the wearing of guns was against the law inside town limits.

A malicious pleasure surged through Ankrom's veins as Windy said to Ratchford:

"Miz Lee said to tell you as how the Ol' Man got hurt this

evenin' an' that she won't be able to meet you in town to-night as requested."

Ankrom laughed at the sheriff's scowl. "Tough luck, Ratchford," he chuckled. "Puts me some in mind of that ol' saw about the 'best laid plans of mice an' men'."

The sheriff swore. "What the hell happened to him?" he demanded. "How'd the damn fool get himself hurt."

Windy shifted his feet. His answer seemed apologetic. "He got throwed from his bronc."

"Throwed?"

Windy gulped. "He was drunk, you see."

Through much experience in diagnosing the various shadings of trouble, Ankrom realized that Windy was keeping something back. This thing must be more serious than was indicated by the puncher's words. Evidently there was something—

Ratchford's rough voice cut through his thoughts:

"Drunk! Hell, it wouldn't be the first time he's been in that condition! How bad hurt is he?"

"He's dead!" the puncher blurted. "He broke his neck."

Slowly, a wide grin broke over Ratchford's face; his eyes began to glow. "Well, now!" he said with heavy pleasantry. "That's sure too bad—poor fella." He shot a gloating look at Ankrom; tensed. Slowly his grin took on a sickly look and faded. The hand holding his pistol dropped.

Ankrom's gun was in his hand, held rigid at his thigh. How it had gotten there Ratchford could not have told, but there it most certainly was, its muzzle covering the third button of the sheriff's vest.

Yet it could hardly have been this fact alone that caused the sheriff's smile to slide and clammed his brow with sweat. It could not have been this alone for he had a gun in hand himself, and but a moment ago had held the drop.

It must have been something he read in the Rafter foreman's eyes that drove the triumph and confidence from him. Ankrom's eyes were a brittle blue and held the metallic glint of that cold weight at his thigh. They were alive with a bleak intentness, a light that seemed to promise immediate violent action if he were crossed.

He turned his head a little, the alertness of his glance never straying from the sheriff's mottled features.

"The responsibility for Trone's death is yours, Ratchford.

It's the thing you've been strivin' to bring about for months —perhaps for years. I reckon it's time you paid."

Ratchford only glared.

"Sheath your gun." Shadow-like, it was—just a blur of motion. Yet Ankrom's heavy pistol had been holstered. Ankrom's hand hung empty at his side.

There was a shake to Ratchford's hand as he pouched his own. Or had Ankrom but imagined it?

"Windy here'll count three," he said. "You can yank your gun any time you've a mind to. I'll fire when Windy hits the three."

Ratchford's face appeared to pale. "You can't—I won't be no party to it!" he muttered. "I—I wouldn't stand a chance against you!"

"What kind of a chance," asked Ankrom coldly, "do you think Ol' Man Trone had against you an' all your hirelings?"

A tremor shook Ratchford's massive frame. "You can't make me do this! I had nothing to do with that old fool's death! It was Claydell that got him drinkin'; Claydell that's been supplyin' him with booze! I had nothin' to do with it, I tell you. It wasn't me."

"It wasn't you what?"

"It wasn't me that's been tryin' to smash the Rafter." He seemed to make an effort to pull himself together, as though his fears were partially allayed at Ankrom's continued inaction. "Claydell's the man you want."

"Yeah?" Ankrom's glance was skeptical. "What about that bedtime story you was spinnin' me about how you was goin' to marry Lee Trone?"

"Hell! I was only funnin'."

Ankrom's lips grinned coldly. "Well, that may be so. Peel off that badge an' hand it over."

He watched narrowly while the sheriff did so. Then he pinned the bit of metal to his own vest, using his left hand in the operation.

"Now we'll stroll up front an' visit your office," he said pleasantly. "Any time durin' these proceedin's you think you've got a break just make a pass at your gun an' find out for sure."

Ratchford only glared.

As they traversed the narrow corridor Ankrom wondered what had become of the frail old jailor. He had not seen the man since he had left him at the entrance to the cells. And the fellow was not sitting there now.

Once the sheriff turned his head to cast a look behind him and Ankrom grinned. Ratchford snarled an oath and Ankrom saw the smouldering fury in his eyes.

It came to him that Ratchford's momentary show of fear might well have been a sham designed to catch him off his guard, even as he himself had turned the tables on the sheriff.

He cast a fleeting glance at Windy as they gathered in the office and Ratchford closed the door. The puncher's face was stamped with an expression telling far more plainly than words that events were moving much too fast for his continued comprehension.

Ankrom faced the sheriff and his jaw thrust forward grimly. "Ratchford—sit down behind that desk an' get out some paper an' a pen. You're goin' to do some writin'."

"Yeah? What am I goin' to set down and write?"

"Your resignation from the sheriff's office. To take effect immediately."

"Are you crazy?"

"We won't argue that. Get busy writin'."

For several moments there was scant sound save that furnished by the sheriff's heavy breathing and the scratching of his pen. Blotting the paper, he leaned back in his chair. "You're bitin off considerable more'n you'll be able to chew."

"You watch my dust."

"This thing ain't over yet."

"Stock phrase? Whyn't you think up a new one?" Ankrom jeered. His cold blue eyes bored steadily into the long smoky ones of Ratchford, who suddenly broke forth in a flood of vile invective leveled at his tormentor. A gleam of quiet derision entered Ankrom's glance. "Turn it off. You're wastin' steam. Get busy an' add to that paper that you're recommendin' me to finish out your term."

"You don't think that'll buy you anything, do you?"

"You do as I say an' never mind what I think. There's a number of polecats still stinkin' up this country. That paper ought to cover me long enough to get 'em exterminated. Far as that goes this office would make a fine—"

Ankrom broke off abruptly, tensing. A knock had sounded upon the office's outer door—and Ankrom's back was to-

139

ward it. He dare not turn his head for he was in a line between the sheriff and the door. He raised his voice:

"Who's there?"

"Craig," there was impatience in the answer.

Ankrom looked at Ratchford. Ratchford grinned and his smooth, unwrinkled forehead expressed a mighty satisfaction. "My deputy," he chuckled. "Your game's up, fella. I gotcha where the hair's damn short!"

The calm tranquility of Ankrom's glance was disconcerting. His chuckle matched the sheriff's. "Think so? Go ahead an' call him in."

For the space of a dozen heart beats there was stillness in the office; a lack of sound that was tight with danger, wherein the clicking of clashing thoughts was almost audible; a silence strained and electric—a thing to cock one's muscles, to set one's teeth on vibrant edge.

Across this hush, oblivious to the puncher's presence, the two men stared malignantly, each striving to eye the other down.

Slowly Ratchford's face went purple. His black hair bristled with the strength of his antagonism. His smoky glance seemed to flash with flecks of flame. His lower jaw was thrust forth pugnaciously and his heavy lips were bulging. A vein swelled throbbing on his forehead, yet he did not speak; not yet.

Ankrom was leaning a trifle forward, arms hanging at his sides. The lines of his face were harsh; seemed deeper etched than usual and his wind-scoured cheeks held a reddish glow. His grin was satanic in its brazen mockery and a wanton gleam was in his eyes.

"Go on, Ratchford—call him in," he purred.

Ratchford appeared to choke. His lips worked several times before words came, and when they did his voice was shaken by the repression with which they were uttered:

"Go back to the men, Craig. I'll be with you in a minute."

With a short laugh Ankrom straightened. "Shucks, Windy," he drawled "this Ratchford's just a whizzer. There ain't no bottom to him—ain't no sand in his craw."

He crossed to the desk and picked up the paper Ratchford had written and tucked it in his pocket, while Ratchford hung there tense with anger, his eyes wild with humiliation.

Ankrom sent a contemptuous glance across the sheriff's burning features. "You're not sheriff any longer, Ratchford," he said evenly, "you're just an ordinary man. As such I'm warnin' you. Never set foot again on Rafter territory." He backed to the door with Windy; opened it.

"If you do," he finished, "I'll see that you're planted there."

And with a final taunting grin he stepped out, rejoining Windy, and closed the door behind him.

CHAPTER XIX

RATCHFORD PUTS
HIS CARDS ON THE TABLE

A LARGE moon, aided and abetted by the lamp on the telephone pole across the street, made the space before the sheriff's office fairly bright. The two machines which had been parked beneath the light had disappeared. But the group of horsemen were still gathered. Most of them were in the saddle, but two or three stood beside their mounts engaged in a low-voiced conversation. These looked up as Ankrom and Windy emerged from Ratchford's office.

"What's holdin' Ratchford?" called one of the group.

"He's windin' up one or two matters," Ankrom said. "He'll be with you boys in a jiffy, I shouldn't wonder."

He knew these men would not recognize him as a Rafter hand for he had not appeared in town since the day he had driven the phoney Struthers' in from El Paso. But some of the posse could and probably did recognize Windy.

"Better git in the car with me," the puncher muttered. "Somethin' tells me we better hump ourselves."

"Don't put on like you're in a hurry," Ankrom cautioned softly. He caught the glint of the sheriff's star where he'd pinned it on his vest; with the sight came inspiration. He raised his voice sufficiently that the posse might overhear:

"All right, fella," he said. "Don't try any of those gags on me—I've been in this sheriffin' game since who laid the chunk an' I reckon to know all the tricks. This your car?"

"Huh? My gosh, you oughta know—"

"Get it started then. You heard what Ratchford said. I've

141

just about got time to get there. How're your tires?" he asked as they climbed into the Rafter's rakish touring car. "Ain't expectin' any blow-outs, are you?" Windy's shin got a heavy kick.

"Them tires are all right. If they're good enough for Rafter, they're good enough for the likes of you," Windy grunted sullenly, and jammed his foot down on the starter. With a roar the engine came awake. Ankrom thanked his gods he'd thought to borrow Ratchford's star. It was that glint of metal on his vest, he thought, which so far had held the posse silent. Without that star their natural curiosity might have spelled disaster.

Windy let out the clutch and the car began to roll. Just as he shoved it into second, the door of the sheriff's office banged open and Ratchford appeared with a rifle. He did not seem to pause, but dropped at once to a knee and whipped the long gun to his shoulder.

Ankrom swore. "Here's Ratchford on the prod. Duck low an' give this can the juice!"

Windy ducked and his foot slapped hard.

Zang-g-g! Zang-g-g!

The motor's roar as the car leaped forward into high drowned the reports of Ratchford's rifle, but it could not obliterate the ominous sound of lead ripping through sheet metal nor the *pingg-gg!* of bullets knocking splintered holes in the windshield's shatterproof glass!

Windy's foot on the accelerator went down to the floor and stayed there! To Ankrom the rushing *whoom* of the whistling wind was a beautiful sound as the car sped down the tarvia road.

They were just out of rifle range when Windy, via two wheels, swung a corner and put the car on the smooth, wide macadam of the state highway. Ankrom saw him turn his head to voice a question.

"Keep your damn' eyes on the road or we'll both wake up in hell!"

Windy's head jerked front again and Ankrom said more softly:

"Straight for the ranch. Ratchford'll probably follow so keep 'er wide open an' watch what you're doin'. We've got a pretty fair start. He won't be able to commandeer a machine right off, so we're that much to the good—see that we don't lose our lead."

142

"What's he up to, anyhow?"

"He's after my hide. He's the gent—one of 'em, any-ways—that's been tryin' to bust the Rafter. Old grudge's still workin' on him, likely. Got a new inducement, too. Some railroad's figurin' to lay track between El Paso and Amarillo. Have to cross the Rafter. Ratchford wants to cash in."

Windy whistled. "So that's what it's all about. This business sure has had me fightin' my hat. Best thing for you right now is to get clear outa the country. Ratchford'll be after you sure as Gawd makes little apples! He can hate like an Injun!"

"I'm a pretty good hater, myself."

Ankrom relapsed into silence. Talking was a strain on the vocal chords at the pace they were traveling.

One thing was certain, he thought; regardless of how many different factions were trying to break Trone and get the Rafter, Ratchford certainly was one! There was no longer any doubt in his mind about it. Ratchford certainly was doing his damndest—by hook or crook he was set on getting the ranch. And wanted Lee thrown in!

Claydell? Well, Claydell might also be striving to possess himself of Trone's domain. He admitted the possibility and would have been willing to consider the plausibility as well, could he have found for the boss of Swinging J a motive sufficiently impelling. But he could not. Claydell was a big rancher—not as big as Trone, perhaps, but a large owner none the less. He was a politician—one of the big men in this country. It would be a mighty risk for him to dabble in this business; a much greater risk than was Ratchford's since he had more than Ratchford had to lose

Claydell was suave—a cool customer. If he went after something, as Ratchford was going after the Rafter, his chances of success would be much greater than would Ratch-ford's, Ankrom thought. For Claydell was a thinker; he had, Ankrom felt, a keener mind by far and well knew how to use it, as was attested by his present prosperity in contrast to the all-but-empty pockets of the majority of his neighbors.

If Claydell— Checked by a sudden motion, Ankrom's thoughts stopped there. No man, he'd abruptly realized, could be in a better position to start Trone on the down-grade than could Claydell—a trusted friend.

Ankrom shook himself impatiently, striving to rid his mind

143

of the insidious thought. He knew it to be born of Ratchford's imputations, and knew those imputations the result of Ratchford's natural antagonism toward the boss of Swinging J, coupled with the desperateness of Ratchford's own position. The ex-sheriff was simply trying to blacken Claydell's character that Claydell might be made to share some of the blame for Ratchford's acts. This was the long and short of the matter.

But the thought persisted; he could not shake it.

Lee had told him of many little things the boss of Swinging J had done to help her father at various times; the man, according to Lee, was a hearty adherent to the Golden Rule, a man four-square and upright, a staunch pillar of the church.

Ankrom's lip curled. He'd met such prodigies of virtue before. Usually if one dug deep enough—Ankrom softly swore. Claydell was top-hand stuff; there was no sense nor fairness in letting Ratchford's charges and insinuations fill him with suspicions of the man. Why, at one time and another, so the boys had told him, Lee and Claydell had been spoken of as a 'pair who'd soon hitch up an' travel in double harness.'

Ankrom grimaced. Why, he was old enough to be her father!—well, almost, anyway.

Yet he had to admit that as a suitor Claydell would be bound to be attractive. Like Ratchford, the fellow was magnetic, likeable; a good catch for any woman. He was successful in his business, he held good prospects for the future. And the fierce vitality of his dark and lean-carved face—

Ankrom swore again. He'd have to quit thinking of the man in that capacity—any man as a possible suitor for Lee's hand in marriage was bound to evoke his prejudice. He must concentrate on Claydell, 'the trusted friend.'

But as a friend, Claydell would be in a strategic position to bring about Trone's downfall. Ankrom scowled. Those cursed insinuations of Ratchford's—he could not get them out of mind.

He had thought when they'd stepped from the sheriff's that this shove against Rafter was over. He'd bluffed Ratchford to the wall, forced him to step out of office, made him 'take water' before a witness—these things should have marked his finish in this country. By all the rules of tradition Ratchford should now be hunting himself a hole.

But he wasn't! He'd got his teeth in Rafter now and wasn't aiming to let go till Death grabbed him by the ankle. And even then, Ankrom thought sardonically, the burly ex-sheriff would likely do some powerful kicking! The way he'd jumped from the office to send those 'blue whistlers' streaking after them was proof a-plenty that he had not yet given up.

Ankrom snorted. "He's stubborn enough to hang on till hell freezes an' then try an' skate across the ice! But he's out in the open now, an' he won't have the law to back him up."

"Who you talkin' about?" yelled Windy.

"Ratchford. *Hey!* Keep your eyes on the road!"

"I'll bet he's mad enough to chaw the sights off a six-gun! He won't be layin' down again."

"This thing ain't over yet," Ankrom agreed, then grinned as he remembered that these had been Ratchford's words. "We're goin' to have to hire more men an' cartridges. Now that this business is in the open it'll be shoot first an' ask questions later an' hell for the guy that ain't lookin'! It may make Tonto Basin look like a picnic 'fore we shake Ratchford loose. Now Trone's out of the way an' he's got a taste of blood, he'll throw the hooks to Rafter hard. We're goin' to play hell with Trone's bank account."

"Not much we ain't," snapped Windy. "There ain't no Trone bank account—bunch of damn' coyotes cleaned the bank plumb out today!"

"What!" Ankrom half rose from his seat.

"I said it. Lee tol' me tonight right after I brung the Ol' Man in. That's what she was goin' to town for—Ratchford sent her word."

Ankrom sank back heavily in his seat. Here was a blow beneath the belt! No need to wonder was this robbery just coincidence—it happened at much too bad a time for Rafter not to have been deliberately a planned part of the whole affair. This robbery was a skillful thrust—it bore the mark of a more subtle hand than Ratchford's heavy paw. This, mused Ankrom grimly, was the balanced stroke one might expect of having emanated from a mind like Claydell's.

Windy burst suddenly forth in song:

"Oh, give me a home
Where the buffalo roam

145

An' the deer an' the an-te-lope play;
Where seldom is heard a
Dis—"

"For gosh sake, save a part of your breath for breathin'!"
Ankrom growled.

"Huh! Don't you like singin'?"

"If that was singing, it sure was in one coyote key—
thought you was tryin' to give the death-rattle!"

Windy scowled; relapsed into silence. A moment later he
muttered, "By gee, these last coupla weeks you've been touchy
as a peeved snake! Cripes, there ain't no livin' with yuh!"

"Nobody's askin' you to live with me," Ankrom drawled.
"Now stuff a plug in your talk-box an' give a gent some rest.
I'm *tryin'* to do some *figurin'*. When I want to hear grand
opera I'll let you know."

More and more it seemed to Ankrom that Claydell was,
as Ratchford claimed mixed up in the Rafter's misfortunes.
Lee had told him reluctantly one day that her father had always
had a weakness for strong drink. Might not Claydell
have known this and have been encouraging Trone's weakness
for what it might be worth?

After all, despite the exemplary character attributed to the
boss of Swinging J, Claydell had swapped sides once; had
gone from Ratchford's old man to Trone. He might not now
have gone from Trone to Ratchford's son, but was there any
guarantee that he had not turned on Trone? Ankrom could
see none.

One thing only kept Ankrom from considering the cool,
suave boss of Swinging J as the Rafter's chief menace. Strive
as he did, he could find no apparent motive strong enough
to lure or force the man into risking all that he now had on
the chance of smashing Trone. He could find nothing which
the man might possibly gain that would be commensurate
with his losses should he lose.

To be sure, Ratchford had *claimed* to have found that thing
which Claydell was after. But had the former sheriff actually
made such a discovery, or was this but another of his smoke
screens designed to further Ankrom's belief in the rancher's
possible guilt?

Ankrom shook his head bewilderedly; he did not know.

The devil of it was, he somberly told himself, that so much

night be hanging on the issue. And upon his correctly gauging
t. If Ratchford alone was responsible for the calamities
descending so steadily upon the Trones, things would indeed
be sufficiently bad. But if Claydell, too, was having a hand
n them, one might as well admit that Rafter was licked. He
and the three Rafter hands might possibly hold off Ratchford
and his unofficial posse if it came to an open fight—leastwise,
as long as their supply of ammunition held out. But Ankrom
and Trone's punchers could not fight off the whole damned
country!

Ankrom's chin sank momentarily forward upon his chest.
It was hard, he told himself, bitter hard to know what a fix
Lee Trone was in and to realize at the same time that he
could do nothing toward alleviating matters.

Then abruptly his chin came up and out. His grim jaws
squeezed hard together, causing the muscles beneath his tawny
skin to stand forth like stiffened ropes. He could not sucess-
fully combat the united forces of this country—but he could
make one hell of a damned good try!

Ratchford, when he had left the Rafter T with Betty Struthers that afternoon—after Ankrom had gone tearing off to
the southwest line camp to deal with the water-jumping sheepmen—had not gone directly back to town as he had informed
Trone he intended doing. He had gone first to the Swinging J.

He would not admit, even to himself, that he was afraid
of Claydell, or Claydell's interference with his plans to get the
Rafter. Yet such was the case. The boss of the Swinging J
had him badly worried. This, coupled with the humiliation
he had suffered before the Trones at Ankrom's hands, had
put the man in a vicious temper. Bitterly had he denounced
the golden girl for a scheming hellcat, a double-crosser of
the first water, and had heaped abuse and insult upon her head
acidulously. She had reminded him that he had no business
calling anyone a double-crosser after the way he had treated
her. Accordingly, when they reached Claydell's ranch, neither
of them could have been described as being in a jovial mood.
A black frown rode Ratchford's heavy features while a light
of sullen resentment glared from the girl's blue eyes.

They dismounted before the ranch house porch. Claydell
his usual suave and courteous self, met them at the door. No
expression could be detected on his angular, high-boned face
as, gravely, he invited them inside. Seating himself in a heavy

cowhide-covered chair, he motioned his guests to seats upon a nearby couch.

"You came to apologize perhaps for the accusations with which you connected me with Drean's death?"

With an effort Ratchford ironed the scowl from his feature and assayed an answering smile. "Yeah," he said, in what he intended for a hearty voice, "that's so. You've got the uncommon habit of smackin' the nail right on the head. I've discovered that it was that Streeter bird who blowed out poor Drean's light. Miss Struthers, here, saw him fire the shot."

"Well, that's something." Claydell's tone was noncommital. "Have you arrested him yet?"

"Not yet. But I will soon's I gather me a posse."

"Posse?" Claydell's eyebrows climbed—just sufficiently to express contempt. "To arrest one puncher?" he drawled.

Ratchford reddened. Choking his anger down he said, "guess there's one or two things you ain't found out. Evidently Streeter's identity's one of 'em."

Claydell waited; his was the power of silence.

The golden girl was the first to recognize that he had no intention of putting the obvious question. She turned to Ratchford. "Tell him, please."

"Did you ever hear of Blur Ankrom?" he growled. "Farther south he's known as 'King of the Corpse-Makers'."

"Seems as though I've heard the name somewhere," the rancher admitted. "What about him?"

"Well, this Streeter's him! An' you can take it from me that baby can get a hog-leg into action quicker'n hell could scorch a feather!"

Claydell leisurely rolled himself a smoke and lit it. He puffed a few smoke-rings toward the raftered ceiling in thoughtful silence.

"WELL?" Ratchford's tone rang with exasperation. "Ain't you got anything to say?"

"Were you giving me that information for some special reason?"

His habitual caution stirred the smoky gray of Ratchford's eyes. He hedged, "I kind of figured you'd want to know."

"Oh," Claydell expelled a cloud of smoke from his nostrils. Through it he eyed the sheriff coldly. "You thought I'd want to know, eh? It strikes me this sudden solicitude on your part's rather odd, Ratchford. You an' I ain't never hit it off together very well as I recall."

Ratchford got to his feet. Over cautious though he was as a rule, he was nevertheless a man with plenty of intestinal fortitude. He decided that here was a place to prove it.

"Let's be frank, Claydell. You an' me figure on gettin' Trone's spread."

Nothing was to be read upon Claydell's unrevealing face. Nothing ever had been, he reflected bitterly, save when it suited Claydell's book. His yellow eyes displayed no more emotion than twin bits of colored glass.

Though he guessed the ending this business was to have, there was nothing left for Ratchford but to go on; he'd already said too much to leave the rest unvoiced.

"You an' me," he repeated, "are both out to smash the Rafter. I know what you're thinking—you're thinking that I'm after that railroad money and the chance to rear a boom town along its tracks. I am—I'll put my cards on the table."

He paused to let this much sink in. When Claydell still offered no comment he said, "Well, I know what you're after, too! So that makes us even!"

Claydell took the information calmly. "Indeed?" was all he said.

Ratchford, gathering his nerve in both hands, remarked:

"Knowing all this, and knowing therefore that our interests cannot possibly clash, I suggest we join forces—rub Ankrom out an' take the ranch. I'll marry the girl so's to make sure there ain't no hitch an'—"

He broke off in mid-sentence as Claydell came to his feet, a .38 gripped ominously in his fist, its muzzle pointing at the sheriff's stomach.

Claydell's thin lips barely moved, yet his words were plainly audible:

"Get out, you rat, before I forget myself!"

149

CHAPTER XX

"LAWS DON'T BOTHER YOU, EH?"

THERE was a light burning in the ranch house living room when Ankrom and Windy rolled down the long slope descending from the valley's rim and braked the car to a halt before the broad shadow-dappled veranda. As Windy reached out to switch off the ignition Ankrom, leaning toward him, asked:

"When you left for town tonight were the boys still out on the range?"

Windy nodded.

That meant that the boys were out there still, Ankrom mused. After all, there would have been no reason for them to come in. They would know nothing of the sudden turn events had taken. Besides, he had given Ring-Legs definite orders to remain at the southwest line camp and guard the tank Heffle and his men had tried to seize.

Thought of those men with their cold grim faces and narrowed eyes turned his mind again to Claydell. Heffle would never have had the money to hire such a crew of gun-fighters. And he thought it extremely unlikely that Ratchford could afford them, either. This left but one alternative as choice for their true employer!

Ankrom took out his silver watch and held it beneath the dash lamp. He saw that the hands pointed to 2 A. M. Returning the battered time-piece to his pocket, Ankrom thrust his legs across the door and over the car's side.

"Put the can up, Windy, get your rifle an' go sit in a shadow where you can keep your eyes open. 'Most anything's liable to happen round here before mornin'." With a weary grunt he dropped to the ground.

He crossed the broad veranda and opened the ranch house door. He was about to pass Trone's office on his way to the living room when, chancing to glance inside, he saw a dim light burning at the head of a sheeted figure. In the flickering play of the feeble light the room made a depressing picture; it brought Ankrom to a pause.

150

Softly he moved within.

For some moments he stood regarding the sheeted figure without movement. Then slowly he reached down and drew the covering from the old man's pallid face. There was a faint smile upon the cold, still features; no worry was now apparent there, nor fear. Just a wistful smile, and peace.

Ankrom felt profoundly moved as he stood there, hat in hand. Many times had he been in Death's presence, yet never before like this. He wondered if it were pleasant where Trone was now.

"Don't you worry about this spread," he told the still figure quietly. "Just keep on smilin', Old-Timer. I'll see that Lee gets Rafter, somehow."

He drew the sheet back over the waxen features, tiptoed softly from the room.

As he moved down the narrow hall and came abreast the living room door, he heard a voice he recognized; a man's voice—Claydell's. It ceased abruptly and Ankrom knew he had been heard.

Deliberately he opened the door.

Facing him he beheld the six-foot frame of the boss of Swinging J. Claydell's high-boned face was taut; there was a leveled six-gun in his hand. But as he saw Ankrom, a grave smile crossed his long dark face and, relaxing, he returned his gun to the shoulder-holster beneath his coat.

Ankrom's glance passed beyond him, to the cold white face of Lee. Her cheeks, he noted, were colorless, and there were dark circles beneath her eyes as though she had been crying. But she was not crying now.

Stepping clear of Claydell's protecting form, she said:

"What are you doing here?"

His eyes fed hungrily upon the soft, pale oval of her face; upon the halo of her hair which shone like burnished copper in the radiance of the table lamp behind her; upon the cherry-red of her parted lips. And remembering the manner of their parting, he could find no words with which to answer.

"I did not think you would have the impertinence to return. Why have you come?"

The contempt in her soft voice hurt far worse than had her quirt before the cabin.

Ankrom's eyes fell before the scorn and loathing to be read in hers. He stared heavily at the floor.

151

Color flamed abruptly in her cheeks and her green eyes blazed. "Will you answer me?" she asked.

He looked swiftly up, then down again. He could not bear to see her thus. Her beauty made a dull pounding in his heart. He winced when Claydell said, "You might's well let him stay, Lee. After all, we're short on fighting men."

Her jade-green eyes flashed hot with a fierce, defiant light. "I don't need men like him!"

"Ma'am—" Ankrom began, and fell silent before the scorn in her level glance. He stood rigid, stiffly, the deep rise and fall of his breathing making the only movement in his body.

The lines in Ankrom's face looked deep and grim when at last he raised his head and looked her squarely in the face. "There's nothin' I can say, ma'am—except that I'm sorry for what I said this afternoon. Sayin' that I'm sorry don't mean a heap, I reckon. But I've come back here to—"

"I've heard enough," she broke in coldly. "There is one thing you can do for me. Just one. Fork your horse and go your way—but don't come back here ever."

Some of the deep bronze washed out of Ankrom's cheeks, "I'd sort of hate to think you meant that, ma'am." There was pleading in his glance.

"I *do* mean it," she said, though to a person less intent upon her words than Ankrom, a catch in her voice would have been apparent. "I shall be heartily glad to see the last of you."

A poignant silence shut down upon the room. Then Ankrom's jaw came up; a short laugh left his lips.

He said, "I reckon you ain't goin' to feel real glad for quite some time, then."

"What—what do you mean?"

"That I got no intention of quittin' Rafter till this fight for possession's washed up. Whether you like it or not, I expect you'll have to put up with me till one or two polecats have been smoked from their holes an' exterminated."

She turned her back deliberately. "Good night, Ed," she said to Claydell, and crossed the room. Opening a door at its farther side, she entered her bedroom and closed the door behind her.

Claydell looked at Ankrom curiously.

"How come you're sportin' that star?"

It was several moments before Ankrom realized the man

152

had spoken. "What?" he asked. The room seemed cold with a chill that bit to the bone. He shivered.

"I say how come you're wearin' that star?"

"Star? . . . Oh!" Ankrom glanced down at his vest where Ratchford's badge was pinned. He said no more.

Claydell's voice came sharply, "What's the matter with you—you sick?"

"Sick? No," Ankrom drew a sharp breath; pulled himself together. "I'm all right."

"Then why don't you answer my question? Is it a secret?"

"I'm afraid I wasn't listening," Ankrom admitted.

"I said where'd you get that star you're packin'?"

A cold smile crossed Ankrom's lips. "I'm actin' sheriff, now. Ratchford has resigned."

"Resigned, eh?" Claydell's mask had slipped a little. For a fleeting instant Ankrom read surprise, wonder, in his yellow eyes. "What did he resign for?"

"Because I asked him to. Now I'm goin' to ask you somethin', Claydell." A metallic timbre came into Ankrom's voice: "What's happened to Bandera and the rest of them gunslingers you lent Heffle to jump our tank today?"

For a long moment Claydell eyed him silently. Then he said, "I've got them posted round the house."

"Yeah? Outside?"

"Outside."

"Go on; you're provin' a heap more interesting than I'd expected."

"I've given them orders to shoot the minute Ratchford or any of his men show up."

"I sort of played into your hands some when I took Ratchford's star away from him," Ankrom suggested.

"It makes no diff'rence to me who's packin' the sheriff's star," said Claydell coldly. "A man's a man, an' he'll kick off just as quick with a star on as without."

"Meanin' that you're above such things as sheriffs. Laws don't bother you over much, eh?"

Claydell smiled. "When a law gets in my way," he said, "I have it taken off the book."

"Laws pertaining to murder are a little different. They got a way of stickin'."

"If one man was to be bumped off," explained Clay-

153

dell patiently, "there might be quite a stink. But kill enough an' it will be hushed up."

"You won't be able to hush this business up."

"Won't I?"

A bit of doubt crept into Ankrom's mind. The boss of Swinging J seemed mighty confident. After all, Claydell was more than just a big owner; he was a politician, too, and perhaps his political affiliations would tide him over—would smooth away all noisy voices.

He watched Claydell take a slim cigar from the breast pocket of his coat, peel the cellophane from it and, bringing out a lighter, ignite its end. Placing the fragrant weed in one corner of his mouth, the boss of Swinging J thrust his long-fingered hands deep into his coat pockets and stood there coolly smoking, his face inscrutable.

"So you don't think I'm big enough to cut this thing, eh?" he asked at last.

"You might be able to dispose of Ratchford, an' them he brings along. But you won't be getting this ranch, I can tell you that."

"That's where you're wrong," said Claydell smoothly. "One month from today Lee Trone an' I'll be married. Think it over."

"She wouldn't marry you." Ankrom's voice did not contain the certainty that was its custom.

Claydell laughed. "You know Miss Lee couldn't handle a ranch this size herself. She needs someone around to look out for her interest—someone she can *depend* on. That someone's me. She's wearin' my ring right now."

Ankrom felt suddenly old and worn. A bleak chill was in his bones. He crossed to the fireplace; put his back to the blaze. But the coldness would not go away; it seemed to be inside him.

He looked at Claydell grimly where he stood smoking in evident enjoyment of the situation; a cold rage like the rage he'd felt for Ratchford was rousing in him. He seemed to hear the throbbing of distant motors, but he paid the sound no heed.

He said, "There's one thing you're forgettin', Claydell."

"Yes?"

"Yeah—me."

"I'm not forgetting you, my friend."

154

"You'll not get this ranch while I've got anything to say about it," Ankrom's voice crossed the silence recklessly. In this mood he didn't give a damn if Lee did hear him. "Nor you won't marry Lee Trone while I've got anything to say about it, either!" he added savagely.

Claydell grinned. "I'm not worryin' about you. When the time comes—"

"Bribes don't interest me, brother!"

"I wasn't thinking of bribing you," Claydell said, and stopped as a white glare circled the room and the rattle of rifles rent the night outside.

Ankrom with a muttered curse sprang to the wall. "Ratchford!" he snarled, as his left hand swept across the light switch, plunging the room in darkness.

CHAPTER XXI

SHOWDOWN

THIS, Ankrom told himself as in the darkness he turned back toward the fireplace, was the very thing he had ridden into this country to avoid—murder, battle and sudden death. Yet he had found them even as he knew he would. Reaching above the mantel for the rifle he'd seen suspended there on pegs, it came to him more forcibly than ever that, strive as he will, a man cannot escape the destiny that is his.

Somehow he had known, even as he crossed the Arizona border and came into this Texas country, that he would find no more peace here than in other places had fallen to his lot. Child of Trouble, he could not escape the Old Man by a shift in border scenery.

Not that it mattered, he told himself. Since Lee Trone had flung those words at him across this room and turned her back, he no longer cared. He'd deserved the words she'd used on him, and more. His censure was for himself.

The rifle was a repeater. He examined it and found the magazine full. His wide lips pulled downward grimly as he crossed the moonlit floor and crouched beneath a window.

155

A glance across his shoulder showed him Claydell at another; there was the glint of a six-gun in the rancher's hand.

With the barrel of his rifle, Ankrom knocked the glass from the lower sash. Jerking his hat-brim low, he peered out across the argent yard. Some two hundred yards away a pair of touring cars were drawn up in a loose V, its apex pointing toward the house. Bursts of yellow flame blossomed magically in the darkened space beneath.

"Reckon they're all behind those cars?"

"I doubt it," Claydell answered. "They got into position mighty quick, but not so quick I didn't see two shadows flittin' away—one to either side. Those two will flank my men and drive 'em into the house. You wait an' see. Ratchford savvies this Indian game better'n any gent I ever met. We'll have our work cut out for us."

"How many men you got out there?"

"Let's see . . . five. Countin' Bandera."

"How many men you figure there is with Ratchford?"

"I'd say eight or ten, anyway."

"Didn't you cut your string pretty short?" Ankrom's tone held a note of mockery.

"You're thinkin' I was kind of tight on men," Claydell guessed. "Well, I wasn't at all sure Ratchford was plannin' to strike tonight. I only brought my bunch to be on the safe side. I don't see how it is Ratchford's raidin' here, 'stead of over at my place. He knows he'll have to smash me first—"

"He was comin' here for me," Ankrom explained, and shoved his rifle across the sill. "Still, you posted your men outside with orders to open up as soon as Ratchford showed. How come you did that if you weren't expectin' him?"

"I told you—I was figurin' to play safe. If Ratchford came I was ready for him. If he didn't, there wasn't any harm done in bein' ready." Claydell leaned closer to his window, peering out into the drifting shadows. "I wish they'd get out in the open where we could pick 'em off."

"If someone was to give you a house an' lot, you'd not be satisfied, I reckon, less they built you a picket fence around it," Ankrom hazarded sarcastically. "You needn't worry though about Ratchford stickin' too close to shelter. He's in no mood for cautious fightin'. Right now he's feelin' meaner'n a new-sheared sheep. In a minute he'll be kickin' the lid off,

156

an' this jamboree won't last no longer'n a keg of cider at a barn raisin'."

"You talkin' to keep your courage up?" Claydell sneered. "If you ain't, then shut up! I want to hear the music. I've tried for a good many years to maneuver Tom Ratchford into pullin' something like this."

"Ratchford's land appeal to you, too?"

But at that moment a bullet knocked glass slivers from the upper sash of Ankrom's window. At that moment also, he sighted a forward-creeping figure edging houseward from the black shadow of the cars. He elevated his rifle's muzzle just a fraction. His finger squeezed the trigger—the crawler ceased all movement.

Ankrom cuddled his weapon's butt against his shoulder and waited for another target. "You wantin' Ratchford's land, too?" he repeated. "Must be damn' valuable dirt in this country. What's in it, anyway—diamonds?"

"You wouldn't be doin' so much scoffin' if you knew what I know," Claydell answered enigmatically. "Trouble is with you, you don't use even the one brain you been equipped with."

Before Ankrom could find a sufficiently scathing rejoinder, a definite lull became apparent in the sound of cracking rifles. "Well, you were right for once, at any rate," he said. "This won't last much longer. They've driven your coyotes off."

"Not off," Claydell corrected. "Just inside. They'll be with us in a second."

The prescribed second had hardly passed when two men entered from the hall. Their faces, as they entered, were in shadow. Yet by their gear Ankrom picked out one for Bandera. He'd known the Mexican would not be hurt—the fellow was far too careful of his hide.

Bandera swore when he recognized Ankrom by the moonlight that was streaming in the windows. The Mexican's companion said:

"They got Tim. Ed an' Baldy sloped!"

Neither by sniff nor oath did Claydell show his feelings. He continued his watchful scrutiny of the yard.

Abruptly Ankrom realized that someone was crouching at his side. With sidelong glance he attempted to determine who. What he saw brought his head full-around. Anger marked his voice:

157

"You can't stay out here! D'you want to get shot?"

"I'll do as I please in this house," Lee Trone answered defiantly. "Kindly tend to your own business."

Ankrom scowled at her through the semi-gloom. Always, he was thinking, they had had to clash. His scowl grew blacker as he observed a gun in Lee's right hand. She was not looking at him now, but at something behind him. He saw her gun start up and whirling the rifle he flashed a glance across his shoulder.

Across the room Bandera was crouched, one arm above his head. From something in his back-flung hand the moonlight struck silvery gleams. Ankrom hurled himself aside as that upraised hand snapped forward. With a *chunk* a knife buried its point in the sill behind him as flame lanced out from Ankrom's hip, and from the gun in Lee Trone's hand.

Bandera spun, reeled sideways and crashed down across the table.

Claydell's oath was lost in the startled cry of Bandera's companion:

"Quick! They're makin' a rush!"

But the man's warning had come too late to stem the tide of Ratchford's rush. The outer door bulged beneath the onslaught of a battering log. With a shrill scream of rending wood the door was torn from its hinges and smashed to the floor as Ratchford's wolves came surging in with oaths and blazing guns.

Ankrom's heart thudded crazily against his ribs as, brushing Lee Trone behind him, he thumbed swift shots into the huddle of crowding men showing dimly in that open doorway.

Shouting, cursing, Ratchford's crew came swarming in, and the moon-dappled murk was illumined by criss-crossed stabbing streaks of flame. Gun-thunder rose in throbbing waves of monstrous sound.

For red moments all was chaotic turbulence; shouts screams, curses mingling with the steady beat of hammering weapons.

Ankrom did not know his gun was empty, its pin smiting aimless brass, until a steady pummeling of his side caused him to lower a hand, into which Lee slipped a freshly-loaded pistol.

Then through the gloom a towering, rockline form thrust

158

up before him. There was no mistaking that bulging, burly figure.

"Tom Ratchford," Ankrom breathed, and whipped his weapon up. Yet even as his thumb released its hammer, he saw Ratchford's big shape lurch sideways—fall sprawling to the swift trip-hammer beat of Claydell's gun from the opposite window.

A mirthless grin crossed Ankrom's lips as the man collapsed.

He crouched there, striving to realize that the tumult of sound was gone; that the doorway was no longer filled with cursing figures; that the silence was creeping back.

Swift at starting, this thing was as swiftly over.

Drawing a deep breath, Ankrom looked down. A bar of moonlight poured liquid silver across Ratchford's heavy face; revealed his working lips as, stubbornly, the dying man strove to speak.

Words came at last in a broken whisper: "Claydell . . . was after . . . oil."

"Damn you to hell!" swore Claydell and flame burst redly from his hip.

Ankrom's voice crossed the silence raggedly: "That was a dog's trick, Claydell."

Through the murk of smoke and shadow the rancher stood stiff.

"*Now!*" said Claydell, and his gun belched flame again.

A burning shock seared Ankrom's side, but he kept his feet. "Not good enough," he jeered.

Claydell's hand was shaking now. Ankrom could hear the bullets shrill; could hear them *chunk* into the wall behind him. With a bitter laugh he shot coldly from the hip—just once. He laughed again, maliciously, when Claydell, clutching at his chest, crumpled, stretched motionless on the floor.

Then everything went black.

Minutes later he opened his eyes to find his head pillowed on something soft. He turned his head a little, realized that it was resting in Lee Trone's lap. He tried to struggle up, only to find that her arms, clasped about him would not let him rise.

Something hot and moist fell on his face. Tears! Lee Trone was crying!

"Why, ma'am—" he began, but she broke in, and there

159

was unimagined tenderness in the low, throat murmur with which she asked:

"Oh, Abe—why did you make me love you so?"

A tremor ran through his body, the blood pumped furiously through his veins. "You—you don't—you can't mean—?"

"Of course," she said, smiling through her tears at his incoherence. "I've loved you all the time!"

THE END

BREED OF THE CHAPARRAL

For the Cochranes—
Harold and Helen

1

THE FIRST time Tune laid eyes on the girl she had her back to the wall of Madam Belladine's brothel with the clothes half torn from her gleaming body and the look of a tigress in the knife-lifted crouch of her. Tune jumped for the man. The fellow whirled and fired, his slug purring death past the edge of Tune's ear. When Tune caught his balance the girl was gone—gone as swift as the man, gone as quiet, as completely.

That had been Tucson. The *barrio libre*.

This was Oro Blanco, one week and sixty-some-odd miles later. The girl was the same but the man looked different. They were in the mauve shadowed doorway of Riske Quentin's cantina. Tune could not catch the drift of their whispers, but their postures, their gestures, were unmistakable. Threat stood in each line of the man's angry shape.

The girl's head lifted sharply. Her glance met Tune's. The effect of that look was like a touch of pure lightning.

Tune breathed deeply, darkly staring.

She was clad in the rags of a border gypsy. Bare toes, delicately contoured but fouled with the grime of this dusty road, peeped from the open ends of huaraches. But her eyes were blue—Great God, what a blue! Like the eyes of a child! Like the windy blue of the sunswept heavens. And Tune swung unthinkingly out of the saddle.

He could not have said what moved him into this. Impulse, probably—the quickened urge of piled-up hungers. The girl reacted as swiftly. Relief came into the look she swept him—relief and remembrance, and a pithy kind of a halfway promise that brought him hard up

163

against the man, that put Tune's hand on the burly shoulder and savagely swung the man round to face him.

He was big—that man; lithe and brown as a golden snake. Gold flashed from the lobes of his pendulous ears and his uncropped hair was shaggy and touseled where it showed from under the floppy-brimmed hat. His shapeless shirt was of cotton and, like the cotton drawers that covered his shanks, might once have been white. Straw sandals encased his big, muscular feet and his drawers were kept up by a twist of rough hemp. There was a raveled serape flung across his shoulder.

His left eye drooped in a kind of sour wink.

He didn't waste breath and he didn't waste time. There was a knife in his hand and he dived to use it. Tune swayed from the waist and, as the blade ripped past, put five hard knuckles square against the man's jaw. The man's feet left the ground and he went over backwards. His head struck the step and he lay sprawled there loosely.

Tune looked for the girl. She was gone again. He yanked open the nearest half of the batwings but he did not see her inside the cantina. With an irritable shrug he went back to his horse and climbed into the saddle.

He sent the horse down an alley toward Grankelmeir's stable and was building a smoke when he dropped the makings and did an odd thing—very odd, considering. He loosened the bedroll behind his cantle, thrust gunbelt and gun out of sight inside it; then he retightened the roll and rode on.

He slapped at a fly and scowled irritably. That pair and their business meant nothing to him. Sneak thief and harlot.

But he knew as he thought it they had not had that look.

That was what bothered him, what kept his mind on them when it should have been taken up with things more concerning him. What if the girl *did* have blue eyes? Like enough there were plenty of blue-eyed gitanas if a man cared to go to the bother of hunting them.

Just the same . . . There was something about the

164

girl's eyes that stuck with him, unquieting the accustomed run of his thoughts. So like a child's! They made angel's eyes out of that kind of blue!

Tune cursed in his throat and pulled up at the stable, a bleak eyed man in a chin strapped hat who had troubles enough of his own to look out for. He had not come all this hell of a way to be taken and dangled for a plain lack of caution.

He said: "No, by God!" and got out of the saddle.

HE WAS CURLING a smoke when Grankelmeir's stoop-shouldered shape came out of the fetid gloom of the stable. There was a calm and relaxing feel to this place, in the hay smell and horse smell that rose up to greet him.

He licked his smoke and put a match to it.

"Right smart of gypsies rovin' round this town."

The stableman nodded. "Yeah—worse'n a plague o' rats, them fellers. You figgerin' to stay long?"

Tune had no answer for that one.

Grankelmeir said, "Not aimin' to be nosy. Kind o' rule of the house. It's cash in advance if you're just passin' through, friend."

Tune dug a cartwheel out of his pocket.

The man was reaching to take it when his eyes went, frozen, toward the stable doors.

A man staggered into the sun's bright blaze, coming out of the stable back first, bent over, hands clutching his chest, his breath spilling out in choked, whimpering groans. He collapsed on his face with both arms hugged under him.

He was dead. Just like that. They both knew he was dead by the way he had fallen.

It was the stealth of the thing that beat up Tune's temper. Death lurching out of that peaceful aura. The deceitfulness of it sent a chill up his spine.

Rage growled through his arteries. He went into that stable cat swift and cat wary, completely forgetting he wore no gun.

There was nothing to shoot at. No sign of a struggle. No sound of departure. Nothing— But wait! Yes—there was something. Something red and round on the hoof scarred planking.

Tune bent. He picked it up and stood holding it, stood oddly grim, eying it.

He suddenly thrust it into his pocket and tramped outside with cheeks enigmatic. He turned the man over. Grankelmeir clucked.

It was a South Texas face they were staring down into, sun bronzed and stubbled with a three days' beard. The face of a man in his middle forties. One accustomed, by its look, to the giving of orders. No common ranch hand.

"Know him?" Tune asked.

Grankelmeir rose and dusted his knees off. He said, "No!"

Without knowing why, Tune knew the man lied.

He made no comment. He reached down, tugged the knife from between the man's rib bones. It was a long-bladed thing, plain of handle. It had no markings.

Tune was like that, bent above the man, holding it, when two fellows came into the yard from the alley; two men in scuffed range clothes, both talking.

Both suddenly stopped.

The taller man stared with a shape gone rigid. The other man's lips curled. Short and broad this one was, almost dark as a Negro, burnt so by the sun and high wind of this country. He said, "I told the fool them sheepmen would fight."

He looked again at the dead man. His glance touched Tune.

A kind of silence fell. The man looked at the knife still held in Tune's hand. He looked a long time at Tune's gunless waist. He turned with a shrug, with a saturnine quirk of his quick-lifting eyebrows. "Come on—come on!" He pulled the taller man after him off down the alley.

Tune's glance came around to find Grankelmeir watching him.

"I don't suppose," Tune said, "you know those gentlemen, either."

"Never saw 'em before. Look—do me a favor. Stop by the marshal's and ask him to drop over here."

166

Tune said, "Tend to your own dead. He's no kin of mine."

THE CROCKETT HOUSE was the only hotel. It wasn't much. As Tune came into its dusty lobby a yellow haired girl broke her talk off short with an irritable glance in Tune's direction. With an impatient swing of the shoulders she wheeled and went through an uncurtained arch to the dining room. At a table by an open window a young fellow, waiting, got up with a smile and pulled out a chair for her.

The place smelled of cabbage. The desk was a rough, scarred pine affair wedged into an alcove under the stairs. The man standing back of it took his scowl off the girl and, with an ungracious jerk of the hand, got down a key and shoved it at Tune on top of the register. "Number Four," he said—"I guess you can find it."

He kicked back his chair and departed.

Tune, looking after him, picked up the key.

Without so much as touching the register he stepped back on the porch and was that way, considering, when a girl's voice said very cool-like and casual, "Just a moment, stranger."

Tune turned without hurry and met her glance through the window.

It was the yellow haired girl. She had not bothered to rise. She was bending forward. She beckoned imperiously.

Tune went over. He dragged off his hat and then, scowling, replaced it. "Yes?" he said.

The girl's eyes dropped to his unbelted waistline. When they came up they held a pointed interest. Tune cursed the impulse that had shucked off his pistol. He would better have worn it for the unfaded sign of it was plain on his jeans and the lack of it now invited attention.

The girl smiled. "I've got a job for you."

Tune said nothing. He kept his stony eyed look upon her and his mind, behind it, sort of wondered what manner of woman this was who so brashly would go about employing a gun man.

She said, "We run Clover Cross—cattle. Teal could use another hand. Another *good* one."

Tune's mind turned over that moment at the stable when the dead man had come reeling into the sun with his hands hugged over the knife that had killed him. *I'm involved in this,* he thought bitterly, *whether I like it or not.*

His presence at that stable had dragged him into it. But he did not have to stay dragged into it. He could saddle and ride . . .

The girl, with just the right touch of irony, said: "I suppose you would work if the price were made large enough."

"If I did," Tune said finally, "it wouldn't be for no petticoat."

Excitement lay in her look for a moment. Then anger spread its dark flush on her cheeks; and that was when Tune turned his back and left her.

He stepped onto the boardwalk. His glance stopped at a store in a false-fronted building of sun-cured pine. It was four doors down and had the one word *Mercantile* spelled in bleached paint across its front.

Tune, watchful and wary, stepped into the street, a tall gaunted man with a saddle-bound stride whose care was the cost of continued liberty. He thought: *two years of this business can change almost anyone.* He was changed.

He was not a laughing man any more.

One of these days the law would catch up with him. It was the logical—the inevitable end, of all this dodging and hiding. He regarded himself as a man without illusions. He knew he had ought to get out of this town. Two men had seen him holding that knife. One would have been entirely sufficient.

He crossed the Mercantile's porch. He was about to step inside the establishment when the blue eyed gitana came out of an alley and stopped beside him. She was watching him gravely with her look of a child.

Vitality shaped the curves of her body. She had an animal magnetism that got its hooks into Tune's long hungers and unsettled his habits of vigilance and caution.

He let caution slide and looked his fill of her.

168

Her lips laughed back at him, became abruptly sober. "The button," she said, and put out her hand.

Tune looked at her carefully.

Her expression turned urgent. "Quick! *Andale*— hurry!"

"What button?" Tune said.

She let the hand drop and he saw how responsive her face was to the things that went on in her mind. Her mouth showed disappointment. She said, "The button you found on the stable floor."

They looked at each other appraisingly.

"So you were there, too."

"Will you give it to me?"

Tune said, "No," and saw her eyes darken.

It wasn't just anger. It was a kind of wonder, really. A kind of searching wonder that left Tune on edge and displeased with himself.

He resisted an impulse to give it to her.

Her breasts showed the lift and the fall of her breathing. She wheeled away and, at once, swung back. "Don't you think that's behaving rather headstrong and foolish? The button does you no good—nothing good can come of this business." She said impatiently, "Come, *prala*, give it to me."

Tune shook his head.

She left him abruptly.

He went into the store still thinking about her.

A face came out of the store's dim coolness and Tune said laconically, "Box of forty-fives," and watched the man's glance briefly drop to his waistline. The man turned without speaking and went behind the partition.

The smells of this room brought pungent memories and Tune was a man to whom memory was poison.

He picked up an unloaded forty-five from the counter and was that way, hefting it, when a man's voice behind him said: "What do you reckon to do with that gun, sir?"

2

THE GHOST of amusement touched the set of Tune's mouth.

The glare from the street left the man a black shape but Tune would have known that voice at midnight.

He said, "How are you, Lou? Thought you was up in the Tonto country."

The black shape moved forward into the store and, with the change in light, took on depth and character. It became a man, spare and still, ramrod straight, immaculate. Expensive black-and-white checked trousers were neatly pressed as was the black Prince Albert snugging his shoulders. Ash blonde curls set off the stovepipe hat and a heavy gold watch chain crossed his flat middle. His cheeks were clean shaven, pale, expressionless.

"What are *you* doing here?" he said irritably.

"Now, Lou," Tune smiled, "that's all past and done with."

"Nothing's ever done with," the man said bitterly. "I'm the Oro Blanco marshal."

"You always did like the shine of a star," Tune remembered; and stood watching him, waiting.

An edge got into the marshal's voice. "Damn it, I don't like this, Dakota. Why did you come here?"

"It bothers you?"

"By God, I don't want you around!" Bitter eyes told the depth of Lou's feeling. "Why, hell! You must be—" He let the rest slough off as the storekeeper came into sight with Tune's cartridges.

The storekeeper said, "What's this I hear about Teal gettin' killed? Wasn't somebody—"

Lou Safford said: "Teal killed himself over at Grankelmeir's stable."

He looked at Tune. They both looked at Tune.

"Sure," Tune smiled, and saw Lou Safford's shoulders

170

relax. "Putting your money into sheep these days, Lou?"

It caught the marshal off guard and he looked his surprise. Then a dark tide of color crept up his neck and his mouth went together like the jaws of a trap. Yet, with all that anger, there was a faint hint of fear at the back of his stare. Tune saw it and marked it and paid for his cartridges.

He nodded at Lou and with the box tucked under his arm he went out.

SUMMER'S HEAT curled off the road—off those scarred wooden planks grayly flanking the store fronts. Even the dust smelled scorched and stifling. On the balls of his feet Tune looked at the town, seeing all the stray movements, guessing much from the guise of things not too apparent. The clink and clank of the hoof shaper's hammer was a steady and untiring beat in the stillness, rhythmic and natural as the action of the cur before the millinery shop. A saddled roan gelding, ground hitched by the faded two-color barber pole was scratching its jaw with a hoisted hind hoof while, a bit farther on, before the cracked and patched front of Riske Quentin's cantina two cowhands, just swung from their horses, were staring open mouthed at a fast talking third.

Safford came out and stopped by Tune's side.

"Been a long time, Lou," Tune reflected.

Lou Safford said with his gambler's exactness: "One year to the day," and fell ponderously silent. His frowning eyes kept roving the town, kept worrying his mind with the things they saw, kept edgily returning to the trio of punchers before the cantina. "Why did you come here?" he burst out suddenly.

"*You* hadn't anything to do with it."

"I don't care," Safford said. "I don't want you around." His eyes raked Tune, wholly without charity. "What have you done with that precious pistol?"

Tune's glance was amused in a remote sort of way. "I kind of reckoned you'd get around to askin' about that, Lou."

A tenseness showed around the marshal's mouth, but

171

he kept his head, kept a hold on his temper. "I'm tryin' to keep this town quiet," he growled.

"That why you called that killin' a suicide?"

The points of the marshal's cheekbones stood out. Some emotion long bottled inside him exploded. The sudden glint of his eyes exposed hatred uncaringly. *"That's it!"* he snarled. "That's why I don't want you around this town—*you're too goddam nosey!"*

"If you got trouble around here soft-pedaling won't cure it."

"You going to tell me now how to run my business?"

"God Almighty couldn't do that, Lou."

A growl came out of the marshal's throat. In front of Riske Quentin's a crowd had grown. Men stood three deep around the fast talking puncher. The man's quick words were building an effect. He was waving his arms. He suddenly shouted and the crowd shouted with him. The sound of that shout was unmistakably ugly.

Safford caught Tune's arm. "I'm going to tell you something. That dead fellow, Teal, was the Clover Cross ramrod—they been runnin' this country ever since the Indians. That's a Clover Cross hand there that's doing the jawing. That bunch's all ranch hands—a cow crowd. There's a sheep camp out at the edge of Teal's range; he was over there yesterday laying the law down. Now he's dead. And Birch Alder is shooting his mouth off."

Safford locked his stare into Tune's stare blackly. "That's the story. You keep out of it."

He turned on his heel, a tall grim man with a star on his chest, and stepped into the street. He was starting purposefully in the direction of Quentin's when the sound of a solitary shot crossed the wind. It was impossible to tell where that sound had come from. It passed unnoticed by the crowd at Riske Quentin's, but Lou Safford stopped with his feet wide apart. The fingers of his right hand jerked and spraddled. His head came around with an indrawn breath and his bitter eyes sprang at Tune accusingly.

"You see?" he snarled. "Wherever you are, by God, there's trouble!"

There were other words crowding against his teeth

172

when the whole tight look of the marshal's face altered.

Tune trailed that look to the hotel porch.

Every sound in the street went abruptly still. Across that hush a .45 drove violence.

Two men and a girl stood on the Crockett House porch and one of those men was swaying, falling. It was the young man Tune had seen with the girl—with the yellow haired girl who spoke for Clover Cross. It was she who stood now, shocked of face, sharp staring, with a white-knuckled fist caught against her red lips while a stringer of smoke curled above the bright gun snout; while the man with the pistol politely said:

"I am sorry, Miss Larinda, ma'am, but not even for you I couldn't take that talk."

3

TUNE BROKE his stride and stood stopped in his tracks.

Considering this scene with a closer care, the memory of Safford's words came back. This was what Lou meant. It was none of Tune's business.

He hadn't the knowledge to guess what lay back of it, not even acquaintance with the persons involved. He had no way of judging who was right and who wrong. It might not be the brutal killing it looked. The man who had fired might well have been forced to; things beyond his control may have driven him to it. A man couldn't go by the look of that girl—women were a heap too apt to get rattled; they were too crazy-headed to shape a man's judgment in a time like this. That young fellow's hand had been inside his coatfront.

Tune's mind went back through the months to San Saba. To San Saba in Texas. To a scene very like this. To Sheriff Tom Curry sprawled dead on the floor of the Carlton House bar. Tune shook his head to get that picture out of it. The sheriff's hand, too, had been thrust in his coatfront, and the smoking pistol . . .

173

They said, anyway, it had been in Tune's hand.

Sheriff killer!

Tune's jaws went white at the remembrance of that cry. He saw the avid faces that had ringed him round. A cold sweat drenched his body like rain as he stood there, locked on the edge of this dusty road while the hurrying figures went clamoring past him to swell that jostling throng round the porch.

Lou Safford was right. This was none of his nevermind.

He looked toward Riske Quentin's. That crowd was dissolved, gone scampering to augment the bunch round the porch rail. It was ever this way, Tune remembered. Life's gusty interest in death called all classes.

He went down to Riske Quentin's and pushed through the batwings.

He pulled out a chair at an empty table. The place smelled of rotgut and cheap cigarette smoke. Tune well knew its ways, its bar and its women, its squinch eyed, tough faced, gun toting customers. This was the breed Blackwell Stokes had consigned him to.

Breed of the chaparral.

A VIOLIN wailed beside a girl on the platform. It packed her song's maudlin melody with all the wild drear flavor of the hills. With voice and gesture, with an art transcending her lowly station, she was pleading with outstretched arms for someone please to put her little shoes away. So utterly earnest was the pitiful look of her, so heart-rendingly choked were her tones with pathos, three shabby old soaks by the end of the bar set out arm in arm to go to her rescue.

But these things were lost on the man called Dakota. There was a cold chill gnawing the pit of his belly and the bottle the barkeep brought held no comfort. There was no anodyne known that could ease what ailed him, no bar that could bolt the door on his past.

Two years!

The keen eyes in his face were vigilant of things not seen in this room.

He thought of the gun he had cached in his bedroll,

of the way of his life since leaving San Saba; and his lips twisted into a hard thin line.

Two years of hiding from the hounds of the law.

Two years of brush running, badges and bullets.

A considerable time when measured by the speed of a hand smashed to gun butt.

The cantina's noise became a faraway sound. The tireless drone of the gamblers' voices ran on and on. The clink of hard money, the clack of the roulette ball, became as lost on Tune as the oaths and laughter of the booted men round him.

He sat with memory and his cheeks were bitter.

After some time he roused a little. There was no way of telling if the reward bills had come this far yet. The marshal had not braced him, but that did not signify. He knew Lou Safford for a circumspect man, a gentleman filled with odd shifts and dodges. Lou was not the kind to make the same mistake twice. He had tried for Tune once before, and if they tangled again Lou would hold all the aces.

Lou Safford was right. This was no place for Tune. Everything here was stacked for trouble. In the past two years Tune had seen enough trouble to last him a lifetime. But he kept remembering that young fellow falling. He kept remembering the look of that girl.

But for the look on the face of that yellow haired girl he would now be riding, would be losing himself with the winds of the desert. His luck could not hold. He knew that. The long arm of the law was bound to catch up with him. And there were things he must do before that time came. There were accounts to be settled—they cried out against staying.

Yet he did not go.

He sat there morosely sprawled at his table, a saddle whipped man in trail grimed clothing. A man gaunted by travel and dogged by doom—*that* was the way the look of him struck you. He had the ways of a man who had Death for a trailmate.

All the drives of his nature were urging him back to the grim accounting. To the belated reckoning with Blackwell Stokes for the things which had driven him

175

out of his homeland, for the blackhearted treachery which had hounded him here to this waste of cholla and sand and catclaw, to this hell of green-slimed waterholes where only the wolves and coyotes came, where only the chaparral breed could survive.

But through the urge of these things came that vivid picture—the young man falling, the tragic look of the girl. He could not forget the shocked beauty of that face. With the clean silver brilliance of a daguerreotype her features were vividly etched in his mind. In retrospect there seemed to be about their gentle beauty a strange look of remorse. Perhaps it was but some quirk of memory which gave them that odd, that haunting quality. But it was there in his thoughts of her. He could not banish it. And he could no more go with that face in his mind than he could get back those things the black past had stripped from him.

Price! That was what she had said—"if the price were made big enough." Price! What could *she* know of price, with her crew of hired hands and her thousands of cattle! With her uncounted acres!

No matter, he thought. There were things in this world that a man could not do.

Blackwell Stokes had first shown him that. Blackwell Stokes, his friend, high commissioner at San Saba. How well Tune recalled the sad look of the man, that regretful voice as Stokes had said with deep sympathy, "No, I'm sorry, Tune. This thing has gone too far. Neither repentance nor innocence can reshuffle the cards. Sheriff Curry is dead. You cannot change that. You cannot escape your connection with it. There are powerful factions at work in the land . . ."

Tune ground his teeth and got up, blackly scowling.

It was plain enough the powerful factions were here, too. The demands of that girl had to have their way with him; he could not leave her, or any woman, to face by herself the ugliness he saw shaping up here. For this was the old, unforgettable pattern, and a sly, sly hand was lying light on the reins.

He got out of his chair while the mood was on him,

a leather legged man with a broad sweep of shoulder and a wintry chill in the glint of his look.

Dark cheeked and solitary he moved through the crowd, through the swirling layers of blue-gray smoke. He was lifting a hand toward the halfleaf doors when a man, shoving in, brought up hard against him.

The man grinned at him tightly. This wasn't an accident.

The man drove an elbow into Tune's ribs and Tune fetched a fist back and let the man have it. Surprise was a flare in hot off-balance eyes and the look of the fellow turned purely wicked as the doors, shoved back by the thrust of his weight, spilled him heavily onto the planks of the porch.

Tune batted the doors and went through them after him.

The man was up on one knee when he saw Tune coming; the gleam in his hand was a lifting pistol. Tune kicked the gun loose, sent it skittering streetward; and the man surged erect and came tearing into him.

Tune let him come, taking the jolt of those blows without feeling them. This was something he could get his teeth into. He hit the man in the belly. He grinned at him toughly. The man's head dropped with whistling breath. Tune fetched him another, full and square on the temple. The man went down on his back and stayed there.

Tune's glance flashed darkly up and around. All the barroom gun toughs stood jammed around him. They were watching him, wondering; and it was one of these wonderers whose look Tune found interesting.

Sudden warning prickled the hair of his scalp. This was a face he had seen before; the burnt-dark face of the short and broad man of Grankelmeir's alley.

The man smiled thinly and nodded. Then he turned on the balls of his feet and departed; and somebody came with a bucket of water and splashed it across the downed man carelessly, and the crowd broke up.

Tune wheeled his shape in the bright glare of sunlight and struck off toward the porch of the Crockett House. But, midway on his course, something changed his mind

177

and he turned and, instead, went up Grankelmeir's alley.

Someone had been through his bedroll.

With anger dark on his skin he went through his things but found nothing missing. He got out his gun belt and buckled it round him, grimly tying the whang strings that hung from his holster. He got the fresh cartridge box out of his pocket and stuffed the empty loops of his belt, replacing the shells he shook out of his pistol.

He bent his steps toward the hotel again.

There was wildness in this town and he felt it.

Yet the town was no different than a hundred others Tune had been in and out of since he'd gone on the dodge. A border town with the border's stamp plainly, dingily on it. One long crooked street hock deep in dust and two thin rows of falsefronts flanking it. Two lines of tie rails paralleled these, their poles roughly polished by the reins of hitched horses. There were a lot of hitched horses at the tie rails now and a couple dozen wagons helped to clutter the store fronts.

Tune kept to the dusty middle of the road and was uncomfortably aware of things happening around him.

Lou Safford, he thought, had come a far piece since Atchison.

A hulking fellow with a hard and bland face stepped out from the shadow of a dancehall's awning. He looked Tune's way and then eased round a corner.

Tune's glance lifted over the hotel's front. A cold amusement briefly lighted it, for back of a curtained upstairs window some other shy soul was keeping cases. From a shanty with *Minnie's* blazoned redly across it a smile and shapely arm invited.

The hand on the reins was a knowing, sure one.

Heat curled like smoke from the drifted dust, it puffed with the dust from each forward boot thrust. Smell of frying food reminded Tune he was hungry and he scraped his spurs across the Crockett House porch and bridged its emptiness with lips drawn tight. There were watching men along both sides of the street, but these would not stop ambush lead from striking him. The feel of this town was an ugly thing.

Tune passed into the dining room.

He took a table with a wall behind it. He removed his hat and mopped the sweat off his forehead. The hasher's tired eyes revealed a shopworn interest. Tune said, "Whatever's handy," and heard her call *"Ham an'!"* through the kitchen doorslot.

A man got up and came and bent over him. "When you're ready to work I'll find a place for you."

It was the short and broad man who had smiled at Riske Quentin's.

"Usually pick my own."

"You'll find it different here."

The man smiled amusedly while Tune shaped a cigarette.

"'Fraid you're slantin' your talk at the wrong gent, pardner."

The dark faced man did not answer immediately. He fetched out a plug of very black tobacco, bit off a chunk and stood chewing thoughtfully. He stared through the smoke Tune had wreathed about him and had no need to say what he thought for the shine of that thinking lay plain on his cheekbones. He was a type Tune knew with his shotgun chaps and that blue bandanna knotted tight at his throat.

This man was a gun boss and both of them knew it.

The man finally hauled up his shoulders and spat. "Mebbe you better just ride along, Mister."

Brashly Tune grinned.

The man's eyes grinned back at him.

"This ain't San Saba," the man said. "You mebbe wouldn't be quite so damn lucky here."

4

TUNE SAID when the hasher came back with his dinner, "Who was the gent that shot the kid?"

The woman's tired eyes jumped nervously up and met Tune's look with a guarded watchfulness. "Stacey

179

Wilkes," she said finally. "He's the Seven Keys owner."

"And that jigger that just went out of here? That dark faced bird in the shotgun chaps?"

"You must be new around here," the girl said. "Didn't think I'd seen you around before. Just get in?"

Tune smiled at her gently. He put down a cartwheel alongside his coffee cup. "Fellow in the chaps just offered me a job. Forgot to mention what the name of his spread was."

The girl's eyes studied the pink checks of the tablecloth. Her glance touched the coin, touched Tune's face and dropped back again. She took a look at her hands, at their roughness and redness, and rubbed them against the soiled white of her apron.

"That was Crowly, Wilkes' range boss. Quite a friend of the marshal's."

She picked up the coin and went back to the kitchen. Her words lingered with Tune. They kept tramping through him, dragging up memories, disjointed reminders of this marshal, Lou Safford, as Tune had once known him.

Lou had not changed much. This had ever been Lou's nurtured style. The strong against the weak. Where the riffraff ruled you would find Lou as riffraff. Where the law was paramount Lou wore the star—or was able to move it to suit his fancy. The strong against the weak; it had paid Lou dividends.

Yet there was a difference here. Tune considered it carefully. Lou's interest appeared to be geared to the Seven Keys program, yet Lou had himself named Clover Cross largest.

That made things pretty plain to a man who knew Lou.

Tune had known Lou Safford when the railroad boom had been expanding Atchison. Tune had been riding fast in those days, for that was when the chase was fresh and Stokes' star packers had asked no more of fate than to get their gunsights lined on Tune, on this man who had counted Stokes his friend.

Wherever hard cash was to be had from the gullible, there you would find Lou Safford's tent. A river boat gambler, Lou had quit the decks of the great paddle-wheelers for the greater spoils at the "end of steel." As trouble shooter for the construction outfits Tune's path and Lou's had frequently crossed until, one night with his own bare hands, Tune had knocked Lou cold and pulled his tent down over him. Four hours later they had told Tune to travel; the railroad said his job had played out. But Tune understood Safford's friends had brought pressure. They were men in high places.

A smile struck across Tune's lips, hard and thin; and he pushed back his chair and got up from the table. He caught up his hat and went into the lobby.

The natty dressed clerk had his feet on the desk again. He brought them down with an angered abruptness and a scowl clamped the lips around his fat cigar. "It's the custom here to put your name on the register."

"Is it?" Tune said, and went on up the stairs.

On the dim upper landing he paused uncertainly. He wished he had thought to take a look at that register. He could see the door with the #4 on it. He tried his luck with his knuckles on #1.

The door swung open while his hand was still up there. A stoop shouldered man in batwings stood eying him.

"Maybe I'm wrong," Tune said. He smiled meagerly. "I been coddlin' the notion this was Miss McClain's room. Miss McClain of the Clover Cross."

The man pressed his leather-dry mouth together. His stare went over Tune bleakly. "What business would *you* have with Miz' McClain?"

"I guess that would be *her* business, wouldn't it?"

"Oh! Let him in, Ives," the girl's voice said.

Tune moved into the room. The man shoved the door shut. He put his back to it stiffly and his bright, baleful stare stayed on Tune with cocked interest.

The yellow haired girl was in a rocker by the window. The heat of this room was like a clenched fist, yet the girl's cheeks showed no sign it had struck her. She looked at ease, very cool and just a little bit scornful as she lifted her glance to meet Tune's.

It made him wonder if he'd read this aright. Looks

181

could fool you. That young fellow killed on the porch downstairs might not bear any relationship to her.

She said, "Changed your mind about petticoats?"

Tune shook his head. There was a displeased look in the shade of her eyes, and Tune wondered why this was. He figured she should have been pleased to see him. If she had wanted him once she ought still to want him. And he was a little surprised about one other thing; he could find nothing tragic in the look of her now.

There was something of dislike—even a kind of regret, in the way she sat there and eyed him.

He was a lonely man, and suddenly he knew it; a lonely man with all of a lonely man's preconceived notions. He was a gun slung rider of the far dim trails who had known better things and again desired them. But he was, he told himself, practical also, and this side of his nature turned his look briefly wistful as he saw with a numbing clarity how all his days must be like this, how ever and always he must be an outsider to the good things of life. Bloodshed and violence would tramp by his side through all the last days of his life, he thought. By his own hard stubbornness he had made his bed, and there was nothing left now but to lie in it.

All the lines of his face pulled together then and he left the hat where it was, on his head. He had pride himself, and roughed up by the look of her it kept him from saying what he had come here to tell her. He said instead, "That boy—that young fellow you ate with . . . Your brother, wasn't it?"

"You knew that, didn't you?"

He said: "I've no time to waste kicking words around with you. If the man was your brother, say so."

"Certainly he was my brother! Now what do you want here?"

He gave her back angry look for look. "I've come back to say I'll hire on, if you want me. To hire on like you asked me."

He expected some sharp and furious words from her. As a matter of fact it was the man, Ives, that answered.

"We don't need no damned gun fighters!"

A paleness touched Tune's cheeks and was gone.

182

The girl said, "Wait!—I'm going to hire him, Ives."

Ives said: "No, by God!" He slashed a hand down. "You're crazy with grief, girl—you don't know what you're doing. You git into that bed and git you some sleep. If your mind's plumb set on it I'll find you a leather slapper, but it won't be one with the look of this feller!"

A door slammed somewhere downstairs off the lobby and a lift of voice sound reached them and dimmed. Tune's face stayed inscrutable.

The girl said sharply, "What's the matter with his look?"

Ives' weather scoured cheeks showed an impatient anger. "Look! Teal gits kilt. Your brother gits kilt. Then along comes this feller with a gun to rent out to you." There was plain open violence in the man's look at Tune. "I say it's too damn pat! A kid in three-cornered pants would know better'n to let this guy git in gunshot of 'im."

There was pride in this girl—there was a lot of it, Tune thought, watching the changing pattern of her features. Pride and a will that would have its way. She said, "That's prejudice, Ives. If you've any real reason—"

"Reason! You ask me fer *reason?* Didn't I jest see him gabbing with that damn Jess Crowly! That's reason enough, ain't it? Who is he, anyway? *You* don't know —*I* don't know! But he was there at the stable when Teal got that knife in him, and by God that's enough reason for *me!*"

The girl looked at Tune. She got out of the rocker. She said: "Is that true?"

"This fellow works for you, don't he?"

"You're goddam right I do!" Ives growled hotly. "All the time! Every inch of the way!"

The girl never took her eyes from Tune's face. "You haven't answered my question."

"Sure it's true. I had just got to town. Was putting my horse up. I was standing in the yard talking to Grankelmeir—just fixing to pay him—when your range boss come reeling out of the stable."

183

"And Crowly?"

"I was downstairs eating. Crowly came over and offered me a job."

She said, "Why didn't you take it?"

"He did," growled Ives. "He's workin' at it, ain't he?"

Larinda McClain's green eyes searched Tune's face.

Ives said, tight and bitter, "A man don't smash one of Jess Crowly's riders an' get clean away without it's been fixed up fer him! Not in this town of Oro Blanco he don't! There was Seven Keys riders all around this guy and not a damned one of 'em lifted a eyebrow!"

The girl's look at Tune showed a quick, sharpened interest.

She smiled. "Good! You may consider yourself hired. We'll be leaving for the ranch inside the next hour."

5

IVES' WHOLE look was hotly incredulous. His lips fanned out, indescribably bitter. He looked ready to break into violent voice, but his mouth snapped shut without spilling a word. He jerked open the door and slammed it after him.

Larinda McClain's red lips curved again.

She had a generous mouth; and she put up her hands now and swept back the hair that was like spilled gold against the cream of her cheekbones. She said: "That was Ives Tampa. He's taking Teal's place as the Clover Cross ramrod. I guess you know why I'm hiring you, don't you?"

Tune rested a hip on the table and looked at her. "Maybe I'd better hear you say it yourself."

Her glance remained smiling. It became speculative, also.

He said, "You trust Tampa, don't you?"

"Yes—of course. He's loyal. Whatever his faults, that isn't one of them. He's been twenty years running this

184

country's roundups. Dad placed his worth as beyond all argument."

"So you've set him down in a dead man's boots, but you know too well his feet won't fill them."

She pulled up her chin. He watched her take a deep breath. Then she nodded. "There are too many things Ives would never do. Too many things he *couldn't* do. We've got a fight on our hands. I don't mean to lose it."

She stood tall and straight and met his look fairly.

She had sand, all right. She had a courage compounded of things seldom component to a woman's character. She had keenness and insight, and the kind of foresight and determination needed to back them. She had made up her mind, he thought, to fight fire with fire, and she did not want for a right bower in this any man whose hands would be tied by scruples. She had hired Nason Tune because she believed him an outlaw.

It ran through her words. She said, "What do we call you?"

"You hirin' a name or a gun?" Tune asked, and watched her. She didn't get riled.

"We've got to call you something."

"You can call me Dakota."

"Dakota what?"

"Just Dakota," Tune drawled; and he could tell by her eyes his guess had hit close enough.

She considered the brash wintry look of him, nodded. "Have your horse by the porch inside a half hour."

Tune took his hip off the table. "Don't you reckon you'd better maybe post me a little?"

Her knowing eyes raked the hang of his holster. "I see you've found your gun." She grinned a little; put her hand on his shoulder. "You'll do what you have to do. If it's good for the ranch I'll back you till hell freezes."

Going down the stairs Tune thought about that. When he got to the bottom other things took his notice. The lobby was empty.

Tune went through the door.

Trapped heat off the porch was like a fist shoved against him. A look at the street showed less wagons,

185

more horses. He twisted a smoke and got a match from his hatband.

There were too many men on this street doing nothing.

He struck the match with the edge of a thumbnail. That same left hand cupped the flame to his cigarette. Strong fingers snapped the wood splinter and dropped it.

He had lived too long by the feel of intangibles not to be warned by the look of things now. He considered those roundabout men once more and pulled up his shoulders and moved into the street.

The clank of his spurs became loud in the quietness.

A man stepped out of Grankelmeir's alley. The man looked at Tune. Tune saw the man's mossy teeth leer back at him.

This was the fellow Tune had knocked through the batwings. This was the old, old pattern again. There was no need for words—no time for words, either.

The man slashed a hand down and dug for his pistol. The barrel came level as Tune's gun spoke.

Dust jumped out of the man's hand-stitched vest. You could see the man stagger.

He was folding forward like a horse bedding down when a quiet voice said, just back of Tune's elbow: "I'll take that gun, Tune."

TUNE!

The sound of that name locked Tune in his tracks. He stood utterly still in the dust and the sunlight with his mouth stretched thin and each jerked nerve in his wire-taught body shrieking its urge that he whirl and fire. This was the blind hypnotic impulse inherent in every creature that breathes, waiting only the blood-money cry of the scalp hunter to be at once transmuted into violence and bloodshed—the wolf urge of the fugitive.

No man moved to hem him in and that, in itself, held its fierce significance. They had been well placed and well chosen.

A harried light flared in Tune's glance as it raked past each closed way of departure. Desire, utterly primitive,

186

pulled down his shoulders as he saw how they waited, some wooden faced, some drear with an abysmal eagerness akin to the look of a waiting vulture. They *were* vultures, really—vulture breed of the chaparral.

Then he saw Crowly's stiff and still shape by the barber pole and knew whom he had to thank for this trap; and strangely, quietly, tight of mouth, he smiled.

"Your pot," he said, and held out his gun by the barrel, without argument.

It caught Lou Safford off balance. He stared, incredulously, upset, unbelieving, unable to credit such a tame surrender. "What's this?" he said; and then quickly, irritably: "I'm not falling for no trick like that! Throw it down in the dirt!"

Tune let the pistol drop. Safford's look became ludicrous. "I'll be goddamed!" he said. "I'll be goddamed! *Yellow!*"

"I expect some would call it that," Tune smiled.

Safford's look grew distrusting. "I don't get this, Dakota. You know what'll happen if you go back to San Saba—"

"Maybe somebody's kidding you."

"I guess not." Safford shifted his body. The memory of Atchison rolled across his pale cheeks and he said with his eyes gone entirely vindictive: "When you get to San Saba they'll put a rope round your neck. They'll put a rope round your neck and that will be the end of you."

"San Saba," Tune grinned, "is a long way off."

"You think so? Better take another look at your hole card."

"Lou," Tune said, "this is beginnin' to get funny."

"Why, you goddam fool!" Safford gritted. "Do you *want* to get hanged? That fellow's got friends. They'll make short work of you."

"For defendin' my life? Why, the man had his gun clean out of leather—"

"My God!" Safford said. "I ain't talking about *him!* It's the man they just found under your bed! Crowly's boss—*Stacey Wilkes!*"

187

6

LIKE MOST big outfits of that time and place, Clover Cross had been founded on bloodshed and violence and all of its days had seen their full share, but until last fall none of that blood had ever splashed on its doorstep. Last fall its founder, Tim McClain, had been killed.

A fire eating Irishman Big Tim had been, one who seldom called anything a spade but a spade. He had called Stacey Wilkes a *goddam thief!* and Mr. Wilkes had promptly drawn pistol and shot him. That was not the end of the business. It was just the beginning. It was still going on.

These were her thoughts as Larinda McClain, after Tune's departure, went back to her rocker and sat with her composed green eyes casually roving the street while she awaited the return of her irascible range boss.

Stacey Wilkes, she recalled, was of Southern extraction. Rumor hailed him from Shreveport in the early '60s—for his health, he had said; and that was mostly true. When a connoisseur and past master of dueling threatens your life in the gray light of dawn it becomes a matter of health to depart somewhat sooner.

Texas had been the habit in those days—the "fashion" one might almost have said. *"Gone to Texas"* described a lot of folks' moving; but Wilkes had thought Texas a little too close and had kept on riding. It would seem Arizona had pleased him better. In that vast desolation surrounding Oro Blanco he had shucked off his saddle and gone into the cow business. There are some who might tell you he'd have need of his saddle, but these lack perception. Wilkes showed that a personal saddle need play no part in a career made prosperous by longhorn cattle. It was inevitable, in the natural course of events, that he and Big Tim, Larinda's father, should clash.

After Big Tim's death, consensus of opinion thought the feud would die out, but consensus had reckoned without the Clover Cross range boss, one Teal, a case hardened citizen from the gunsmoke end of Texas. Teal did not wait for any grass to grow under him. He struck back at Wilkes while the iron was hot. He mislaid forty head of Wilkes' best saddle stock. He did a number of other things a little less openly.

Wilkes offered bonuses—even trafficked with outlaws, but all to no purpose. Teal's depredations continued until no man in the country dared lift hand against him.

Naturally, Clover Cross prospered.

Mr. Wilkes did not. His pride was touched. There was ribald laughter when his name was mentioned. Laughter ate into Wilkes' soul like acid. Teal ate into Wilkes' pocketbook. Wilkes became desperate.

Larinda did not know quite how it had happened, but suddenly the Clover Cross luck petered out. Teal's raids went haywire. Clover Cross began losing men; some were killed, a few quit, several of the best suddenly turned up missing. So did a bunch of the Clover Cross livestock. And in her own mind Larinda blamed it all on Jess Crowly. Short and broad Jess with his dark burnt face and taciturn ways who had come out of nowhere to be the Seven Keys range boss.

JESS CROWLY was taciturn. But when he opened his mouth he never had to dig round for any special language to express his meaning. He was cooly efficient without brag or bluster. Old Stumpy, the outfit's cook, could have told you about Jess Crowly. Old Stumpy was handy when Crowly arrived.

It was along in the fall, about grass cutting time, that the dark faced Texan rode into the ranch. Around three o'clock of a hot afternoon. Wilkes was dozing on the broad veranda.

Crowly rode up and got out of the saddle. He shook Wilkes awake.

Wilkes glared out of his whisky bleared eyes and came out of his chair like an uncoiling sidewinder. Crowly's smile stopped him before he opened his mouth.

189

"I'm Jess Crowly, suh. F'om Texas. Told you been huntin' a ramrod. Wheah do you want I should put my belongin's?"

"Just a minute," Wilkes said. "I ain't hired—"

Something about Crowly's look stopped Wilkes' talking.

Crowly said, "Sho't lives an' sho't mem'ries gen'lly runs hitched togetheh. You had me hired 'fo' I eveh left Texas. Fetchin' you right up to date you got a bill with me fo' two hundred dollahs an' fifty-fo' cents. Pay it."

Wilkes took a long close look at the man.

"You think I will?"

"Mister, I know it. Five chunks of lead in this gun all says so."

Wilkes eyed the shine of Jess' teeth and nodded.

In many respects Stacey Wilkes was a fool.

THERE WAS nothing of the fool about Crowly.

Wilkes wanted power. Crowly knew how to get it. Crowly knew the sure way to real power was fear.

He got down to the business of making Wilkes feared. The Clover Cross outfit started downhill.

Three of its best men turned up missing. The wrangler asked for his time and faded. Teal took to drink and turned suddenly blasphemous. He understood what was happening but was powerless to stop it. His choicest traps were sidestepped neatly. He commenced to talk of spies. Ives Tampa suggested he go see Safford; that was when Teal really took to the bottle. Safford was Crowly's friend, and Teal knew it. He was as much Teal's friend as a man could be. Crowly had no real talent for friendship. All Crowly's talent was aimed at accomplishment.

Then the sheep moved in and Teal lost his reason.

Crowly stopped Teal in front of Riske Quentin's.

"Heah you've gone in fo' sheep," Crowly grinned. "Tired o' cattle?"

The lift of Teal's shape was a jerk edged with violence and he wheeled full around with the hate in his eyes blazing out bright and naked. Crowly just chuckled and patted Teal's shoulder.

"You want to watch out fo' them fellers. Might git

yo'se'f knifed. Then what's thet Cloveh Cross gel goin'
to do?"

And he grinned up into tall Teal's red eyes. "Might
betteh sell out whilst she's got somethin' *to* sell—though
I'm danged ef I know who would want the spread. Said
as much to Misteh Wilkes jest las' night. But Wilkes don't
want it. Too run down, he says. Not wo'th the botherin'
with."

Teal's look got plain wicked, but some vestige of sense
kept his hand off his pistol. With a final dry chuckle
Crowly walked off and left him.

It tickled Wilkes plenty when he heard of this play.
"By the gods," he declared, "you're a real card, Jess!
We'll have them eatin' right out of our hands. We've
good as got the spread now."

Crowly shrugged.

"Afteh Teal's dead, mebbe. I don't count much on it.
You got t' do suthin' about thet cub, Stacey—the gel's
brotheh. Gittin' notions, he is. Shoots off at the mouth
eve'y time he opens it. Called you a thief in Riske Quentin's last night. A *low-down, sneakin', yeller-bellied
chicken thief!*—them's his ve'y words."

He looked across at Wilkes blandly.

Wilkes' cheeks roaned up and he sprang from his
chair.

"By Gad, sir!" he choked. "I won't take that talk! I
won't take that talk off no one!" And he grabbed up his
gunbelt and clapped it around him.

"Keep cahm," advised Crowly. "He's jest a fool kid.
You don't want t' do nothing——"

"By Gad, I'll *kill* the whelp!"

"Now, now—you betteh think it oveh."

Crowly knew the man he was dealing with.

Wilkes was so mad his whole frame shook. The look
of his cheeks turned apoplectic. He grabbed up his hat
and rushed out of the room.

A door banged loudly.

Crowly loosened his shoulders and sat back, thinly
smiling.

LARINDA WENT through her mind very carefully. She

191

had known all along how much weight Ives could take. But he was the logical man to step into Teal's boots, so she'd stepped him into them. "But he's a weak reed," she told herself. She thought of the new hand—that gun hung drifter—and smiled. She felt considerable satisfaction in thinking of Tune.

Hiring the man had been a stroke of real luck. Tune looked brash enough to fill her need and he was shaped to that need by his own past conduct—by that which impelled him to be what he was, a man come from nowhere and bound the same place.

Larinda saw what she wanted very clearly. She believed she saw how to go about getting it.

She went over and looked at herself in the mirror and smiled in a pleased way at what she saw there. Then she pulled on her gloves and was turning to leave when something she saw through the window stopped her.

DYING SUN lay like fire along the thrust of Tune's jaw. A piece of loose paper lifted out of the dust and was whirled away on a wind from the mountains. No man moved. None took his eyes from the length of Tune's shape. The receding flutter and flap of the paper left a tightened quiet through which Tune scanned his chances without illusion.

The hate of this town could not be mistaken.

Tune looked at Safford. "What was Wilkes doing upstairs under my bed?"

"My God!" Safford said. "The man's dead. With his throat cut."

"And you think I killed him."

"If you didn't," Safford said, "you better start praying. I won't say you had no cause," he growled, lifting his voice up. "Considering San Saba you had cause aplenty. But you ought to know, Tune, that a man can't take the law into his own hands. And that knifing stuff—it don't go around here."

Tune smiled at him thinly.

"I'm afraid somebody's been loading you, Lou."

"Not me. Not this time." Safford dipped his head and stood watching Tune brightly. "Not this time," he said

192

dryly. "Stacey told me about you. About you murdering that San Saba sheriff. And now you've murdered Wilkes trying to hide it."

He made the accusation loudly but there was an undercurrent of fretting unease in the way of his standing, in the way his bright glance kept picking at Tune.

Tune said nothing. He got out the makings and rolled up a cigarette. Every jaundiced eye on that street tabbed its progress and, while they were doing so, Tune found the one thin crack in this business.

There was a gun hawk posted on the porch of the Crockett House; another pair weighted the steps of the Mercantile. Jess Crowly was lounged by the Frenchman's barber pole and, off down the other way in front of Riske Quentin's, two more dark shapes stiffly stood in the sunset.

There were other men watching but Tune ignored them.

There was nobody showing in Grankelmeir's alley.

That was the crack, with its mouth twelve paces from Tune's trapped station. Twelve paces well covered by the snouts of five pistols.

And Lou Safford, the marshal, would have good straight shooting for a clean fifty feet if Tune crowded his luck and tried to get down it.

Bait!

Left deliberately empty to lure him into it.

Lou's love of caution had given Tune this choice. It would look better for Lou if Tune died escaping.

Lou said, and strain was a harsh ground edge in his talking: "If you don't want to swing you better pick up that pistol."

"Sure you want to go on with this, Lou?"

"Damn you, Tune!" Safford shouted. "I'm wearin' a badge! I can't traffic with outlaws!"

"Well, well," Tune said. "You've come a long way since Atchison."

He smiled at Lou then, a smile bleak as malpais; and all the bantering ease fell out of him and he banged his words like bullets at Safford. "You are just a cheap little coyote, Lou, with your lips peeled back because you run

193

with a wolf pack. But you ain't got the guts to *be* a wolf. When the going gets rough you'll slink for timber— and it will get rough, Lou. When I'm roped into something I play for keeps."

"Pick up that pistol!" Safford yelled, half strangled.

One of the pair on the Mercantile's steps growled, "Yappin' won't kill him. Throw your lead into him."

That had been Safford's plan. He had tried to work up to it.

Hate was a bitter bright look in his eyes. Desire for destruction was pounding him, spurring him, shoving him fiercely; but there was no satisfaction left on his cheeks and there was no comforting sureness left in him, either. A man was burnt in the heat of those moments, and that man was Lou; and every eye on that street that was watching him saw it.

Another full moment Safford stood there with that beaten incomprehensible look on his features. Balked rage was in the cant of his shoulders and rage was a consuming fire inside him, but Lou had lived too long with caution. He was done in this town. He had picked this place and he had been left holding it. The wolves would not feel quite the same any longer.

He threw his leaden eyed look around. A wind inside him puffed out his cheeks. He kept his look away from the barber pole.

"Jail's at the end of his street," he growled. "Get movin'. Get movin'." He shoved at Tune bitterly.

7

LARINDA MCCLAIN turned away from the window with something akin to impatience in her look. It had ever been this way, she remembered. The old days were gone but their flavor lingered, staining yet this land's activities. And the old ways lingered, changed but little. Death still slunk by the side of life and so it would always be,

194

she thought, for this was the same drear story, same country, blood and hungers that had staged the hectic past.

She must watch her step.

This was a desperate game she played, a long-odds game in no-limit country where law was a thing you strapped in a holster and death lone reward for the man who failed.

She must not fail. She *would* not!

Boots came up the creaking stairs and briefly stopped before the door, and the door was opened. Jess Crowly came in and shut it after him and settled his weight against it while his knowing glance played over her cheeks and openly admired the curves of her body.

He gave her a darkly taciturn smile.

She put her words at him coldly. "What do you want?"

Crowly's smile continued. "Jest wanted to tell you. It was a good idee, but it didn't come off. And the' won't none of 'em come off long's you play 'em against me. Might's well make up yo' mind to it."

"Did Wilkes send you up here to tell me that?"

"You reckon I'm playin' houn' dawg fo' *Wilkes?*" Crowly said to her finally: "Stacey Wilkes is dead."

"Dead!"

Her eyes showed a sharp curiosity, but it was not concerned with the Seven Keys owner. She was marveling at this tough featured Texan who had pulled Seven Keys from the dust by its boot straps. He was big—though not in the same way that Tune was big; he was shorter than Tune and considerably darker. He was heavier, more massively framed with his wide brawny shoulders and hair matted chest. Power was inherent in the man's every gesture. He was a masterful man, and no one knew much about him.

She found the look of his eyes could make you tingle.

Abruptly she remembered what Jess Crowly had said. "Dead!" she repeated, and her glance came up sharply.

He saw the sudden dark glint of her eyes and he shook his head at her solemnly. "You ought to keep track of what yo' hired hands do."

Larinda said, "Whatever in the world are you talking about? If you've something to say to me, say it and get out of here."

"I say Wilkes is dead in this hotel with his throat cut. The marshal's takin' yo' new man to jail fo' it. That plain enough?"

"*My* new man?" She looked at him blankly.

But Crowly grinned. "Yo' new man. What I said, ain't it? No need to play hide an' seek with me, gel. I'm talkin' about Tune—thet drifteh, Dakota."

Her intention had been to deal coolly with this man, to hold herself above him. But how had *he* known she had just hired Dakota?

Crowly saw the break of that thought in her features. He grinned brazenly.

"Betteh unpin yo' hopes from these driftehs an' hitch yo' wagon to a man thet's goin' places—to a man thet will *stick*. To *me,* he said, and crossed the room and was suddenly before her.

He heard the quick pull of her deepened breathing and his eyes grinned into her eyes understandingly. He saw the rise of her breasts and excitement changed the shape of his face and he put out a hand and touched her lightly.

He stood perfectly still with his eyes locked on hers; and then he took a deep breath and pulled her to him, pulled her hard against him and put his mouth hard against her mouth and kept it there until her hands jarred up and shoved him back.

She stood with her shape filled with tumult, watching him. Her eyes looked bigger and darker. They told Jess Crowly what he wanted to know. He shrugged and smiled and stepped back away from her.

She said with an attempt at her old composure, "taking quite a lot for granted, aren't you?" and an angered look jumped into her stare and, when he would have reached for her again, she knocked his arms down.

"All right," he growled, and stepped clear and put his broad back comfortably against the wall. His grin came back and changed the dark look of him. He said with a

196

gusty confidence, "We could go a long ways, me an' you, gel."

"Maybe I like it here——"

"Sure—sure. What I mean. Cloveh Cross. We could make it the biggest spread in this country. The *only* spread! Hell!" he said boldly, "the' ain't hardly nothin' me an' you couldn't do—togetheh."

She reached up and tucked in the edges of her hair. Her look was soft; she was smiling. "I think we'll talk again. You had better go now, I'm expecting Ives Tampa."

He took another deep breath, still watching her. Then he jerked his head in a nod and went out.

THEY WERE passing the store, Dakota Tune and the marshal, when a horse came around a far building before them. The girl in the saddle was the blue eyed gitana. Tune kept his face blank but his thoughts commenced building. Ideas came crowding as he watched the girl slide out of the saddle and carelessly toss her reins at the hitch rack. She went at once up the steps and entered the dwelling.

Tune sent another edged look at the horse. A big yellow claybank, long legged and rangy. There was plenty of bottom tucked away in that horse. Tune wasn't guessing—he *knew*. It was his horse. He could see the bulge of his bedroll plainly.

This was no accident. This was planned.

Another trap?

Tune studied Safford from the corners of his eyes. The marshal was paying no attention to the horse. No interest canted the set of his features. They were bitterly blank as pounded metal. They belonged to a face hacked out of flint.

And Crowly was gone from his place by the barber pole.

Four of the others fell in behind Safford who tramped back of Tune with a naked gun. Tune knew these fellows weren't going for the walk.

Once again he looked over his chances.

It could be a trap. It could be one more slick scheme of

197

the marshal's to rid them of Tune in a way that would afterward look quite legal. Legality was a complex of Safford's makeup.

Tune thought about that.

There were times when a man found life good and used caution. There were even occasions for shrewdness and stealth. But there were times—and this looked like one of them—when it were best to forget all that and act.

They would pass within ten feet of that horse.

Tune walked with his head tipped forward, apparently fully absorbed with his thinking. The lines of his shoulders looked dejected; but his eyes were small as they roved the street and the slant of his lips was hard as a well chain.

Droning flies filled the still-hot air with their clamor. The sun's last light came no lower than the warped looking chimneys of these flimsy shacks. Soon full dark would roll over this land.

They approached the horse. It was now or never.

Blindingly sudden Tune appeared to go loco. He threw up both hands with a startled yell and dropped flat down on his knees and elbows. Safford, screaming one maniac curse, slammed terrifically into him and pitched sprawling headlong. Tune snapped the pistol out of his hand and whipped Lou grimly across the head with it. He whirled to his feet and fired twice swiftly. Three of the four behind him scattered; the fourth man was hit and stayed where he dropped.

Tune snatched up the reins and dived into the saddle. The rangy claybank lunged into action. Three scattered gun fighters dug for their pistols and lead was a cold thin whine past Tune's shoulders. They went careening around a corner, into an alley between two buildings and the gunfire and cursing died behind them and flight was a cooling wind in their faces.

Tune rode into the McClain yard at daybreak.

8

A MAN came out of a chair on the porch and stepped into the yard with a Spencer rifle. The man was Ives Tampa, and dislike was a stain spread over his cheekbones.

"Turn that horse and ride out of here."

"Maybe you didn't hear the boss say I was hired?"

"We're not hirin' outlaws. Turn that horse and ride out."

"I think not," Tune said. He put his hands on the horn and considered Ives calmly.

The range boss' mouth twisted into a crease. "Ride out!" he said. He lifted the rifle. "Ride back to the Seven Keys where you belong!"

The screen door suddenly opened behind him and Larinda McClain came out and stopped, stopped with an audible intake of breath, the sight of Tune changing her look completely. "Why, I thought . . . I thought you were in jail," she said.

"It don't have to disappoint you, ma'am. I will be, likely. Soon," Tune said.

Color briefly touched her cheeks and vexation put its mark on them. She considered him intently while the shading of her eyes grew darker, and she did not use the words she first thought of. Instead, watching Tune, she spoke to Tampa. "This man's going to work for us. Put him down as *Dakota*. His job with the ranch will be strayman——"

"Why don't you hire Jess Crowly?" Ives said.

Larinda swiveled a look at him. "Perhaps I shall."

"Now look—" Ives growled, refusing to believe that. "I'm prob'ly old-fashioned. I don't like outlaws. I'm prejudiced as hell. But I'm goin' to tell you I've been around this country, man an' boy, and I've yet to see the owlhooter that ever done anybody any good. When the

199

goin' gets rough they'll slide out on you. They'll leave you holdin' the hot end of the iron. If you can't trust a man what the hell good is he?"

Larinda said, faintly smiling, "According to your argument he wouldn't be here at all."

But Ives waved that aside. There was a doggedness about him that would not be sidetracked. "Use your eyes, girl! The feller's a spy! A man don't smash one of Jess Crowly's riders an' get clean away without it's been fixed up——"

"It's been fixed up," Tune said. "I killed him."

Ives just looked at him. He didn't seem to find that worth answering.

Larinda said: "Put his name in the book, Ives."

The ramrod's feelings were a color in his skin. "By God, I won't use him!"

"*I* will," the girl said. "He will take his orders direct from me. There are ways to this thing you don't understand, Ives. Wars are the same no matter where you fight them. There is no fairness in it. Seven Keys wants control of this country. They will not control me! When brute force is brought against me I will meet it with brute force."

Ives said, "So there's ways to this fightin', is there? Ways I don't understand, eh? Well, you'll learn your lesson but it will be too late. This Seven Keys spy will dig your grave—the same grave he digs for Clover Cross!"

"You take care of the ranch work, Ives. I'll look out for Clover Cross."

Larinda looked at Tune and smiled. "I'll talk with you inside, Dakota."

Ives Tampa's eyes showed dark, inscrutable. Tune watched the range boss tramp away and there was respect in Tune's regard of the man. Respect, and a kind of pity.

The girl led the way to her office and closed the door behind them. She tossed her hat in a corner and shook back her yellow hair. She faced Tune much as a man might have done, cold purpose holding her shape erect.

Morning sun, flowing in, threw its light against her. She was something to look at, and Tune's eyes said so.

"Ives," she said, "was right about one thing. That Seven Keys crowd is a pack of killers. It's a *bravo brand*. We fight or we fall. I have no intention of falling."

Tune watched her, keeping his thoughts to himself.

"You don't quite approve of me, do you?"

"When you want something," Tune said, "fight for it."

She searched his face. She turned a little away from him. He was struck again by her fullness, by the deep and womanly ripeness of her. She was a cup filled clear to brimming and the look of her hit him hard.

He halfway started to move toward her, then he realized his unfitness and stopped. He locked his arms behind him, but he could not lock back his words that way. They were out and gone before he could catch them. "You're a brash and handsome woman, 'Rinda—too brash and too handsome for your own good, probably. I have never met a woman like you."

Her eyes came up from behind dark lashes. "Do you always talk to women that way?"

Color came into Tune's cheeks. He was embarrassed. Then he scowled and said gruffly: "I seldom bother to speak with women," and color touched *her* cheeks briefly, and she took her eyes away from him.

She drew a long breath. She turned in the way she had turned in the mirror. "Let's keep this on a business basis." She stepped back and lowered a hip to the edge of her desk. "We've got five men left from a crew of twelve. Our oldest hands; we can probably trust them. But they won't go out of their way to hunt trouble. Hunting out trouble is going to be *your* job." She paused, took another long breath and said: "I want those damn sheep moved. I want you to go over to that camp— What's the matter?"

"Ain't that what Teal did?"

She stood still a moment searching his face again. She moved away from the desk and went over to the windows and stood looking into the sunbaked yard.

"What would you have me do?" she asked finally, and when he did not answer she came back and faced him. She stood close before him and observed how her nearness put pressure into the corners of his mouth. "What would you have me do?" she repeated. "Quit and crawl out like a yellow cur? You think that would become me? You want me to throw up the ranch and get out of here?"

"It's your place," he said, "and your problem."

"You're a real help, aren't you!"

Tune looked at her then. "Wanting has nothing to do with reason. If you want a thing bad enough, sense has no part in it. It's something inside you like a lash or a spur that drives you on and won't ever be done with you."

She continued to watch him, green eyes still questioning.

He said, "If you want a thing bad enough, fight for it!"

She smiled at him then. "I intend to."

WHEN THE day's heat finally slacked off a little, Tune got off his bunk and stepped out into the evening glare. He filled a bucket with water at the creaking pump and soaked his tousled head in it and, afterwards, felt better.

His glance passed round the empty yard, noting the horses in the pole corral, aware that Ives Tampa's mount was there and considering the fact in relation to himself. Then his restive gaze traveled off to the mountains.

Blue they were and hazed by distance, serenely aloof to man and his problems. The mountains did not care whether he lived or died. What difference to them if this ranch changed hands? They would be as they had been since Time's beginning, little altered by man's noisesome passing. There was a power in this country, the power of indifference.

He went to the cook shack and ate some cold meat scraps with his glance turned inward and backward, considering accounts that were yet unsettled, looking over each facet of this Clover Cross wrangle in terms of its relationship to the persons involved.

It was, after all, just the same old pattern. The same lusts still struck sparks from folks. The same greeds urged to thievery, the same desires to violence. The world, he thought, did not change much. Only the methods varied.

He was not surprised by Safford's non-appearance. Lou

Safford was a man Tune understood. He would be busy now patching up his conduct, but he would not forget and he would not forgive. He had made a play that had not come off. It had lowered Lou's standing in the eyes of his fellows; but maybe the power that was back of this setup would not care for too strong a badge toter. In any event there was bound to be more of the same before long. There would be reprisals, repercussions. That business of yesterday would not long go unanswered. Lou Safford was merely biding his time. That Lou had no authority outside of town meant nothing. When the iron was hot again Lou would strike—or the power back of Lou would.

Tune nodded. This was San Saba all over again. San Saba dressed up and refurbished a little.

Jess Crowly had known all about San Saba—his words in the restaurant were proof of that. But *how* had he known? Who *was* Crowly? Where had *he* come into Tom Curry's death? What part had *he* in Tune's flight from justice? Had Crowly been someway involved in that deal? What was Crowly's place here?

Tune wheeled with an impatient lift of the shoulders and went outside, went across to the horse pens. He stood looking over the horses awhile and then turned and found Ives Tampa watching him. No catchable expression curbed Tampa's cheeks but his tireless eyes sucked up every movement and the thumbs of his hands hung over his gun belt. Tune wondered with a tempered amusement how long it would be until this man's black notions bred results in gun smoke.

Tampa stood against the pole corral and watched while Tune roped out his horse. He was still there, watching, when Tune finished saddling. He was still there when Tune rode away.

THE SHEEP would be somewhere near the southwest boundary; at least the sheepman's camp was there—Lou Safford had told Dakota that yesterday. It was possible, of course, that the sheep had been moved, but they would probably be in that general direction. Sheep were not given to traveling fast. Sheepmen did not leave strays behind for a strayed-away sheep was a dead sheep. Sheep were born with the will to die and Tune thought it likely they would get their wish hereabouts. Another thing: Sheepmen seldom moved without backing, seldom came into a cow country this way. So it must have been Wilkes who had brought them in here. Part of the Seven Keys plan to smash Clover Cross. After all, it mattered little who owned these sheep. They had been brought in for a purpose and, now that Wilkes was dead, what would Jess Crowly do with them? Lose interest?

No, he would follow up Wilkes' plan very probably. Push the game to the bitter end.

All across the West things like this were shaping up as cattle barons and would-be barons fought tooth and nail to increase their holdings against that time when the law should step in. This age was violent, an age of transition. Woe to the man who stood in greed's way.

And woe to the girl left alone with a ranch that was bigger than many a seaboard state. There would be no peace until the Seven Keys outfit ruled this entire range, or was smashed.

Tune had given some thought to this matter. The man who had killed Larinda's brother was not up to driving this breed of horse—not in Tune's mind. Wilkes had neither the brains nor the vision required to build such a plan or prosecute it. A craftier hand was on the reins than his. And, by this reasoning, Wilkes' death could make little difference to Clover Cross. The plan was to steal this entire region. It was a bid for empire, really. The kind of thing corporations dreamed of.

Was the Seven Keys ranch a syndicate?

It could be. It could be a land and cattle company.

Where had Wilkes found the money for such a spread? By forming a company he could have raised it easily. But had Wilkes seen that? Had Wilkes the wit to realize that? Or had someone else pointed out the fact to him? Crowly, perhaps?

It might have been. Certainly the place had taken on new life since Crowly's advent.

Tune's thoughts moved again to that Crockett House shooting, to young Tim falling on the Crockett House porch. Stacey Wilkes, Tune thought, had been coached to that shooting. By someone who wanted young Mc-Clain put away.

Had the syndicate wanted McClain put away? Or had the someone been Crowly?

It was by no means certain that there *was* a syndicate. Who had knifed Teal?

And who had knifed Wilkes?

Had the same hand wielded the knife both times, or had someone willed to make it look that way?

The quickest way to get a range war brewing was to turn every outfit against its neighbor. While neighbor fought neighbor there was good chance for pickings.

Was Crowly the spider so busily weaving? Or was Jess but the hammer for a syndicate tool?

The man was in this thing someplace. Crowly knew about Tune who had come from San Saba. And Tune did not mean to forget that.

They cruised steadily along through the yellow flow-ered greasewood and, though he thought as he rode, Tune had an eye out for trouble. This was first class country for a man with a rifle.

The late afternoon drowsed on toward twilight and a dreaming stillness lay over this land, this tawny land stretching mile on mile to the misty blue of the faraway mountains.

There was little sound but the claybank's footfalls. An occasional lizard scampered over the trail, but mostly they rode through a vast kind of silence whose only company was the everlasting heat.

Just short of full dark the country's contour changed. The sun's molten copper was behind the far peaks and the greasewood flats had given way to a series of rolling slopes and cutbanks when Tune, coming leisurely out of a wash, caught the wink of a distant campfire, and a girl's voice suddenly, sharply said:

"Pull up!"

TUNE STOPPED.

Surprise pulled down his eye corners. He released them with a whimsical smile. "You sure get around, ma'am. You surely do."

205

It was the blue eyed gitana.

She did not smile.

She wore levis now, denim pants stuffed into hand-tooled boots. She wore a man's woolen shirt. She looked surprised as he'd been.

"I want to thank you," Tune said, "for fetchin' my horse. It was an act of charity." He would have said more but she broke in swiftly:

"Where do you go to, prala?"

"A man always rides where fancy takes him. What do you do here, Blue Eyes?"

"But here!" she cried. "Why should you ride here, prala?"

"Where a girl blocks a trail with a rifle, there is bound to be some reason for it."

"But I was not blocking the trail. I—I was hunting rabbits, prala. I heard your horse and I was frightened."

"What's to frighten a girl in this country?"

She shrugged slim shoulders and looked away from him.

It was Tune who finally broke the silence. "I don't believe I've heard your name. I am called Dakota. I shall always remember your goodness, chiquita——"

"Then go," she said quickly. "Go back to that yellow haired one who sent you. There is nothing——"

"Nothing, querida?"

"My name is Panchita. No—nothing for you."

"There are sheep," Tune said. He could hear the sharp catch of her breath in the stillness.

"Have the sheep hurt you?"

"Sheep hurt the grass——"

"Not if they have a good shepherd with them."

"Cattle will not eat where sheep have been——"

"That is foolish! With my own eyes I have seen them eat!"

"Well, you've got to admit they spoil the water. Neither cattle nor horses will drink after sheep."

"So you would kill them! Is that your kindness, prala?"

"I am not a killer of sheep, Panchita."

"Then go back where you came from. Go back to that woman and tell her so!"

"But the cattle came first, chiquita. All this land is cattle country. It will remain so. You must turn your flocks and take them out of here."

She said nothing to that, and Tune said more sharply: "Do you hear, Panchita? You must get your sheep out of here."

"They are not mine. They belong to my uncle."

The wink of the distant campfire seemed brighter. It made the shadows seem deeper round them. Out of this darkness the girl spoke abruptly. "Come—come, prala. You shall speak with my uncle."

He saw the quick turn of her shoulders, heard the thud of her bootheels going off from him.

He walked the claybank after her; and a man's raised hail came down the wash and the girl's voice lifted, answering him.

They were not unprepared, he thought grimly. But if this girl belonged with these sheepmen, what business had taken her to Tucson? And how had she gotten there? And what had she been doing at Madam Belladine's brothel? And her language, too! That was not the talk of an ignorant gypsy.

She had the lure of mystery, this girl with the so-blue eyes.

Tune followed her into the sheep camp warily, searching the night for dark eyes behind rifles. But the night was too black for him to observe very much; the fire raised a wall of shadows which no human eye could pierce.

Tune watched the girl throw wood on the fire, fresh greasewood branches that burned like fat; and a voice came out of the shadows angrily. "Little fool! Would you have us all killed that you make such a brightness?"

"Come out of your hole, Tio Felix," she called (*Faylas* was the way she pronounced it). "I would have you talk with this caballero."

"These gringos—I cannot talk to them well. Is it about the sheep?"

"Yes. I would have you tell him about the sheep."

A little bent old man hobbled out of the shadows. He was like a little gnome in his soiled white cotton so pungent of sheep. But his eyes were kindly. He did not

207

look like a fighter. He did not look quite the kind to do much good in a range war. It made Tune wonder why the Seven Keys had picked him.

"Tell him about your sheep, Tio Felix."

"Tell me, rather," Tune said, "why you brought them here."

"I brought them here for the grass, your honor."

"Yes, of course. But who suggested you bring them here—the McClains?"

A brightness flared in the old man's eyes. They burned into Tune's like hot coals. "God forbid! Never would I do those robbers—but you would not understand, your honor. I have brought them back to the land of my fathers."

"That's all very well," Tune said, "but this is cow country."

The old man turned to the girl, his glance anxious. "What does he want with us? What does he want with my sheep? Why does he come here, Panchita?"

"He comes from the yellow haired one," the girl said. "He says we must move the sheep out of here."

"No! No! No bueno por nada!" the old man cried. He shook his gnarled head; shook his stick in the air. He muttered a lot of swift Spanish.

Tune said: "The sheep cannot stay here, compadre. This is country for cows and the sheep are no bueno. You must move them, amigo."

Words tumbled out of the old man fiercely. Spanish words, too swift for Tune's catching.

Panchita looked at Tune. "He says——"

"Tell him to take it a little slower."

The old man mumbled it over again.

"He says——"

"Yes, I heard him. He is wrong. It makes no difference what the marshal told him. The marshal has nothing to do with this land. Tell him so. Tell him the marshal lied to him. This range belongs to the Clover Cross. He will have to move——"

"Never!" The old man glared at Tune angrily. "Never!"

"It makes no difference," Tune told the girl. "I am sorry about this, but the sheep must go. Marshal Safford

208

was lying. His permission means nothing because he has no permission to give. You will have to get the sheep out of here——"

"Not a foot! Not a incha!" Felix shouted.

"Would it not be better to move them yourself than to have the cow boys move them for you?"

"But we can't!" the girl cried. "Tio Felix can't move them—he has no hombres—no man! They were frightened of Teal and have run away!"

"You could move them yourself if we gave you time——"

"It would take us too long. There are too many," she said.

"How much time would you need?"

The old man's eyes turned crafty. "Two weeks."

"Three days," Tune said, and Tio Felix cursed. He shook his stick at Tune angrily.

But Tune stood firm, for he knew he could not give them longer. "You will move the sheep in three days' time or the Clover Cross cow boys will come and shoot them."

9

TUNE FELT no pride of that scene at the sheep camp. There was in him the feeling they had bested him someway. He could not put his finger on it, but the feeling stayed with him. There had been something—Take that girl waiting out on the trail with a rifle. That big, winking campfire with nobody round it but that one old man. And he had seen no sheep. Tune remembered that now.

He stopped his horse with an oath.

That was it! Where were the sheep? Where *were* the sheep?

They were not at that camp or he would have known it. He'd have heard them. Why, he had not even *smelled* any sheep, except the sheep smell on the old man's clothing.

That sly old man had made a fool of him! While he'd kept Tune by that campfire, talking, the sheep had been moving—moving deeper into Clover Cross!

A look came back to Tune then. The look he had seen in Lou Safford's eyes when he'd sprung that question about Safford's money and sheep. Whether Lou had put money into sheep or not it was a pretty safe bet he was mixed in this deeper than any marshal's badge could have warranted.

Tune swung around in the saddle and threw a quick look at his backtrail. But there was a bend in the wash between him and the camp and he could not see the wink of its campfire.

Could there be any gain in further talk with old Felix?

Tune's shoulders moved impatiently. Then an odd thought caused him to swing from the saddle and lead his horse deep into the brush that so rankly grew beside this trail. He stood by the claybank's head and listened, and a thin unamused little smile crossed his lips and he clamped a hand to his mount's swelling nostrils.

The sound of a traveling horse came plainly.

Horse and rider flashed past like gray ghosts in the gloom and Tune took his grip from the claybank's face. That would be the old man, or it would be the girl riding by his order, gone to warn the men with the sheep or to give them some new change in direction.

Tune could find those sheep by tailing the rider.

But did he want to, right now?

He decided he did and was lifting a foot to swing into the saddle when muzzle flame burst from the night's crouched shadows. The claybank went up—went away back on its haunches; but Tune went up with him, went into the saddle. He flung himself forward and raked the big horse with his rowels. The horse lunged forward. Tune flung two shots toward the faded flash. He drove the horse all through that brush but there was no further firing and no sign of the firer.

He cut south for a ways, well clear of the trail, and a mile farther on returned to it with a gun held ready for trouble. And he had good reason to be glad of that. There was another horseman cutting in from the right, angling down from the brush stubbled slopes very carefully.

"Hold it!" Tune yelled, and heard a rattle of rocks as the downcoming man sat his horse on its haunches. The deeper black of the man's arched shoulders and hatted head vaguely showed against the lesser dark of the trail beyond.

"Kind of late for ridin', ain't it, friend?"

The man sat his horse stiffly still, unanswering. He must have guessed Tune had a gun trained on him, must have sensed in Tune's voice the degree of Tune's temper, for he kept his horse still, kept his hands still, also.

Then something about the set of those shoulders pulled up Tune's chin, and he said through tight lips, "Some of your habits stand in need of alterin'. For two cents, Ives, I'd take care of that for you."

Ives said: "You'd better get out of this while you're still able."

"Meanin' next time you might have better luck maybe? Don't count on it. Next time'll probably be the last chance you'll have at it."

Ives said nothing.

Tune said, "Maybe I'm figurin' this wrong, friend. I don't like a man that gets his duck from——"

"Why, you driftin' hound! When I come after *you* it won't be from no ambush!"

Tune could feel the man's glare. They sat their horses barely twenty feet apart, sat several moments without saying anything. Then Tampa said: "What you doin' rammin' round in the night?"

"Just what I was thinking of asking you."

"By God," Ives snarled, "I've got a *right* to be ridin'!"

"So have I," Tune said. "And I'll tell you something else, Mister Ives; I will ride where I please. Where I please and when I please. Remember it. If you want to play Mary's lamb with me——"

"Go on—keep swingin' it. I can wait," Tampa choked through the spleen in his voice. "What was you jawin' so long with that girl about?"

"So it *was* you!" Tune breathed softly. "Let me give

211

you a little advice, Ives. When you make up your mind to shoot a man don't wait till it's dark and get into a thicket——"

"I'll guarantee you one thing," I'ves shouted. "If I'd been gunnin' for you you'd been dead an' planted!"

"So maybe you was thinkin' to run a little bluff, eh?"

"You've had your warnin'. Make the most of it. Clover Cross is too small for you an' me both."

"I shall hate to see you packin' your warbag. But if I find you again with a gun pointed my way I shall see that the boys get some digging to do. Two can play at this flip-an'-shoot business, and when *I* play I play for keeps."

TUNE WATCHED Ives' shoulders fade away. But not until Ives' sound had grown dim did Tune put away his pistol. Then he started thoughtfully home. He was still undecided about Ives Tampa when he rode into the moonless Clover Cross yard.

There was no one about, which might mean much or nothing. Tampa's horse wasn't in the corral. Tune unsaddled the claybank, hung his gear on the fence and leaned there, making a cigarette and smoking it, considering the various angles of this business. Were those sheep Lou Safford's? Or were they really Felix's?

After all, thus far, he had seen no sheep.

Leave them alone, ran the nursery rhyme, *and they'll come home, wagging their tails behind them.*

Well . . . maybe. At any rate, he knew too little about this range to go ramming around it in the middle of the night. The sheep would keep, some other things mightn't. Any moment now might bring a raid from Crowly. Any moment might bring trouble for the cattle; the ranch itself might be attacked, besieged to pen the crew inactive. But these were matters within Ives' province and had best, for the moment, be left there. Tune's was an outside job as outlined to him, his part to harry the enemy.

On sudden impulse he decided to ride.

He stubbed out his smoke on a pole of the fence, took his rope and went into the round enclosure. The horses

212

rushed away from him but he settled his loop on a line-back dun and quickly, afterwards, saddled him.

He rode from the yard at an easy canter.

He would go to town. He would find Lou Safford. What good this might do him he did not know. It was a hunch and he would follow it. The danger to himself he discounted. If by seeing Safford he could save one life, could shorten this thing by only that much, he considered the risk well taken.

Lou was mixed up in this, and probably more than by his friendship with Crowly. Lou's self-seeking soul was a deal too canny to get mixed into anything simply for friendship. The marshal would be in this war for a profit and Tune must convince Lou the cards were against him.

He stepped up the dun's easy pace a little. The horse was fresh and a willing mover. The long and rangy look of him, his depth of girth and powerful muscles promised speed and a deal of stamina back of it. There was a very good chance they might need that bottom.

Oro Blanco's lights came before them presently, and it was then Tune wondered who had lost that button, the little red button hand carved from mesquite wood, he had found on the planking of Grankelmeir's stable.

Not the girl—surely not Panchita? Tio Felix, then? Was that little old man concerned in this?

Something recalled to Tune then the shot he had heard as he stood in this town with the marshal, Lou Safford, casually watching the crowd collect in front of Riske Quentin's—that sudden lone shot just ahead of Wilkes' pistol when Safford had cried out so bitterly: *"You see? Wherever you are, by God, there's trouble!"*

Lou seemed to be right about some things.

But who had fired that lone shot and at whom was it aimed?

It was plain to Tune all these things had meaning, some particular place in the web of evil that some dark spider was so slyly weaving. They were not random things, disjointed happenings whose trail led nowhere. They were parts of the sinister whole, tiny cogs, marshaled and aimed at this land's enslavement.

Tune's lips got a little tighter, and he turned the dun

213

toward Lou Safford's office that was back of the jail at the end of this street.

IT WAS not Ives Tampa's intention to make the mistake big Teal had made. Spectacular plays and ultimatums had no part in Tampa's strategy. Both Larinda and Tune had counted him short when balanced in the light of things imminent and drastic. But Ives was full measure in his own odd fashion. He did not like trouble and could never invite it. For itself, that is. His stubborn nature saw no benefit in change. He liked old things. He liked all things to remain as he knew them. So long as he could he continued doggedly to shut his eyes to the things he could not countenance.

But shutting his eyes did not bring Teal back, nor could it undo the cold blooded killing of young McClain. That killing warned him of the things to come, finally opening his eyes to the danger of them.

If the spur were sharp Ives Tampa could act.

The spur was like a thorn in Ives' side as he whirled his horse and rode away from Tune. He distrusted the man and hated his calling. When he was sure he had passed Tune's hearing he rode for town by the shortest trail.

He would as soon have trusted Jess Crowly or Wilkes as this drifter Larinda had hired for strayman. Ives had not spent forty-seven years in the saddle without picking up a few bits of wisdom. That wisdom told him Tune was a man on the dodge.

So his course was plain.

There is no man so set against sin as the once-erring man brought at last to the fold. By this same paradox, there was not a man in all Arizona so intolerant of outlaws as the Clover Cross ramrod, once an outlaw himself. "Who will live by the gun will die by it," he said; and it never occurred to Ives to doubt his judgments.

Larinda he regarded as both foolish and headstrong. No girl was fitted to run a ranch anyway. Running a ranch was entirely a man's work. Ives realized now they would have to fight for Clover Cross. He could understand the desire which had prompted Larinda to hire this

214

gun fighter. Desire for revenge was a common failing, and in this instance desire and necessity rode the same bronc. But Ives could not understand the girl's blindness. What folly! What madness! To pick a Seven Keys man to fight the Seven Keys!

It was Ives' intention to rectify this blunder. If there were sheep on Clover Cross the sheep could wait. As Tampa saw it, getting rid of Tune was a heap more important than shoving a bunch of sheep back in the greasewood. Sheep he could manage. Nobody could manage a goddam outlaw!

Ives had known Safford casually for several months. He was not acquainted with the marshal's politics. His knowledge of Lou went no deeper than a few good drinks exchanged at the bar. He had always found Lou impeccably courteous, an open-minded gentleman comfortably inclined toward preserving law and order. Ives could not think how Tune had escaped Lou. He figured Seven Keys trickery must have had some large part in it. That Seven Keys outfit was a nest of snakes.

Ives expected the marshal would feel pretty happy over the prospect of taking Tune back into custody.

IN THE MARSHAL'S office Lou Safford was uncomfortably fiddling with a penknife and trying to look engrossed with the business. Three pairs of uncharitable eyes were on him and apprehensive shivers were playing with his spine. There was no use making up tales to account for it; he had let that gun fighter get clear away from him. Tune had done what Lou had hoped he would do, only in Lou's intentions Tune had not got away. Lou was right now wishing he had never heard of Tune.

He did not like the way Crowly was eying him. He did not like the way any of them were. This pair with Jess were not town grifters; they were tough hired guns—this Loma Jack packed two.

Loma Jack's cold sneer set Lou's teeth on edge.

And Cibecue, with his mismatched eyes and twisted foot had always made Lou feel uneasy. Loma Jack never trusted anyone, but a man couldn't tell what that Cibecue was thinking. Lou had sometimes wondered if he thought at all.

He took a slanchways glance at these fellows.

The cast of their features did not calm him any. "You yeller-bellied rat," the reedy Cibecue snarled, "I've a notion t' bash your face in!"

"Wait!" Loma Jack murmured softly.

Jess Crowly's mouth shaped a civilized smile. "Guess you played into a little tough luck, Lou. Might have happened to any of us, but the boys is naturally feelin' put out a bit. They're kind of figurin' what you done was mostly deliberate. But thet ain't my notion. I don't think you're thet kind of a felleh. I'm allowin' you'd like mighty well to prove it. Fact is," Jess said, "I come by to give you a chance t' prove it."

With his backbone feeling like red ants were at it, Lou made the try to look pleased with the prospect. But it seemed like his tongue had swelled up and petrified. He couldn't get out the word of thanks that looked called for. He couldn't, right then, say anything.

But Crowly didn't seem to notice.

Crowly went on urbanely: "Yep. I'm figurin' to give you a right good chance, Lou. I know how it is with this gun packin' business. The breaks sometimes go ag'in' you. What I got in mind now don't call fo' much luck—jest a eve'yday piece o' routine, as you might say. It's a chore I could give to Jack, heah, or Cibecue. But I want you should hev yo' chance to convince them. I want—" Crowly smiled. "I want you should get rid of Ives Tampa fo' me."

"Ives Tampa!" cried Lou. "Why Tampa, for God's sake?"

"Because thet gel has made Tampa range boss. With Tampa gone Tune will be her top screw, an' with Tune roddin' Cloveh Cross we won't need t' figure the plays so damn ca'ful. This Tune is a flip-an'-shoot killer an' we can plaster his outfit with the same kind of rep."

Lou Safford looked round him uneasily.

"We will see that it does," Loma Jack smiled thinly.

Crowly said, "This will be duck soup fo' a man of yo' talents, Lou. Jest rid us of Tampa—that's all we ask,

216

Lou. With Tampa out of the way the gel will make Tune her boss—bound to. Then we'll pull a few strings an' git you made sheriff."

"But," Lou said nervously, "I still don't see how that's going to help much."

"Why," Jess smiled, "we make Cloveh Cross look like a outlaw hideout. Then we ride in an' smash it. That's simple, ain't it? We're tryin' t' clean up the country—tryin' t' make it safe fo' the women an' kids."

"An' we'll do it, too," Loma Jack grinned sourly.

"But what about these other outfits——"

"They needn't git in yo' hair," Crowly told him. "I got deals on the fire with most of 'em anyway. Them I ain't can be scared out easy. Let 'em heah what's happened to Cloveh Cross. They'll be rollin' their cotton in a hurry."

Lou dabbed several times at the sweat that was on him. The sweat kept coming. It was colder than hell with the blower off.

Lou said, "It seems to me we're kind of crowdin' things. What's the rush? It looks——"

"The only looks you need to be botherin' about is the looks of Ives Tampa," Loma Jack said bluntly.

Crowly considered Lou tolerantly. "That's right, Lou. That's all you got to worry about. And I'll give you some help. I'll give you Cibecue here for a deputy."

"I don't need no deputy——"

"You're goin' to hev one, anyway."

Crowly's smile worked on Lou like a sunstroke. He sank back in his chair like an old, old man.

10

COULD Lou Safford have known whom this night would bring riding he would have done quite a number of things differently. He would have stage-set the scene and had things watchfully ready like a whole string of fire-

217

crackers tied to one fuse. For Lou was a man who liked
all the trimmings and he was a man, above all, who liked
things safe. This was not so attributable to any fear bred
in him as it was to the educated habits of his calling. A
professional gambler likes the odds in his favor, and Lou
had been professional all of his life.

But he had no means of foreseeing the future. After
Crowly had left with his gun weighted bravos Lou
slouched moodily a considerable while in his chair. It was
all the fault of that damned Dakota. Lou had known the
moment he had seen Tune that the nice Old Lady was
going to fold up her tent. He should have taken his hunch
then and quit this place; he should have gone as far as a
good horse could take him. He should have gone at
once.

Lou was not afraid of this Dakota Tune. He was not
afraid of him in any physical sense. It was psychologi-
cally Tune had Lou whipped.

Lou had thought when he saw Tune he had ought to
get out of this, and he was asking himself if that were
not still a good notion when he heard the rumor of an approaching rider. The horse came along and stopped at
Lou's tie rack.

Saddle leather creaked. A boot thumped ground. A second boot followed and came up the steps with a measured tread and spur sound scraped the planks of the
porch.

Lou pulled the desk's top drawer a little open.

He was facing the door when Ives Tampa walked in,
and the look of his gambler's cheeks showed nothing.
His nod was courteous, and he said with the tone he
reserved for this man, "How are you, Ives? A fine evening, isn't it."

Tampa grunted. He brought his stoop-shouldered shape
inside and closed Lou's door and stood a moment shaping his thoughts.

"Drag up a chair and sit down," Lou said affably.
"How's the cow business these days? How's Miz Mc-
Clain? I can't tell you how shocked I was about that
killing. I'd have arrested Wilkes if that gun fighter,
Tune——"

218

"I came in to see you about Tune, Lou. He's out at the ranch—the girl's hired him," Ives scowled.

Safford brought up his look with a show of interest. He flexed his lean fingers thoughtfully. "He's out at Clover Cross, you mean?"

There was a lean, hating look in the depths of Ives' eyes.

"Yeah, I figured you might like to know."

Behind his gambler's face Safford's thoughts moved swiftly. His fingers drummed a lazy rhythm. He wondered how much this gaunt Tampa knew. The man had not ridden in just to do Lou a favor. What *had* he come in for? In fear lest Tune cut him out of a job? Was that feeling strong enough for Seven Keys to use? Would there be anything in this for Lou Safford personally?

Lou said, "You ain't figuring on hunting new pasture are you?"

"What put that fool idea in your head?"

Lou Safford shrugged. "Miz McClain shouldn't have put that outlaw on. Hate to see that girl . . ." Safford shook his head. "Two wrongs never made a right in this world———"

Tampa said impatiently: "You better git you a posse an' git out there after him. While you're swingin' your jaw———"

"Hell!" Safford said. "I've no authority outside this town."

Tampa's eyes turned black. "You ain't goin' to let that stop you, are you?"

"Well, hardly," Lou smiled. "Makes a difference in how I go at it, though. I've got to think this out. You going to be here a spell?"

"I wasn't figuring to be. If you're wantin' that feller you better be gettin' on out there."

Lou said: "I'll get—" and, like that, quit talking. He was froze, half turned on the edge of his chair, when the door banged open and the man with the mismatched eyes limped in.

Irritation lifted Lou's shoulders.

"Cibecue," he said in a held-down voice, "try knocking some time. You will find it good practice. *Now what do you want?*"

219

Cibecue brought his look off Ives. "You fergot t' give me my tin," he leered. "What kinda deppity would I be with no badge?" His unfocused glance skittered back to Ives. "Who's this?"

Lou opened another drawer and tossed the gun man a nickeled star. "There you are. Close the door on your way out, will you?"

Cibecue's vacant laugh rattled forth. "I ain't gone yet. Who *is* this feller—ain't Ives Tampa, is he?"

Ives Tampa snarled: "Yes! Now git the hell out o' here!"

Cibecue's half-witted face gleamed with pleasure. He scrubbed a hand on his dirty trousers. "Ives Tampa?" he said, limping over to Ives. "I'm right proud to know you. Say—what's that you got all over your hat?"

Ives snatched off his hat and Cibecue thumped Ives' head with a pistol.

Ives dropped down on the floor without argument.

Cibecue's mismatched eyes flicked to Lou. "What you been waitin' for? What do you want I should do with him now?"

Lou said drily: "I sure as hell don't want him left here."

He looked at his hands and flexed his fingers. "Get him on a horse and take him out to the ranch."

"Take him out to the Clover Cross?"

"Hardly. Take him out to Seven Keys. I'll tell Jess——"

"Jess ain't in town no more."

"Where is he?"

Cibecue shrugged. "Hell! He don't tell me."

"Never mind. You take Tampa out to the ranch—and don't be seen doing it. I'll get hold of Jess someway. I've got an idea—Do you want any help getting him onto his horse?"

"Don't you worry about me."

Lou picked up his hat. He smoothed down its knap with a careful elbow and, while Cibecue watched with a sneer on his face, set it jauntily atop his corn-yellow curls. He buttoned his coat and picked up his gloves.

"You look like a goddam dude! growled Cibecue, and

spat on his hands and heaved Tampa's limp shape across his shoulder.

Lou nodded. "I'll still be looking like one long after you're planted."

TUNE, well knowing the risk he ran, stepped into Lou's office and found it empty. But the lamp in its bracket on the wall still burned, so he thought it unlikely Lou would be away long.

"Might as well wait," he thought, closing the door. "Probably down to Riske Quentin's."

He put his shoulders against the wall and leaned there awhile and frowned at the windows. He regretted that Lou had not drawn the shades. It would not be smart for him to draw them himself. Someone might see him or Lou, when he came, might notice. Better stay where he was, just inside the door. Lou would probably come in and head straight for his desk. At any rate, this way, Lou wouldn't see him till he got clear inside.

He wouldn't see Tune's horse for Tune had left the dun in a clump of brush at the edge of town. He felt reasonably certain he had arrived here unheralded.

He got to wondering about that blue eyed gitana. She didn't look much like the old man, he thought. She didn't seem to have much in common with him, either. Maybe it was the sheep that bound them together. She used a pretty good brand of Spanish for a gypsy. He was aware of an increasing interest in her. A fellow wouldn't have to exert much effort to get himself interested in a girl like her. Yet it was odd, he thought, how well he remembered her, each trick and shading of her mobile features. He could only remember the yellow haired girl as she'd been on that porch when Wilkes shot her brother.

He was like that, considering, his eyes roving around, when abruptly his glance sharpened into grim focus.

There was a battered old hat tumbled under the desk. A hat with a faded tigersnake band. It had not been placed there of deliberate intent; it looked to have rolled there, to have been forgotten.

Tune knew that hat. It belonged to Ives Tampa.

Unthinkingly Tune stepped away from the wall.

221

He was bending to pick up Ives' hat and examine it when a girl's scream loudly sheared through the night and a window, behind him, broke into fragments as a gun beat up wild echoes in the street.

11

THERE ARE some kinds of men who naturally gravitate toward women and Birch Alder, the Clover Cross bronc peeler, was of this persuasion. Obviously looks have little to do with it for Birch was a heavy handed, rough sort of man with a blue-black jaw and eyes frankly cast on the gimlet pattern. A cud of tobacco usually bulged his cheek and there was a knife scar over his opposite eye, giving his look at the world a kind of uncaring truculence. A good many women, despite this, had built fond dreams around Birch Alder.

According to Birch the world owed him plenty and he was out to get it any way he could. He was a man who had worked for many outfits and at each place, or within its vicinity, he had always managed to find him a woman. He preferred them young and with fire in their veins, but any kind would do if it had to. "Hell! It's only their names that's different," he'd say, and be off with a wink to find him another.

An old dog can be taught new tricks yet its essential character remains unchanged. It was that way with Birch.

After signing on with Teal to ride rough string Birch had one day seen a certain look he knew in the eyes of Larinda McClain. She was on the top rail in her levis, watching him.

A wink was as good as a nod to Birch.

With his own eye, as ever, strictly on the main chance, he had taken himself right in hand from that moment. He knocked the rougher edges off the worst of his manners and took to aiming his expectorations where they showed least later. He even gave up the habit when Larinda was around him. He shaved more frequently, talked less about women.

Clover Cross was a damned fine ranch.

Birch believed in signs when the signs were favorable, and he found plenty of signs he was on the right track. Take that time she had picked him out of the bunch to go with her to look at cows in Tubac. Or that more recent time, not a week gone by, when she'd taken him with her to inspect the watershed. Why, he'd even had her right up against him!

She might be the boss but she was plenty human!

It was, therefore, with considerable of a shock that, right after Teal's death, he found she'd made Tampa range boss. It was a dirty damned trick and Birch was not forgetting it! Why, that damned old Tampa was old enough to be her grandpaw!

Birch fumed and smouldered with enraged resentment. What kind of a woman was she? Kiss a man and make another guy foreman! Why, she hadn't no more ethics than a goddam jackrabbit!

Birch commenced to look over some things in his mind. There was a heap of things could happen to a man when he took to riding nightherd in this country. Lots of guys had fell over cliffs—there was such a thing as justice, by God!

While he was deciding how best he might aid it, Larinda sent for him up at the house.

Full dark had fallen and she had the lamps lit. He found her standing before a little piece of mirror propped up on the mantel. Birch stared at her, startled. She was doing up her hair and taking both hands to it.

Birch found it hard to keep his mind on justice. She hadn't much on underneath that wrapper.

There was times, Birch decided, when a coal-oil lamp could be a real satisfaction.

Without turning, Larinda asked through the pins in her mouth, "Where's Ives and that new fellow?"

"What you wantin' them for?"

"If it concerns you, Birch, you will probably be told when the time is right for it."

Birch liked neither the words nor the smile with which,

223

like an afterthought, she garnished them. All the black thoughts in him began to boil up and he said with the words gritted out through his teeth:

"So it's Birch the Hired Hand you're talkin' to now, eh?"

The tone of his voice brought her eyes around to him. She eyed him a moment across her shoulder. Then her red lips curved in that warm kind of smile and he felt desire climbing out of the ashes. He cursed, and a down-swinging blow of his hand thumped the table. "By God," he cried, "can't you never stay put!"

She laughed at him then and went back to her primping. Birch, still scowling, blackly watched the way of the lamp with her contours.

"Are they still around?"

"Them rannies? I dunno," Birch growled like it strangled him.

"And Crispin's out with the cattle . . . Where's Wimpy Gilman?"

"He's around someplace—I see him awhile ago fixin' his saddle." Birch considered her more carefully. "What's up? What you wantin' that little wart fer?"

"How do you feel about taking a ride, Birch?"

Birch perked up. "I allus feel like ridin'—with you."

She swung away from the mirror then, swung round to face him. She had her hair up now. Shimmering braids of gold, like a halo. She grinned. "Not *that* kind of ride." She got a pair of levis and a man's rough shirt from the corner closet, and Birch Alder's thoughts put a shine in his eyes.

Larinda saw that look and she smiled a little and Birch came across the floor tumultuously. But she put both hands up against him, and holding him that way let him kiss her. Just once. Then she pushed him back. "Later," she said. "Later Birch—later. We haven't time now. The Seven Keys' payroll is on that stage from Ajo. We'll take Gilman—Hurry! Catch up the horses while I get into these clothes."

12

JESS CROWLY, a long while back, had used to claim he hailed from El Paso—and he might have done it, but not originally. As a matter of fact, Jess' mother had borne him on the opposite side of the River in an eight-by-ten mud shack of a house that belonged to a one-eyed Indio. The place didn't have any windows, and the only door was a tow sack strip that didn't come down to below a man's knees, and the Old Man had killed three Rurales through it when they'd come dropping around for a chat with Jess' mother. It was right after this Jess hailed from The Pass.

The Señora Crowly had been a mighty fashionable looking woman in her day; right many a guitar had been plunked by her window and she had been trothed by fond parents to a man of fine family, old Jesus Juan Bravo y Vandalera, the Alcalde of Juarez. But these plans had gone agley someway. Just prior to the ceremony Jess' mother had chanced to be passing the jailhouse and glimpsed the rogue face of Kane Crowly grinning back at her.

Ah, those were the days!

Red heeled slippers and caballero spurs. Lips gay with laughter. Sweet hours of madness when blood was hot and quick to run and the way of a maid needed no explaining. Those were the days! Moonlight and stars through the breeze-swayed trees. Writhing bodies and the sharp click of castanets. Frijoles y cuchillos. José Cuervo in a gleaming glass and wild cries winging through the hoof-torn night when a man's life hinged on the speed of his horse and only the bold had their way with a maid.

But life with Kane Crowly proved a little too fast. Few were the hearts that could stand the pace. Dona Ysabel died stripped of her youth and stripped of beauty. Speed was the measure of an outlaw's passion and speed,

225

the begetter, packs its own wild challenge and the time always comes when the pistol drops from the paralyzed hand; and so it was with Kane Crowly one night. From that hour on it was young Jess Crowly against the world.

He was only a kid, but the border blood burned hot in his veins and he was swift to learn the ways of the land. No humdrum honest life for Jess! He preferred to die with his boots on, and said so. He took to the gun and, with his agile wits and ready hand, took the top of the Wanted list in no time. Banks and stages were his special dish; then he heard of the James boys, the Youngers and Ketchum, and decided he could tame the Iron Horse, too. He stopped one close to Pecos one night; stopped a second not far from Shakespeare. Then he took his bunch to the Cherokee Strip and Doolin's gang wiped Jess' bunch plumb out.

Jess went back to Texas a wiser man, but not near as wise as he figured he was. The Border Patrol caught Jess one night with a bunch of wet cattle coming out of the River on the U. S. side, and the next few years he took a course in rock breaking. At the State's expense.

But all things pass if you can wait long enough. Jess had little choice in the matter. When they let him out he was a reformed character. He had not changed a great deal in appearance; he was the same dark, short and broad fellow he had been—more quiet, perhaps, more given to thinking and more controlled of temper. It was all in his head, but the boy they had set to breaking up rocks walked out of the jailhouse a man full grown. A man fundamentally different as night from day; a man gone wrong to his rotten core. A man haunted and hounded by the things in his mind, by the repressions of those years and by the imagined taint they had put upon him.

The inherited tendencies were also there, much strengthened—nurtured and intensified by those years on the rockpile, grown and bloated by those years of brooding that only a prisoned man can so nourish. Two things only were gone from his heritage—love of nature and the gift of laughter. Those were gone, burnt out in the ashes of those cooped-up years. The wind and the stars, the

226

vast silence of deserts, the majesty of mountains held neither meaning nor interest for Jess. Not for him the lonely campfire or the way of a moon playing through white clouds. Not even the feel of a good bronc's barrel between his legs could bring any answering thrill to this man he was become. Recklessness and that wild fierce temper still rode with Jess, but caution held a leash on them now, and they were fused by subtlety, polished by craft. His was the same atavistic nature, but sharply honed now by perception, by the thoughts engendered of past experience.

Jess Crowly knew what he wanted now.

He wanted power and he knew how to get it.

He had tried out his talents and the knowledge of power was yeasty in him. All things come to the man who can wait. Every man gets what he wants if there is enough determination in him to keep after it. What you get, Jess believed, is a matter of your own intensity, the intensity of your desire and the measure of your endurance. Given bottom and will a man can have anything. This was Crowly's creed, the refined result of observation and experience.

After the warden had said goodbye to him Jess had covered a deal of territory, just drifting and watching with his ear to the ground. San Saba had presented Jess with a set-up ripe for his talent. A young rancher named Tune was hip deep in trouble. The bone of contention was a vast spread of grasslands Tune's father had held under lease and developed. The elder Tune had had vision. He had improved the property with buildings and fences; irrigation and industry had done away with the native growths until today the Tune range was an evergreen series of lush meadows knee-deep in the nourishment of succulent fodders. It would feed well upwards of six thousand cattle. A good fat lease, just what Jess was hunting for.

He had studied Tune's various envious neighbors, seeking their weaknesses, discovering their virtues. The inroads of prowling cinch ring experts had reduced young Tune to a minimum of cash. His sole negotiable assets were four-footed ones, line-bred horses and those fine white-faced cattle he'd been building up with the aid of

227

four imported registered bulls. The lease money payment date had been extended and was now again due when Jess rode into San Saba one morning.

The outfit back of Tune's rustling troubles was a syndicate spread which operated under the somewhat ambiguous title of the Lone Star Land & Cattle Combine. They were after Tune's lease. They would have to pay for his improvements, of course, but they were well heeled with capital and eager to do so—if they couldn't get hold of the place any other way. Tune was not well liked, he was too desperately envied. He was considered an upstart by those less fortunate.

Jess looked around. He found the man with the most influence in Tune's community was one Blackwell Stokes, the High Commissioner.

Jess, in the guise of an out-of-state cattleman, cultivated Stokes with care and circumspection. He suspected Stokes of the common hunger and he subsequently found his suspicions well founded. Like the syndicate outfit, the admirable Stokes was after Tune's lease. Stokes was the town's most solid citizen, an institution almost, a pillar of the Church. Not only was Stokes High Commissioner, he was also president of the local bank. A very choice state of affairs, Crowly thought, and proceeded to fit himself into things.

It seemed the greatest obstacle to Stokes' ambition was the Lone Star Land & Cattle Combine. It was Jess who ironed out that angle for him. Jess laughed every time he thought of that business.

Tune, finding himself increasingly short, became increasingly unlikely to scrape up enough money to renew his lease. Tune consulted his friend, Banker Stokes, and inquired if there were any way in which he could save his stake. Why certainly, Stokes said, the bank would advance the money. Naturally Tune would have to assign his lease-hold over to Stokes as security, and the loan, unfortunately, could not be extended over a longer period than ninety days. That was all right, Tune said. He could still gather up and market sufficient good beef in that time to more than pay off this obligation.

So, with the lease money due by noon on the morrow,

228

Tune had come into the bank next evening, just before closing time, and completed the deal. Stokes had given him the money, a substantial sum, in hundred dollar bills. Jess, posted outside, had watched Tune putting the money away. When Tune left the bank Jess followed him.

Jess idled in an adjacent doorway while Tune ate supper in a nearby hash house and dawdled over the evening paper. It was almost dark when Tune finished and left and, as Stokes and Jess had figured he would, stopped in at the Grubstake Saloon.

Almost any man would with his worries lifted suddenly as Tune's had been.

The Grubstake was a cowtown place, typical of its kind. Some folks called it the Carlton House Bar because it stood next door to that hostelry and the hotel had no bar of its own. There was nothing pretentious about it. It held a pretty fair crowd that evening and the games already were creating excitement for this was a Saturday night in San Saba and payday for many of the roundabout ranches. Jess, looking in through the batwings, saw Tim Curry, the sheriff, alongside the bar not far from Tune's elbow.

A sagebrush orchestra—one fiddler and a swarthy Mexican strumming a guitar—was furnishing the noise and the light was furnished by three hanging lamps just over the bar.

Jess took a good look over his shoulder then whipped out his pistol and fired four times.

Pandemonium filled that place on the instant.

The hanging lamps came down with a crash, and through the murk Jess wove like a cat. Shouts and oaths made a battering din while Jess slugged at Tune through that wild press of bodies and abruptly shied off with a hand round Tune's wallet. He got off with it, too; and when the bartender got his candle lit there was Tom Curry sprawled dead on the floor and Tune crouched over him with a smoking pistol.

"Goddam sheriff killer!"

It was Jess cried that from outside the door, but the crowd took it up and Tune left by a window.

Tune had not seen Jess—did not know Jess from Adam.

229

Jess trailed him over to the banker's house where Tune went to see Stokes in Stokes' capacity as Commissioner. Stokes appeared sympathetic. He listened gravely while Tune excitedly told what had happened. How he'd been in the Grubstake getting a drink when some damn fool had up and shot the lights out. In the ensuing darkness and resultant confusion, someone had snatched Tune's wallet; Tune had fired, hoping to drop the man. When the bartender's candle had brought things back into focus Tom Curry, with a hand thrust into his coatfront, lay dead on the floor.

Stokes' hand had gone worriedly through his white hair. He had finally, gloomily, shaken his head. "I'm sorry, Tune. This has gone too far. Neither repentance nor innocence can reshuffle the cards. The man is dead—you cannot change that. You cannot escape your connection with it. There are powerful factions at work in the land . . ."

Stokes had sighed like the world's whole weight was on him.

"I hate mighty bad to say this to you, son, but it looks like you had better travel. For awhile, anyway. This town is too riled to split hairs right now. You'd better dig for the tules and stay hid for a spell. That was probably a frame-up to get Tom Curry—no telling who killed him; we may never know. The man had powerful enemies. But when the authorities get to the bottom of this you will doubtless be cleared and can come back to your own again. I'll take care of your lease . . ."

Jess gave him that—Stokes had certainly intended to.

It was a slick piece of work all around, and none of it slicker than the part Stokes wasn't aware, of the part of the business that was yet to come. Jess Crowly's big part.

With Tune gone larruping off into hiding Stokes had made haste to protect Stokes' interests. He paid the annual rent on the lease. He put a big crew of riders armed with guns on the place, for he held bonafide notes on the most of Tune's cattle and had no wish to be done out of them. He allowed Jess Crowly to keep the money Jess had got from Tune's wallet, hinting there'd be more ere the deal was finished.

230

That was Crowly's notion, also.

It was Jess who had seen the real chance in this business. What a fool Stokes would be, he had pointed out, to keep that lease and bring the syndicate down on him. That lease, Jess declared, was a hot potato. There might always be trouble over that damned lease—hadn't the syndicate mighty near ruined Tune to get it? Did Stokes think they would stop because the lease had changed hands? That L.S.L. & C.C. crowd wouldn't stop at anything. So why not make a deal with them? Why not sell them the place and to hell with them?

"Don't forgit," Jess said, "you still got Tune t' consider. He ain't goin' to like this a little bit. The guy holdin' this lease is like t' stop a few bullets!"

"If you'd gunned the fool according to plan——"

"Plans," Jess said, "is subjeck t' human limitations. I done what I could, but I ain't no cat—I can't see in the dark no better'n the next guy! Could I guess Curry was goin' t' jump in front of him?"

Stokes had muttered but he'd finally come around. The syndicate could afford to pay well for that lease. But Stokes had himself been having some trouble with them— Jess knew this, he had himself engineered it. Stokes said he doubted if they'd do business with him.

"I'll take care o' that," Jess told him. "You leave it t' me. I can deal with those tough guys, I know all about 'em. Will fifty thousan' take care o' you?"

"How much are *you* thinking to pull down out of it?"

"I'll git mine from you after the deal's finished. Name yo' price an' I'll see what I can do fo' you."

So, while Jess was carrying on negotiations, Stokes had got busy on the law end of things. He took the business to court and sued to foreclose on the note the outlawed Tune had given him, and to have the court transfer the lease which Tune had put up as security for the note, and to have it set over into his, Stokes', name. By the time this was accomplished Jess had a deal lined up with the syndicate.

"But they don't want t' pay mo' than fo'ty thousan'," Jess said, looking to see how Stokes would take it.

"They'll pay fifty thousand or I'll peddle it elsewhere

231

—what do they take me for?" Stokes demanded. "There's plenty outfits round here would like that lease. And tell them I want the money in War Bonds—I don't want none of that 'bearer' stuff. I want Civil War Bonds—Series X."

Jess scratched his head like this was all above him. He said: "They ain't goin' t' like it, Blackwell. Thet's a touchy bunch—meaner than gar soup. They been figurin' to give you a check—"

"They can figure again. I want Civil War Bonds! They'll do this *my* way—or someone else will! That lease won't go begging for fifty thousand!"

So Jess rode back to the syndicate again, and the L.S.L. & C.C. finally agreed to Stokes' terms; and that was how Jess had come to leave Texas.

Stokes made out the papers and called in some clerks to witness his signature. "Here you are," he told Jess, folding them into an envelope. "Tell those highbinders to get those bonds in the mail right away; you stay right with them and be damned sure they do. Don't give them these papers—Hold on! Wait, let me think."

Stokes had sat there scowling at his desk for a moment. Then he'd looked up at Jess and nodded, like he was putting the go-ahead sign on his thinking. "Guess you'd better fetch those bonds back yourself; those crooks might stick up the stage, or something. A bunch like that will stoop to anything."

"Yeah, they're salty all right," Jess grinned at him. "But I'll watch 'em! Er . . . How much you figurin' my time's been wo'th to you?

Stokes looked at Jess from under his eyebrows. "I never forget my friends," he said solemnly. "You got five thousand dollars coming the minute you put those bonds in my hand."

That was the way Stokes had got Jess figured; and it kind of riled up Jess' bowels that anyone should take him for such a dumb cluck.

He must have showed his face pretty satisfied though, because Stokes kind of sniffed and took his look off Jess and commenced rattling papers the way bankers do when they've used up time beyond a customer's value. Jess halfway looked for him to dust off the seat just so quick as Jess got his bottom out of it. But that was all right with Jess. He was being well paid to take insults.

He picked up the envelope and put on his hat. *"Al garanon no le inporta lo que el patrio dija de el,"* he murmured, and Stokes jerked a nod at him absently, his mind gone already to another transaction.

That was the last Jess had seen of him. He delivered the papers, got the bonds from the syndicate and took the next train out of Texas. Blackwell Stokes, he considered, was a plain damn fool.

LEAVING THE MARSHAL'S office, Crowly took his two gun men down to Riske Quentin's and bought them a drink; then he gave them instructions and took his departure.

For just a bit things had had Jess rattled, the way this thing was developing. But it was all right now. The end was inevitable. With Tampa out of the way, the girl, if she would not play along with Jess, was bound to give Tune Tampa's job. And that was all Jess asked for. Let her make Tune boss and Jess would get Lou Safford made sheriff and the rest could be left up to Safford's posses. Not even Safford's cold feet could make any ultimate difference then, for Jess meant to pick the posse men himself and he would pick the kind who would do as he told them.

The world, Jess thought, was filled with damned fools.

13

BLACKWELL STOKES, the San Saba banker and county commissioner, was a hypocrite and a pernicious rascal and, under his country gentleman guise, he was one other thing—a disliker of children. He would not have them around. They disrupted the ordered run of his thoughts. They took his mind off more profitable matters. He disliked the sticky feel of their fingers, their shouts and shrill

voices, their bickering and whining. Nonetheless, in the
early days of his marriage, he had tried for a son to carry
on his business. Childbirth had cost him the life of his
wife, and the child she bore him was one without tassel—
a sniveling, blubbering brat of a girl which he shipped
off at once to the care of relatives. This had solved her
problem for awhile until divorce had forced him to find
other caretakers. He never spoke of her, never wrote to in-
quire of her welfare; his checks were regular and the full
extent of his interest in her.

After eight years of being farmed out, she was placed
in a convent at Corpus Christi. There she remained in the
sheltered obscurity of eight other years. On her fourteenth
birthday Blackwell Stokes came to see her and was completely dumbfounded by her charm and beauty. He at
once gave thought to her possible marriage and thought
over the names of possible husbands. He decided he would
have her come home for a bit. He inquired if she might
come home for the holidays. Mother Superior thought it
quite possible if Mr. Stokes would provide suitable escort.

It was thus arranged, and for a handful of days in her
fifteenth year Mary Jaqueline Stokes visited the home of
her father. She found everything strange and exciting. San
Saba of those days was a rough community of crude board-
walks and false-fronted buildings that had been slapped
up of planks and tarpaper. It had much quaint charm to
delight the child's vast energy and interest; but Stokes had
had no time to waste on such foolery. He had not brought
her this long way from Corpus to spend his time in showing her the town; he had brought her here that the town
might see *her*—or such of the town as he deemed advan-
tageous. Collectively he held his neighbors in low esteem,
regarding them privately as uncouth backwoodsmen de-
scended from the illicit unions of ruffians and hurdy
girls; his daughter was not for any such trash. She was bait
for cash balances and met only the most affluent of the
bank's clientele, three wrinkled old rakes whose accounts
ran into the six-figures bracket and whose lecherous
looks made the girl blush hotly. She disliked particularly
the tall skinny one with the parfleche face whose contin-

234

ual grin showed repulsive rows of decaying teeth and whose breath was a blast beyond endurance.

So when, one summer's evening in her sixteenth year, Sister Teresa unhappily disclosed her father's plans to her, Mary Jaqueline's voice rose in whole-souled rebellion.

"But I don't *wish* to marry that awful old man—I don't wish to marry *anyone!*" . . . .

"Hush, child," the good Sister admonished. "These are matters for older heads—what could one so young know of marriage? Such matters are best left to one's parents; besides, it is the custom. The child's duty is obedience to family. You will find it will all work out very well. Parents consider these things in the light of experience. Your father is a prominent man in his community, he would not make other than suitable plans——"

"But——"

"Hush, child. You must have faith. Your father tells us it will be a fine match——"

"With that old goblin!" Mary Jaqueline wailed. "Why, he's old enough to be my great grandfather! He has bleeding gums and mossy teeth—his eyes are like black spiders, Sister!"

Mary Jaqueline felt she must talk with her father. If she could explain her feeling she felt sure her father would not insist on this marriage. Arranged futures might be the custom, but at least let the arrangement include a man more personable. She felt sure she could make her father understand. She must go to him at once!

She went with the money he had given her for Christmas; stole away from the convent, crept away like a furtive thief in the night.

It was also night when she arrived in San Saba, night and full dark with the town gaily lit by saloon-front torches and kerosene lanterns. Her father's house showed a lamp in the study. The door was unlocked and she let herself in quietly, lest she disturb her father's housekeeper, a timid old soul who probably needed her sleep.

The girl knew her way from previous visits and, thinking how delighted Stokes would be to see her, went at once to his study and opened the door.

He had company that night, a short and broad man

235

with a dark-burnt face and burly shoulders whose muscles showed ropelike through his pongee shirt. This man grinned disagreeably as her father talked. Several times he nodded and rubbed at his cheek, but always his mouth showed that dark sly smile.

Her father seemed to be outlining some projected program concerned with some rancher he contemptuously referred to as 'that fool Tune.' So engrossed were the pair with developing their plans they failed utterly to notice the wide-eyed girl in the doorway.

Her words of greeting died away unspoken. She stood very tense and straight visioning the things her father was unfolding. She would have cried out against them but no words would come; she would have fled undiscovered but the cold calculation of their villainy froze her, anchoring her there as with chains of steel.

She remained and heard, repelled yet fascinated as a bird is fascinated by the look of a snake, by the snake's sinuous body, by its weaving head. It was all too monstrous, too unreal—incredible. Yet there they sat, her father and that man, nodding and smiling like two old friends talking over old times.

She found it revolting, nauseous; it someway made her feel unclean. Yet she stood there, listening, unable to leave.

And then the dark man saw her.

His brows went up, the cruel mouth went down; the rest was a dim blurred nightmare of horror. She had fled from them blindly, spurred by panic—by the look of their faces; and always the dark man thumped behind her and her father's shrill cursing turned her blood to water. She found a door before her and she jerked it open and rushed out into the cool night air.

14

TUNE, REACHING for Tampa's hat where it lay half concealed under Lou's desk, heard the girl's shearing cry, heard the window back of him burst into shards and then all other sounds were hammered insensible by the nerve-sledging crash of pistol fire. Splinters stood up on the desk before him. Holes appeared in its side like magic. An old coat of Lou's fell off the wall. Another shot cuffed at the brim of Tune's hat; then his own gun kicked up an angling fire and the lamp flared once in its bracket and died.

Tune, with his belly pressed flat to the floor, felt the whole back side of the building shake. Whoever it was they were out to get him. With his knees, belly, toes, with the points of his shoulders, squeezed hard against that gritty floor, Tune inched around till he faced the window. He knew when he faced it by the deeper dark round it, by the cool night air flowing over him from it. Flare of the guns played like Northern lights over it and then Safford's high angry voice smashed through it, ordering his bravos to rush the place, to storm it and take it through their sheer weight of numbers.

Tune listened with lips thinly peeled from his teeth. He crouched and held still as their boots crossed the hardpan and were chopped up and lost in the round-about echoes. But he saw no shapes in the wind harried shadows and knew by that what was in Lou's mind. Lou's strategy was plain; he meant for those men to come in through the back and drive Tune through that shot-out window.

It was a first class plan and might work if Tune waited.

But Tune had no intention of waiting. He went scrabbling backward like a crab on his belly till he felt his boots come against the rear wall. Then he got his shoulders flat against the timbers.

Safford's mob struck the door with a rebel yell. With a squealing groan it came off its hinges and was banged underfoot by the shadow-blurred shapes bounding in across it. Tune left the wall as they crowded past, hunting him —left the wall carefully and insinuated himself brazenly into their ranks and, with them, probed the curdled gloom.

Red fire gushed suddenly out of his pistol as he drove his flame at Lou's fallen coat that was just a black smudge in the room's far corner. And all Lou's gun slam-

237

mers triggered, too. Someone yelled through that murk and gunfire rocked the shack with its pounding and the acrid smoke was for all the world like a stinking canopy flung over hell.

Tune had thought being one of them would afford the best cover, and it had. Moving with them, firing with them—in every way appearing to be one of them, had served to mask his presence from them; but now he was trapped by the pressure of them round him. He had joined their ranks but he could not safely leave them—nor could he safely continue to be one of their number. Unless——

Some man outside yelled long and full and Tune went suddenly stiff in his tracks and gasped and let his knees fold under him and felt his shape fall through those crowding legs to the floor. The press milled around him and then was gone past, each man with his gun snout riveted on the dark still smudge of Lou's coat in the corner.

Tune shoved to his knees, got one leg under him and came erect. He slipped out the door like the ghost of a shadow, and he humped his pounding boots toward the brush, toward the yonder greasewood where he'd cached his horse. A shout burst out of the street, and Lou Safford's voice slammed a halt order at him, and muzzle lights bloomed and slugs cracked through the branches round him as Tune, bent double, dived into the thicket.

The uproar of Lou's tricked men at the office came racketing through the gusty gloom, and Lou's voice yelling they had lost Tune, cursing them; and the guns, beating up a renewed thunder, as Tune snatched reins and slogged into the saddle.

But, just as he would have gone lunging out of there, just as he lifted spurred heel to slash downward, dim through the night he heard the girl's cry—the same frantic cry he had heard in the office, Panchita's voice, lifting vibrant with fright.

Tune stayed the descent of that lifted heel. He hung that way, balanced, with a hand to the horn, with his ears strained into that raucous dark trying to make out the source of the girl's scared cry.

Through the uproar he heard it again, dim through the

gun sound, through the rack of men's cursing. Dimmer now and gone toward panic.

She was out on the desert. He was sure of that. Out on the desert and running, he thought, running deeper into the drifted sand. He dug in his spurs without mercy. The Clover Cross dun went off like an arrow, with Tune crouched low he tore through the chaparral. A treble tongued shout went instantly up. Guns belted the night, streaked the gloom with cross fire. The wind from those slugs screamed high and shrill but their aim was wild and Tune sped on. With the reins in his teeth he fumbled fresh loads to his heated pistol. And then he saw the girl's shape there ahead, a vague blur, to the left of him.

His knees signaled the horse. They went rocketing toward her, and muzzle flame licked a white line past her shape. Something jerked at his vest and Tune's bleak face went indescribably wicked as he saw the dark blur come apart, gyrate wildly, and abruptly resolve into two struggling figures locked writhing below the dull shine of a pistol.

One of those twisting shapes was the girl—he could hear the fierce pant of her labored breathing.

Tune hit the ground on skidding bootheels. The man saw him coming and tried to jerk free—succeeded, sent the girl sprawling and lifted his sixgun. Tune, reaching for his own, found it gone.

He hurled himself slanchways. Lightning winked from the crouched man's middle. The fan of that shot was a too close thing, and Tune knew the fellow would never quit firing till his gun was shot dry. And he was right.

Fire gushed red from the fellow's gun snout. But Tune was rolling too fast to target in that murky light the man had to shoot by. Before the man could slap hammer again Tune was into him, jerking him, slamming him backward in a jolting fall.

Tune held no exaggerated views of his own ability. He knew himself to be plenty tough, but he knew there were others who were probably better and this man facing him might well be one of them.

He wished he could see who the fellow was, by some trait or gesture guess whom he dealt with; but you could

239

not tell in this cloying murk. He had a shape to deal with and, beyond that, all he could get was a hazy impression —thick muscular legs, burly shoulders, a chin-strapped hat with a floppy brim. He saw the man roll and come to an elbow, saw him shove to his knees and come off the ground. There was no glint in the man's hand now and a pleased kind of growl welled out of Tune's throat. His lips fanned out in a savage grin as they came together in a meaty impact.

The fellow took Tune's slogging fist with a grunt and shook it off and came back swinging. A left-handed jolt raked along Tune's ear and, by the feel, took the ear along with it. Then a lifted knee skidded off his thigh and Tune knew then he was in for something. He fell back, giving ground with the world redly reeling, and a roll of his head barely got him clear of the too-anxious fist that went whizzing past it.

Tune lurched in. He put his knuckles hard against the man's chin—felt chin and head snap backward fiercely; but the man got that bony knee up again and excruciating pain rushed all through Tune's body, and he doubled over; and the man came boring in like a pile driver.

Those sledge-like fists reached out like pistons and all Tune's will and footwork could not keep him entirely clear. Every blow the man struck rocked Tune to his bootheels, and he caught the dull shine of the man's grinning teeth through a kind of red fog that got darker and darker.

He stumbled backward but there was no respite. Those bone-bruising fists came rocking after him in a rain of blows that was beating him senseless. Through the roaring howl that was in his head Tune knew the end could not be far off. Queer that it should come like this, that it should be a man's fists and not lead that got him . . .

It was almost over. Tune was flat on the ground, spread-eagled there, numb and past caring—or so he thought. It was the bark of the gun that brought him out of it; a gun's explosion not two feet from his head. He sensed that the girl was crouched there by him, that hers was the hand that had fired that pistol.

He heard the man's startled curse with sharpening

240

senses; saw the blur of a shape go slamming past—heard the girl scream as the man's fist struck her.

That jerked Tune off his back like a rope—jerked him onto his shaking knees; and cold willpower alone got him onto his feet, and the man's broad back was just before him.

Instinct, or that sixth sense that is born of danger, turned the head on those burly shoulders. The man's eyes saw Tune coming. He stood in his tracks in a kind of crouch with his fencepost legs spread wide apart. And when Tune got within reach the man hit him, two brain racking overhand jolts of lightning that exploded against Tune like sticks of dynamite, that knocked Tune off his feet like a mallet.

But the fight spark, that killing urge buried deep within him, still shed its glow in Tune's fogged brain. It dragged him up off his aching back and pulled him over onto hands and knees; and five groping fingers scoring the dust found the butt of a pistol and balefully closed on it, and balefully came up with it as the girl screamed again. Tune lurched upright, stood there swaying, trying to focus his sight through the black fog around him.

She was out there somewhere. The man was still after her, after her with a haste that had no more time for Tune. Or maybe the fellow figured Tune was done for. He had gone anyway without making sure, and that in itself spelt a need for hurry. Every move the man made seemed geared to haste. What was the pressure? What fear spurred him so? Fear of Safford's men yonder? Did he think they were after *him?* Did he think Tune one of those cursing others?

They were getting nearer. Each widening circle was bringing them closer. Was it fear of the law that rushed the man so? And why was he after Panchita, anyway?

Tune scrubbed his eyes with the back of a hand. Every fist-thumped bone in his body ached; every nerve screamed protest of further movement. But the girl was running—running blindly with panic. He could hear her now, the racking sob of her breathing, the sand muffled beat of her headlong flight.

241

Tune shook his head impatiently to clear it. If only he could get his damned mind to functioning!

He knew they were somewhere off to the left. Off there in the murk not far away. He was starting for there when a rush of ponies coming out from town hit a high lope of sound and he knew it was Safford's gun fighters coming, pulled this way be the recent firing.

Closer he heard the thud of a body plummeting into the warm loose sand—heard the girl's stifled cry, an exultant grunt from the man; and by this Tune guessed the man had found and caught her.

He flung himself into a shambling run.

15

THROUGH THE crisp still dark of the moonless night came a low muted mutter of wagon wheels. The metallic click of chains came, too, and the slowed clup-clup of the tiring horses.

Gilman levered a cartridge forward. Birch Alder pulled up his neckerchief. The Ajo stage was nearing the bend, heavily climbing the grade on that long second loop of the S-curve. The creaking of harness mingled now with the chain sound as the labored breathing of the straining wheelers drew the lumbering vehicle ever nearer and nearer. Old Pap Bennett's gnarled voice could be hard lifted occasionally above his chawing to snarl some sulphurous curse at his horses; and the bite of the iron-rimmed wheels in the roadway.

The Ajo stage was arriving at last.

They could see it now through the interstices of the dark massed foliage flanking the road, could see it coming slowly behind the plodding horses. They could make out the shotgun guard beside Pap, with his chin slid down on his chest, head bobbing.

"It's about time," the girl said, and both men looked at her.

There was something about Birch Adler's shape that suggested reluctance, a kind of unease. "Are you sure you want to go on with this?"

"Why shouldn't I want to?" The girl's voice was sharp.

Birch hesitated. "Well . . . you bein' a woman, an' all——"

"What's that got to do with it?"

"Well . . . but if it ever got out——"

"Who's going to let it out? *You*'re not thinking of talking, are you? Look here," she said. "Put yourself in my place. Should I sit there at home with my hands primly folded and let Jess Crowly run me off this range?"

"You don't know it's Jess Crowly——"

"All right. So I'm guessing. It's the Seven Keys, anyway——"

"You don't even know that."

"Maybe *you* don't know it but *I*'m losing cattle! *I*'m losing horses! Men have quit me and left the country; some of my men have simply vanished! At work in the morning and gone by noon! I'm getting mine back any way that I can!"

"There's other ways," Birch Alder said earnestly. "Stickin' up stages ain't no chore for a girl—you wanta be another *Belle Starr*?

"If you're afraid——"

"Hell! I ain't afraid of anything!"

"For a man that ain't scared you do a heap of talking."

"If I act like I'm scared," Birch growled, it's *you* I'm scared for. What you goin' to do if you git shot? How you figurin' to explain off a gun wound?"

"I'm not going to have to. C'mon! Let's get at it!"

Birch didn't like it a little bit. He liked neither the business nor her attitude toward it. She was too damned cool —too hard! Like granite!

He didn't know as he *liked* girls that way. There were a lot of things Birch could countenance, but he had strong notions on the fitting and proper in regard to a woman, and he hated to see these notions tromped on. Some way her talk got under his skin. He was all mixed up in his mind and—Hell! he didn't know what he thought hardly. But if anyone had told him so recent as yesterday

243

he'd be robbing a stage at the whim of a woman he'd have told that fool to get his head looked at!

Birch didn't see anything funny about it. It made him feel like riding plumb out of the country—and he'd have done it, too, only then it might look like she had had something, hinting he was scared. And it wasn't that he was yellow—or was it? Was it the thought of robbing this stinking stage that was bringing this clammy sweat out on him?

The time taken up by Birch in this thinking was infinitesimal—no longer, in fact, than it took him to turn and climb into his saddle. He was a man of strong hunches and the hunches were hounding him, urging him fiercely to ride and get out of this. But he quietly put his horse through the brush and eased it down to the road with Gilman's.

He wondered what Gilman was thinking.

With the sweat feeling cold underneath his collar he drew his Winchester and stepped with Gilman to the center of the road.

"HALT!" Birch shouted; and Gilman's rifle jumped to his shoulder and flame gouted whitely out of its muzzle, the reports fanning into the squeal of brake blocks.

The Ajo stage careened to a stop. Dust billowed up in a dun colored gale and the guard was cursingly hunting his shotgun when Gilman's rifle streaked flame again. The guard straightened up like a rope had jerked him. The buckling hinges of his knees let go and dropped him forward between the squatting wheelers who screamed their fright and went lashing into a terrified tangle.

Pap Bennett said "Hell!" and grabbed up the shotgun, and Alder's swung rifle knocked him off the box. That was when both doors of the stage banged open and spewed out Seven Keys hands like hornets, and each of those erupting men was triggering. Birch fell wordless out of the saddle and Gilman's scream was lost in the uproar.

Behind the dark massed screen of the chaparral, Larinda McClain clapped spurs to her horse and fled, badly shaken, into the night.

244

16

TUNE PAUSED once to stare through the murk while he hefted the weight of the gun in his hand. He had no remembrance of how it had got there, of how he had found it deep in the dust; and without even thinking what his fingers were doing he emptied its cylinder and filled the bored holes with cartridges fumbled fresh from his belt. And all this while he was listening, gauging, measuring the speed of those oncoming ponies against this thing which he knew he must do. Blood and death growled through this night and a little more blood would not make much difference to a man already doomed to be hanged.

Dust was a lifted smell on the wind and, cocking his throbbing head that way, he caught the slap of flesh on flesh, the panting grunt of breaths hard caught, the beat and thud of boots swift tramping; and a senseless surge of anger plunged him forward again in that shambling run.

He could not guess, and told himself bitterly he did not care, why this blue-eyed gitana should be always in trouble. She was none of his business and he hotly resented the attraction she had for him. His mind, he thought, was a sight too keen on weaving a web of mystery around her, on building her up into something of glamor just because she was young and on her own in this country. On her own? He didn't even know that for sure. After all, she had that damn sheepherding uncle!

By grab, he'd trouble enough to look out for without going around with his mind full of gypsies. Trouble with him, he'd been too long alone; his animal hungers were painting him pictures. To a man two years on the dodge like he'd been, *any* girl would probably look like a million! He was a fool to waste thought on her. Man on the dodge had no right to a woman—no right to even be *thinking* about one; and he was already involved in the worries of one woman. But the girl with the golden hair was paying him. That made it a job and took it out of the realms of this other thing.

Thought of a woman was an obvious weakness and, if it got known, could be used against him. It could trap a man and spill his blood and get him put into a hole in the ground. Weakness was a luxury no man on the dodge could afford.

The girl was in trouble so he had to help her. She had helped him; he had to pay that back. But that was all there was to it—it had *better* be all there was to it! Her being Panchita had nothing to do with it.

He found it important that he get this matter straightened out in his mind. And, while he was still trying to do so, he saw them up in the gloom ahead—two dark lurching twisting shapes, panting, grunting, wildly swaying as they fought with the fury of desperation. The girl, lithe and wiry, was hard as an eel to grab and hang onto, and she fought with the strength of panic. But panic was not enough, nor was courage. Slowly the man's brute weight was telling. He had hold of her now. He was forcing her backward, bending her savagely, deliberately striving to snap her spine. That purpose shouted from every braced line of him, from the arched bulging muscles, from the grunt of his breathing.

"Let her go," Tune said.

Emotion, passion—the battered shape of his lips, made Tune wonder for a moment if the voice were his own. A rough wind was shouldering out of the south and the hoof-slapped sound of those onrushing ponies came stronger and stronger across the land. But the man heard Tune's words, understood their meaning. He let the girl drop. He snapped broad shoulders square around and crouched in his tracks with a hung-up breathing. He was a black silhouette against the sand and, because for the past two peril-packed years he had stayed alive by the skill of his ability to translate men's postures, Tune knew the fellow was going to leap.

He was—he did!

Even as the man's booted feet left the ground Tune brought up his pistol and squeezed the trigger. There wa no mercy in him. The man deserved none and Tune meant to kill him. He pulled the trigger with a remorseless savagery. When your life is at stake you do not worry overmuch about anything but saving it.

But pulling the trigger did not save Tune's then. The pin of the hammer never touched the cartridge. The gun's mechamism jammed. The gun was filled with grit.

Tune swore. It was too late now to get out of the way. He had barely time to drop to his knees. The man's knees came hard against Tune's shoulders and half the breath was spilled out of Tune. But his wits were at work and he rolled—rolled for dear life to get clear of those fingers, those fingers that could ball into rock hard fists; and he came up onto his feet, eyes glinting, and swung with the pistol.

He felt the barrel carome against the man's beefy shoulder. He heard the grunt jounced out of the man's burly throat. But the man did not quit. He kept boring in, harshly growling, bear like, every blow he landed shaking Tune to his bootheels. The man's staying powers were terrific—maddening. It was like fighting a nightmare. Nothing you tried could prevail against it. Those killing, hammering fists kept coming.

Then a knife gleamed suddenly in the man's upraised hand. Tune felt its edge down the length of his arm, like the bite of hot iron from wrist to elbow. He staggered sideways. The man bored in. Again that lifted blade was coming. But a lucky blow of Tune's pistol loosed it—sent it spinning off into the brush. And a change came suddenly into this fight.

Tune sensed it in the lessened ferocity of the man's bull rushes. He was no longer giving everything he had; it was as though he were fighting with only half his interest. You got the impression the man was listening, trying to gauge this thing by the sounds of impact—but that was crazy.

Then Tune got it. The man *was* listening! He was trying to gauge what time he had before those horsebackers should come up with them. You could hear them out there beating the bushes.

It was unthinking impulse that lifted Tune's voice.

"Here he is!" he yelled. "Right over here, boys!" And off in the darkness, hoof sounds lashed the dust like thunder. Safford's pack came tearing headlong.

Tune grabbed for the man, bitterly cursing his folly. He wanted to be caught no more than this other man! His fingers slipped from the bulging shoulders—caught in his shirtfront; but the fellow tore loose and bounded away. He was lost in the dark, in the thunder of horse sound.

Tune knew by its feel what lay gripped in his fingers. Knowledge burned the palm of his hand. The thing he held was another of those buttons he had picked off the floor of Grankelmeir's stable! And he'd let the guy go!

Through the pain of his arm, through the aches of his body, Tune burned with that knowledge. That had been the man—he was sure of it; the knife-wielding killer of Teal and Wilkes. It explained why the fellow was after this girl. It explained a whole lot of things. Panchita had been in the stable when Teal had been stabbed. He had known it, or guessed it, and that was why he'd been after her!

Tune had no time to think further then.

The girl's hand came from the darkness and touched him. "Quick! *Andale*—hurry!"

He followed her into the whirling shadows.

He stumbled after her, impotently cursing.

17

WITH the sprinting speed of a Quarter Horse, doom swept the Oro Blanco country. It fell like a darkness over the land, and no man knew where next it would strike unless, perchance, that man was Jess Crowly. The hour was come, and not even to further mature his plans, or to consolidate his forces, dared Jess delay the avalanche longer. The iron was hot and he must strike. Clover Cross had dug up the hatchet and further delay might cost dark Jess not only his goal but his very life; for Tune had again slipped through his hands and there was no guessing what the man might try now.

But Tune had served Crowly well after all. Regardless of job or capacity, the man was obviously associated with Clover Cross. Jess could daub them from hell to breakfast with all the infamy of this man's reputation. But he need no longer depend on that. At last Clover Cross had come out from cover and had committed last night an act of lawless violence beyond excuse or repudiation. They were a pack of thieves and murderers and no court in the land but would back him up in it. They had stuck up the Ajo stage with rifles, faces masked with neckerchiefs, and four men lay dead as the immediate result. They had killed the shotgun guard. They had shot Pap Bennett down like a dog, and would have got clean away with the Seven Keys payroll but for the canny foresight of longheaded Jess who had put several men on the coach as passengers. These had surprised the robbers, had shot down two of them, Birch Alder and a man named Gilman, both well known to be Clover Cross hands. There had been some more of them back in the brush, but they had fled.

Crowly had good right to feel pleased. That stage job last night had turned the trick for him. Clover Cross had come out from cover and now no man could rightly blame Jess no matter what devilment came of this. The rivers could run blood red. Human bones could lie picked and bleached and no man could call Jess Crowly accountable. He might have to shoot a few people, he might have to run a few out of the country, but only in defense of his rights and interests, and whatever he did it would have the law's sanction. Jess Crowly would be acting in self-defense.

Things had really moved last night. Folks had gone plumb haywire, it looked like. Open warfare had broken out. Arson and anarchy had stalked through the land. Ten or twelve men had been dropped with their boots on, gunned by the greed of that red-jawed wolfpack that was holed up at Clover Cross and led by that renegade Mexican, Tune. Whether he took his orders from himself or the girl made little difference; if the McClain girl

249

didn't approve his acts his name would not be on her payroll.

Down valley, a pair of masked riders had ridden into a small farmer's holdings and burned him out. Had he offered resistance they would probably have killed him—they were that breed of men. Half a dozen miles east another weedbender, New Ground McCune, had been shot on his doorstep and riddled with bullets, with a rock-weighted note left upon his body ordering all dirt farmers to pull their freight under threat of being fed the same medicine. Four men, riding horses marked with the Clover Cross brand, had slaughtered a herd of cows belonging to the Bar O, and had hamstrung four of the outfit's best saddlers; and the rancher's twelve-year-old daughter, left alone in the house, had been scared half senseless.

In mid-morning, a man on a lathered bronc came tearing into town hunting Crowly. After speaking with him Crowly had smiled his feline little smile. He had beckoned a couple of his handiest gun slingers and sent them off with the man on fresh horses. Then Jess went home and changed his clothes.

Men were riding all over the range that day. Rumor was rife. Crowly heard each story of pillage and arson with a face that hourly grew more indignant. At times he would pound his fist on the table and the cords in his neck would swell like ropes as he listened to the outrageous stories brought him.

Such things were not to be countenanced. Such deeds cried aloud for punishment. Clover Cross should pay to the last steer packing their brand, he swore. If the law couldn't do anything the Seven Keys would!

But first the law must be given its chance. There was a brand new sheriff in the saddle today. Lou Safford, the former Blanco marshal, had just been appointed and expected the co-operation of every honest man in the country. And he would get it, too! There would be a mass meeting held this afternoon. Until then . . .

18

WHEN TUNE first went stumbling after the girl it seemed a thin hope to try and outrun Lou Safford's horsemen. But the girl soon proved she wasn't trying to outrun them. She was trying to elude them, to evade, get away from them —to lose them in the brush and cat-claw that here abounded so thickly and tangled the place more resembled a jungle than desert. She seemed to know what she was doing, too, and her way of doing it bred new hope in him, and he followed her with increasing confidence as, through the wind harried shadows, she led off along an old rabbit run that angled through the slapping branches and took them deeper into the desert. He was amazed at her seeming knowledge of the country; he could not reconcile it with the fact of her so-recent arrival.

"It was Tio Felix who showed me this trail. I always take it on my trips to town. It is a short cut from our camp near Clover Cross. Tio Felix was born in this country. He was brought up on a part of the Clover Cross range."

The old man's father, it seemed, had once had a ranch here, but had been driven out by Tim McClain when the Clover Cross still was building. "That is why," the girl said, "he was glad to come back here with sheep to eat the Clover Cross grass. They have played on his hatred of the McClains—on his bitterness. He has taken care of me ever since—But, quick! We must hurry—no time for talk now. We must make him see how these men are using him—You have that button?"

Tune grunted; kept casting quick looks at their backtrail. "We'll never make your camp without horses——"

"But we will *have* horses!"

"What kind of Aladdin's Lamp are you packin'?"

Panchita laughed softly. "That Aladdin! He was smart —Tio Felix is, too; you will see. Just a mile or so now—

251

just a little way more. We will both have horses—good ones! There is a gulch up ahead that has a little cave in it and that is where we keep the horses—these extra ones —'just in case,' as Tio Felix says. Sometimes the saints are too busy to hear one."

Already, Tune noticed, the trail was tipping downward. Its descent, at first, was barely perceptible. Then it dropped more rapidly until, abruptly, Tune found himself in a narrow gorge whose walls, at the top, were almost joined together. It was very dark down here. It made the stars seem nearer, brighter. The girl moved along with a sure-footed grace, pausing to warn Tune every little while of some snaky turn or fallen boulder. And every now and again they could hear the rumor of traveling horses.

But Tune, for the time, had forgotten Lou Safford. A paralysis gripped his mind, born of exhaustion—of the battering he'd taken; and all his aching bones and muscles, every dog-tired nerve and sinew, was lifting up its agonized howl at each new-added foot of their progress. How blessed it would be just to drop in his tracks, just to welcome oblivion for ever and always and never have to get up again.

In the ghostly unreal light of this gulch he could barely make out the girl's shape before him, but something about the free swing of those shoulders was balm to Tune, like a breath of cool air through the down-smashing slant of a noonday sun. It was someway remindful of other and happier days in the past before San Saba, and all that town stood for, had shoved him onto the Boothill Trail.

Shoved him onto it? No, it hadn't done that; a man made his own kind of hell in this world. Only Tune himself could be held accountable for where Tune's boots had taken him. No use to put the blame elsewhere. Society might set up fancy rules, custom might dictate modes of conduct, but a man lived by his own conceptions and by his own acts, or failure to act, shaped and surcharged the world he lived in. If that world be not to his liking let him look to his own lone past to find where his boot left the hard-packed trail.

252

Tune saw that now. Too many times since that fatal night had he relived the past to mistake where the faults of the present had sprung from. He had been a fool to sign over that ranch—he had been a fool to think he needed that drink. If he'd never stepped into the Grubstake Saloon he would not be tramping this black gulch now; so it all came back to a man's own doing. Man made his own bed and, if he was a man, he climbed into it.

Which was not to say Tune felt less bitter toward the man who had taken advantage of his trust. Tune was growing, all right, but he had not grown that much. He hated Stokes with a bitter intensity and if ever Stokes' trail cross his again it was going to be just too bad for somebody!

THE GIRL'S VOICE roused him.

Her hand was on Tune's arm and, even through the lethargy of pain and exhaustion that draped his mind as with tatters of fog, he could feel her tremble—could hear the sharp gasp of her indrawn breath as, instinctively, she shrank away from him. It came to him then with a sense of bewildered surprise that he was no longer walking —was no longer on his feet. He was on the ground, kind of crumpled there like, with his face uncomfortably against the trail's gravel. He squirmed around, got his head off the ground; with every ounce of will he could muster he got his good right arm beneath him and worked himself up to a sitting posture. Cold sweat stood out all over him.

"You're hurt, Dakota—your arm's all blood!"

He could see the gray blur of her face bent over him.

"I guess I'm not so tough as I figured. If——"

"Wait! You cannot go on losing blood like that . . ."

But Tune, with a growl, was grinding his boots hard against the gravel. He felt weak as a chicken but he kept on straining and finally his labor got one leg under him and, with the girl's help, he lurched erect. He stood there, swaying weakly. It was like the shakes had got into his knees and only the girl's steadying grip kept him up.

But she couldn't seem to get her mind off that blood.

253

"Your wound, prala . . ." She said urgently: "We must tie it up!" and he felt her grip go briefly away from him, heard the rip of cloth, felt her hands come back to him; and presently she was saying, "It is not far now. Listen! You hear the horses, prala?"

Tune grunted, bearing harded and harder against her. He made a strenuous effort to get hold of himself; made a try to go on without her help but his breath came shorter and shorter and the sweat rolled into his eyes like rain and he reeled to a floundering, all-in stop.

Once more the girl's hands were on him, holding him. She got his good arm over her shoulder. "Let your weight come on me, prala. I will be your rod and your staff—it will comfort you."

A bitter laugh growled up out of him and he said between the harsh grunts of his breathing, "You've already got all the weight that's in me." He shook his head, trying to get some sense into it. "It's no good, Panchita. You go on—you go on without——"

"But it's just a little way—just around the next bend. Look! You can almost *see* it. In the right-hand wall. A tiny opening just back of the brush. There is food and blankets—Can't you make it prala? Can't you go that far?"

She looked at him, worriedly biting her lips. For the last half mile he had leaned on her heavily, struggling on in a kind of half stupor that told her better than any words how near he was to the end of his strength. He was out on his feet, and if he fell again . . .

She wouldn't let herself think of it. "Would you rather wait while I fetch the horses?"

"No—No, I'll make it, I guess. Hang hold of me—Now then!"

They lurched on again and he wondered at her pluck, at the unexpected strength she had found for them. And then his mind quit all attempts at coherence and he was conscious of only an interminable lifting and lowering of legs that no longer had any feeling, of dragging feet that were like mud-gripped anchors.

A shallow creek purled underfoot now, swirling and gurgling around obstructions, and the cold wet feel of it

254

partially roused him. He tried to be of some help to himself as the girl carefully guided him over and around the slipperiest stones.

They stumbled out of the water at last and onto a shelving beach, and heard the near-by nicker of horses. There was a smell of damp and growing things and the night seemed not so dark as it had been.

"We're almost there," Panchita said. "Just a few more steps—just behind that brush over there to the right"; and he went staggering after her through the wet branches and through the dark slit in the canyon wall.

The horses made whinnying sounds of welcome. The girl struck a match and found a candle stump in a bottle, and lit it. He saw the horses then, a pair of them. Chesty sorrels. They were penned in a corner roped off for them, and there was baled hay spilled on the ground about them; and these familiar smells of hay and horses gave to the place a homey feeling that was infinitely soothing.

There was a welter of blankets dumped in a corner and Panchita helped him over there, and his knees let go and dropped him onto them. He smiled tiredly, his cheeks faintly edged with color, that he was so little able to control his actions. And Panchita said, "Rest. God will look out for you. I will find Tio Felix and bring——"

That was all Tune heard. Exhaustion had its way with him. Sleep drugged his eyes and he heard no more. He did not hear the girl saddle or go; he did not know how she first stood and looked at him, or how changed and reserveless her eyes then became before she turned away, oddly wistful, and left him.

IT WAS late afternoon when Tune opened his eyes. His body felt like it had been through a rock crusher and pain knifed through him when he moved his cut arm, but his head—thank God!—was clear at last.

He placed the time by the look of the sunlight spilling in through the slit in the wall. It filled the cavern with a mellow glow that was like the intensified flare of a lantern. He guessed it was probably the restive stomping of the gelding which had roused him.

But it wasn't.

His first intimation of danger came when he, very carefully, started to get up. A booted weight ground the shale of the floor. A man's voice said, "Take it easy, bucko. You ain't goin' no place."

The jerked turn of Tune's shoulders was hard enough and quick enough to send hot pain rushing through his arm. And what he saw pulled his breath up short.

There were two men watching him, flanking the speaker. The man who had spoken Tune knew by sight. A wire-thin shape in a pinto vest with two forty-fours strapped around his middle—a very hard customer. Loma Jack Marana was the name he went by. He'd been a one-time boss of the border dope runners, though right now he wore a deputy's badge and was palpably enjoying the airs that went with it.

Light yellowed his cheek bones and threw back its brightness from cat-lidded eyes that were tawny and watchful and aglint with amusement. He said, "I'll take that gun you got stuck in yore pants, Tune."

Tune shrugged, saying nothing. He made no move to produce it.

Loma Jack rolled a smoke with his cat-sly eyes going over Tune blandly. He said, "Skeet, go get it," and one of the gun toughs siding him slid forward and got it and went sneeringly back with it.

Tune, still motionless, appeared outwardly calm and wholly indifferent.

Loma Jack raked Tune with his hard yellow eyes. "Takes a heap of imaginin'," he said, "to fit some guys to their reps around here." Then he said in his quick, sharp, arrogant way: "Where's the girl?"

"What girl?"

"Come on—come on," the gun boss growled. "Do I got to fetch you a look at her picture?" He sifted a handful of grit and said, "When I shove you a question, by God you answer! Get off them blankets!"

Tune got up, but he managed it badly. He did not quite smother the groan that came out of him.

"You're liable to have somethin' to groan about if you don't git that jaw to workin'. Where-at's that girl?"

Tune shook his head. He said reasonably, "If you mean the McClain girl . . .?"

Loma Jack just looked at him. "Okey," he said. "By God, if you want it the hard way, bucko—I guess you better be showin' him that charm, Skeet."

The fat-faced Skeet moved up to Tune again.

"Look here," he said, thrusting out his left hand; and when Tune looked, Skeet hit him. Between the eyes and it wasn't a love pat.

When Tune got his eyes pried open again he was flat on his back on the lumpy floor staring up at a roof that was swinging in circles. His face was wet, and his hair and shirt, and he knew how come when he saw Skeet chuck a bucket in the corner.

The gun boss said, "You better be givin' a little thought to this, bucko."

The man's hardcases grinned, and Tune painfully got himself off the floor and it wasn't just acting that made him groan this time.

Loma Jack smiled pleasantly. "Where's the girl, Mister Tune?"

Tune dragged his good hand across his face and wished Loma Jack's wiry shape would quit jumping. Then the three shapes presently settled into focus, but the place where Skeet had hit him felt raw and bloated. He put careful fingers up to it gingerly and almost passed out from the blinding pain of it. When the gun boss' face got still again Tune looked at the blood on his fingers and winced.

Loma Jack said: "You goin' to talk, or ain't you?"

"I don't know where she is," Tune said.

"You come here with her——"

"But I was out when she left."

"I expect you could guess where she went if you tried, mebbe."

Tune said nothing.

Anger darkened Loma Jack's lean cheeks. He looked at the fat-faced Skeet and nodded.

Skeet stepped over. A grin tugged his lips.

Tune said, "If you smack me again you better make it damn final."

"Now look," Loma Jack said earnest like. "I could kill

257

you as easy as guttin' a slut. But what would be the good in it? I got nothin' ag'in' you, personal. So here's what I'll do. I'll make you a trade. You give me your word to get out of the country—an' tell me where that damn girl has gone—an' you can climb on that geldin' an' get the hell out of here."

His cat-yellow eyes went over Tune carefully. "Well? What you say? Is it a deal?"

"I don't make deals with polecats."

Color crept blackly through the gun boss' cheeks. Flame flecks showed in the narrowed eyes and his jaw came forward heavily, angrily. Standing that way he made a dark crouching wedge against the refracted sun glow; there was in the fixity of his posture a quality that was more ominous than any spoken threat. His fists splayed out above the butts of his pistols and he looked in that moment exactly what he was, a killer who killed for the sheer lift it gave him.

He began to shake with the passion inside him.

His right hand dipped, whisked a gun from leather. He stood like that with his whole face working and the heavy six shooter waggling in his hand. "By God," he snarled, "you ain't a-goin' to have her! You got one slut an' she's enough for you! That blue eyed tidbit belongs to me an' by God I'll have her! I been chasin' round after her long enough. If I don't get her then I swear t' Christ there won't nobody get her! An' that goes fer Jess Crowly, too, by God!"

Tune heard his wild talk without remark. The man's whole shape was shaking. Sweat was a shine on that writhing face and the veins at his temples were swollen and purple. His bloated face was not an arm's length from Tune; and, outside, the sun shone bright and warm and the creek ran its joyful way, softly gurgling. Here in this glowing cliffside pocket the flies were droning their interminable song, and the chestnut gelding was restively stamping his unshod feet and hopefully waiting for the time when freedom would send him whirling out over the desert miles.

But there was no freedom possible for the man who stood in Dakota Tune's boots; and Tune knew that.

258

There was just the bare chance of a few more hours before some gun, or the law, finally got him. Yet he found in retrospect that life was still precious, still something to be cherished and fought for; and he brought his right hand naturally up from the waist and brushed his moist cheeks with the back of it. And he observed the set placement of Loma Jack and his gun-dogs, and he felt the hot wind that kept flapping the pages of a yellowed paper; and then he sent that raised arm in an outward arc that quit like a rock against Skeet's fat face and sent the man staggering across the floor. And Tune's other arm, that pain-shot left one, came up like a mallet, unsettling the aim of Loma Jack's pistol; and Tune seized that pistol and wrenched it away from him as the man doubled up with Tune's knee in his crotch. Tune, whirling then, brought that seized gun across the third man's face in a vicious swipe that wilted him down like a tallow candle.

The gun boss caught his breath and his balance. Curses spilled from his writhing lips and he clawed his second gun out of its leather; and the bloody-faced Skeet, half across the room, came onto a knee with a lifting pistol; and the gelding reared, squealing, in a frenzy of terror while sixguns crashed and bullets whined in ricochet and the weaving shadows of men's frantic shapes played out the pattern of foreordained fate.

Crouching, Tune dived for the sunlit portal, for that water-cut gash in the standstone wall. The gun boss' pistol bucked in his hand, that shot brushing blood from Tune's ear to his cheekbone; and Tune knew then how unlikely it was that he ever would really get out of this, but he fought on, working his trigger till the gun clicked empty, firing into that smoking maelstrom.

He was a lone, crouched shape bluely wreathed in gunsmoke whose bared teeth gleamed through bitter lips. He shot to kill and he shot without mercy. These men's only code was kill or be killed; they knew nothing else, cared for nothing better. They were border vermin—breed of the chaparral; and all Tune's thoughts in that hideous moment were for the one who waited in trust that he would save her, that yellow haired girl back at Clover Cross.

259

He fired till his gun clicked empty; and he saw the fat Skeet suddenly wilt in his tracks and spill grotesquely through the swirls of powder smoke. He saw Loma Jack drop behind baled hay, horribly cursing, epileptically mouthing; and he waited no better chance. He flung himself through that brush-grown slit, tumultuously he went through it and out into the hot sun-gilded open, and found it good just to be alive.

Three ground hitched horses were not ten feet off, the mounts of Loma Jack and his crew. The animals looked up expectantly, one swinging its head down and pawing at the ground. Tune looked them over, swiftly noting their points. He picked the one that was pawing, the apron-faced bay. He would chouse off the others, drive them with him to choke off at the start any chance of pursuit. Then he shook his head, remembering the chestnut gelding, the big-boned sorrel, that was still in the cave for Loma Jack to use if he were still in shape to climb into a saddle.

So Tune started for the horses, fumbling his shell belt to find fresh loads. He could still hear Loma Jack's vicious cursing. The man was alive yet, anyway.

He had just shoved the last load into his pistol and was beside the forward-pricked ears of the bay. He was lifting a hand to reach for the horn when a group of riders burst round the bend. They saw him and yelled, and one loud voice, Lou Safford's bull bellow, sailed against the rocks and the whole bunch started triggering.

The bay jerked once and dropped dead in its tracks.

19

WHEN HE saw that shudder writhe through the bay's frame, even before the struck animal started to fall, Tune knew this was it—the end of the trail. With Loma Jack, or one of Jack's gun throwers, due any moment to burst out of that cavern, with Safford's bleach-eyed wolf-pack deputies avidly watching him over their gun sights, nobody had to tell Tune he was licked. He stood there, upright, beside the bay's body and saw the end of all he had run from, the end of each dream, of each thing he had fought for; and he realized then what a fool he had been. He should have known he was whipped from the very start. This was the end Blackwell Stokes had planned for him, the end of a fugitive, the gunsmoke payoff. The inevitable end of an owlhoot rider.

He would have surrendered then but for the chessy-cat grin on Lou Safford's face.

This was Lou's proud moment. This afternoon's work would reinstate him in the eyes of all those who had seen him humbled. Tune stood trapped, straight and plain in the open, and by his rock Lou grinned derisively. He had been a long while on this fellow's trail, all the way from faroff Atchison, but now he was come up with him; the end was in sight and it looked good to Lou. Out here in the brush Lou could make the account balance. These weren't cattlemen, these men who rode with him; they were a breed of the chaparral—gun toughs, vultures, and would care precious little what happened to Tune. They would care no more than they cared for justice, for the even break, for the rules that guided more solid citizens. Tune was nothing but cash in their pockets, and he would not be that until they had him dead.

A few looked at Safford and Safford nodded. Lead sang its song through the evening sun.

Thoughts come sometimes faster than light, and that was the way it was with Tune as he stood and watched the bay horse fall. He had his small regrets in that moment and he thought of the girl; and then the guns started pounding the cliffs again and he dropped by the horse and raised his pistol.

Lou's men on their horses made mighty good targets until he had hammered a pair from their saddles; then panic jumped in and changed that charge through a brainless milling into headlong flight. But even as Lou's men whirled crazed horses, a gun began blasting from the brush back of Tune. Its lead hit the bay like blows from a cleaver. Lou's men took heart and came back to their purpose. Tune, counting himself already dead, whirled up on his feet and flung two shots at the cavern portal. Loma Jack went suddenly back out of sight with his mouth spread wide in a soundless yell.

Like a flash Tune ducked and rolled for cover. Lead snapped brush all around his body and, twice, slugs ripped gouts out of his chaps. Then he was back of a rock and jamming fresh loads in his smoking pistol.

Safford's men grabbed the lull to fling down off their horses. They dropped out of sight behind nearest cover, melting like dew under the lash of sun. Tune lifted his head two inches and saw nothing. He drew a deep breath into his sweat-streaked body and lifted his head a full half hand higher.

"Come out of there, Tune," Safford yelled. "Come out of there!"

Tune said dryly, "Come get me." And he peered again, cautiously, around his rock and through the ferned foliage of a low mesquite. But no men showed but the two he had dropped in that first swift exchange, and these did not show any prevailing interest.

"What's the matter with you—scared?" Safford taunted.

"You bet!" Tune said. "I'm scared you ain't going to get out of this, Lou."

"If you'd get up onto your hind legs and fight——"

"I'll get up any time you want to stand with me. I'm not worrying much about them rats you've got with you, but any time you want to make——"

"Words!" Safford scoffed. "I come out here hunting a hell-bending sheriff-killer, and all I find is a goddam windbag! You better come out of there while you're able."

Tune could hear him whispering with some of his outfit. Came the sound of a hard-galloped horse, swiftly fading; and Tune wondered uneasily where and for what Lou had sent that man dashing. His arm ached intolerably. He cuffed the sweat from his eyes with torn knuckles.

This was it, all right. This was going to be it unless he found some way of getting out of here pronto. There was a cold in his bones that the sun didn't get to, and he found himself kind of wondering about that. He had never felt premonition so keenly.

Then, across this thinking, stole the piquant features of the blue eyed gitana; and he wondered if she had found Tio Felix and whether she had made the sheep boss see how these crooked sons were using him, were using his hatred of Clover Cross to help them smash that grand old ranch. Very probably, Tune thought, he would never know. Just another unsolved mystery. Just one more of those things for the mind to pick at, like that one fleeting glimpse of stark emotion he had caught in the eyes of the yellow haired Larinda. So plain he could remember her! So vividly he could yet see that look that had been in her eyes as she had stared down upon the lifeless clay of her brother stretched stark and still on the spur-scarred planks of the Crockett House porch.

Thought of the girl brought fresh sweat to Tune's cheeks. No telling what deviltry Crowly was hatching. Having set his new sheriff to tracking down Tune, he was not of the kind to be lolling idle. Even now he might be raiding Clover Cross, might be gutting the place, bent on ruining it utterly to serve as a warning for other stubborn ranchers. But, romantic and fine as the old spread was, it was no feeling for the ranch that shaped Tune's look. It was plight of the girl, of yellow haired Larinda so slim and straight in the face of odds; it was of the undreamed lengths to which Crowly might go . . . of the things he might do . . . of the shame——

"*God!*" Tune breathed, and it was like a prayer. It was a desperate wail flung against these winds—against these winds of adversity, against the creek's gurgling racket and the suddenly increased sound of gunfire that was sweeping from Lou's snarling wolfpack.

They were coming for him now. They were stealthily creeping through the grasses, creeping round the boulders, creeping through the branches—maybe even through the gurgling waters of the creek; creeping, creeping, with all a spider's noiseless stealth suddenly to pounce and sink their fangs in him, to close his eyes while the sun was bright and warm overhead and the earth beneath

263

his shape was moist and smelling of green things growing . . .

The sparkling creek ran shining past and in his veins
Tune's blood turned cold and sluggishly moved like boot-
churned slush; and a crazy impulse jerked him up and
muscular reaction grabbed him suddenly and flung him
headlong through the brush and toward that half screened
gash of the cavern he had so lately left with the hope of
freedom. It was a desperate long-odds chance for a horse
that was sending him back, the last-hope chance of a
man long doomed.

He scoffed at himself, for the sorrel was dead. It *had*
to be—in his heart Tune knew it. What horse could have
lived through such leaden hail as had ricocheted off
those rocky walls with Tune and Jack's gun hawks shooting it out?

He dashed for the cavern anyway, well knowing the
chance he took in this. There was no chance at all back
there in the rocks on that shelving beach. Sheer amaze
must have frozen Lou's men in their tracks. They let
him get almost out of their sight before their guns started
up again.

If that horse still lived—that sorrel gelding—and Tune
could get a leg over its back . . .

Thought of that animate barrel under him, of the joy
of those fast legs bearing him off, brought new life to
Tune's leaden limbs. By the narrow cleft of the cavern's
entrance he whirled and loosed a couple more shots, and
saw one man throw his arms out wildly. Then he jumped
Loma Jack's sprawled moveless shape and threw himself
inside the portal, and change in light for an instant
stopped him with his back hard shoved against the nearest wall. The place swung into grim focus and he glimpsed
the fat Skeet on two knees and an elbow trying to stuff
fresh shells in a pistol.

The man jerked up the gun and fired.

Tune saw the flame gout out of its muzzle. But the shot
jarred off and rock dust dribbled down from the roof as
Tune's lifted boot took the man in the throat and
slammed him into his rising partner. Both men went down
in a squirming heap and the squirmer, the bloody-faced

man Tune had hit on the head, was too fight drunk to leave
it there and madly reached for the gun Skeet had dropped.

Tune let him have it—and a bullet with it, and the man's
long shape folded floorward loosely. Hard on the heels
of this man's fall a volley came racketing through the portal, and somebody outside yelled like a maniac, and a second gunblast shrilled through the cleft and knocked chips
off the sandstone walls.

It was then Tune's glance found the sorrel gelding and
he knew he had swapped the witch for the devil. He had
bent all his hopes of escape on this horse, and there the
horse lay, dead with glazed eyes on the cavern floor.

For a moment Tune stood with his look gray and
bleak. The bones of his knotted fists showed whitely. He
was trapped beyond hope. His own scuffed boots had
brought him here, his own battered flesh and unbending
will. But these could not get him out of this place. Safford's men could sit back and wait till hell froze; they had
him now and they knew it this time. They could bottle him here till starvation killed him, till he died of thirst
or of his own bitter thinking. They could lie in the cool of
the chaparral's shade and let plain madness do their work
for them.

For a man could *go* mad trapped like this!

But what of that girl with the golden hair whose first
glimpsed look had brought him here?—whose desperate
straits had hired his gun?—whose pride and pluck had
sowed the seed whose growth had snared and kept him
here?

What now of *her*? She could not wait!

And what of that other—that gypsy waif whose pluck
had twice saved Tune's own life?—whose eyes were the
blue of angel eyes . . .

With mouth awry Tune bitterly cursed.

20

THE WOLVES sat down in the chaparral to wait and Tune could hear their snarling voice sounds. These told him plain he had cut his stick too short this time.

The sun went down red as flame in the west and the sawtoothed peaks turned the color of blood. Tune's sunken eyes, deep pouched in misery, looked around the cave and uncaringly saw the sprawled dead shapes; and he lurched against the wall and leaned there. A great weariness gripped him, a lethargy that took no account of time or need. He was a dead man—the one dead man who hadn't fallen. The one dead man doomed to go on thinking and feeling and caring, doomed to go on fighting though his hour had come.

His glance touched and left the last man dropped. It fastened on the fat-faced Skeet between whose eyes the hair was smeared in a wanton streak and clotted there like an actor's mask. The feel of those eyes was like a curse as they followed Tune round while he picked up the guns and flung them into the outside brush. The fat man almost cried when the last gun fell beyond his reach.

Tune went to him then and patched him up, what little he could, though the man's only thanks was that black look of hate that burned like peat in his unwinking gaze. Half of the lead Skeet packed would have killed other men. But this obese Skeet was like a broken-backed snake he would strike if chance offered. In the venomous mind behind those eyes there was no other thought, no better wish.

Tune stood there too dog-tired to think and heard the wrangling snarls of Lou's men without even trying to make sense of them. Why had the man he had fought last night been so intent on killing the blue eyed gitana? He *had* tried to *kill* her; it *might* have been him who had tried before. Outside the walls of Madam Belladine's brothel. In the blue shadowed doorway of Riske Quentin's cantina.

But *why?*

What could that little gitana know that should make her death so imperative to him? Did she know *anything?* Or was the reason, rather, in something she had done to him, or in some thing she had failed to do?

Tune felt the two buttons that were in his chaps pocket. He fetched them out and stared at their round red shapes in his palm. Two hand carved buttons of dark mesquite wood. Alike as two peas.

With a grunt Tune put them back in his pocket and filled the emptied loops of his belt from the long row of shells that gleamed in Jack Marana's. He dragged off his hat and pitched it aside and put Loma Jack's soiled hat on his head. He peeled off his vest and painfully wriggled out of his shirt. He replaced these also from the dead outlaw's garb.

The dying Skeet came up on an elbow and his twisted lips drew back in a sneer. "Ain't you goin' to put on the dead man's boots?"

"Why not?" Tune grunted, and made the swap.

"*They* won't git you out of this." He leered at Tune wickedly. "You're a cooked goose, boy—cooked for a gal that wouldn't turn a hand for you! Cooked by the same kinda smile that cooked Jack—Oh, she had him throwin' his weight around, too, till Jess showed him what a damn fool he was. Jess'll tame her—but *you* won't be around to see it."

Skeet laughed through the clogging blood in his throat, laughed till the tears rolled down his fat cheeks. But Dakota, after that first quick look, discounted it all for the work of venom, for the feverish imaginings of a twisted mind. He would not believe such hate ridden words. Maybe she *had* tried to hire Jack's guns—it was convincing proof of her desperation; but that she could see any— "Phah!" Tune grimaced. She was not the one to trade herself like a stinking Judas for a sackful of coins! She had no call to sell herself, to pass out her favors for a little help. A man's help was her due, it was a man's acknowledgment of her high character, of her sweetness and goodness, resolution and pluck.

Skeet's talk was wild. It sprang from a plain wish to hurt Tune—that was it! From the man's wicked wish to make Tune think he had thrown away his chance to help out a woman who wasn't worth helping . . .

Tune suddenly spun with eyes gone narrow and stared intently toward the last shine of sun where it gilded the thorny brush by the passage. One word from that outside welter of talk had cut through his thinking. One word.

Dynamite!

It had been Lou's voice that had used the word. Lou's voice, quick and terse with command; and now another rider was pelting off, was clattering over the creekside shale and pounding away to do Lou's bidding.

Dynamite!

That was the answer. That was how they aimed to be rid of him.

That was Lou, all right. That was Lou every time. Play it safe! Lou could polish Tune off very neatly with dynamite. Dynamite would not tie Lou to it. He should have expected smart Lou to think of that. He would call on Tune to surrender and, when Tune refused to come walking out to him, he would throw his bundle of yellow sticks and the result would be all anyone could ask for. It would be the same if Tune *did* surrender. For they would then pin Loma Jack's death on him—a deputy killed in performance of duty.

The game was Lou's any way you played it.

Tune turned with a shrug and met Skeet's eyes. "They're bringing in dynamite," he said. "Fetchin' it up from one of the abandoned mines. If you want to get out of this I'll give you a hand——"

Skeet grinned. "Not on your life! I wouldn't miss this for a million dollars! I'll be right here with you. I want to *see* you die!"

Tune said with a snort, "You don't think I'll wait for it, do you?"

"You'll wait all right. I'm goin' to see that you do!"

"Yeah?"

"You know it! First try you make to get yourself out of here I'm goin' to shout my damn head off. Get it?"

Tune looked at the man and Skeet's twisted lips curled back off his teeth.

"I've got you pegged, boy. You don't fool me! You're tougher than fish eggs rolled in sand—but there's a soft streak in you. You been raised too good. An owlhooter's got to take care of his chances; he can't go soft like you done for that girl. You can glare your damn head off but you *can't down a man that's unarmed in cold blood.*"

He lay back with that blood-choked gurgling laugh. "You wasn't cut out for a owlhooter, boy. You ain't got the guts to take a gun now an' finish me!"

It was true, Tune realized. Skeet had called the turn.

21

TUNE STARED out into the gathering dusk.

It would soon be dark. If night beat the man who had gone for that dynamite——

Night didn't.

Tune could hear the dim flutter of faraway hoofs. Safford's men, gathering stuff to build their watchfires, also heard; and they set up a cheer. They threw fresh taunts at the cavern. Swiftly the wind bore the hoofbeats nearer. Safford's men quit gathering wood and Safford's voice shoved them back to their posts again, and all was the same as it lately had been with the sound of that horse getting steadily closer.

Through the gloom Tune could feel Skeet's unwinking gaze. If he tried to get out of there Skeet would yell, thereby killing the chance. If he stayed, Safford's yellow sticks would make short work of him.

Tune stared at the man through the creeping shadows. He went over, bent down and examined Skeet's bandages. They were sticky and the man's skin was hot as fire. Yet he wasn't delirious. He looked up at Tune with his twisted grin. "Don't worry about me. I'm goin' to enjoy this."

"Maybe so."

Skeet peered through the gloom trying to read Tune's face. Then the croaking laugh rolled again from his throat and banged thin and harsh against the rocks. "Quit churnin' your bowels. You ain't goin' no place."

"Maybe not." Tune grunted, "Roll over on your side."

Sudden fear flashed into Skeet's feverish glance. "You ain't quittin' this place . . ." He said it less certainly. He said it with something of fright in his look.

"I'm makin' my try," Tune told him. "And I'll tell you for sure it's goin' to be a good one."

"You won't like dyin' with lead in yore guts!"

"I'd as soon die of lead as of hangman's rope. Get over on your side———"

"No!" Skeet said. "No! You wouldn't dass gun me!" He licked at his stove-hot lips and cursed. "It would ha'nt you all the rest of yore days———"

"I———"

"You ain't *killed* a man, boy—you don't know what it's like! It won't be like that San Saba business. You know damn well you never killed that feller! You'll be seein'—"

Tune stopped the man's talk with an outthrust hand.

The sound of a horse clattered into the gulch. Voice sound rose, excited, exultant. Tune bent over Skeet with a sense of urgency. "Get your arm round my neck———"

"God's watchin' you, boy!"

"Quick!" Tune growled. He bent lower. "Get your arm round my neck. I'm going to lift you up."

A shudder ran through the fat man's shape. He cringed away with a blubbering snarl. He said aghast: "A human shield!" and recoiled from Tune's hand like a snake had touched him. "I won't! I won't do it—I'll yell!" he cried.

"Christ!" Tune said. "I'm tryin' to get you out of this!"

"You're not!" In the thickening murk the man's eyes looked like saucepans. He drew a ragged breath. He shook his head unbelievingly. "Mean you'd risk your neck fer a feller like me? . . . No guy could be softheaded as

270

that—it's a ruse! *You're lyin', boy!* You want to hold me up like a shield for their bullets!"

Tune sighed. "I could whack you on the head just as well."

He dropped to his knees and got one arm half around Skeet's waist. "Let yourself relax . . . Catch hold of me now . . . I want to get you over my shoulder—that's it!" He came erect with a hard wrench of muscles. "Now then!

With his free hand Tune got his gun from its scabbard and, crouching low under Skeet's heavy weight, staggered toward the cave's opening. On second thought he shoved the gun back in leather. Its dull gleam might show and betray their position. Safford's men would spot them quick enough anyway.

He paused by the opening to shift Skeet's weight. Safford's voice, down below, said "All right," very clearly and a concerted movement, as of men scattering out, came upslope through the night's thickening shadows.

"I'm going to try it now. Keep your face turned away from them."

Tune could feel Skeet shudder. "God's watchin' you, boy."

Tune damn sure hoped nobody else was.

He stepped through the cleft like he was treading on glass and night closed in dark and cold against him, and he was suddenly lonely and drearily wondered where all this would end. Could ever a man fully know life's answers before death tapped his shoulder and put all knowing to a final end? He tried to think what life could mean to a man like Skeet. To these gun hung men of the backtrails life could hardly be much but quick farewells, gunsmoke and sunlight and death at the end. A fading memory, perhaps, of something briefly glimpsed in a woman's eyes. He thought life must be for everyone mainly remembered glimpses of things they had never attained.

He moved into the chaparral.

Night curtained the land like a stuck-fast fog. Like a fat wet hand pushed against your face. Like the pennies laid over a dead man's eyes.

Tune could sense the shifting of Safford's men and he

smiled enigmatically into the darkness. They would be watchfully spreading upslope toward him, creeping and crawling with their guns thrust before them like little black beetles with their heads to the earth. They were a definite pressure that was carefully maneuvering him. And over and above any other feeling was the threat of those yellow sticks Lou had sent for. Any moment the world might explode in one shattering, final burst of light. Any moment Dakota Tune and one of those crawlers might come face to face across lifted guns; yet Tune dared not hurry lest his feet betray him.

His ears got tired with the strain of listening. His mind rebelled against this needed caution, yet he clung to it. He yearned to run like a deer and get out of this but he continued his tedious advance along the gulch wall, creeping over and around and, sometimes, through the bushes. A thorny branch slapped Skeet and the fat man groaned, and a challenge jumped out of the dark to their left.

A cold sweat filmed Tune's scowling cheeks and a streak of flame left the yonder murk and lead whined past his stiffened shape. But he held his fire, listening to that shot's wild echoes slamming along the canyon walls. Lou's voice came angrily up the slope and, thereafter, silence closed like a fist about them and, gradually, Tune heard again the advance of Lou's men.

He wondered why Lou did not use his dynamite. Had Lou failed to get it? Was the man's ride in vain?

That must be it, Tune thought; and again took hope.

Yet he stayed where he was with Skeet on his back and stared toward the place the gun had flashed from. That man, angered, would be doubly alert and Tune dared not risk drawing fire again.

Then he saw a shape silently drifting toward him and the tension proved too great for Skeet and sound broke out of the fat man suddenly. Skeet's arms closed strangling tight round Tune's neck and Skeet's croaking voice cried crazily: *"Here he is! He's right amongst you! Right——"*

With a surge of strength Tune broke Skeet's hold and the man let out a shriek and slid, a loose dead weight, down the backs of Tune's legs as Lou's men loosed a rattling blast that shook the brush like a gust of wind; and shale bounced like hail off the canyon wall.

Relieved of Skeet's weight Tune ripped out his gun and fired point-blank at the shape before him. The man buckled forward and one more shot sang past Tune's face. A bullet slapped off the ground in front of him. Another cuffed a flap of his chaps.

He flung himself up the canyon trail. Three long, sprinting, rushing strides he took and was caught in the tide of charging men—black crouching shapes in the gloom crouched round them. Cursing, panting, struggling shapes with fire wreathing out of the snouts of their pistols. Dim-seen, fleeting phantom shapes that struck and swung and triggered round him. A man's shoulder hooked him hard in the chest and Tune batted that man with his gun weighted fist and saw the man's shape reel back and away from him. He stumbled headlong over another. He clawed to his feet and tried to get into the brush again but could not make it. A man welled out of the ground in front of him and Tune's brought-up knee caught him in the groin; another man got an arm round Tune's waist but Tune shook free and went plunging on.

Muzzle flame ripped and crisscrossed the darkness. Powder smell rolled with the rising wind.

And, suddenly, Tune found himself out of it. Out in the clear and running, stumbling, lurching on through the black and gusty night. Men's shouts and gun sound dimmed away.

Ahead was clean unbroken dark.

HE HAD NO idea where he was or how far he had come from that canyon shoot-out. But he was clear of the canyon. He was out on the broad sweep of desert again with its studdings of yucca and cholla and the thorn spiked branches of twisted mesquite.

He thought he had tramped for hours but the east hadn't cracked to day's coming yet. The eastern skyline was too black to see and his feet were like lead and twice as unmanageable. His legs were sticks on rusty hinges and he was never quite sure if he were lifting his feet or just making ready to set his feet down. He thought about this

273

for a while and, when he caught himself doing so, knew how near whipped out he was.

He felt pretty sure he was going the right way. Clover Cross must be off here someplace. He was out on his feet but he wouldn't admit it. He *had* to keep going. He had to reach shelter because if daylight found him still out in this open the wasteland sun would make short work of him. Of course, the sun might not get a chance to. It wouldn't if Safford's men came across him.

His slashed arm felt like fire was in it. It was swelling, too.

Up foot, down foot—mile on reeling endless mile. Up foot, down foot; he had never guessed this desert was so big. It seemed to stretch to eternity and there were no landmarks to set a course by—not even a star shone down to guide him. He made shift to count his weary steps but there was too much sameness. It was like tramping all night on a treadmill. You made a lot of movement but you never seemed to be getting anyplace. Up foot, down foot. The same pools of shadow always ringed you round, the same ghostly cactus forms and huddling brush shapes marched on with you and stopped when you stopped.

Maybe, Tune thought, he wasn't moving. Maybe he just thought he was. Maybe he had stood all this time in one place.

The notion finally took such a hold of him he got down onto his hands and knees and crouched there, groggy, looking at his tracks. He stared a long while before he remembered why he was staring. But he could only find one set of tracks—a kind of wabbling, weaving, fool sort of tracks. But there was just the one set. They were his, and none of them looked to have been stepped in twice. There were no tracks ahead of him.

It took quite an effort to get up on his feet again but he finally made it and staggered on.

Up foot, down foot, up foot, down foot. Someplace a coyote lifted its voice, and other coyotes happily answered until their ululating calls made a kind of chorus, a mad symphony of sound rushing over the sand and swiftly lost.

There was a black ugly shadow up ahead a ways that

274

Tune was sure he had passed before. It resolved, when he reached it, into a jaggedly weatherworn outcropping of sandstone. He was sure he had passed it no less than twice already; and he got down onto his knees again and commenced crawling around it in search of tracks. There were none, however—just the ones he was right then making, freakish indentations such as might have been made by Stone Age Man trying to scoop up the mental waters of a mirage.

Struggling upright Tune cursed himself for a loco fool. A fine lot of good he was doing Clover Cross! A hell of a trouble buster *he* was! Just about as much help as a twenty gauge shell in a Spencer rifle! With all the helling around he had been to, not one good blow had he struck for the ranch—not one!

Might be a good thing all around if he took out his six shooter and——

That was when Tune saw the light.

It was away off there to the left someplace—the faint shine of a lamp. But the glory of it, the hope it offered, bolstered him up like a shot of red-eye. He scrubbed battered knuckles against bleared eyes and found the shine still there. It was lamplight, all right.

He stumbled toward it, muttering.

He knew very well he could have reached it easily if the confounded thing would have only stayed still, but it wouldn't. It kept dancing away just beyond his reach, first on the right of him, now on the left. Bitterly he cursed its rambling propensities. But he kept stumbling after it, lurching and staggering like a barroom drunk—even sometimes crawling. He would catch that damned light if it took all summer!

And then, finally, long ages later, he *did* come up with it. And it *was* a light—real lamplight. And it was coming from a window. A window in a building that seemed to be a ranch house.

But it wasn't Clover Cross.

It took him quite a while to realize that.

It was so damned confusing because Ives Tampa, the Clover Cross range boss, was there. Tune could see him plainly. He was sitting down in a wooden-backed chair listening to a couple fellows who seemed to be doing quite a pile of talking—real earnest turkey talking. And Tampa's face didn't seem very cheerful. And those other guys didn't look pleasant, either. Tune could not hear what they were saying, but they sure were slinging their jaws around. And it kind of seemed like he had seen those fellows before—ought to know them. Especially that short and broad one. That gent with the dark-burnt face.

Tune stood outside the lighted window and stared.

Something uncommon odd with that picture.

What was Tampa looking so dried-up about? What was he doing here if this wasn't Clover Cross? What the hell was he doing with his arms tied back of him? And if he didn't like what those gentlemen were saying——

Tune sighed like a weight was pressing on him. He wished the damned building wouldn't rock so. He put an arm to the wall to steady it. To kind of hold it in place and make sure that light didn't go sneaking off again in case he closed his eyes to kind of clear them sort of.

It sure was downright odd about Ives.

Might be he had ought to go in and find out about it. Ives was his boss—remember? Ives hadn't seemed to care too much for him, but Ives was the Clover Cross boss all right—no getting around that. And *he* was the Clover Cross strayman. So if Ives was in any kind of trouble . . .

Yes, he guessed he had better go in.

He pulled his arm away from the wall. Easiest way to go in was the window. Wouldn't be much trouble to bust out a window.

He dragged out his sixgun and staggered toward it.

He had no remembrance of striking the window. He did not hear the crash of breaking glass. He *thought* he heard a sound like hoofbeats, and the figures in the room seemed oddly still and unnatural, like that windowful of dummies he had seen at Albuquerque. The dummy faces had looked a heap more real.

Funny thing about faces—take that dark fellow's mug, now. The way it was——

"Hell! That's Crowly," Tune thought. "Jess Crowly!"

Sure! And that other guy, that long lean jigger with the

276

ismatches eyes—that was Cibecue, Crowly's ace gun
inger.

Then somebody said, "Well, damn my eyes! If it ain't
the bad penny turned up again!"

That was the last thing Dakota Tune heard.

Something hard and hot clipped him side of the head
and he saw yellow flame gushing out of Jess' pistol. Then
the floor kind of swayed and rose up and came at him,
and the window frame slapped him round the middle; and
chair came skittering across the floor and the floor
caught hold of it and jabbed at him.

The lights blanked out in a burst of stars.

22

TUNE GUESSED rather likely he was running a fever so he
wasn't much surprised that his next recollection was of a
dark-haired angel with smooth cool hands who had his
head in her lap and was sort of patting him or something while her salt, salt tears dropped onto his cheeks.
He couldn't think what she was crying about; it made him
downright uneasy. He wanted to do something about it
but, about that time, she kind of drifted off from him.
There came a time, however, when, opening his eyes, he
saw things in their proper semblance. At least he guessed
he did. He seemed to be lying in a bunk, lying flat on his
back. That, anyway, was the impression he got, though
he was not at all sure because all he could see was a
complete vast whiteness. A heap too white for an Arizona
sky. So what the hell was it? Kind of seemed like fabric
and it smelled like sweat, and . . .

It was! That's exactly what it was! It was a sheet
draped over him; and his hands, kind of odd like, were
folded on his chest just like he had seen them fold up a
dead man's. In fact, if he'd been grabbing hold of a lily
he'd have figured he *was* dead!

And then he got it. *He was supposed to be dead!*

They had got him laid out like he was in a coffin!

Cold sweat broke out of him clammily and he wa
about to spring up, about to dash that sheet aside in pro
test, when the sound of approaching voices stopped him
There were two voices, arguing. One was protesting, shor
and indignant; the other was a full-throated growl. Jes
Crowly's!

Booted feet clumped into the room. Spur rowels raspe
the floor and stopped. There was a moment of absolut
silence. Tune scarcely dared breathe. Then the resume
and nearing spur clank warned him and he let his mout
fall slackly open and prayed he would not be looked a
too closely.

A hand grasped the sheet, a hand impatiently savage
The sheet was whipped away from his face and he coul
feel hot eyes staring skeptically down at him.

"He don't look dead to me," Crowly said, and fetche
Tune a cuff with his open palm. Twice more that roug
hand cuffed Tune's face, and it took all his will to kee
playing dead.

Crowly let go the sheet with a grunt and turned. "H
don't look dead to me," he repeated. "But we'll dam
soon see—an' if he ain't he will be! Now then! What di
you throw them shots at me fo'?"

"I have told you," Tio Felix's voice said, "we were firin
at this bandido loco——"

"Never mind the lies! I reckon I know when I'm sh
at! Where's the girl?"

Tune could almost feel Tio Felix cringe. But the man'
voice was smooth—too smooth, Tune thought. "Qui
sabe, señor—I do not know."

"By God, I've had enough of yo' lies!" Crowly raspe
Tune could hear him crossing the floor toward old Feli
and only the remembrance of the gangling Cibecue pre
vented him from going at once to the old man's assist
ance. It was hard, bitter hard, to lay in that bunk an
know that Jess Crowly's back was turned and still d
nothing about it.

But he stayed where he was, luckily.

And a moment later was glad he had, for the man cam
stamping in. He said, "I've looked all over this godda

278

place and I can't find a sign of her! She's got away, right enough!"

"How *could* she git away?" Crowly snapped. "How *could* she git away? Her hawss is still out theah. The only two people she's interested in—Did you look in the feed bins? Git back then an' look in 'em! And *look* this time! Don't come back heah without her! If you haven't the wit t' do any betteh, git a lantern an' track her down—git the dawgs!"

Tune heard the gun fighter go clanking off; then the sound of a blow—Tio Felix's protest. Crowly snarled, "You talk an' talk quick or I'll break ev'y bone you got in you!"

There was that in Crowly's voice that warned Tune. The man was in a fit mood for murder. Events that for awhile had marched according to Crowly's slightest whim were threatening now to get out of hand and the man was reverting to natural instincts. This war was not going just the way he had planned it, and the two-bit outfits clinging by their teeth to the skirts of this thing were showing an unexpected stubbornness in their rabbity refusal to do the expected. They were not ganging up on Jess. They were taking their beatings like yellow curs, and Jess wanted action. Action to make it look like the Seven Keys outfit was being forced to take things into their own hands to save themselves. Even Tune had not acted as Jess had thought he would. He had not run Felix's sheep off or slaughtered them; he had not made one overt move that Jess could exploit to his own advantage. Only the girl had played into Jess' hands; and Tune didn't know this. But he saw that the veneer of easy tolerance was gone from Jess. Time could defeat him. Crowly must force the issue or admit himself licked. An empire lay within his grasp and he was not the man to lose it calmly.

Tune sensed something of this in the mood of the man; it was in the timbre of Crowly's voice. Unless Felix talked Jess Crowly would kill him. Crowly was done with fooling, and with bluffing. He was going to batter the old man senseless; from Jess' point of view Felix's use was ended. So far as Jess was concerned he had not *been* any use!

279

Felix said, as though recognizing this, as though only now he were realizing his peril, "What would you have me tell you, señor? What——"

"You can tell me wheah that damn' gel's got to!"

Crowly's talk wasn't nearly so careful now. With the baring of his baser self Crowly wasn't keeping up his Southern drawl; even his accent was frequently missing. His words were clipped, his tone grown ugly. There was no sign now of the cool crafty schemer who had hoodwinked Stokes and Stacey Wilkes. This was the real Crowly talking—the man Jess had striven so long to hide.

Without guessing Crowly's past Tune sensed these things; they were there in the man's tone of voice and look.

Tune carefully lifted the sheet back off him but Felix's scared eyes gave the move away and a pistol, placed beneath the sheet, fell noisily off the bunk to the floor.

Jess Crowly slewed his dark face around and his cold jawed mouth twitched downward wickedly as his brown right fist blurred up with a gun. Tune could see the hammer go whacking back and the lurid flame that burst from its muzzle. But that flame went up and into the rafters and its lead went harmlessly through the roof as Tio Felix, springing, got his arms like a vise around Jess Crowly and bore him backward in a cursing fall.

Some remote recess of Tune's spinning mind knew an instant of wonder for the man's brash courage; but he had no time to think of it then. He must find the gun he had knocked from the bunk. He must get his hands on it quickly; for even now he could hear the pounding boots of the hurrying Cibecue.

He saw the gun's shine in the light of the lamp. It lay just under the edge of the bunk, and Tune dropped down and bent to get it. Yet, even as he grasped its worn-smooth butt, the lamp wildly flared to a sixgun's explosion, and his backward thrown look saw Felix teetering on buckling knees. The sound of the old man's fall was lost in the trip-hammer blasts of Crowly's gun. Tune could hear the thwack of Jess' bullets round him, but the man's ragged nerves wouldn't waste time for aiming. He was firing blindly, in the grip of fury, firing as fast as he could fan the hammer.

Tune threw one shot and saw dust jump from Crowly's vest; but Jess wasn't much hurt, he was gone on the instant, whirled away through the doorway in tumultous flight. A hall hurled back the sound of his leaving—a sound suddenly lost in the crash of impact. A gun went off in that outside dark and Cibecue's voice cried, "Gawd A'mighty!" Then Tune was at the door, pistol lifted; but they both were gone. There was nothing to shoot at.

Feverishly Tune plucked shells from his belt. He was fumbling them into the pistol when presentiment gripped him, a premonition of danger so acute and strong it was almost as though he heard Larinda's voice calling over the empty miles to him. It froze him there in his tracks, tense and staring.

Every urge of his blood bade him fly to her side—bade him larrup across the hills to find her; but he stood where he was and finished loading the pistol. There were things here he must see to first if he would truly aid her. He must find Ives Tampa and, if he was ever to make any security for her he must seek out and kill Jess Crowly—he *must!* It was all very suddenly very beautifully clear; it was simple as that, *he must kill Jess Crowly!*

As the lightning sweeps the dark aside, so the webs of doubt were swept out of Tune's mind and he saw the issue as it really was. He must kill Jess Crowly.

The Clover Cross fight was one for survival, the last desperate stand of a grand old ranch struggling for life, for continuance, battling the powers of greed that would seize and destroy it. It was, in Tune's eyes, the magnificent courage and pluck of one girl pitted against an unscrupulous wolfpack. There was no choice for Tune if he would help Larinda. He must locate Jess Crowly and kill him, for naught but Jess' death could stop this.

Gun loaded and ready he was about to go catfooting down the dim hall when a voice, softly coming from the room he had left, wheeled him round in his tracks with widesprung eyes.

It was the blue eyed girl, the gitana, Panchita.

281

23

STRAIGHT AND SLIM she stood with the lampglow back of her, with its yellow shine streaming through her hair, with her frail arms braced against the sides of the door.

Always, he thought, she had come like this, unexpected and sudden as a face from the fog. It occurred to him, ironically, that all their contacts had begun this way, with the two of them, motionless, staring back at each other. He tried to make out her face and catch what emotion was enlivening her features, but could not. The light was against him, shining full upon him; and he wondered what she saw, if her child's eyes could see through the fight scars and grime to the man he had been, to the deep solid core of him. And if they could, what they found there—if what they found seemed worth having.

It was a curious thought in that time and place. Yet it seemed to him to be of great import, a thing he needed to know; and still it did not occur to him to wonder why or how her opinion could matter.

She said: "Please—will you come now and look at him? I think—I'm afraid——"

Tune pulled himself out of his thinking and followed her into the lamplit room. Felix lay where he had fallen, grotesquely sprawled, unmoving, a dark stain clotting the goods of his shirtfront.

Tune dropped onto his knees, but the man was dead.

Tune considered this thing with his upsweep glance taking in the drawn shades at the windows.

He met the girl's eyes and shrugged wearily. Hunger gnawed at his bones and he could not think when he last had eaten. He took a deep breath and got onto his feet. "We'd better get out of here."

She stood with her round eyes watching Felix. "He was a good man." She said it simply, like a benediction, and tears made a shine at the edge of her lashes. "A good man

282

. . . but wrong. He tried to take God's judgment into his own hands. He did not understand God's ways."

She crossed herself, murmuring some phrase in Latin, and grew still with downcast eyes, silently crying.

Tune put a hand to her shoulder. She was so like a child, he thought. In her distress she was so alone. "Come, little sister—" He spoke in Spanish, and abruptly stopped, aware that inside him something did not care to think of her that way. The words were distasteful to this inner self, and he changed them. He said, "Come—I must fetch you out of this."

But these words did not please him either. They implied an importance he did not feel. He felt humble when he thought of this girl. It was odd . . . And he felt inadequate to console her. Words were but sounds, and one suffering such loss did not want sounds. Words were pads strung together to cushion life's ways for the timid. This gitaina was not timid; she had strength and character. He hadn't thought of that before; but she had these and she cried, not out of weakness, but for love.

And he wondered, strangely, if she would cry for him.

When he spoke his tongue felt thick and unwieldy. "What will you do now without your uncle? Who will you go to? Have you someone . . .?"

She came to him. She clung to him, wetting his shirt with her tears.

He patted her clumsily, acutely conscious of his extreme inadequacy. Strange thoughts and stranger feelings touched him; and he winced when he thought of Tune, that border renegade, that plaything of destiny, trying to comfort this stricken child. Tune, the leather slapper—that gunsmoke king of corpse-makers! It was almost blasphemy!

But Panchita clung to him, and he did not put her away from him though time was a-wing and time was precious. She clung to him fiercely and a kind of comfort came of this union, and then she pounded his chest with her fist. "Oh, Mother! Mother Mary!" she cried through her sobs, "—Guide me! Guide me!" And she clung to Dakota more tightly, tight as death, with her tear-wet face squeezed against his shoulder.

Then, abruptly, she was staring up at him—was pulling

283

his head down, hesitantly. In the manner of a child she touched her lips to his face. And, more suddenly still, she caught his rough face in both her hands and, fiercely, almost defiantly, she kissed him hard on the mouth; and stood back.

"I will go with *you*," she said breathlessly.

24

THERE WERE many things Tune needed to know, but the answer to that was not one of them. He looked at her, and the eyes he suddenly snatched away were haunted eyes and hunted. A sound broke groaningly out of him and he wheeled away lest she sense the cause and divine the depth of his misery. Better by far had he never seen . . . He *could* not take her—he *dared* not. Ives Tampa had put the name to him. "Gun handy," Tampa had called him; and that was the way all the world must see him—a hardcase gunman without compunction.

"You can't!" he said, keeping his eyes away from her. He spoke through clenched teeth and the words came out harshly.

She looked at the back of his head. Her lips trembled.

"I would be very quiet—I could keep out of sight . . ."

"It ain't that, Panchita—You don't understand. You—I'm a chaparral rat—a man wanted for murder—an outlaw with a price on his head!"

"Oh, but that—" she said; then she looked at him oddly and stopped. "Don't you think I could be a chaparral rat, too? I've lived in the brush with Tio Felix——"

"Living with your uncle——"

"Oh, but he wasn't—I mean, not really. Only by courtesy——"

"I couldn't even be a fake uncle to you!"

She looked at him quickly and, tremulously, smiled "Don't leave me, Dakota. Don't *ever* leave me——"

"You're a child. You don't unders——"

"I am not a child! I'm eighteen!" She said indignantly: "Of course I understand. You're trying to protect me from stuffy conventions—from what people might say—from what they would think. What do you suppose they are thinking now? Convent bred and in the brush with old Felix!"

She came nearer, laid her hand on his arm. "Dakota, life can be good or it can be very bad—life is what any one of us makes it. Life is a *personal* responsibility; it usually becomes whatever you think it is. For two years I thought it was terrible—looking back on it now I am not so sure. God works His will in strange guises, but belief will help. If you *believe* you are right—I mean *honestly* believe it— what matters it what the world may think? What is the world but a lot of foolish rumors?—a lot of bewildered people very strangely like ourselves, Dakota."

Tune stared, baffled.

As though she would clinch the matter she said, and quite seriously, "I am old enough to know my own mind——"

"Then you're old enough to know better!"

"Lots of girls are wedded and bedded——"

"Good God!" Tune cried. *I* can't marry you!" Then his cheeks got red and he scowled and fell silent. "Would you want to live with an *outlaw?*—with a fellow who's killed an' will probably kill more?"

"What has that got to do with it? Where there is love——"

"Love! What kind of love do you think *I* could give you?"

She was silent a moment, looking down at her feet. "I suppose it's the waiting that's always the hardest—on the woman, I mean. But I've lived two years with that kind of waiting——"

Tune said midway between a groan and a snort, "Come on! We've got to find Tampa—we've got to get of here!"

But she stood there, unmoving. Color got into her cheeks. "I didn't ask you to *marry* me—only to let me go with you. I could make myself useful. There would be clothes to mend and meals to be cooked——"

"More than half the time there wouldn't *be* any meals. Come! We've argued enough——"

"Am I so ugly, then? Do you find me so hard to look at?"

Tune groaned, and his clenched fists tightened till the bones shone white through his skin. A pressure of months was bursting in him, all the hard ways of his life cried out and he knew he dared stand there and talk no longer.

He said harshly, "We'll argue this later, Ives Tampa——"

"He's gone—if you mean that man who was tied in the chair. We looked. The ropes had been cut; the man was gone. There was blood on the chair . . ."

Tune thought: *They've killed him. They've killed him and hidden his body to make it look like he's quit the country.*

"Then we'd better get out of here."

But it was the girl that made their leaving imperative. He would rather have stayed to hunt for Jess Crowly—to hunt for Jess Crowly and kill him. It was a bitter thought, but Jess' death was all that could now save Clover Cross; and Larinda McClain was depending on him. And she had that right, for he'd passed his word. But he had to get Panchita out of here.

It was all kind of mixed up and complicated. Even in his mind it was complicated—especially in his mind. There was that knife-handy killer to be reckoned with, the man who had killed Stacey Wilkes and Teal and now was trying his damndest to get this girl. If you could just take the job one thing at a time; but a man never could. Life didn't run that way in this world. Like goodness and badness it was all mixed up till no one but God knew the straight of it.

He said, "Where are the horses?"

She gave him a small little smile like a child might have offered a bit of striped candy and turned through the door and led off down the hall that was like a black tunnel dug straight to the pit.

Tune followed, recalling again that unexplained shot he had heard in the town just before Stacey Wilkes had killed young McClain. That shot, he guessed now, had been

286

fired at Panchita. By that same man he'd fought with, probably. That fellow was sure out to get her all right—but *why*? What did she know that they didn't want told? What had she seen with her so-blue eyes? Who was she? No common gypsy, certainly—they didn't raise gypsies in the quiet of a convent!

Tune closed the kitchen door screen softly.

It would soon be light. The night was fled and, already, dawn's crimson banners were burning up into the eastern sky. Sunrise would soon be upon them. It was time to be gone—it was past time.

Tune's glance raked the roundabout buildings. There was too much quiet in this yard; it rasped across Tune's nerves like a file.

He moved after the girl toward a thicket of squatting cedar. Jess Crowly and Cibecue would be somewhere close . . . somewhere close, sharply watching with rifles. He could tell by the feel of his cringing muscles. Crowly wasn't the kind to pass up any bets.

Of a sudden Panchita stopped and whirled toward him.

"Look!" she cried, catching hold of his arm—his good arm. And Tune, swinging his head, discovered that Crowly had not been idle. They had talked too long. The whole back wall of the house was aflame! Dried by the years it burned like tinder. Already the flames were spreading and twisting; glass was falling from the windows in sheets; and Tune cursed. He saw in this Jess Crowly's answer to the small ranchers' lack of aggressiveness. They had failed to strike back as Crowly had wanted, so now he was striking back for them. He was burning his place and he would raise hell about it; he would use this fire to fine advantage. And if Ives Tampa's body were found in the ruins . . .

Something, whacking the ground, flung sand on Tune's boots; and he caught the girl's arm, started running. He knew what had thrown that sand without guessing and, as though in confirmation, a rifle slammed sound from a bunkhouse window.

"Quick!" he cried, pushing the girl toward the cedars. "Get under cover!" He thumbed a wild shot at the bunkhouse, well knowing the range was too great for a pistol.

Panchita let out a stifled cry and Tune, pounding into

the thicket, found her crouched on the far side peering through the dark mass of the branches, staring wide eyed at a pair of tied horses.

There was dismay in her glance. "They've moved them —the horses, prala! We tied them in here——"

Tune nodded. His eyes were sharply probing the shadows, the flame-harried shadows of a low line of timber some dozen or so feet beyond the tied horses. They were buckskins and good ones. They were hitched to a stump and the stump was a long forty feet from Tune's station. A smart man would have hidden those broncs, but what Jess Crowly had done was more smart. He had left them in sight, knowing Tune would try for them. And while Tune tried Jess would not be idle.

"I'll have to get them," Tune grunted.

"But you *can't!* They'll kill you—that's what they *want!*"

"Sure. But we can't get away from here without horses."

And that was the plain hard truth of it. And to remain much longer in this thicket would be suicide. Time was with Jess Crowly. Time was what Jess wanted right now; time for his men to see that fire and come running. It was possible Tune couldn't reach those tied horses, but——

"You can't!" wailed Panchita. "They'll kill you!"

"They'll try," Tune said. He grinned toughly. "They'll try whether I go for them horses or not. Mebbe I'll be lucky——"

"No!" There was a very real fright, a very real concern, in the dark haunted eyes that looked back at him. "I will not *let* you go!"

Tune smiled at her then, smiled compassionately. "Don't you see? Don't you get it, Panchita? This is what it is like to be tied to an outlaw. This is the kind of a life you would share with me. Buck up now—stick your chin out, pardner . . . That's more like it. Stay here now and help me. I've got to have a free mind to get those horses. You stay put where I'll know where to find you."

He patted her shoulder; shoved fresh loads in his pistol. Six chances to live if he could dodge their lead. Six chances to go out with company.

One of those two, Jess Crowly or Cibecue, would be watching for him now, watching for him to make this break, wickedly watching across the sights of that rifle. The other would be up ahead there someplace, probably in that timber just beyond the tied horses.

But there wasn't any way he could do this differently.

He had to get those horses.

It was neck meat or nothing.

25

THE FLAMES roared with the sound of a high wind. Sparks and bits of exploded planking fell through the resinous branches and set up little spirals of smoke; and one piece, about the size of a quarter, flaked down on Tune's hat and ate through its brim with a smell of scorched hair.

Tune raked the timber with his hard gray eyes. He saw no sign of movement, no glint of weapons. No scolding bird gave the man's place away, and yet Tune's judgment told him there would be a man someplace in that still-dark undergrowth, and the man would fire soon as Tune left cover.

Bitterly Tune's glance went back to the horses.

A blue whistler jerked the crown of his hat and left a new part in the hair at his temple and the sound of the rifle slammed out of the harness shed.

So the man in the bunkhouse had quit his post. Either that or this had been the second man firing, and Tune didn't quite believe that. It would not be like so good a general as Jess to pass up the timber, to have no man there to stop Tune.

It was anyone's guess but the truth was needed.

Heat from the house was like a breath from Hell's furnace.

Tune changed position and another slug screamed, dropping twigs from near branches. Rifle sound lashed from a rain barrel midway between the harness shed and this thicket.

The man was closing in. Or maybe—but Tune hoped not—some of the Seven Keys crew had arrived.

Tune parted the branches, flung a look at the girl. "Take care of yourself," he said, and was gone.

Two forty-fives drummed lead from a treetop, hammering the ground with its thuds all around him. One shot withered past his cheek; then another. He glimpsed the wild roll of the tied horses' eyes. One of the pair suddenly reared up, snorting; and Tune groaned, certain the reins wouldn't ever hold it. He drove his legs madly but was still out of reach when the strained leather parted.

The horse went into the air like a rocket.

Tune, keening the trees with bitter eyes, saw muzzle light break through a dense clump of foliage, briefly disclosing the sniper's dark shape; and Tune fired on the instant and a man came crashing down through the branches. The loose horse lunged toward Tune and he hurled himself at its neck in swift tackle, and one hand caught in the cheekstrap and held, and he threw all his weight into dragging that head down.

The frightened horse stopped, blowing hard through its nostrils. It flung its hind legs up, pitching. Tune caught the horn and let go of the cheekstrap. Around and around they went, the horse squealing and kicking, before Tune got a leg finally over the saddle. The rain-barrel rifle was bang-banging frantically when the girl, all wild-flying hair and bare legs, swept past Tune on the other buckskin.

HOW LONG they rode, or how far, did not matter. All that mattered was the gaining of distance, the putting of miles between them and the roaring inferno of Wilkes' Seven Keys Ranch. The sun was well up when they finally stopped on a low rise of ground and quested the long roll of prairie before them. A huddle of buildings ten miles due west showed a spatter of white against the dun hills.

"Clover Cross," Panchita said, pointing.

Tune thought a moment, debating the wisdom of taking her there. There was no real reason why he should not, of course. Larinda could put the girl up; would probably be glad to. And right now, he thought, while they breathed their horses, would be a good time to get a few of those answers which had so long been eluding him.

He said, "How'd you happen to show up when you did?—I mean, back there at Seven Keys after I'd passed out."

"It was Tio Felix," she said. "When I told him how Jess Crowly was using him, he refused to believe it. I offered to bring him to you so that he could see that button you found in Grankelmeir's stable, but he would not listen. He started right out for Seven Keys to see Jess; he seemed sure Jess would admit it if it were so. So of course I came with him. We were just riding up when we saw you smash that window. I guess we flogged up our horses. Jess must have heard us—he probably thought all Clover Cross was coming. Both he and that cross-eyed fellow were gone when we came in and found you. You were lying half across the window sill, kind of folded there, stunned. There was an overturned chair with some blood on it, and another chair all broken up on the floor just under you."

"But you didn't see Tampa?"

She shook her head, pushed the black hair out of her eyes again.

"We saw him through the window just before you smashed the glass, but not afterwards. When we got inside he wasn't there, just the blood—like I've told you. We came in through the kitchen. They could have left some other way."

"I reckon they've done for old Ives," Tune muttered.

He cleared his throat, looked at her. His face was thoughtful, embarrassed also. "Where did you come into this mess? There's a powerful lot of things I'd like to know about you—you're no common gypsy——"

"Why not? What's the matter with me?"

He ignored the so-innocent look of her eyes. "Your language, for one thing. You don't talk like a gypsy—you've been educated. Didn't you tell me you were raised in a convent? I'll admit you had me fooled for awhile, but you're not gitana—gypsies aren't brought up in convents. You're a Texan, aren't you?"

"Are there no gitanas in Texas, Dakota?"

Tune gave her a scowling look and grunted. "How did you come to fall in with Tio Felix? Who's trying so damned hard to kill you?—and why? Who was that fellow I saw you fighting with in front of Riske Quentin's? Was he the man that was after you last night?"

Her eyes laughed back at him. "So many questions!"

"Yeah. And I've got a lot more that I'd like to get answered." He looked at her blackly, scowled and grunted. "You got me fightin' my hat for sure. First time I see you is outside a Tucson sportin' house, tryin' to fight off a man with a knife. Then I see you in Oro Blanco, fightin' another guy. Then you're following me up on a store porch and high-and-mightily telling me to fork over a button I found in a stable. You don't get the button, but a couple hours later you go out of your way to fetch me a horse I'm needin' so bad I could taste it. And that ain't all! I give Lou the slip and get out of there. Then I find you guarding a sheep camp that's got no sheep and nobody in it but old Tio Felix. Then I come back to Blanco and you're there, too, hollerin' for help again, like usual. But first, you let out a shout that saves my bacon; then you're off, dashing into the desert, with half the scum of the town foggin' after you. Then I find you with a guy trying to break your neck. What is it you've got?" He gave her a baffled scowl. "I don't get it!"

She laughed at the comical look of him. Then the gayness faded. Her eyes grew sober and searched his face. "Perhaps it is those buttons, prala."

"Buttons!" He looked at her. "You're pretty sharp, ain't you. How'd you know I'd got hold of another one?"

"But you told me—just a moment ago you said 'those buttons.' Anyway, I saw you jerk it off of his chaps. He was wearing those same moleskin chaps when he killed Teal and Wilkes—at least, I *think* he was. I saw them plainly after Teal was killed."

"Then you know who he is!" Tune exclaimed excitedly. "You know—Hell!—beggin' your pardon, ma'am; I mean, that's why he's been tryin' to kill you, of course!"

"I'm not sure. It *might* be."

"Huh!" Tune gave her a slanchways look and grunted.

292

"I suppose I'll know all about it some day—if I live long enough. Don't hurry it none on *my* account, but when you get round to it give me the nod. It's Crowly, ain't it?"

"I *think* it's Crowly."

"What's that? Didn't you just get through saying you saw him wearin' those moleskin chaps?"

"I didn't say that, exactly. I didn't see him when Wilkes was killed—I wasn't near Wilkes when he died. But I *did* see Jess coming out of the stable that day, and he was wearing them then. I mean the day Teal was knifed. I *think* it was Jess—anyway, it was somebody wearing those moleskin chaps, and I saw Jess once with them on."

Tune sighed. "Look—do it over. Start with Teal. What were you doing in the stable that time?"

"I wanted to talk with you, privately—I mean, I didn't want to be seen with you, because that would have meant putting you under the same threat . . . Anyway, I hurried to the stable, figuring you would go there—I mean, after I left you outside of Riske Quentin's. I meant to wait in the stable till you showed up. I slipped in through the back; but just as I did a man brushed past me, leaving. Going out the back way. He was walking fast, not making any sound. I saw the chaps but not the man's face. It was later I saw those chaps on Jess Crowly. He was wearing them when he shot Wink Parr——"

"My God!" Tune said. "Who's Wink Parr?"

"He was the man I was struggling with at Riske Quentin's. He was trying to persuade me to go back home. You remember when Wilkes shot that boy at the hotel? There was a shot just before that——"

"I remember," Tune said. "I figured it was fired at you——"

"But it wasn't! Crowly fired that shot. It killed Wink Parr——"

"But who is this Parr?"

"He's a halfbreed Mexican who used to work for my father—he was janitor at my father's bank."

"So you *have* got a father!"

"Why, of course! I ran away from him. I ran away from home. I think my father hired Parr to find me——"

"What did you run away for?"

"At the convent one of the Sisters said my father had made plans for my future. She told me the plans; they were distasteful to me. I was to be married to a man I could not love. I didn't think my father realized my feelings. I ran away from the convent and hurried home, intending to explain my feelings and plead—Anyway, he did not know I was coming. He didn't expect me. He had company that night, a visitor—Jess Crowly. They were talking about a man, a rancher, who was going to be forced to borrow some money——"

"Does Jess Crowly know you saw him kill Parr?"

"I think so. I ran—I managed to get away. But I think he saw me; I think he tried to catch me. He chased me that night in San Saba after I heard them planning to ruin you——"

"Ruin *me!*" Tune stared, startled, unable almost to credit his ears. "To ruin *me?*"

The look of her eyes was so young and so earnest. "They called the man 'Tune'—Didn't you tell me you were wanted for a killing in Texas? Was the name of that man Sheriff Curry?—Tom Curry?"

Tune's look was incredulous. The bones of his cheeks stood out white as ivory.

Panchita looked frightened. She backed away from him.

"What—What have I said? What *is* it?"

Tune stood in his tracks, stiff-staring and frozen, searching her face with his blazing eyes. And, suddenly, there was a strange dismal feeling inside him, a sensation that was almost a pang of dismay.

"Good God!" he breathed hoarsely. "Who are you?"

"Mary Jaqueline Stokes."

Tune stood utterly still.

Mary Jaqueline Stokes!

A short ugly laugh broke across his lips.

He swung into the saddle and, without a backward look, rode off.

26

TUNE RODE in a red fog of anger.

His mind was too filled with her revelations, too crowded with conjectures roused by them—too poisoned with hatred, to have any room left for charity. He thought of her, yes—but only in connection with that treacherous "friend" who had driven him into the chaparral to die. He knew this turmoil for the pestilence it was, for a gangrenous passion unworthy of him but that must ever dog his weary tracks till he faced Blackwell Stokes across the glint of a gunsight. It was a scourge of fire redly licking his veins, a spark that could flare into devastating fury whenever he permitted his thoughts to touch it. He had lived with the hope of revenge too long to discard it now, or to be swayed by things which might once have moved him. Let her look to herself! Let her try out the cure of her old man's medicine!

From the start Tune's problem had been to save Clover Cross, but they had kept him too much on the jump to get at it. Yet he might fool them all, for there still might be time to kill Jess Crowly.

And he would not have to seek Jess far.

Safford, for instance, was a gambling man; there was none of that bravo stuff mixed in Lou. He played to win and he kept his cards held close to his chest. When the deal wasn't right Lou could pass it up. He had passed many deals up and, for all Tune knew, he might be sloping right now, digging for the tules, getting out of the country. Not that Tune had accomplished so much, but because Tune, despite all the things they had thrown against him, had managed to keep going. That, from Lou's side of the table, would look rough. If it looked rough enough Lou would pitch in his hand.

But not Crowly. Jess Crowly, if Tune gauged him right, would head straight for the ranch, straight for Clover

Cross. He was, Tune thought, the kind to bull his way through. Scornful of odds, Jess Crowly in the last analysis would hammer straight on. He would hammer straight on though he knew it might be the death of him, for Crowly could never admit defeat. He wasn't built that way; he couldn't bring himself to acknowledge a besting. When everything else failed, when stratagems and wiles went by the way, Jess would bull on until a bullet stopped him.

Tune was sure of this and, because he was, he felt sure dark Jess would come to Clover Cross. Jess would come to the ranch for the showdown, for the spoils or the bullet payoff. He would come if only to make sure of Tune's death.

So long as Jess had been able to keep Panchita away from Tune—and thus keep his part in Tune's ruin secret —he could have felt in no personal danger from Tune. And by this same token, all the girl's troubles—all that chasing, all those attempts made upon her life—had stemmed from the chance of her talking with Tune. Jess had figured to keep himself out of that, he had figured to let Stokes catch all Tune's vengeance.

But now Jess would know that the secret was out. Tune and the Stokes girl had gotten together and Jess would know what that could mean to him. He would have to kill Tune to protect himself.

But what had dark Jess got out of the deal? It didn't look like a man slick as Jess could ever be satisfied with the role of accomplice. A hired gun slammer in the employ of Stokes? Tune was damned if he could see Jess in *that* part. And there hadn't been any gun slamming in it, except for the shooting which had dropped Tom Curry.

Except for the shooting which had dropped Tom Curry!

Tune reared back in the saddle. He pulled up the buckskin with narrowed eyes. Had Crowly been that supposed drunken dimwit who had shot out the lights in the saloon that night? Had *Jess* dropped Sheriff Tom Curry? Was dark Jess the man?

Why, God *damn* Jess Crowly!

In the heat of that moment Tune was sure he had solved it; but as he rode on again he wasn't so sure. The

296

role of boot-licking gun thrower didn't fit Jess Crowly with any degree of snugness. Jess was not the kind to fill a back seat when the time came for splitting the profits.

Jess was a schemer. The man who could vision what Crowly saw here—and have the brains and the guts to go after it, was hardly the man to sit calmly by while the profits of enterprise went to another. Yet, against this logic was the irrefutable fact that Tune, when he'd so trustingly borrowed that money from Stokes, had assigned his lease to the banker—to Stokes. Jess couldn't very well change that!

Tune shook his head, still baffled. If Crowly had killed Tom Curry that night—and the man was, anyway, mixed up in it—then Jess was at any rate equally responsible for the unpleasant things Tune had undergone since. For those years in the chaparral—for the blood-money price the law had put on Tune's scalp!

Maybe death and Jess Crowly wouldn't fetch the right answer.

A corner of Tune's twisted mouth twitched.

A vision had come to him out of this blackness, a vision of himself exonerated, a chance for complete restitution, for the return of his heritage—for the recapture of all those lost things he held dear.

A Jess Crowly facing a jury could talk. A dead Jess Crowly was no good to anyone . . .

The vision faded and the face of a yellow haired girl took its place. "You will do what you have to do," she had said. She had put her trust in Tune to save Clover Cross and he had failed her miserably. So long as Jess Crowly remained alive the evil things Jess had started would go on propagating—would crawl on to fruition. Crowly's organization would carry them out. Only Jess Crowly's death could ever tip the scales.

With his jaws tightly clenched Tune rode into the yard.

There was a strange horse standing, head down, by the porch and Tune looked, oddly, a long while at it; and something turned over at the back of his mind.

A man, at that moment, stepped out of the house.

He saw Tune and stopped.

Across ten paces their eyes met and locked.
The girl had been right!
God's will took strange guises.

27

GOD'S WILL . . .

The man on the porch was Blackwell Stokes.

Stokes drew back, half starting a hand toward the bulge of the holster strapped under his coat. But he wasn't quite up to completing the gesture.

Tune's lips curled as Stokes' hand fell away.

Stokes' hooded eyes showed a terrible intentness. There was fear in the look of his waxen cheeks.

Tune said, "How are you, Blackwell—Still trimming the customers, are you?"

Stokes wet his lips several times before he could get any sound across them. "I—I had no idea you were out here, Nason. I—I suppose I should have guessed it though when Parr failed to——"

"I had nothing to do with Parr's death, Blackwell."

"You'll have a hard time convincing a jury of that."

Tune looked at him somberly.

"Perhaps it won't get to a jury," he smiled; and the color crept back into Stokes' gray cheeks. He discarded the meaning of Tune's words for their tone and he mistook Tune's smile for an attempt at appeasement.

The wrinkles hardened about his mouth. "Your luck's played out, boy—you can't beat the law. I say you can't go on taking life with impunity! I wouldn't have your dreams for all the gold in the Denver Mint."

His shoulders managed an effective shudder. "My boy, I'm sorry for you. I would not have believed you could be so misguided. I have tried to think of you in a kinder light. It is a sad, sad thing to see a lad of your propensities —of your background and promise, go bronc in this fashion and turn against his kind. I've made allowances for you—for your youth, for the fact you'd been drinking; I tried to show Curry's death as an accident. But I was wrong——"

"I expect that's one of the things we can both agree on."

The Commissioner stared. His brows drew down, iron gray, without charity. "A man wastes his time trying to reform a blackguard!"

"I guess we can agree on that one, too. Aren't you a little curious to learn what has happened to your daughter?"

"That lying hussy!" Stokes said: "I have no daughter! She relinquished all claim to my concern when she left my roof——"

"Then I expect Parr was out here on other business."

Tune looked at Stokes straightly.

The banker's glance slid away. "Parr! What's—" Stokes' glance came back, turned crafty. "As a matter of fact——"

"Don't bother lying," Tune said, and got out of the saddle. "I expect I can still make out to add two and two. You had Parr hunting Crowly."

"I beg your——"

"Crowly," Tune said. "Jess Crowly."

Stokes opened his mouth, but something he read in Tune's face must have scared him. He went a half step backward. He said in panic, "That lying scut's been trying to poison your mind against me!" He made a visible effort to pull himself together. "I'm going to tell you the truth! —I *did* send Parr here to hunt Jess Crowly. I was going to surprise you; I'd have let you know but I hated to awaken false hopes in your breast. I—I have reason to believe Crowly killed Sheriff Curry—I have had Parr trailing him for several months. I felt bound to prove your innocence——"

"Very kind of you, I'm sure. Is that why you had Crowly out to your house——"

"I can explain that!" Stokes cried hoarsely. "You must not believe Mary Jaqueline's lies. It was the night you applied for the loan—Crowly, acting for the Lone Star Land and Cattle Combine, came out to make me a

299

proposition. I don't know what lies that ungrateful girl told you, but———"

"All right," Tune said. "Where's Miss McClain?"

"I beg your—Miss McClain? I don't know. I presume she's in the house———"

"Then I think we'd better be going in, also. I think she'd be interested in hearing this account."

It was very apparent Stokes did not relish the notion. But he had no choice. With a plain unease he put the best face he could on the matter and held open the door.

"After you," Tune smiled.

Sweat was a shine on the Commissioner's features. But he nodded and went jerkily into the house.

Tune followed.

LARINDA MCCLAIN's look at Tune lacked interest.

"Is this the man you've been running away from?"

She spoke to Tune and the languid flick of her hand was toward Stokes.

Tune looked at her sharply.

She was very lovely in the bright morning light streaming in through the windows. Lovely, and cool with a kind of aloofness that made Tune uncomfortably conscious of his own draggled look. Her yellow hair was fresh combed and carefully contoured. The laundered starchiness of her gingham dress looked prim as her composed features and Tune found it hard to think of her as the girl he had carried so long in his thoughts—as the girl whose pleading eyes and whose promise had been so often before him through the smoke and bedlam of the cartridged past.

"Have the boys turned back that sheep———"

"I don't think I care to discuss sheep with you. While you've been off helling around with that gypsy I have concluded other arrangements. You haven't answered my question. Is Mr. Stokes the gentleman you've been running away from?"

Stokes' cheeks had a little more color now.

Tune brought his look back. "I expect you could put it that way," he said.

He hadn't remembered this room as so big. It was as though she stood far away from him. It was as though

300

he were some casual acquaintance, some chance connection she was trying to bring into her memory. And all this thinking piled up in him, and he pulled his shoulders away from the wall and suddenly all the drive was out of him. Yet still he did not feel as he should feel. He was being heaved out like a wornout coat. He had ought to be angry. He'd ought to feel resentful. He felt relieved instead. It didn't seem to matter what she said to him.

"I'm to take it then you're through with my services?"

"Your services, indeed! When did I ever have them?" she said, and curled her red lips disdainfully. "I told you the way it was, before. I'm afraid we can't find a place for you here, Tune. This ranch can't afford to hire gun throwing outlaws——"

A door opened someplace at the back of the house and a man's heavy boots dragged spur sound toward them; and a man's voice said, "Larinda? I've decided to take——"

Jess Crowly came into the room and stopped.

Hate blazed out of Stokes' widening stare. His hand jerked out of his coatfront, glinting.

Crowly fired from the hip.

Yet even as Stokes staggered back he kept squeezing the trigger of that short-barreled pistol, kept throwing his lead into Crowly's braced shape as though he would smash the man down with sheer weight of it.

But it was Stokes who fell. His fingers let go their grip of the pistol. He sagged a little in the middle and teetered. He pitched suddenly forward on his face and lay still.

Jess Crowly sighed like all the breath was out of him.

Tune knew Jess was hit, but he knew the man's strength, too, and he looked for trouble. He looked at Jess' reddening shirtfront and left his gun where it was in his holster.

Crowly's face was ghastly. It was full of hard purpose. He put the flat of one hand to the wall and leaned there. He stared at Tune and drew a hard, ragged breath and, that way, still with that bracing hand to the wall, he started moving toward Tune.

"Jess," Tune said, "lie down and die decent."

301

"I'm—" Crowly let out a grunt. His shadow weaved wildly and he collapsed on the floor.

Tune was watching Larinda.

She pulled her eyes off Crowly. She let them come full around until she looked at Tune. She said: "Get me out of here."

He looked at her and found nothing to say. He picked up his hat and turned doorward.

"Tune! *Tune!*"

That cool expression was gone off her face now. She was running after him, just a badly scared woman still wanting her way.

"Tune!"

She caught at his arm. She tried to bar his way from the door.

"Tune—wait! Please! Listen! Jess told me all about it —I can prove your innocence—*I can prove you didn't kill Sheriff Curry!* I can———"

Tune shook off her arms.

He went past her silently.

There was a girl dismounting in the yard outside. A ragged gitana, bare of foot, brown of face. A gypsy lass with eyes like a child's. *This* was the girl! It had been this girl all the time inside him. He knew that now. He understood now why Larinda's words hadn't mattered. He hadn't ever *cared* for Larinda. He had had to keep thinking of Larinda to get this other girl out of his mind.

But he was done with all that.

He wasn't fooling himself now.

He was going right out there and tell the girl so.

THE END

THE KID FROM LINCOLN COUNTY

I

Coming out of the hills and their smell of high pines with the ache of long travel ground into my bones, I sat with both hands shoved against the flat horn and took my first look at Post Oak's single street.

A teeming place—no doubt about it, and hard to believe I was still in Arizona. But this was what gold, and the lust for it, could do. Like an epidemic, I thought, staring down at it; a fine situation to sheer away from if a man set much value on longevity or good health. This, anyway, was Tucson's view of it, the folks I had talked with being angrily vehement, some few plumb aghast or sardonically amused that a button of my tender years and frail appearance would even consider putting out for such a hole.

I had my reasons. And here I was, peering down at the place through the night's blue-black gloom, hearing the hellish sounds lunging up like prodded beasts wild to rip and tear.

Lamplight gleamed from half a hundred gashes, doorslits and windows, spilling out across the yellow

dust and the turmoil that churned like something fe
tering there. Fiddle screech clawed above the lift
voices, skreak and rumble of passing wagons, shou
and curses and E-string laughter, the flurry of sho
and the tin-panny thump of a tired old piano.

Clint Farris is my handle. Five foot eight and w
be seventeen time the cattle crowd get their fa
roundup over. No kith nor kin. Far back as I can r
member I been doing a man's work—not a prou
man's, mind—just the bastardly jobs no one el
could be hired for. Missouri and Texas, the Indi
Nations. Fort Sumner and Tubac—by God I had
bellyful.

I put the bay gelding down the rough trail and in
the press of that traffic-crammed gulch where Po
Oak sat on its haunches and howled. The noise a
the stinks were near overpowering. As I passed tl
front of a place labeled GUNSMITH, three gents pac
ing shotguns busted out of an alley and got prompt
cut off by a six-mule hitch on a loaded ore wago
The guy they were after, a frock-coated galoot with
gory knife in his fist, ducked panting between tv
hardfaced riders and disappeared between the b
wings of a nearby saloon. Five frolicking cowpro
ders burst from another, whooping and yelling fit
wake the dead; one of them, jerking a sixgun, fir
five times straight over his head. The shotgun tote
swung about and tromped back.

There were more saloons and gambling establis
ments, from what I could see, than there was anythi

lse. The street was a riot of color and movement.
Oil flares orangely painted the dives' high fronts and
spilled smoky light across the hawk-faced spielers
full-throatedly barking their wares and incitements.
Just across, to the left, was a rambling structure of
whipsawed pine which looked and smelled like a
honky-tonk. Drawed across its wobbly-topped
front were the words BOLL WEEVIL BAR - JEFF
PAYNE, PROP. Two barkers out front in tails and silk
ties were reciting the blandishments of the goodies
and games.

The walks were so jammed quite a jostle of hu-
manity had taken to the street, adding their blas-
phemies to the raucous shouts and popping black-
snakes of irate drivers. I had never got into such a
racketing confusion. And then, compounding it, a
tassel of pistol-banging riders came whooping and
ripping into town from behind me. They were spread
six abreast and taking everything with them, walkers,
stray riders—even two rigs filled with giggly females
in curly-feathered hats. Off to the right of me eight
tied horses snapped a rail from its uprights and tore
off like a twister, people diving right and left to get
out of the way of that murderous rack.

I backed my horse up on the arcaded walk and let
the fools slosh by.

"Damnfool punchers!" some feller beside me
growled.

"Punchers, hell!" another exploded. "Them's
—" Right there he spotted me and let the rest of it go,

fading hastily from sight behind a pair of green ba
wings.

Kneeing my gelding back into the untangling tra
fic I said to a head-shaking frock-coated horsebacke
"What outfit was that?"

"Mark Harra's boys; caution, ain't they?"

I said, "What's a man do in this town when he
hungry?"

"You might try the Four Flowers—that's it u
ahead."

The grub cost me twice what it was worth, but
filled me. Then, just as I was leaving, I heard
couple of fellers talking about a stage that had bee
stopped some place between here and Tucson, th
bandits getting away with a chestful of silver. "N
trouble figurin' who's back of that!" growled one, an
his companion nodded.

Going back to the street I climbed into my saddl
Plenty of food for thought around here, impression
too strong to be casually rid of—like the law, fo
one, being crooked or helpless. And this Harra. Wh
was he that his men rode roughshod through th
town? That bunch had been wearing range cloth
but they hadn't much looked like any cowhands I
known.

I slanched another probing squint up and dow
the noisy street, weighing the never-still patterns
light and shadow, listening, watching the faces
some of the louder talkers, the ore wagons rumblir

through gray ribbons of dust. What I was hunting was a place to put up at.

Neck reigning the bay between two rigs, barely clearing a wagon high-sided with lumber so freshly milled you could smell the sap, I pushed the horse toward a sign that said DROVERS INN.

A careening stage jolted past as I rounded two laughing riders. I got down by the steps, dropping the reins across a tie rack. Tramping the porch I went in, abruptly coming to a stop.

It was plain right off I had walked into something. The loutish grins on the faces of the pair by the desk swivelled my glance to the sorrel-top furiously struggling to break the grip of the galoot who had hold of her. It was a foolish thing I did then—I couldn't help it. "Ma'am," I said, "is that whippoorwill botherin' you?"

The feller twisted his neck, showing a hard, scowling mug. "G'on, beat it!" he growled, and went on with his fun.

It was that, I suppose, this contempt, that set me off. I could feel the dark heat coming up through my sinews. With never a thought in that gust of wild hate I caught up a chair and brought it down across his shoulders and, as the girl sprang clear, I hit him with the rest of it. The hinges of his legs let go. He struck the floor all spraddled out.

Still holding the broken back of the chair I considered bare-lipped the pair by the desk. Their jaws hung down; they couldn't believe it. "You boys," I said, "want to buy into this?"

Their grins had departed. One licked his lips, gray-cheeked, shook his head. The other one, though, had more spunk. He was fixing, I reckoned, to claw for his gun handle. I flung what was left of the chair at his face.

He threw up a hand, flexed his knees and got under it. But it cost him the deal. Next thing he saw was the snout of my shooter looking right down his windpipe.

I said: "Well?"

He hung there a moment, stiff and scared, with his cheeks like old putty. I had him cold, and you could see that he knew it. He was mad sure enough, but he wasn't plumb crazy. He fetched both hands over his galluses and uncomfortably swallowed.

"All right," I said. "Get out of them gunbelts. Toss them on the desk—that's right, *careful*. Now get away from them."

A groan came out of the guy on the floor. I moved over far enough to kick the shooter out of his holster. "All right. Get him out of here, and don't come back."

Pretty sullen they looked but didn't shoot off their mouths none. The guy on the floor, the one who'd had hold of the girl, was a long, dark-faced jasper. They got him onto his feet, an arm over each of them. His eyes fluttered open, pale as a snake's. "That's right," I said, "take a *good* look, mister."

He never opened his mouth. Still holding him up, the blood darkly smeared across his cut cheek, they went out.

One thing was for sure, they wouldn't none of them forget this.

The girl's sorrel hair was tumbled down around her shoulders. Through that bodeful quiet I heard the breath she sucked in, felt her stare taking hold of me. "You oughtn't to have done that."

Her eyes looked big as walnuts. "I don't mean to sound ungrateful, it's just that . . ." She looked away, then back. I saw despair in her eyes. "It's just going to make more trouble, and—"

"Trouble," I said, "is a two-way street."

"Not in this town, stranger. That was Geet you knocked down, Harra's wagon boss." She talked like that was pretty near the worst thing. She was mighty upset, the whole look of her darkening. "They'll be laying for you."

"This Harra," I said, "must be a pretty big switch."

She just kept looking at me, nervous, the worries pushing hard at her. Her eyes were a brown that was almost gold. She wasn't my idea of pretty: her nose was turned up, the mouth of her too wide, and she was freckled like a spotted pup. She didn't look old as I was even. Now her cheeks fired up and I flapped into talk, asking what chance there was of getting put up.

"You better climb on a horse and tear out of here!"

She was blunt, all right, if she wasn't nothing else. Matter of fact, it was what I wanted to do; I got hot just wondering if it showed that plain. I managed to dredge up a grin.

She said, "You poor darn fool! You think they're going to let this drop? They'll bury you, boy—that's what they'll do! There ain't a more revengeful skunk in this town than that gun-crazy Geet . . . unless it's Mark Harra." She got powerful earnest. "You jump in your saddle and light a shuck out of here."

I picked up Geet's pistol and put it by the trappings of them others on the desk. I was scairt, all right. I could see better than her most of the things probably getting chalked up for my future; I ached to fling myself in that saddle. But I knew from experience it wasn't the answer. I said: "About that room—" and she glared, exasperated.

"Can't you see that your staying will only make things worse?" She clenched her fists. "I know these people!"

I knew them, too; at least, their kind. They'd work me over if they ever got the chance; it was the least they would do. Being a orphan, and puny seeming, I'd been pushed around aplenty and was fed to the gills with it. It was time I found out if I was man or mouse. I'd took a stand at last. I'd be done if I run now.

Her eyes bored into me. "I don't want your death on my conscience!"

"That's a pretty hairy kind of talk. You treat all your customers to that sort of gab you won't be long in business, ma'am."

I thought for a minute she was going to bawl, then her look got fierce. She spun away with a snort, and went back of the desk putting up her hair. "It's your life, I guess." Her tone said *Go ahead and get yourself killed*. She made quite a show of consulting the book. "Only room I've got vacant will have to be scrubbed. Scanlon's room—they only just got him out of it." She pushed the guns out of her way and shoved the register around. "You'll have to sign." Her look slanched up. "Better write down some place where your belongin's can be sent."

"Ma'am, you're like to beat that dog plumb to death. All I've got is a horse outside and the clothes on my back."

She said with a sniff, "Just another dumb drifter!"

"Ex-drifter, ma'am. Don't work so hard at it. I'll be gone quick enough if you've called the turn." I bent over and wrote with a flourish *Clint Farris*, then printed after it *Saint Jo, Missouri*.

"The charge is five dollars a night, Mister Farris." She looked at me stubbornly. "I'll be wanting it in advance."

I counted out ten dollars. She said, picking it up, "I hope you know what you're doing," and tucked the bills into the bosom of her blouse, dropping the two cartwheels into a drawer. "You may be tough as

313

a white oak post—for your own sake, Farris, I hope you are, but don't bank too high on it. There've been six gents killed in this town since morning. We buried three yesterday and two the day before. Have you eaten?"

I nodded.

"You can put your horse, if you're bound to stay, in the corral out back, or take him around to Doane's livery." She fussed with her pile of red hair some more. "You want to get up any special time, case you're still, come mornin', among the hearing?"

I allowed there was nothing special about me, that I'd get up when I woke up.

"Your room's thirteen, at the top of the stairs. I'll try to get at it while you're beddin' down your horse."

"Don't you have no help? I mean," I gulped, seeing the wild look she give me, "a place big as this . . . I know it's none of my business. It just sort of struck—"

"You spoke the right word there," she cut in, eyes turning hard. "I guess you're tryin' to be kind, but I don't want your help. I got troubles enough. You look like a Texican! My Dad came out of that country, Farris, and all he ever brung home was grief. Why don't you get out of here?"

That last pretty near was a wail, way she said it. Sure fetched me up short. "You father's dead?"

"What else would you expect of a man fool enough to stand up to Harra? They rubbed him out the night they took over his Aravaipa claims!"

THE KID FROM LINCOLN COUNTY

A voice, while I was staring, coolly said from the door. "You must learn, my dear, to state these truths less ambiguously. It's loose talk of this sort that's behind all these shootings."

II

Graveyards is full of impulsive gents.

Like a possum I hunkered for perhaps half a minute, letting the sound of those words slide through my noggin, while the sorrel-top's cheeks brightly stiffened with anger.

His tone of reproach was a masterful show of tolerance sharp-pulled over the bones of danger. When my look finally swiveled to where he showed it was more of the same, Prince Albert coat and Ascot tie, wolf's grin back of that pussycat smile.

"Who's this?" he said, like turning over a rock.

"Some guy from Missouri, name of Clint Farris." Though her look was stony she seemed cool enough now. "Farris, meet the mayor of Post Oak, Mark Harra."

He was a spare six-footer with a fluff of goat's whiskers sprouting out of his chin. Never bothered to shake my fist. I gave him back his curt nod, watched his glance take me in from busted boots to brush-clawed shirt and sweat-stained hat.

"You figure to be around here long?"

"Hard to say." Then I caught myself, not wanting to seem cagey. "Be gone mighty quick if I can't rustle up a job."

He kept peering at me, bright as a tack. "You the feller hung those scabs on that gunfigher?"

"Well," I said, getting set for trouble, "some of them, I reckon—if you're meanin' Geet—could be chalked up to me." Then, feeling pushed, "You got a ordinance against it?"

He astonished me by chuckling. Amusement winked from his look at the girl. "Where'd you find this sport?" His eyes, dancing back, didn't wait for an answer. "You done just right; that rascal's needed taking down." Now his glance kind of sharpened. "Ever ride shotgun?"

"Maybe you better make that plainer."

Harra grinned. "That's what I like about you. We got a good camp here. Might not hold a patch to Deadwood, but plenty of color if a man can get it out. That's the joker, Farris, getting it out.

"Nearest smelter's over to Galeyville, where that Curly Bill and his bunch hangs out. We've had to come to terms with them buggers—shoved our cost up considerable. Can't say we're rich but we were doing pretty fair till these mask-and-gun guys come meanderin' in."

He steepled his fingers, set a hip against the desk. "Some of the smaller operations have had to close down. A few have sold out, disgusted. Guess we'll all be shutting down pretty soon if we don't find some way around these road agents."

"You mean," I stared, "they're making off with the *ore?*"

"No, they let that through. Nearest bank, though, is Tucson. Miners have to be paid. Don't want ore or promises; they want the cash in their fists. We can't get enough through to chink the ribs of a sandflea." He scowled reflectively and twiddled his watch fob.

"Don't you get checks from the smelter?"

"We get drafts on their account with Lord & Williams, merchants at Tucson. Cash for our payrolls comes up from them—anyway, they ship it."

"How?"

"That part don't seem to make much difference," Harra said, look fiercening. "Whether it comes by stage, private carrier or what, damn little gets past the guns of these vultures."

"That's why you keep guys like Geet in your string?"

"Part of the reason." He didn't say what the rest was.

I said, "There must be a leak."

"Tucson end's as tight as a drum. If the other boys dealt with L & W there might be cause to figure something like that. Only two of us does. Crench, Bloch and Phipstadt do business with the Jacob Brothers' Pima County Bank. The others ship in through a variety of carriers, horseback, and wagon—Sullivan ried getting it in once by mule pack. These buggers top everything."

"They didn't stop me."

He looked at me sharply, tugged his goatee. The girl went off someplace and he said after a moment, "I tried putting some of my boys on the stage. On dry runs they got by. Last Thursday they brought up a load of cash. Lost it not two miles west of town."

"Looks like the insurance people would—"

Harra snorted. "We can't *get* insurance. Companies won't risk it. Every cent we lose comes straight out of our pockets!" He got his hip off the desk and moved around like a deer fly. Seventh time past he clapped on the brakes. "How'd you like to go to work for me?"

It was the one thing I hadn't looked for him to ask.

"I dunno," I said, wishing the girl would come back. "What'll I take for pay with no cash comin' through?"

Harra's stare banged into my face. "I can scrape up enough for that!" he said.

"What about this Geet? Think he'll cotton to it?"

"He'll stay at heel," Harra said. He stood with both hands deep-shoved in his pockets.

"But why me?" I said. "You don't know me from Adam!"

"Bunch that's grabbing these payrolls don't, either. Look," he growled, "I'll go a hundred a trip! Win, lose or draw. And every time you come through without losing it, Farris, I'll match it with another by way of a bonus! Can't beat that, can you?"

My thoughts juned around like a hatful of hoppers. I thought of them gunfighters swaggering through town, what the girl had said about her old man; but with pay like that I could pile up a stake. It was powerful tempting.

I looked around the dingy lobby, back through the memories of all the gut-chewing yesterdays, and the things I had done—the whacks and crap I had taken just to keep myself from starving. I said: "Who all will have to know about this—the times, the route an' method?"

"Fix that up anyway you want. I don't care when or how, long as it's soon and we get some cash through."

I peered at the eyes and them bony gray brows set squarely above them, and sucked a breath deep into me. "All right. I'll take a run at it."

"Good boy!" Harra said, and popped out his watch. "How soon can you start?"

"I'll put some thought on it directly."

He eyed the watch again, then put it away. "Might be smart if we kept this just between the two of us. If it should happen to get around you could get yourself killed."

"If it leaks," I growled, "I'll know who to blame. Just keep that Geet jigger off my back."

A door shut someplace. A thump of heels came

ward us. Harra said, "You're right," with a great
eal of firmness. "This camp won't be safe for women
nd kids till the most of these thieving rogues have
een hanged. I'll do all *I* can toward it."

The girl came in with a bucket and mop. She
lanced at him unreadably and went behind the desk.
guessed his last remarks had been chucked out for
er. Now he said, "What Post Oak needs is a vigi-
ance committee, something that will put the fear of
iod into these ruffians. It was the Lord that steered
ie onto this gold and with His help and guidance I
iall run this riffraff hell, west and crooked."

"Well, more power to you," I said, beginning to
vonder if he was some kind of a nut.

"It's time," Harra said, "to test the souls of men.
'd be remiss in my duty if I was content to sit by and
ee these thugs take over. This camp is at the cross-
oads; if we don't want it made into another Gomor-
ah every God-fearing Christian has got to take a
tand—isn't that so, Miss Quail?"

"It's gettin' pretty fierce," she said.

"Well, a better work awaits my doing," Harra
rowled. "You think about what I've said, young fel-
r. When the trumpet of the Lord is blown I hope
ou'll be on the right shore, brother."

The Quail girl didn't take long, once he'd gone, to
how what that talk had done for me. "Well!" she
aid, the sound of it matching the curl of her lip, "I
an see no one needs to fret and stew about you!"

I said, halfway graveled, "Don't go grabbin' up t‍
pepper."

Her chin came out about a foot and forty inche‍
"You . . . you *carpetbagger*, you! To think," s‍
cried in that withering voice, "I was fool enough
—" With a sniff of disgust she let the rest of it g‍
"Go on. Get out."

"Now see here! I paid for a room in this place."

"And I figured *you* for a Texas man. Texas!" s‍
said with her eyes bright as glass. She sloshed up
shotgun standing back of the desk, snatched the bi‍
from her blouse and flung them at me. "Git!"

"But, ma'am—"

"If you want to hitch up with that kind of varmi‍
you sure ain't about to stay here, Clint Farris. Hit
lope! Start making tracks or sure as my name's He‍
Quail, by godfries, I'll blast you into the middle
next week!"

Outside, pushing through some red-shirted Cous‍
Jacks clomping up the steps, I'd got as far as the b‍
tom, looking for a chance to cross the walk, whe‍
something I saw at the hitch pole drove the last ga‍
of tolerance out of me. A sharp faced galoot in
green-and-black striped shirt was picking n‍
gelding's reins off the rack.

I gathered myself. "Get away from that horse!"

Something tugged at my sleeve. I heard the ba‍
of a shot. That walk cleared like a stampede had go‍
over it, folks jumping every whichways. I got a f‍

322

THE KID FROM LINCOLN COUNTY

n my shooter as a second clap nearly snatched the
at from my head. Clouting the brim off my nose I
apped a slug toward the flash.

Somebody screamed. Some guy called "Damn!"
he horse rustling party in the green-and-black shirt
ot an arm across the saddle and tried to cork
ie with a quick one. I ducked and whirled left, was
ying to get him in my sights when someone grabbed
iy shoulder and spun me clear around.

"Drop that," this jasper said, "or I'll blow—"

That far he got. My fist went *splat* against the side
f his jaw. It knocked him reeling across the planks
nd into the yellow dust of the road; and just as he
ent flopping I saw the glint of the star on his vest.

III

Looked like the smartest thing I could do was pi
into leather and cut a streak for the tules. It was
powerful fine notion and, regardless of temper,
would probably have done it except that ranny in tl
two-colored shirt already had wropped himse
around my saddle and was pounding a hole throug
the wind with my bronc.

I still had hold of the gun, but what with the du
and all them people I hadn't a Junebug's chance
connecting. Putting it away I went over to the bad
packer.

He was a small wiry gent with a face like boile
leather. He was up on one elbow, groaning, glarin
trying to get the legs under him. Despite his hard lu
he seemed to look pretty capable as I got him on
his feet, brushed him off and found his hat. He had
mort of restraint—I got to hand him that. Some
the gab going round wasn't learned at no womar
knee, and not a few of this bunch that was lickir
their chops appeared the kind that would enjo

324

watching somebody get the bejazus knocked out of them.

He didn't say much straightoff, but stood looking me over with them elk colored eyes, opening and shutting the bottom half of his face like to maybe find out how much that jaw was still good for. "Don't believe I caught your name," he said finally.

"Clint Farris," I told him. "I'm pretty new around here."

"Have eye trouble, do you?"

His tone got sharper. "You make it a habit to go round beltin' marshals?"

"Sorry about that. Never noticed the badge till after I'd conked you," I said, knowing he was riled and thinking probably he had some right to be. "I was kind of excited."

"Anything wrong with your hearin'?"

"Now, look," I said, with the rage clawing up again, "I told you I was sorry!"

"You had a gun in your fist. *I* told you to *drop* it."

It wasn't only this. All the times I'd been pushed around other places got to churning and squirming and clouding my judgment. I kept trying to stay cool, trying to see this guy's side, but I could feel it piling up. In that bunch crowding round there was grins and eager looks enough to let me know this could be damn rough if a man wasn't careful.

"All right," I said, "If you hadn't grabbed hold I might have used better sense. I didn't stop to think—

but who the hell would when he's watchin' some jasper getting set to lift his horse!"

The marshal heard me out then looked around, presently saying, "You don't seem to have much support for that statement, Farris. What kind of horse was it?"

"A bay gelding," I told him, "with a beat-up Hamley saddle", but only one of the bunch around us gave in to having seen such an outfit, and he wouldn't own to being positive about it. Another said, "Longly, I wouldn't be surprised if this whole thing wasn't hogwash," and three—four hardfaced watchers nodded.

Longly, it appeared, was the marshal's name. He said, "What sort of lookin' jigger was this feller you claim took your horse? Fat, skinny, tall or short?"

"About average, I reckon. Face like a hatchet."

"You really *see* this guy?"

I guess some of the heat that juned up in me showed. While I was trying to get on top of my temper he said like he figured the whole deal was plain bunk, "Let's see your bill of sale for that nag."

I didn't fish through my pockets because I'd nothing to fish for. I'd swapped a roan filly for that bay about six months ago in the Indian Nations, never thinking to have my right to him questioned. I told the marshal I didn't have one. He scowled a while and gruffly asked what brand the horse was packing.

"Never had no brand," I said, feeling trapped, "but

the guy that took him had on a green-and-black shirt with pearl buttons."

I can't say why, but I got the notion it was about the worst thing I could have told this gazebo. He'd been scowling already; now his face sucked in around the shape of his teeth and it looked for a minute like he was going to lay hands on me. I saw mouths flop open and grinners grinned fiercer, but all that flint-eyed badge packer said was, "Farris, don't be around here come mornin'."

I thought of several things I might of said to him, but time I latched onto them he'd got the traffic going and was dragging his spurs up the other walk. The crowd had broke up. But some gents was still around, with a hereafter shine about the way they stood watching. Sweat began to crack through my pores. I chucked myself between a pair of batwings, burrowed up to a bar and dropped some money on a beer.

It wasn't much cooler than the planks outside, but it was wet.

Some frail in a short skirt joggled my elbow. Half sliding off the white of her shoulders was this peek-aboo deal of some thin colored fluff you could of put pea soup through and never lost a drop. Blue-black hair piled against a red comb, a full mouth of teeth bared now in a grin with a kind of secret-feeling ooz-ing out of that look that told me plain I had better get lost because, in spite of them duds, there was something damn queer. No paint on her cheeks, and things bulging out of that jumpity stare so laced with panic you could mighty near taste it.

I had come to this camp hunting greener pastures but this was a little too green for me. Gripped by confusion I was shaking, plumb edgy. Any fool would of known that was coffin bait, yet I swiveled my ears for another quick squint.

I saw him then. Big as a blowed-up toad and gray. Shoe-button eyes in the shaved-hog scowl of a three-chinned face that was livid with fury as he whipped out a knife and come to his feet. It wasn't clear who he planned to skewer—her or me—nor I wasn't about to wait around to find out.

I sure wasn't hankering to be no dead hero.

When his arm went back I went over the bar. I lit spraddled out, came off the floor full of fright and spied this apron coming for me with a bung-starter. I swept up a bottle, let him have it in the gut. As he went down I saw a door. With a gasp I had it open. Something tore it out of my hand but, crouching low, I flung myself through into a dark that was blacker than the scairt dame's hair.

What with all the racket and the heart barging in me like a battery of stamps, I wasn't too cool and optimistic myself. I'd got into a storeroom—this much I could tell by the sourish stink. Some light splashed in from that open door, but before my sight could begin to take hold my ears picked up a thump of running boots. With both arms out in front of me like feelers I skittered around maybe eight or ten barrels and come head-on into a wall of stacked crates.

Bottled goods. I reckoned it was pretty near time I was digging up something that might slow them down a little.

I could have chopped out a tune on my shooter, but seemed like there had ought to be something less drastic I could do to improve things. When the crates began to sway I knew I'd found it. I reached the end of the line, ducked behind and crouched there, trying to keep the breath from whistling through my teeth.

The clatter of boots got louder and quit. I knew they were standing there, peering and listening, waiting for me to give them a cue. I mighty near done it. A floorboard skreaked with the shift of weight, and, not fiddling for nothing, I put both arms against them crates and shoved.

The whole works toppled with a hell of a crash.

Just back of me now was the dockside door. I flung up the bar and dived through with the guns and shouts beating up a wild clamor. I didn't say no good-byes. I hit the ground running and plunged into the night.

Like the marks set into a tally book all the things I had done in this camp came slithering back one by one through my confusion to beset and confound me. Every reflex, each habit cravenly endorsed to duck trouble, stared aghast at such audacious tomfoolery. How could I have been so incredibly stupid!

These were my thoughts, my silent shivering companions of the interminable eternity I crouched beneath that honky-tonk dock waiting for the hubbub I had loosed to quiet down.

Never in all my life had I so much as even laid hands on a man, not before I had come to Post Oak. Sure I'd been tired of it, fed to the gills with inching around like a cat-watched mouse, cursed, cuffed and spat at like some broken-down swamper in a rivermouth tavern. But it had kept me alive.

When a guy gets orphaned at no older than eight, staying alive can get to seem mighty important. That kind of figuring can surely take hold of you to where, pretty soon, a man will put up with anything.

Still—

I wasn't sure now I'd not been right in the first place. Oh, I'd felt pretty fine swapping gab with Mark Harra, making out to be someone he could afford to spend time with. Now I was scairt even to recollect such craziness—me, riding shotgun to a fortune in specie! The meek might never inherit the earth but at least they were part of the observable community.

It's the inconspicuous ones that stay longest, the ordinary Joes no one takes a second look at. The forgotten people. Their name is legion. I'd have traded every hope I had of the hereafter to slip back again into that hated obscurity—and don't think I wasn't thinking about it.

The forgotten people—how pleasant they seemed,

those inconspicuous ones, but the worm had turned too far for that. There was too many now had seen and heard. That scairt dame upstairs. That triple-chinned tub with the Arkansas toothpick—they wouldn't forget me. Or Mark Harra, or Geet that I'd broken the Quail girl's chair over, or that horse-grabbing weasel in the green-and-black shirt! I hadn't even the means of skinning out of this burg, just them eight paper dollars and maybe a handful of change. Might buy a stage seat, but would they let me climb into it?

It was quiet out there beyond the dock's edge now. Peering into that dark my tongue was dry as the flowers put away between the pages of a Bible. More I stared the more reluctant I was to move even a finger.

My legs was cramping. I knew I had to crawl out, get some place where I could comb a little sense from the muddle of confusion juning round inside my noggin. I could hear the far sounds of turning wheels and horse hoofs, fiddle scrape and tavern noise, but the blackness of this alley lay as still as a gut-shot gopher.

There'd be trash underfoot but the best chance I thought would be to sashay along the dark backs of these buildings, and that was what I did. For as far as I was able. But, stumbling along through the heaved-out junk, I came all too soon to a point so choked with broken crates and splintered boxes I couldn't see no way of getting past without a racket. The gulch wall had pinched in and was too rock-studded and steep for tackling. I could sense this much.

I began to sweat, not wanting to go back, not at all anxious either to wade around in that stack of kindling. I couldn't even see how far it went; and, while I was staring, trying to make up my mind, something slapped against wood like a scrabbling of claws. A door hinge skreaked. Labored, panting breaths spilled out of a slather of struggling shapes, a heavier black against the door's open hole. I couldn't wiggle a toe until, out of a grumbled mumble of cursing, sheared the jumpity climb of a woman's thin screams.

My eyes pawed them then. It was too late to run, and no place to dash for without I could barrel past into that room—but they were too near for that. Grabbing out my shooter I looked for a head to hit, but this mealy gloom was thicker than porridge and the way they were swirling there was too much chance of clobbering the girl.

While I was hopping from one foot to the other some cluck in the next shack threw up a shade, light from that window pouring into the alley. This pepper-neck yelled, "What're you damn fools tryin' to do!"

I never wasted the twist of my jaw on him. Every thinking fiber of me was clapped like my stare to the stamp and sway of that pair of locked shapes, to the two-colored arm wedged beneath the girl's chin, black and green in a grip that was choking her life out.

I lit into him with my gun-weighted fist, busting to see the blood spurt. I didn't care about the girl. With the fury swelling through me I had eyes for only the damned chisel face of that horse-thieving son who had left me afoot. His arms slashed out. Shaken loose of the girl he went reeling back in a clatter of rowels. Before he could drop I tied into him again, clouting him hard across the throat with my pistol. He went down like a dog that's had the wind kicked out of him.

I was wild enough to finish him, but the girl dragged me off.

"Quick!" she cried, and I could feel the pant of her breath on my cheek, the frantic need in that cry getting through to me finally. "We've got to get out of here!"

That nump from next door was still yelling his brains out, but the sharp urgent edge to her words fetched my face around. "You!" I growled, and got stiffly up, hearing the thump of hurrying boots.

She was pulling the ends of her torn blouse together; and this wasn't the frail which had triggered the rage of that knife waving slob in the Boll Weevil either. This was Heidi Quail, the sorrel-haired Harra hater—her of the Texas temper that, because I'd seen fit to swap gab with the mayor, had refused me a room I had already paid for and driven me at gunpoint into the street.

I took another hard look at the guy on the ground, a hatchet-faced rat if I ever had seen one. A couple more cuffs with the barrel of a pistol and he would be about ready to cough up my gelding. I started for him again but the girl spun me round.

"Ain't you done enough now?" She tugged impatiently. "Come on hit a lope."

"Hold up!" someone snarled. But, stumbling and cussing, she yanked me along through that tangle of crates with no regard for the shouts that was churning up back of us. A pair of slugs whistled past as we dived into the dark. It was just beginning to look like we'd make it when a wide-shouldered shape speared up out of the gloom and a gun's bore dug into the wince of my belly.

"That's about far enough!" a tight voice said maliciously; and there was other dark shapes piled up solid behind him. I shoved both fists high above my ears. "All right, Geet," this guy said, "fetch the lantern."

IV

Boiling under my breath, I knew one thing for sure: If I got out of this bind you could dunk me in bean sprouts and call me "Chink" if I ever lined up on the short side again.

The guy with his gun in my gut was the marshal, Jim Longly. "So it's you again, Farris!" There was a hard satisfaction a-tramp in his tone. "We'll step along to my office." He slanched a look at the girl. "I guess you better come with us."

He motioned with the pistol and the crowd opened up, Geet striding ahead into the street with his lantern.

"What's the charge?" I asked, trying to uncover some hole. When nobody bothered to give me a hand I recollected the advice this great seizer had given me right after I'd got done brushing him off. It wasn't all I remembered. There was the matter of that chair I'd busted over Geet's head, and the guy in the Boll Weevil I'd smacked with the bottle. They wouldn't have much trouble working up a charge. Least I could expect was a couple of weeks in the Post Oak pokey.

A lather of thinking rampaged through my noggin
none of it calculated to bolster my hopes much, bu
there was no point getting the girl dragged into it.
told Longly so. I said, "She don't know me from
Adam."

Began to seem like these jaspers was all deaf a
gateposts.

When we got to the jail, Geet with his lantern, wen
up the steps first, then the girl still holding her blouse
pulled together. Be a fine pass if they claimed I'd pu
hands on *her!*

I swabbed some of the sweat off the back of my
neck. The marshal's eyes shooed me after them and
it sure didn't seem like I had much choice. In all tha
bunch of staring faces I couldn't find one that held
any encouragement. My shooter was in his pocket
and the one in his fist was peering right at me. I
sucked in a fresh breath and went reluctantly up
hearing Longly, behind me, advising the crowd to get
on about its business.

He came in, slammed the door, parked a hip on
the desk. He said real quiet, "What's it going to be
Farris,—reasonable or painful?"

I allowed I would do my best to co-operate.

"Smart boy," he said, and waved the girl into a
chair. "You can start by tellin' us why you killed
him."

I looked to see if he was funning. He wasn't. "Hell's
fire," I said, "I ain't killed nobody,"

The place got so quiet you could hear the clock.

Longly finally got off the desk. "That your idea of co-operation, Mac?"

The edges of a frown kind of framed his smile, and it was traipsing across my notions we could all come out of this considerable nicer if we'd made a real effort to stay on top of our tempers. Having lit on this gem I said, to seem hopeful, "If we could sort of come up on the off-side . . . maybe a different approach?"

His eyes stared at me across the fold of his arms while the outside noises sort of drifted away. "All right. You've got to Post Oak. Work it up from there."

I didn't know what to say, hardly.

"What was the first thing you done?" Longly asked, thinly patient.

"Stopped at a hash house. It was just gettin' dark."

Geet said with a sneer, "Then you went to the Boll Weevil?"

"No, that was later." My look skittered off the dark loom of his face. "I figured I had better find some place to put up at."

"So you went to the Drover's," Longly said. "Then what'd you do?"

My mouth felt stiff. This cat-and-mouse deal of ask and answer was running cold chills across the ends of my neck hair. I tried not to notice Geet's plaster-patched cheeks or the brightening shine of his gunbarrel stare. I said, "Harra come in," and saw them swap pleasured glances.

Nobody mentioned my little spree with the chair.

"Well?" Longly said with his tone bland as peach fuzz. "What did he want?"

You could almost see their ears lean out, waiting. I'd be no good to Harra without I kept the most of that stuff to myself. As things stood he looked to be the only hole card I was like to come up with. While I was mulling which way to jump, the Quail girl said, "He dropped by to see me."

It should have taken me off the hook, but you could tell by the quiet how much it had helped. Nobody looked at her. She might better have stayed out of it I thought, watching Geet.

"Having been raised right, not wanting to get in the way of a man's courtin'," Longly chucked at me, obnoxiously polite, "this pilgrim takes himself over to the Boll Weevil. That how it sounds to you, Geet?"

My tongue got dry as a last year's leaf. Harra's gunfighter said with a bully-puss grin, "You want I should loosen him up a little?"

Longly dropped back to rest his rump on the desk, eyeing me like he was giving some thought to it. "In a camp like this a marshal has to learn to budget his time. Now I'm a reasonable man." He tipped his head to one side. "I try to give every guy the best shake I can."

"You've convinced me," I said. "I went over there."

"Now," Geet grinned, "we're gettin' some place. So you got cozy with Dayne and he dug up this deal."

"I never saw no Dane."

"*Jeff* Dayne," he said, like that should mean something to me.

I twisted a glance at the marshal.

"Look," Geet scowled, shoving out his left mitt. When my head tipped down that fist flew up like the hoof of a mule.

I woke up in a chair, the whole front of me soaked, water running off my chin and both ears. I couldn't see extra good and the middle of my face felt like it wasn't there no more.

I shook my head and wished I hadn't. When the room quit whirling Harra's gunfighter had me by the front of the shirt. He hauled me out of the chair. I slammed into a wall. I thought, by God, he'd broke the back of my skull.

When I got back enough sense to realize he hadn't, he still had me pinned there like a bug on a board. I was too badly shook to pile much of a mad on, too scairt I'd catch more if I opened my mouth. "You oughta watch where you're goin'," he grinned.

He let go of me when he judged I could stand. Longly, the marshal, said, "Let's start again. This time, Farris, try to be more careful." He gave Geet the nod.

The gunfighter said: "You went over to the honky-tonk. What happened then?"

"I had a beer at the bar."

"You talk to anyone?"

It wasn't easy to think after what I'd been through.

My head felt like it was opening and shutting, like bubbles fritterin' up out of a bog and going *plop*. "I don't think so," I said, and saw the nastiness start to come out on his face again. "This dame drifted up—"

"Which dame? What'd she look like?"

"Well, she had black hair pulled back around a comb."

"Verdugo," Longly said. "Go on."

"Anyway, while she was giving me the eye, this hog-fat jasper back among the tables comes out of his chair with a face like thunder. Next thing I know he's got a knife up to throw. I got out of there fast."

I couldn't tell about Longly, but it was plain by Geet's look he wasn't buying any part of it. "You beat a knife?" he said.

"I went over the bar, smacked a apron with a bottle, yanked open a door, got into this place filled with barrels and—"

Longly said, "That's pretty hard to believe."

"Looks like you could check it."

Through the sneer on his puss, Harra's gunfighter said, "Sounds to me he's about ready for Lesson Number Two."

"Let's hear the rest of it," Longly decided.

I told them the truth, even to how I'd ducked under that dock. I said to the plain disbelief on their faces. "When I figured they'd quit looking I moved off down that passage, thinkin' it might fetch me out near enough that, with any kind of luck, I could make

to the Drover's. Somebody jumped
em back doors—"

"Yeah," Geet said with his teeth skinned. "To
is kid o-rate half the town's got it in for him!" The
arshal, swinging his leg, observed, "Some guys is
e that. Can't hardly get out of bed without splittin'
eir britches." He pared off a chew and popped it
to his jaw. "You got any more questions?"

"Gettin' back to the Drover's," Geet said, "why'd
u kill him?"

They had me so jumpy I was scairt to say any-
ing. Longly said, quiet, "It's a fair question. Answer
"

I was sure enough caught between a rock and a
rd place. If I told them the truth I would probably
t smacked again, and not to say anything would
rtain be asking for it. If I could have got word to
rra, or fetched him into this someway—but it was
in if I did I'd be worth less than nothing, far as
was concerned. That job he had mentioned was
pposed to be kept quiet. "Is there a lawyer in this
mp?"

It came out pretty meek but I saw the quick shuf-
of looks them two swapped. Longly got his butt
the desk. "He was found in your room, kid. Why
n't you own up to it?"

"I ain't *got* no room!"

Longly's eyes fastened to me. "What kind of talk's
at? You just told us you was hopin' to get back

341

ook. You signed for th
."

been in it," Geet said.
n than a barrel of monkeys.
growled—"I never even be

wonder why I kept squirmi
from the start this pair aimed
scuttle . . . ose hope dies hard when your wh
life's ahead of you. You got to recollect I was o
seventeen, that I was pretty shook up and that,
spite of my experience, I still thought a marshal w
made of better clay than most. When Heidi Qu
spoke out to vouch for my contention I dragged i
fresh breath and come away from the wall. I felt f
already and was working up a grin when Longly sa
looking hard at the girl: "You puttin' in your
again?"

She got white around the mouth but shoved b
back stare for stare. "He never had anything to
with it!" she cried. "Look at him, for heaven's sak
he's *only* a boy!"

"Some rattlers is young, too," Geet sneered, "
you can croak just as sure from them as any others."

"I tell you he never saw the room."

"What is he," Longly said, "some sort of da
fool? Signin' for it, payin' for it—"

"I gave him back his money, told him this ca
was no place for a kid."

342

Longly, staring, said from the side of his mouth:
"Frisk him, Geet."

Harra's gunfighter, grinning, fetched something
out of my pants and held it up where the both of
them could see it. "If you sent him packing," the
marshal said, "what's he doing with that key in his
pocket?"

V

I seemed to remember her pushing it acros
the Drover's desk, but that was as far as my recollec
tion took me. That golrammed Geet was shining u
his fist again.

It wasn't clear what connection he might have wit
the marshal but it was plenty apparent if I didn't tal
quick I'd soon be in no kind of condition to. "Is th
ape packing tin? Some kind of deputy marshal met
be?"

"Just a public spirited citizen who happened to b
along when I ran into you," Longly scowled.

"Then what about taking a couple of good looks i
him? When I first went over there huntin' a room th
'public spirited citizen' just happened to have bot
paws on this girl and she didn't look like she was ei
joyin' it none. She—"

Geet swung. I ducked. The marshal, red-face
yelled for Geet to back off; and, behind him, Hei
Quail with a hand still gripping her blouse bounce
onto her feet like hell getting ready to take off on ca
wheels.

Geet, voice filled with protest and bluster, hauled his wide shoulders round to fix Jim Longly with an affronted glare. "You swallerin' that crap?"

The marshal looked at the girl. He seemed a little embarrassed. She said, "Why don't you ask him how he got so banged up?"

"Aw," Geet said, "I told you about that."

The girl said, pinkly furious, "Did he tell you this fellow broke a chair over his head?"

Longly's elk-colored eyes began to look riled. "If you been using my badge—"

"Chrissake!" Geet yelled, "you gonna—"

Longly said sharply, "Either stop that shouting or get out of this office." He was white around the gills and it looked for a bit like Geet, all swelled up, was going to sure enough make tracks. He half wheeled to do it, then got hold of himself. "It wasn't that way at all," he growled, looking misused and sullen. "All I done—hell, I told you about him!"

The marshal peered at me again, and I thought maybe he didn't know what to believe. He sloshed a look at the girl. She pulled her chin up, flushing. She said, hotly scornful, "I always figured, Jim Longly, that you was anyways *honest!* I didn't think being turned down by a girl would warp you into—"

"We're not investigating me," the marshal said stiffly. "Geet claims this feller's a pal of Charley Bowdre, Bill Scroggins and Doc Scurlock—a back-shooting killer, wanted over in Lincoln County. One of the sort, Geet says—"

"Geet says!" she snapped. "He's a fine one to talk about back-shooting killers! You ever think for yourself? Or do all your judgments jump full-grown from the unsupported say so of Mark Harra's gunslingers?"

Longly, pulled two ways, cried, "That's not fair!" Then, probably reminded they were not alone, he wiped the torn look off his cheeks and swiveled that bitter stare back to me. "I understood, Farris, you come from Texas. Why'd you write 'Saint Jo' in that register?"

Why does a guy do a heap of things? I just scowled and shrugged. But the girl, still riding the blood in her eye, didn't look like she would back off for anything. "I don't know what you're trying to pin on this boy, but I'll swear on a stack of prayerbooks he never once had that thing in his hand!"

It was the second time she had called me 'boy'. I could feel the blood pounding into my head; the marshal and Geet wasn't tickled none, either. Geet was opening his trap when he said, whirling on him, "Any mean-minded skunk with a key in his fist can make like he's took it out of someone else's pocket!"

"That's a . . . she's just tryin' to git even!" he snarled, turning ugly.

Kind of seemed like Longly was beginning to wake up. Lip on lip like two chunks of granite he peered a mighty time at that squirming polecat. "Even for what?" he said, soft as spiders.

Spluttering, Geet went back a couple of steps. "Why . . . uh, hell, you know dang well she's had it in for Harra's boys. Ever since her ol' man fell down that shaft."

Longly's cheeks was pale as a puff of smoke, them elk-colored eyes of his shining like glass. Geet's look got a little wild, and he swore.

If I had kept still then the whole cc :se of this deal might of took a different turn; but ı cried out, just remembering, "Say! That feller back there!"

All their heads swiveled round. I said, obsessed with it, "He's the one got away with my horse, daddrat him."

Longly's darkening stare went from me to the girl. "You got any idea what he's jabbering about?"

Heidi shook her head.

I stared like a nump. She looked completely at sea. "That pinch-faced sport in the black an' green shirt," I said, "the one you was wrasslin' with."

That girl wasn't helping me one dang bit. You'd of thought I was ready for a string of spools. The marshal said, "He sounds like his needle's stuck."

The girl glowered back at him. "I think your pal must have scrambled his brains. You ought—"

"But he's back in that alley!" I cut in, bound to have myself heard. Of course I was graveled; who wouldn't be? This seemed like, to me, a chance to get myself cleared of whatever it was they were trying to pile on me, if I could prove I'd been tangling with that son of a buck. "You could anyways look!" I told Longly, fuming.

"I got other fish to fry right now," the marshal said. "We're going over to the Drover's and have a look at that corpse—you, too, Geet. You can lead the way."

In the Drover's tiny lobby the girl pulled up by her desk. "I believe, if you don't mind, I'd just as soon wait here."

The marshal's look was searching. "I should think you'd want to—"

Heidi Quail shook her head, folding brown arms across the mauled blouse. "To tell you the truth it's getting monotonous. You might as well know I've been seriously considering throwing in with Buck Peters in that coffin and headstone business he's got. Every guy in this camp that's picked to throw in the sponge seems to wind up in this place to get the job done."

"I've noticed that," Longly nodded. "Geet, help Farris navigate them stairs."

We went up to the second floor, the marshall fetching a lamp off the desk. A long hall opened up; to the left and just topping the stairs was a closed door on which, in white chalk, was the number 13. Longly, passing the lamp to the Harra wagon boss—at least that was his job according to Heidi—dug out the key Geet had fished from my pocket. "After you," he growled, and threw open the door.

I followed Geet in. He held up the lamp, watching my expression from the corners of his eyes. He slipped the lamp in a bracket. "I see you know 'im," he said nastily.

"That's dumping considerable weight where it don't rightly fit." I took another squint at the guy on the floor. "I got stopped alongside him on the street —it was when you rode in from wherever you'd been with that bunch of yippin' hooligans. We was crowdin' the walk and I asked how come the whole town ducked for cover. He said you was some of Harra's gun hands."

"What else did he say?" Longly asked from the door. He hadn't hardly been civil since I'd popped it at him to go look at that feller. He hadn't hugged Geet either. He would growl out this talk and scarcely notice what it got him, like there was something gnawing his mind that figured to be of larger importance.

Like now. Never bothering to wait for any answer, he gruffed, "Let's get out of here."

Back in the office it was Geet that took over, Longly appearing satisfied to hunker in the back seat like a chicken with the pip. If this brooding bothered Geet it sure as heck wasn't much apparent. He said with his snoot six inches from mine, "You're stuck with this, kid, so make it easy for yourself. What'd that chump hev on you?"

I couldn't help sighing. "He didn't have a thing."

"Then why'd you kill him?"

"I didn't," I said, and wondered which hand he would take to me.

"He was killed in your room, kid."

"I can't help that. When I went up there with you was the first time——"

"Kid," he said, "I got that key from your pocket. The marshal seen me, so don't give us that. It's the only key there is to the room."

"Just because you say so don't make it a fact."

He stepped back a bit and held up his fist. "You want me to knock you through that wall?"

"You might's well tell the truth," Longly said. "You saw I had to use the key to get in there."

Before I could find any answer to that the jail office door was flung protestingly open and heavy steps made the floor skreak. Geet's eyes narrowed warily and Longly said irascibly, "What do you want here, Jeff?"

I jerked one fluttery look and knew I had come against the end of my string. It was the three-chinned jasper who'd sprung up with that knife just before I went over the Boll Weevil's bar.

VI

His shaved-hog face appeared as smooth as a mill pond. There wasn't a particle of menace, yet the crackle of frost seemed to hang in this place plain as cut mistletoe strung from a rafter. Geet scarcely breathed. The marshal looked like he'd been caught in a melon patch.

The faintest tug of a grin twitched the newcomer's mouth, but nobody appeared to be finding much fun in it. "What have you got this kid in here for?"

Longly couldn't get enough spit to talk with. It was Geet who presently got around to saying I was being asked some questions in connection with a killing.

The fat man paid no attention to Geet. Eyeing the marshal he said: "Some more of Harra's back-of-the-bush stuff?" His scorn fired Longly's cheeks. "When are you going to get onto yourself?"

"One of these times you'll push me too far!" Longly flared, but the words seemed to carry more bluster than threat. He looked doughy and sick, and he jammed shaking hands in his pockets to hide them.

It wasn't till he took off his steel-rimmed cheaters, blinking near-sightedly as he huffed and polished them on the front of his shirt, it became apparent to me the big guy wore spectacles. I could see the wild thoughts juning through Geet's stare, and the wanting of it tugging him so bad you could taste it, but for all that he stood there like a chunk of stuck machinery.

But the fat man's next words woke me up. "How much bail you holding him on?"

The marshal said with a plain reluctance, "No bail's been set. He ain't been arraigned."

"You mean," said the fat man, hooking on his cheaters for a long, and careful look at me, "Geet hasn't been able to pound a confession out of him?"

"I don't have to take—"

"You'll take it, Jim." The fat man sighed. "Have you got any evidence at all against the boy?"

"I've got enough," Longly glowered. "He put up at the Drover's. 'You Bet' Farley was found croaked in his room. Door was locked an' the key, when we found it, was in the kid's pocket!"

The big guy done some more quiet looking. "Suggestive," he nodded, "but hardly conclusive. Somebody else, one of Harra's hardcases—"

"Guess you ain't heard about them new locks Heidi's put on the doors. Take a special key, and there's only one key given out to each lock, all different. He had the key on him. No one else could have got in."

352

"How'd you know this dead shyster was in there?"

Geet took to twitching like a tromped-on centipede, but the marshal's stare looked froze in his face. I watched his tongue scratch across dry lips; even then I had to stretch hard to hear him. "In where?" he said, like it had come from his bootstraps.

"In the kid's room. If the door was locked and he had the key with him?"

It took perhaps three seconds for their jaws to fall, and I wasn't no quicker to catch on how marvelous these two barracudas had slammed into the bait, caught with full mouths of the porridge cooked for me.

Geet looked pretty ugly, but what was there to say? This slickery pair had yapped too much already.

The fat guy's cheeks were smooth as a biscuit but the eyes behind them steel-rimmed cheaters wasn't missing a trick. "Kid, pick up your hat. We're clearing out," he said.

Longly stood there looking sick while I filched my shooter out of his pocket, caught up the hat and dragged my spurs across the floor. The night air was cold as we tromped down the steps, myself turned jumpy as a cart full of crickets, watching him slanchways from the corners of my stare.

In the street he stopped, then faced me square "You got no cause to be afeared of me, boy. If so be you're a mind to, turn loose of me here; there'll be no hard feelings on my part."

I was tempted, believe me. I could still see the fright in Verdugo's crouch and remember them moments when, by yanking that knife, this smooth-talking walloper had give such a hard time to me in that deadfall.

Nothing I put my thoughts to made sense. I wasn't halfway sure he hadn't fished me out of there to take care of personal. One swipe of that Arkansas toothpick could do it; and them fair words he'd spoke wasn't blinding me none. I'll own up I was anxious, but this seemed like a chance to get a few of the things that was gnawing me answered.

I said, "How come you was trying to hook that knife in me a while ago?"

"Wasn't *you* I was after," he grumbled, peering about. "Tell you soon's we get off this street." His stare kept picking at the black between buildings, and his voice came out gruffer. "You stringing along?"

"I'll take a samplin'," I said, and stepped after him warily, one hand nervously fisted about the butt of my shooter. I reckon that was childish, set beside everything else, but I still had in mind that last look a Geet, and the burning fury I had seen quivering out of him.

We got into Dayne's bar without no untoward incidents, though the relief of having done it pretty nea unstrung me. Some of the custom shoved back to make a place for us at the mahogany. My big friend called for a double shot, said, "Boy, git that inside of you."

I've never drunk nothing that burned like that; I could feel the stuff climbing through every sinew. And while I was gagging, trying to catch my breath, a hand on my arm was moving me confidently into his office. I dropped into a chair. He pulled out a desk drawer to prop booted feet, watching me through the thick shine of his cheaters.

"As you likely have guessed, I'm Jeff Dayne," he said, frowning. He pulled in a deep breath and scrubbed a hand over his jowls. "I didn't even see you when I grabbed that knife; skunk I had my mind on was back of the bar."

"The guy I slugged with the bottle?"

"No." He shook his head at my disbelief. "Pat's square enough. Grant's Pass was the bugger I was fixing to skewer. He come out of that door. While you was tangled with the barkeep, and before I could get a clean swing, he got back through it—you were right on his heels."

I couldn't help being astonished. I hadn't even suspicioned there'd been anyone ahead of me. "But that black haired—*Verdugo!* I'd of swore she was scairt half out of her wits."

"Sure. I guess she was. She's in love with the bugger, or thinks she is. My fault, in a way." He heaved a dour sigh. "I'd better tell you, I reckon. Kitty Verdugo's had some pretty hard knocks. She was born in Durango. When she was ten her pa and her mama were rubbed out by Apaches. I had her with the Sisters up to three-four months ago; told me I'd better let her come on home."

He studied a spell. "She works in this place; insists on earning her keep, and she does. But she's straight." His look challenged me.

"If that's so," I said, "and, like you claim, she's in love with this feller, why was you fixin' to heave that knife at him?"

"Damn two-bit romeo!" the fat man growled. "I ought to skin him alive, and mebbe I will if he don't stay clear of here! Just because she's a Mex. Jim, anyway, was a real gent once, but that damn Grant's Pass, as they've all took to calling him—Hell! Let's find something better than a woman-chasing pissant to occupy our jaws with. What'd you do to get that pair so put out with you?"

It was my turn to stumble around. Watching me, Dayne said, "Probably none of my business, but that Geet seems to have took a real violent dislike to you."

"Yeah." I couldn't honestly see what harm there was telling him. "He was botherin' that Drover's frail. I busted a chair over his mug. In front of witnesses."

"Sure enough? My!" he said, looking me over with a plainer interest. "Wonder you ain't got a lily in each fist." Rubbing his chins he considered me some more. "What's Longly's beef?"

I dug up a parched grin. Told him about that whippoorwill making off with my horse, about dragging my shooter and the marshal taking hold of me.

Never seein' that badge, I hung one on his kisser; did help him up, though, even brushed him off," I said.

"And both of them plumb public," Jeff Dayne chuckled, shaking his head. "You really been humping, boy. Short of pulling our he-kangaroo's goatee you couldn't hardly have piled up more grief quicker." He peered a little more close at me. "You didn't by any chance tangle with Harra?"

"No," I said, and, tightening up, sloshed a look around the room. "There was something, though." I told how the marshal had happened to glom onto me, that set-to in the alley when Heidi had come busting out of that door trying to get loose of them unwanted attentions.

"This jigger," Dayne gruffed. "You happen to catch a look at—"

"Dang right I did. An' give him somethin' to remember me by! It was that chisel-faced jumper that went off on my horse!"

"Think you'd know him again?"

"He'll be packin' the mark of my gun barrel a spell." I told how I'd whacked him across the throat. "Even without that green an' black shirt—"

"Grant's Pass!" Dayne swore, quivering cheeks turning dark. "A pity you didn't break his damn neck!"

It was my turn to stare.

Account of Kitty Verdugo, of course, he had his mind on the man; but it did seem odd him naming

357

him like that, and my description getting no respon[se]
from the marshal. It seemed uncommon strange, pa[r]
ticular remembering me telling Jim Longly the g[uy]
was out in that alley and him refusing even to loo[k]
I said so.

Jeff Dayne, settling back, continued to regard m[e]
Out of the piled-up silence he finally said, "It's [a]
great wonder. That maverick's his brother."

Hallelujah! I thought, and a whole heap of thin[gs]
suddenly begun to make sense.

The fat man grinned, but it was more like a g[ri]
mace. His stare never left me. "You sure, boy, y[ou]
ain't been sucked in by Mark Harra?"

I could feel the heat pounding into my cheeks. [His]
look softened a little. "Sho," he said. "There's so[me]
things, at your age, can seem mighty personal. [I]
reckon nobody likes to be taken for a fool."

I said, bitter, scowling, "Ain't been proved ye[t]
have." My cheeks got hotter, remembering Jim Long[ly]
"All right," I growled, "he offered me a job."

"Riding shotgun," Jeff Dayne nodded. "That f[ig]
ures, boy. You took it?"

"Suppose I did?"

"Then you're in for trouble. *Killin'* trouble."

"Maybe you better chew that finer."

"Well," he pawed his perspiring chins some more. "He probably told you this camp's been kind of hard put during the past couple months to fetch in enough cash to meet payrolls, that certain unnamed parties have been grabbing all shipments. That about the gist of it?"

"Close enough."

Dayne nodded. "Then likely he pointed out about the only chance he can see to beat 'em is to get somebody the mask-and-gun gentry wouldn't have no reason to tie in with folks here, with the owners, that is. Some stranger, like yourself. Might be, trying to put the best face he could on it, he left it to you to come up with the way and means for delivery. I expect he offered a pretty good inducement. Like a hundred bucks, say, each trip regardless . . . and double that, mebbe, whenever you got it through?"

Talking about pulling hats out of a rabbit! "You vas there?"

Dayne's round cheeks smiled. "Seemed a logical premise; but you mustn't overlook the trees for the woods. It will occur to you presently most of the practical steps have been taken."

I peered at him. "You tryin' to say I can't pull this off?"

Jeff spread his hands in a Mexican shrug. "You're missing the big thing."

"That there's a leak, you mean? But Harra claims —You think *he's* in back of it?"

"Heidi Quail's the camp's best authority there." He considered me patiently. "Best brains we've got have been chipping away at this but, like you, the most of them have rammed right over the unvarnished obvious."

"That feller! The guy they found in my room, was *he* diggin' into this?"

"Might have been," Jeff said without divulging an opinion. "Something else for you to take up with Heidi Quail."

"Why her?"

" 'You Bet' Farley, frock coat and all, was the nearest thing her daddy ever had to a law man. He was a disbarred attorney who made bottle money out o cards." Now Dayne said, coming out with it, "You ought to line your sights more nearly at Tucson."

I could only stare, not making no sense of it. I had the feeling he thought I must be almighty stupid. But he just grinned, eyes still watching me. "You don' get it?"

I shook my head.

"Tucson," he said, "is where this whole thing takes off from. That's where the money is. No matter what schemes is hatched up here, that's where it's got to come from."

And Farley, I remembered, had been on a horse.

The night, I noticed, had cooled off considerable, or maybe it was me. There was still hitched horses at some of the racks, and almost out of sight, heavy loaded by the sound. Two freight outfits strung out for Galeyville was having hard pulling getting up the grade.

The street itself, here in town, loomed empty. Must be getting on toward morning, I thought, uncertainly considering the silent walks and peering, nervous, at the blacker slots between buildings. I'd refused Dayne's offer of a cot to tide me over. All the signs I'd been given a look at seemed to be arrowed in the direction of the Drover's as the most likely place a man could get a tooth hold this side of the county seat.

It was there I had made the acquaintance of Geet. Outside the Drover's I'd run into the marshal and his horse-grabbing brother, Grant's Pass, who, by Jeff Dayne's tell, had been shining up to Kitty Verdugo, notwithstanding the back-alley didos he'd tried on Heidi Quail.

There was the girl herself, and me tied into it account of a guy who'd been teamed with her father being found dead inside the locked room she'd linked to me. And there was Jeff Dayne's testimonial naming her the camp's top authority on Harra.

All I'd got out of that place was trouble, yet here I was traipsing back again. I guess you'll think I had a hole in my head, but sense had nothing to do with it. The Drover's was where I had run into Harra, though I sure didn't look to find him there now.

Something about it—I wouldn't let myself believe it had anything to do with Heidi Quail; yet there was this pull, and her face was plainer to my mind right then than the handle of the shooter heavy banging against my hip.

I was drawn even while the thinking part of me, protesting, peered askance. And the nearer I come to that dim lobby lamp glow, away from what sound was left in the night, the more I had consciously to lift each boot. A danger-laced wildness seemed to lurk in the crouch of them bastardly shadows. I had to clamp my teeth—even then I was shaking. The ching of my spurs was like chimes in this stillness.

At the porch edge I twisted for a last cringing look. Nothing moved. I had an impulse to shout some crazy defiance if only to slap back the creep of that quiet.

I died a dozen deaths in the skreak of them planks. I went through the screen like a panicked badger.

The lobby was empty, the lamp turned low.

It took pretty near forever to get up them stairs, what with squawks from my weight and the breath-caught stops while I hung there expecting half the camp to bust in.

I hung some more at the top, shaking, listening, eyes clapped to the number chalked on the door. The corridor's dimness was filled with the snores of sleeping men, and their smells crowded round till I could scarcely breathe. I got one fist around the door's china knob; finally got hold of enough wind to turn it. I careful pushed and it opened, so easy and unexpected I was halfway into the room before it come over me some barefoot walker was right on my heels.

I mighty near climbed the goddamn walls when a hand, steadily pushing, come against my back. "Step right on in." Just a whisper, it was, but fierce and ungiving as the prod of cold iron.

I wasn't in no good shape to argue. The door latch clicked and in that mealy black for about a split second I figured this whippoorwill had shut me in. Then a match sprung to flame and in that orange light I saw Heidi Quail with her eyes like half dollars. They looked just as hard as the gun in her fist.

She said, blunt as always, "What do you think you're doing in here?"

"Well," I felt some put upon myself, "I sure didn't come to lovey-dovey with you!"

Her eyes, spilling out the kind of look a skunk might have got at a parlor social, took me in from head to foot. "Get the chimney off that lamp on the bureau." She bumped the wick with what was left of her match just before it got too short to hold.

I shoved the chimney back in its brackets. There was a pile of things I might have said, but I was still too riled from the fright she had give me to be digging up much in the way of chin music. She was barefoot, all right, had a blue wrapper round her, that red hair fanned out back of her shoulders. I reckoned she would just as like shoot as not.

"You can tell me," she said, "or you can talk to Jim Longly."

I sure wasn't minded to *habla* with him. "I don't expect you'll believe it," I finally got out, "but I come for another look at that stiff."

"You think I was fixing to keep him all night?"

I let that roll off. Then she said, more civil, "He was hit on the head, with a gun barrel probably. You keep sniffing around you could catch the same thing." Her eyes got all funny. "Why don't you get the hell out of here, Farris?"

I still ain't rightly figured how it happened—no such tomfoolery ever entered my head—but suddenlike both my arms was round her and both her arms was wrapped around me.

When we come up for air, first thing she said was, "Did you really come back for a look at Farley?"

"Sure," I said, and saw her eyes kind of darken. You'll reckon there's a heap I don't know about women. It's the golrammed truth—I don't make no bones of it. "But mostly," I said, "I come back to find out what you can tell me about Harra."

She seemed to be trying to read past them fool words, to guess what was behind them, to find the real me. I didn't catch that much then, it sort of come to me since. I saw her nose crinkle up, she give a bark of a laugh. Pulling loose, not making no sense, she said queerly, "I used to dream about this, thinking how it would be," and shook her head, mouth twisting. "I think you must have a one-track mind."

"Is he on the level?"

She considered me gravely. "I don't honestly know. The whole thing's so muddled—all those toughs he's hired, that crazy talk."

"But what do *you* think?"

"I think he's a crook! And a hypocrite, too! It was my pa, Farris, who made the discovery strike in these hills. There was nothing here then. What you see— all this," she flung out an arm, "came after. Post Oak, everything. There was a regular stampede; people came from all over. A lot of riff-raff moved in—dice men, cardsharks, pimps and their women. You never saw such a mess. Inside six months there were twenty-three saloons."

"All I've seen's three, and that's countin' Dayne's honky-tonk."

She nodded. "One by one Jeff took them over. Those he couldn't buy got busted up—mostly tent houses."

I said, scowling, "An' Harra?"

"Harra came later. Gave out to be interested in growing businesses, something, he said, that might give him a proper run for his money. He was thicker than splatter with Dayne for a spell, then they must have fell out. He got a horse and took to riding the hills. Then he hired him a crew, brought in some cows, bought a couple small ranches and threw them together. One he bought out was Jim Longly."

"And then put a star on him?"

"Jim was marshal already. Most people liked him. He was square, a good sport." She seemed lost in her thoughts.

"Humph!" I said. "What about this Grant's Pass?"

"After the ranch was sold he started running with Harra's bunch. Charley always was weak—he never used to be vicious. Getting free of his brother kind of went to his head. Took to calling himself that ridiculous name. He's been mixed up, I guess, in some pretty shady deals. He hires out his gun," she said, sounding worried.

"About your pa. If he made the original strike—"

"Never developed anything. His fun was in the hunting. He had this string of claims he'd staked but about all he did was gopher around. He turned up one good pocket; it went into this hotel. About the time Dayne and Harra got fed up with each other Harra made Pa an offer for those Aravaipa claims; I don't think Pa had any notion of selling. He never talked that way. Then, last May, that's a year ago, he

366

went off with a burro, hankering to turn up fresh ground."

Her look turned grim. "The afternoon of the day 'a set off, Mark Harra told around he had bought hose claims."

I said, "Mebbe he did," but not too hopeful. Some things she hadn't put to words I could feel. The dark thoughts looking out of her, the lift of her chin, churned uncomfortably through me. "What did your dad say?"

"They never gave him the chance. He was found he next week at the bottom of a shaft."

We stared at each other. "What's the duff on this Farley?"

"He was supposed to have looked over the papers or Pa. That's what they said, anyway."

"An' he give 'em the nod?"

"Apparently."

"If he hadn't been killed— What happened to the money?"

"It's a pretty good question not to ask around here. Harra says he paid cash." She smiled wryly. "Thirty housand."

Pretty raw, I thought, whistling. "Farley never said othing?"

"He suggested I take a trip to the patent office. Everything had been transferred; there was nothing I ould do. For a 'dollar and other valuable considerations' Harra had a clear title. The property is recorded as The Twelve Apostles Mine. I could have howled, but who would notice? Those gunfighters are a pretty good insurance." She said with them gold-brown eyes digging into me, "How do you feel about working for him now?"

I felt sick, no use denying it. I told her what Dayne had said about that deal. She said, "I wish you hadn't —" Her eyes got big. *"Killing trouble."* It was pretty near a whisper. She got hold of my arm, kind of hugging it to her. "Oh, Clint!" she said in what was almost a wail. "Don't do it!"

VIII

was fed to the gills.

All the sneers and harassments, them contrived dignities, the whole sorry mishmash of what I mounted to, rose up like a maddening flood in rebellion against the lousy run of cards life had chucked me. I said, never thinking how it might look to her, "It could be the last chance I ever have to do anything."

"But he's *right*, Clint—Jeff's right! They've killed every man who's been put on that run. Don't you see? They can't afford to let anyone live who might name them!"

Every snarling misery boxed into my memory broke loose in wild yammer to temper and toughen his brash determination, to set it up like veins in stone, her resistance curing it as smoke cures meat. I had the bit in my teeth and no power could turn me.

She had sense enough to know when she was whipped. A forlorn kind of sigh came out of her, the barest tremble of sound, but no tears, no reproaches.

I saw her then, the shaken look of her cheeks an
them staring eyes. "It's the only way we can eve
know the brass tacks truth of who's pullin' the string
—whether Harra's the one or it's somebody else."

"When will you go?"

I patted her shoulder. "I'll go see Harra now."

"Oh, Clint, *do* be careful!"

"I'll be careful," I said, seeing a number of thing
I hadn't noticed before. The dark ins and outs of th
thing had no end to them, wheels within wheels, bu
behind all the greed, all these bits of skulduggery
there'd be one biggest spider that had to be steppe
on—one weaver, one planner all the rest was tied into.

"What can I do that will help?" she said then.

I looked at my thoughts. "You reckon Dayne'
back of these stickups?"

She stood there a moment. "Jeff can be pretty ruth
less; I don't think he's dishonest."

"Do you know how Farley got into this room, o
where Geet got that key?"

She shook her head. "I didn't know Farley had go
back; he's been away. As for the key, anybody,
guess, could have slipped in and got it. I picked it u
after you'd gone and put it back on the rack."

"Dayne," I said, "seems to figure if there's a lea
it's at the Tucson end. All the arrangements, h
thinks, has to be fixed there. On account of th
money."

Something jumped in her look. "Farley! Do yo

suppose that's where he's been? Perhaps," she said, brightening, "you ought—"

"No! You put your finger on it. The nub of this thing is in the grabbin' itself, the fact they can't afford to let a witness get away. I don't know how it is, or why, but—"

"Farley was never a witness, Clint."

"He was *supposed* to have witnessed the sale of them claims. And he goes off on this trip. Maybe his conscience caught up with him, or mebbe," I said, "he got nosey. He certainly got rubbed out, that's for sure!" I took a turn of the room, wheeled abruptly and faced her. "What was you doin' back there with that horse thief?"

She half opened her mouth, then her chin come up, closing it. With her eyes gone tight and hard she lammed past, slipping down them stairs like a wet-footed cat.

I could have kicked myself when I seen how it sounded; the fact that I'd spoke like she was something I owned wasn't figured to calm her ruffled feelings much neither. I reckoned I had better stay out from under foot until that redheaded temper got worked off a little.

Digging out my watch I found with surprise it was a sight nearer daylight than I'd had any idea of. Another hour at most was all I had if I was minded to be out of Post Oak by sun-up; and, besides seeing Harra, I still had a horse to find.

It didn't seem too likely I'd be getting one from Harra. There was that livery Heidi had mentioned, but them eight paper dollars I had wouldn't buy much more than a wore-out bridle, not in a camp like this anyway. I thought of Jeff Dayne.

But that wasn't quite the same. The loan of a branded horse, any pony that could be traced back, could tie him to me a heap closer than he might care for. Still thinking about him I blew out the light.

He'd already took up for me.

Leaving the door where it was I stepped over to the window which was in the back wall, and, summoning what tatters of patience I could, got up the sash, trying hard to keep it quiet. A mutter of voice sound come up from somewhere. Mighty careful, I peeked out.

Like I'd half suspicioned there was a piece of roof, about a four-foot ledge, directly below. This shrunk my view of what else might be down there, like maybe Jim Longly or that gun-throwing brother who had got me warned not to be here come morning. This piece of roof could be ten foot from the ground. There was an empty pen sticking out of the dark and a couple of scraggly hackberries beside it, but too far out to hold any help. By hanging from my fingers, if I could land and stay on it, that ledge shouldn't be more than a three foot drop.

I pushed a leg over the sill and, without waiting longer, skinned over and hung. I had some pretty bleak thoughts before I finally let go. The damned ledge pitched some worse than I'd figured and there was nothing to grab onto. That slant threw me out. I lost my balance and went over.

I banged into the ground like a broken roped bucket hitting the bottom of a well. Felt like every bone in me was busted, and half of them driven clean on through to China.

No telling how long I lay there. It was hard to get back even enough wind to cuss with. To tell you rank, I might of been there till Christmas, I was that cairt to move, if the hard slap of boots hadn't jerked me out of it. They had come off wood and was thumping round the Drover's like the devil beating tanbark. I had one thought—a lamp bright picture of cold-jawed Jim Longly—and come up off that ground like a cottontail rabbit.

I got clear; don't ask me how I done it. My hide ached like mules had been drove over me. Every bone let out a shouting, every muscle stiff as a Charley horse, but I run. I guess nobody ever seen nothing like it. I sure as hell wasn't seeing much either till I come hard against the Boll Weevil's back door, and nothing I tried would by God get it open!

Of course I didn't pound; I wasn't trying to hang up no record for racket. All I wanted was to climb on my horse and get me out of this camp ahead of Longly; I had a mighty bleak hunch if he put hands on me again, any hereafter I had coming wouldn't last no longer than two bits in a poker game.

When the roaring inside me began to slack off som I seen pretty clear what a fool play I'd made, not i ducking that marshal but scratching at this doo There wouldn't be no horse inside a dan honky-tonk!

Time was getting away from me. The shadows w: beginning to show streaks of gray and I could hea empty wagons rattling up through the shale on thei way to the mines. I could strike out for Tucson with out seeing Harra, but getting that money was goin to need his okay.

Then I noticed this shed off the alley back c Dayne's. It had closed Dutch doors like they put o horse palaces and, just on the chance there might b a nag in there, I cut over for a look.

There was a length of strap iron across both door and a hasp, but somebody had been in too much of hurry. The padlock holding this rig hadn't latched— a piece of sheer luck if I had ever bumped into one.

Before lifting it free I sloshed a glance at th roundabout shadows. The animal inside begun t show his impatience. A good sign, I thought, becaus no coldblooded cart horse would paw the ground tha way.

A cooler hand, maybe, might of read that sign di ferent; I might have myself if I'd been under les pressure. I got the strap off, all thumbs though I was and swung open both doors.

It was still pretty dark. About all I could be sure c was this big, muscled rump and a sleek combed-ou tail ending short of clean hocks. A dark bay or black, and he was snorting now, nervous. There was the shine of his eyes peering over a shoulder. Tied, he was, too.

I was watching them legs, edging in to get round him, when a girl's angry voice cried, "What are you up to!"

Holding a bucket, she wasn't three steps away. Kitty Verdugo, and all set to yell.

Great! I thought, disgusted. A caught horse thief! No better than Grant's Pass, and without—

She come forward, peering sharper. "Oh. It's you; Mother of God but you gave me a turn! I thought . . . did Jeff send you out here to take care of Aguila?"

Right on a platter. You couldn't have it no better, and all I done was just stand there, goggling, them words of hers squeezing my insides until it hurt.

"No," I said, like a gold-plated ninny. "I was fixin' to grab that bronc an' take off!"

IX

You'll think I should have been bored for the simples.

I was aghast at myself. Against the brightening outside light I could see the comb poking up from her head. No need of them eyes or the shock of her mouth with her shape gone so still in the gray of that doorhole.

Then she laughed. I felt like Jericho's walls about the time old Gabe bent to pick up his tooter. "When you're finished," she said, "you'd better come in to breakfast."

I stared after her, bug-eyed.

Sick with myself I picked up the measure of oats she'd come in with.

No telling, when I didn't come round, what she'd say to Jeff Dayne, or what he would do when this stud turned up missing. The horse was plain enough now for me to know he cost money. He was short on the top with a long underline that held out the promise of both speed and bottom. I dumped the oats in his feed trough and, while he was eating, found his rig and got him ready. I wasn't hunting no hay. Quick as he quit chewing I shoved a bit in his mouth, rammed the bridle over his ears and, hanging onto the cheek strap, danced him through them open Dutch doors.

Hauled up, peering, I could scarcely believe it. Fog, like gray smoke, was thick outside as feathers in a pillow. No sign of the Boll Weevil—ten foot off I could only just barely see the end of its dock.

The horse mighty near got away while I was staring. I piled onto him then, not taking no chances. Moving him past where I figured Dayne's place was it come over me sudden I hadn't any notion where I was supposed to find Harra. Looked like he'd of told me. If he had I couldn't recollect.

I got onto the street, still fretting and fuming, knowing the guy would have a office here someplace, anyways a house—a gent important as he was.

It seemed lighter out here, the fog not so clinging but what you could pick out the nearer buildings with the tatters of mist piled up in layers around the shine of whatever lamps was yet showing. But you couldn't read signs without getting right up to them. The only live things in sight, and that wasn't fooling me, was a couple of hitched broncs humped over a tie rack.

Someone had told me the name of Harra's mine was The Twelve Apostles, not that I was fixing to romp around hunting it. I wasn't craving at all to run into Jim Longly or them *buscadero* bully-puss johns he chummed around with. Nor it didn't look smart to duck into the Boll Weevil, though that was what I done. I was too durn scairt of picking up a blue whistler to stay any longer on that street than I had to.

Knotting Aguila's reins around a porch post I pushed through Dayne's slatted half-leafs, heart pounding, knowing right then I wasn't cut out for this.

The only guy in there was a bent-over swamper spreading sawdust from a bucket who didn't even bother to twist his neck or look up.

"Where'll I find Mark Harra?"

"Sleeps over his office."

"Where would that be?"

He sloshed a look at the clock. " 'Leven doors down, other side of the street." Dumping the last of his sawdust he reached for a gaboon.

I backed out, slipped the reins and got into the saddle.

Eleven doors down. Seemed a powerful piece looking off through the curl of that fog. It was thinner, maybe lifting, with a ground breeze rolling up from them south flats. Trying back lots would be risky, too. I nudged the stud with a knee.

He moved away from Dayne's porch, and I could tell straightaway he was feeling them oats. It took a strong hand to keep him down to a head-shaking three-cornered walk.

Part way down a guy stepped out, ducked under a

hitchrail and come up, staring. My heart come up, too. It started beating my windpipe. Just as I come even, trying to make up my mind if I should reach or sink steel, the galoot turned away and staggered off between buildings. Which didn't leave much chance for studying doorholes or shadows.

It was while, soaked with sweat, I was trying to get back some of the breath I had lost, I saw the place I was hunting. No lights showing. Evidently he hadn't got up yet.

I scowled, peering round. I sure didn't want to leave this horse on the street. Something then, some skitterish notion, hauled my eyes to the place next beyond.

Every hair come off my scalp stiff as wire. It was the Drover's and Geet, in the lamplit lobby gone as still as a Injun, was staring straight at me!

It was kind of a shock.

I must have hung froze a dozen seconds hand-running before, with a shuddery grab at fresh breath, it passed through my head he hadn't seen nothing, not with the shine of that lamp in his face.

Not exactly calm, but certainly trying to be reasonable careful, I put Dayne's stud up the crack of dark passage between Harra's building and the shuttered tore this side.

Getting off that street seemed a likely thing to do. Smartest move I could make with this big devil under me was to get as far and fast as I might. There was too many here who would like nothing better than to stretch my hide to the nearest wall, and Jeff, soon's he went for this horse, would be one of them. You just can't argue with a stem-winding bullet!

But it was in my mind, too, I hadn't come no great ways in my campaign to start over. I'd never had it so rough. And, besides, there was Heidi. Seemed the least I could do was give Harra's proposition the whirl I'd already promised.

Behind his place I was anchoring Aguila in a half bare stand of yellowing salt cedar when this bang hit my ears like a burst paper sack. First thing I thought of was a coat-muffled shooter. Geet jumped into my head, and I come within a ace of getting back on that horse.

I even had a foot up.

It was uncommon hard not to follow it into leather, but someway I couldn't. Easing it down, watchful as spiders, I catfooted closer to the back side of Harra's, drawn there like a rope was hauling me.

Though a full two storeys, tall enough for his importance, it wasn't much better than a square mud box, not near so deep nor broad as The Drover's. Didn't look to have more than a room to each level. Like a blockhouse, kind of, or the tower to something that had been tore down. There was a door in the end and one lone window with a pulled-flat shade that, even as I watched, turned lemon bright, throwing out the black shapes of two bent-over men.

With the flare of that lamp, and them shadows to scrinch at, I guessed the sound I had heard was a door, maybe snatched by the wind from a careless hand; might even of been the one they slipped in by. What really shook me was the astonishing resemblance of this nearest bent shape to the galoot who had told me to be out of here by morning. My cold-jawed friend, the Post Oak badge-toter.

If this was him, and I'd have bet on it, who was with him? And what were they doing in Harra's office?

The other shape was too dim and muzzy for any clear shot at a name to clap on it. You couldn't begin to even gage the size of him but it was plain enough he was teamed with Jim Longly. Geet, more than like, or his Grant's Pass brother!

The window was shut. All I could catch was a grumble of voices, no words, nothing usable. Even a ear against the wall didn't help. I couldn't think waiting was going to get me much, either. No matter which hole I covered there was no guarantee they wouldn't leave by the other. And, scrooched up against the place that way, I kept thinking what a bind I'd be in if someone else come along or that big stud of Dayne's nickered.

Then, impatient, he suddenly did.

Both shadow shapes stiffened. I had just about time to go into my rabbit act. Fright and despair, those insufferable well-wishers, was shoving me hard

THE KID FROM LINCOLN COUNTY

toward a lunge for the tules. Sick with the bitterness
of self-disgust I watched for the lamp in Harra's office
to die.

Before they could kill it I was at the door, hammering like mad in the brashness of panic.

IX

"What the hell!" Harra snapped, angrily yanking it open after freeing the bar.

Light come against my face like a mallet, and over his shoulder the marshal's elk stare was as coldly ungiving as a wall of dressed granite.

"Well, if it ain't the kid from Bitter Crick!" With a jeering laugh he stepped away from the desk. Then the grin quit his face. "You playin' stickup or somehin'?"

With that gun in my fist I felt a sure enough fool. There was nobody else, just them. And though his hin hair bristled there was nothing about Harra's cowling attention to suggest I'd come onto things he idn't want told.

But there was something, the feel you get around spooky bronc, a restless kind of chilled steel waitg that kept me hung to that shooter.

The glint in Longly's stare got brighter, and again

I saw on the screen of my mind this pair with their heads bent over that desk. What were they up to? *Why were they here at such an hour with the shades drawn?*

This fix was bulging worse with each breath. Even with this hog-leg affronting the proprieties I wasn't going to keep them stood up much longer without I was ready to shoot or be shot at.

"How's the trumpet of the Lord this mornin'?" I said, watching Jim Longly settling into his tracks. He had a shorter fuse than what was built into Harra. His patience was thinner, or maybe his conscience had a trickier load.

He looked just about up to letting go all holds when Harra, coolly nodding, took the play away from him. "I suppose you're here, Farris, about that—Oh, you needn't mind Jim; he's as much concerned as—" He broke off to say testily, "You can put up that pistol!" and to peer at me sharper round the beak of his nose. "It seems I won't be needing your good efficiency."

"Mean you've hired someone else!"

A polite regret looked out of his smile.

"Him?" I said with a flick of my gun snout.

"Point is, you weren't around when I needed you. Many are called but few are chosen," he said, warming up to it and getting right into his hell-fighting voice. "When the bridegroom cometh—"

I said, "Never mind that," beginning to think I'd

got hold of something. "If no one's been gettin' any payrolls through— *Stand still, Marshal!*"

Them two swapped glances. Longly's shifted weight brought his burnt-leather look a little deeper into shadow and I said, pushing the thought around, "A pretty slick stunt, sending Farley up with it, then shutting his mouth."

Harra's face jerked around. He seemed to catch himself, chuckling, but it didn't quite hide the wicked shine of his eyes.

"Looks like I better find a place for you, Farris."

"I don't want no place like you found for that shyster!"

"Well," Harra said, and turned unwinkingly moveless while the marshal's look got tighter and darker and, too late, I saw where this brashness had took me.

Only a fool could doubt any longer what was going on here, or what was back of it; and Longly it looked like, account of his brother, had been sucked into where he had to go along.

The door I'd come in by was back of me someplace, but if he went for his shooter I was due to get planted. Placed like they was with six feet between them it wasn't in the cards I'd be able to get both.

Harra, grinning, didn't bother to speak.

A Mexican standoff. Sweat was cold on my skin. I felt the pressure of panic.

Like there was sand in his voice, Jim Longly said, "You don't want to be no dead hero, do you?"

Desperate to get him stopped I cried, "I won't go alone."

"Take Jim," Harra laughed, stepping back.

I saw Longly's cheeks, wild as a willie's. The contempt and easy coldblooded scorn in which Harra without hesitation had withdrawn his support, clearly had pushed the man beyond reach of anything.

His mouth went back like a cornered rat's. Like enough my own probably done the same. First shot, I was thinking, better go for the lamp or Harra would have me before I could swing. *And it would have to be blind!* I didn't dare twist my look off the marshal.

I was tipping it up, praying for luck, when across the room the front door banged open. One frightened glimpse I caught of her eyes before all hell jumped out of the skillet. The lamp went up in a burst of blue flame. Slugs, whistling and whining, smacked into the walls as, driven from a crouch, I went through the window in a frantic dive.

A tin roof wouldn't have made more racket. Shots, shouts and cursing built a bedlam behind as I come off the ground in a rolling lunge shook loose of the shade and pelted for the cedars where I'd left Dayne's horse.

He was there, snorting and pawing in a lather of excitement; my breath was like a saw ripping logs as I fumbled, all thumbs, to get the damned knot out of them tangled reins. I could hear Harra shouting, and the snarls of the marshal above the scared scrabble of a girl's frightened questions.

My time was shorter than the tail holt on a bear. Even as the reins came free and I went up, blue whistlers begun to slam through the cedars. I raked Aguila both sides with the steel and we tore out of that brush with the guns popping back of us and lead swarming thick as a hatful of hornets.

Cuffing him around I got him lined out on a up-hill scramble pointed toward the Globe road. It climbed north through the mountains but, quick as I figured we'd cut off Harra's view, I cut him sharp right, going down a long tangent in a slather of shale that fetched us, shaking, into the top end of town. Not waiting to catch no breath but walking him care-ful through that gray chintzy light, I come up back of The Drover's.

Crazy? You bet! Yet who but a fool would think to look for me there? Not them, I didn't reckon; and seemed like I was right. It was quiet next door, as a goosehair pillow. Looked like they had all took off hellity-larrup.

I come out of the saddle, softly tapped her back door, hanging onto the reins and peering two ways at once. Don't think I wasn't nervous; I felt about as unlikely as a tenderfoot trapper slicing out his first skunk. I only hoped she'd had time to get over her mad, and that wasn't all I was thinking of, either.

There was still more than somewhat about this Post Oak mess I hadn't caught up with. I didn't understand even all I knew about it.

When no one answered I tried to ease the door open. Like I figured, it was barred.

I could feel the sweat cracking through my hide and a bunch of cold prickles chasing up and down the back of my neck. I was scared to call out, afraid to leave without seeing her.

Being timid's plain hell. I must of died a dozen deaths scrinched up against that door hanging onto my breath, picturing a hundred things that could happen and wondering, back of everything else, if Geet was still hunkered alongside that desk.

I rapped again, about ready to fly when sound come barefootin' up to the door.

"Who's there?" Heidi called, no louder than a cricket.

"Me," I said. "You gonna stand there and yak?"

Looked like, for a minute, she didn't figure to talk no way. "Is Geet in there?" I said, some urgent.

The bar snicked back. She pulled the door open and, hand on it, stood there, me feeling about as welcome as a mutt coming home with a nasty bone.

Her eyes come wide open. She had seen the gun. "Well!" she sniffed, "so you *were* mixed up——" It was then, I guess, that she took in the horse.

"You gone plumb loco?"

"Shh . . ." I growled. "Not so golrammed loud! All I want——"

"Git in here!" Her arm shot out, fastened into my shirtfront. You wouldn't think for her size, she had that much strength. But the next thing I knew, there I was in the kitchen, still gripping them reins, with the door shut behind me.

XI

I held the reins out, waggling them, looking, I reckon, more stupid than usual.

No one had run off with Heidi's tongue. "You think I'm going to take *him* in, too? Throw them down," she cried, "he ain't goin' no place."

The kind of look she gave me—without it come from his wife—no guy with gumption would of took for a minute. She stepped back, arms akimbo. "What have you been up to?"

"Geet?" I said, nervous, peering over her shoulder.

"He went hightailin' out of here soon's that row started. Come on, let's have it, who've you killed now?"

So I unlimbered my tale. She stood taking it in, saying never a word till I come to where Kitty Verdugo showed up. "Whatever that bunch has been up to," I said, "she's into it plumb to them black Spanish eyes!"

"She's straight," Heidi said. "She probably stepped over there hunting for Charley."

"Charley . . . who's he?"

"The marshal's brother. Grant's Pass."

"Oh," I said, scowling, reminded of the horse I'd been done out of. "Mebbe."

"What are you trying to do now? They'll be back, you know."

"That's why I come over here." I put up my shooter, annoyed that she figured I couldn't see that. "Seems like Harra's been havin' a pretty good thing, sendin' guys down there secret, then rubbin' 'em out after they've fetched up his payrolls."

"You're just guessing," she said.

"I ain't got no proof but . . . I thought you was bustin' to fix his clock!"

"What's the point in all this? He's not paying his miners."

"Prob'ly usin' it," I growled, "to pay off that gun crew that's pullin' the stickups. Cripes! He can afford to close shop if the rest of these owners can't take out no ore. An' if they can't pay their men—"

"What I told you straight off. If the others get hard up enough he can buy them out at ten cents on the dollar. Maybe if you talked to them—"

"You think they'd listen? Hell," I said, "you was right in the first place. Proof's what we need, and I've a notion. . . . But I've got to have help."

"I'll help."

I told her, scowling, "You're a prejudiced party. I've got to have someone these owners'll listen to. This Harra's dug in, but if he's sent for more cash—"

"He won't stop his *own* man. He don't have to; you've shown that. If you've got it in mind to catch them red-handed we better put out some bait." When I stared, she said: "A payroll shipment for one of the other mines. By stage, of course, but *secret*."

"How you gonna work that? An' if it's secret," I said.

"They'll get onto it," she told me. "How secret did *you* stay?" She caught up her hat. "I better get moving. That feller Harra hired in your place, has he gone yet?"

"You seem to be wearin' the pants for this deal!"

She come back to put her hand on my arm. "If we pull this off it will be a joint effort, Clint. Farris, Quail and Company." She wrinkled her nose at me. Squeezing, she said, "I'll go see if old Phipstadt will risk a little cash."

"And who do you figure to talk into siding?"

"Jeff Dayne will go with you. They'll take *his* word."

It was him I'd had in mind. But now, with her putting his name in the pot, I couldn't see him for hell. I said, "How about Longly? He's the badge-packer here."

She looked her surprise. "I thought you reckoned he was tied in with Harra."

"How do you know that saloon keeper ain't? You forgettin' Verdugo? Come right in, she did, never a knock! Besides," I said, scowling, "what about his horse?"

She considered me, sighing. "Jeff told you about Kitty. Where else would she go to find out about Charley?" It was plain she thought I was being unreasonable. Probably I was, but a man likes to feel he's got *some* of the answers—once, anyway.

She said with that gamin grin on her mouth: "As for the horse, why don't you step over and see Dayne 'bout him? A brash, string, upright, handsome galoot like you shouldn't mind facing up to a trifle of that sort." And off she went, with a sniff, trailing trickles of laughter.

I felt like the fool with the sack at a snipe hunt, not as a blanket after a hard ride. She could sure cut a man down to size in short order.

I went out with the reins and climbed into the saddle. She hadn't left me much choice. What I ought to have done, thinking back to it now, was taken Aguila and dug for the tules; or maybe this was just the spleen working out of me. I'd been dancing to other folks' tunes all my life. A hard turn to drop. But I had come to Post Oak to face up to myself, and if I was ever going to do it right now was the time.

"I'll show her!" I growled, and kneed the horse

around, right into the street and down its dead center
like a storybook sure-shot, ignoring the stares I could
feel swinging after me. Straight up to the front of
Dayne's honky-tonk I rode and, jaws clenched,
stepped down.

Tossing the reins over the pole I went in, remembering that other time. "Boss here?"

The guy in the apron jerked a thumb toward the
office.

"Go tell him," I said, "there's a horse thief out
here wants to swap *habla* with him."

I don't know what I expected. Not what I got. Jeff
Dayne's bulging cheeks and three chins showed up,
with the apron's popped eyes goggling back of one
shoulder. I couldn't read what he thought from that
moon of a face, gage his intent or temper. I stood
brittle stiff but I stood, damn her eyes!

Dayne suddenly chuckled. "Hi, kid," he grinned.
"Better get that chip down offen your muscle an' tie
into a drink before them knees of yours give out complete. Fetch it over to the corner table," he told the
barkeep. Looking, I suspect, pretty hangdog and
sheepish, I followed him over and took the chair he
pushed out.

I perched on it like a caught fence-crawler. Reckon
my tongue must of run off and hid. This shaped up
to be harder even than I had figured. Sweat moved
around on my lip like a fly and, sudden, I couldn't

394

eem to hold it no longer. "You'll find the damn horse ied out front!" I blurted.

The apron come with a glass and a bottle, plunked hem down and went back to the bar. "Go ahead," Dayne said. "I sell the stuff but I don't have to drink t."

I told him, glowering, I didn't have to either. And here we set with that table between us and the not-nowing silence piling up chunk on chunk till the lurn squirming weight of it was not to be borne. "He in't hurt," I snarled, "if that's what you're thinkin'!"

"I haven't lost any horse."

I looked at him, hard. Borrowed or whatever, I ad still took that stud, and if he figured to overlook t I aimed to have him say so. "He come out of your hed."

"Must be Kitty's horse, Aguila."

It took me square in the wind. *Was this what had etched her over to Harra's?*

"If you were going to light out," Jeff Dayne said, why didn't you?"

"I took the horse to go after that job. When I got to Harra's place the marshal was with him. Harra told me he'd already hired somebody." I mentioned how had been, me sandwiched between them and longly all set to go for his shooter, and the girl show-ng up and me knocking the lamp out. "You know nis bunch a sight better than I do; you reckon he's xin' to send Longly after it?"

The fat man, studying his fists, finally shrugged. "Hard to tell."

I put him next to our notions about Farley. All the change I got from that was a nod. A fish-belly shine was beginning to come out of him.

"If it's Aguila," I growled; and his look, coming back from some far place, kind of tightened and shuddered. "Take the horse," he muttered. "I'll take care of Kitty."

Something about the way that sounded pulled my eyes around. If what he meant was he'd 'square' it, why hadn't he said so?

"If you're trying to get rid of me—"

Starting to get up, he settled back with a growl. "Them boys, you know, ain't playin' for peanuts." He looked like he wished I'd drop into some hole.

What I couldn't figure quite was why. But it come over me now with considerable astonishment all that yap he had given me before about Tucson was a pile of damn hogwash, something connived to get me out of this camp. And I looked at him harder, trying to see how this fit.

"Keep away from them, kid, or you'll end up on a shutter."

And then a sigh rumbled out of him. "So she got to you, did she? I was afraid she would." He said, leaning forward, "Don't it scare you thinkin' of what happened to Farley?"

"There's other things scares me worse." I was able,

ven, to grin at him a little; and I saw his look darken.
ome of the things that was bottled inside him, des-
eration and anguish, began to come through, but I
as figuring now we spoke the same lingo.

I said, more confident; "Your hands've been tied
ccount of Verdugo. You're too square a gent to rest
asy on your butt while the rest of this camp gets took
r a cleanin'."

The big feller snorted.

He took off his cheaters, puffing on them, rubbing
em. The shape of his cheeks seemed more forlorn
an angered. It was hard to be sure with a face
mooth as his. I said, "We ain't got much time."

He hooked the wires back over his ears. "You just
an't romp around exterminatin' people."

"If we come onto 'em while they was up to their
ecks in it."

"You wouldn't have nothing but punkinseeds, Far-
s."

"If we caught Geet—" I began, but Jeff shook his
ead.

"Geet's just a bully boy, the threat, not the medi-
ine. To implicate Harra you've got to hit closer.
ustin' the gang up ain't going to stop him."

"Grant's Pass Charley?"

Them cheaters hid the look of Jeff's eyes, but a
lain reluctance was in every line of him. This was
hy he'd set back and stayed out of it, account of
at crazy mixed-up girl that had it stuck in her head

397

Longly's black sheep brother was some kind of tin-pants saint on horseback.

"Well, hell," I said, "she's gonna be hurt no matter *what* you do. If she up an' runs off with him—"

Dayne sighed again. "Yep." He scrubbed a sleeve across his jaw. "Charley's the nub of it. He's the lodestone that's hung round her neck. Harra's black-jack."

I saw it, now. All the bits clicked together. Blood was thicker than water; Longly went along because there was nothing else he could do. Harra pulled the strings around here, and the rest of these yaps was more ready to cut off a hand or both legs than bring on a visit from the boss-man's adjuster.

"But, damnit—" I growled.

Jeff shook his head. "People, kid, once they've give in, will take a mighty lot to hang onto what they've got. Most of them's still living. The memory of them that's gone works for Harra—that's his system. Hope, luck, and some reminders of Charley."

He blew out a bitter sigh and got up. "Fork that horse, kid, and—"

"Help's what I'm huntin', not a way to get out of this!"

"You can't buck the whole camp."

"If we can catch them redhanded—"

"God, but you're stubborn! Look, you can't catch the ones that will do any good. Grant's Pass and Harra! How will you get at them?"

"Bait. Heidi's goin' to have Phipstadt—"

His narrowing stare had gone over my shoulder. I heard the batwings slap shut and steps coming lightly over the floor, and just behind me they stopped. Heidi said, "It's all fixed. The money'll come up tomorrow by stage out of Tucson. Every last nickel Phipstadt's got in the bank."

XII

Dayne, not much liking it, finally gave in.

He didn't think they'd go for it. Even if they did we didn't know, he said, where Harra's hyenas would make their play. If we cleared these hurdles and managed to save Phipstadt's cash he still couldn't figure an outside chance of bagging Grant's Pass without killing the bugger. "We have to bring him in dead, what the hell have you accomplished?"

"At least," I said, "we'll have proved it can be done."

The fat man, snorting, went off with Heidi to sack up the grub.

It didn't look too promising even to me; but if someone back along had been willing to put his neck out maybe, I thought, there'd been no need of this now. You never knew what you could do till you tried.

And there was Heidi, of course, and that Twelve Apostles Mine her dad had been done out of, not to mention his death, which could be laid, it seemed now, at the door of the marshal's shoot-and-run brother along with a passel of other people's troubles. And, back of everything else, I still had to know if it was guts I was packing around or just fiddle-strings.

When Jeff showed up with the grub, and two filled canteens sloshing round on their straps, there was something different in the cut of his eye which impelled me, caught up, to peer hard at the girl. "What's the matter?"

"Nothing the matter with me." She tossed her head. "Jeff can't get used to the notion of havin' me along."

"You! Hell's fire, you're not goin'!"

"Who got Phipstadt to put up the money? Whose idea was it that we catch them redhanded? Who," she said, chin up, "has a better right?"

"But . . . but . . . for the love of Mike, Heidi. A deal like this—ain't no *place* for a girl! Godfries!" I said. "Them buggers ain't playin' for peanuts, you know when them guns get to poppin'—"

"Mine will be poppin', too. Take the grub," she said, "and let's get to whackin'."

She took the canteens from Dayne and, slipping the straps bandoleer-fashion over her shoulders, went off through the batwings without a backward look. Jeff, wryly grinning, handed me the grub sack, then got me a rifle and two boxes of cartridges. "Happy days," he said. "I'll catch up with you later."

We camped that evening in a tall stand of jack-pines thirty miles south and not too far off the Tucson road. While I took care of the horses Heidi opened the grubsack and fixed us some sandwiches. I could of done with some java but she wouldn't risk a fire. We washed them down with some of the warm water from the canteens Jeff had loaned us.

We were still in hill country. After the sun sank behind the Tortolitas it began to cool off. I fetched Heidi her blankets and got into my brush jacket. We hadn't swapped much talk in the past three-four hours and now, with darkness settling over the land, a kind of constraint sprung up between us. She put her back to a tree, blanket over her shoulders, and I hunkered against another. Tongue-tied and grumpy I scowled at my thoughts, wondering if Harra's gunnies was still combing the ridges. They must have found out by now we had skipped. Once clear of town we'd got onto the Tucson wagon road and hadn't left enough tracks to trip up an ant.

We watched a yellow moon creep over Biscuit Peak and somewhere off in that lonesome quiet a coyote pack set up its awful yammer. "You warm enough?" I said, and saw her face tip toward me.

"I'm all right."

"Tomorrow," I said, "you better take the Winchester and let me have that .45-90."

Everything considered it was a hell of a conversation. For two people that was supposed to be gone on each other we was sure letting a pile of good time slip away. But there was things on my mind.

I don't know when I quit thinking. Next thing I knew, something had hold of my shoulder. I jerked open my eyes, some surprised to find it wasn't more than a cuss and two snorts to wide-awake morning.

In this cold gray-shadowed time that was not quite night nor yet day neither, the bent-over blob of the girl's concerned face swept the cobwebs out of me as nothing else could have.

"Clint," she whispered, "there's something out there!" and pressed her dad's rifle into my hands.

I don't know if it was the comforting weight of that gun or her fright—the dependence and trust—that done it but, strangely, I felt cool as a well chain. My ears caught the foxlike drift of his progress, the low scuff of sound coming over damp needles, the nerve-twisting pauses while he peered and listened.

I got out of my boots. "Stay put," I growled, and the confidence I felt was like a heady wine. I knew exactly what to do, just how to go about it, circling the sounds to come up downwind of him. *Regular Tom Horn!* I told myself, marveling.

Off thirty yards I picked up the dim shape of him, writhing like smoke between the poles of the pines.

I snicked back the bolt.

The horse threw up his head with a snort, froze beneath the clamped muscles of his rider. The guy, never twisting his head, said, "Farris?"

A quiver run through me. "Why the hell didn't you sing out!" And Jeff Dayne's laugh only riled me fiercer. It was good, just the same, to know he had got here. He was the chiefest thing I'd been wondering about.

Even Heidi looked pleased in the freshening light. "Coffee, Jeff?"

He peered around as we come up. "I expect we can risk it."

"Better keep it small," I grumbled.

While I got into my boots he give us the news, all, anyways, he figured was good for us. Harra, it seemed, was still around town but his crew was gone, presumably off to catch up work at the ranch. "Looks," Dayne grinned, "like they figure you've sloped; Longly's gone, too." He glanced around at Heidi. "Put in most of yesterday watching your place. Just short of chow he rode off, pointin' south."

Right at that moment I didn't care where he'd went. Suppose, I was thinking, we'd read Farley's moves wrong? "Do we actually know Charley's on Harra's books?"

"Well . . . no," Jeff said, thoughtful, "I don't reckon we do. Harra's not stupid. But if they wasn't hooked up what would the marshal be doing in Harra's office? Before breakfast, too, with their heads together and all the shades drawn? By your account they seemed pretty upset; didn't you say Longly was all set to blast you?"

It had sure looked that way, but there was things in this deal that seemed queerer than that. After all, I'd knocked him flat on his butt, called his brother a

se thief, and been in their hair at pretty near every
1. "Wonder," I said, "if Phipstadt sent for that
ney?"

eff's eyes wheeled behind the glint of them glasses.
hy wouldn't he?"

Everything considered, he ain't got much
ain."

Ieidi stopped what she was doing to stare at me
ly. Jeff, kind of laughing, said, "Didn't you know
ad his hat set for Heidi?"

Ier throat fired up. You couldn't tell from her
< if he was kidding or not. "I got the impression,"
owled, "he was older than Moses."

The fat man laughed. "What's that got to do with

poured some more java, gulped the last of my
t. "Verdugo say anythin' about bein' over there?"

eff shook his head. Presently he said like it come
n his bootstraps, "She ain't been back."

That brought my head up.

No fault of yours," he growled. "Expect she's
e skallyhootin' after Charley."

There was something mighty grim in the sound of
remembered Heidi saying he could be pretty ruth-
. She caught my look and scuffed dirt over the
ls, up-ended the blackened pot and reached
und for the emptied cups. "Where," I asked Jeff,
you reckon they'll stop it?"

Most likely place is Burnt Woman Crossin'."

Heidi said flatly, "Red Rock!"

I stared from her to him and back again. "Tha
a change station, ain't it?"

Nodding, she said, "They've already used all
most likely places. They've hit Burnt Woman twi
Last time they tried the stage got away; two of th
chased it better than three miles before they were a
to take off the driver—they'll not want that kind
chance again. Nor won't have to at Red Rock. Th
can make their play while the horses are be
changed."

"Too many witnesses."

"There'll be only one man at that station—
Fred."

Jeff said skeptically, "What about passengers?"

"Killing passengers hasn't ever bothered them l
fore!"

"They're cold*blooded* enough. Probably sh
their own mothers if they got in the way," Day
grumbled. "What I'm sayin', there's more risk."

"Risk is a gambler's stock in trade." Her glar
whipped to me. "What do you think, Clint?"

I was thinking of what she'd said about passenge
From all reports these payroll jumpers never left
witness. If they'd had to chase after their quarry
last time it could only have been figured out fr
the tracks, and if what Jeff had said about Char
was true— The glance I pushed at him was a ha
way apology. "Looks like I'll have to be votin' w
Heidi."

"We guess wrong, we're stuck with it. There ain't going to be any chance to start over."

I seemed always to wind up with the women and kids. "Red Rock," I said, and his mouth twisted wryly.

"All right," he grumbled. "Heidi, you better give the kid back that rifle. We bump into that bunch he's goin' to need every bean in the cylinder."

I said, "A .45-90 is too heavy for a woman," and could see my yap didn't set none too good with him. "I'll go fetch the horses."

"No hurry about that. Be middle of the afternoon before any stage out of Tucson pulls into Red Rock."

It was plain he hated to give up on Burnt Woman. "It's a five hour ride right from here," Heidi said, "and I'd like to talk to Fred if we can manage it before the fireworks."

She had her way. I fetched the horses. But some six miles this side of the station her mare threw a shoe and there was no means of fixing it. Before we'd covered another three the animal was limping. By the look of the sun it was about one o'clock.

Dayne peered at his watch. "Twenty after," he said. The heat was stifling.

Heidi chewed at her lip. "Well, there ain't no help for it, I guess," Jeff remarked, mopping at his chins. "You an' the kid are goin' to have to ride double."

It was lucky I happened to be on a stout horse. I hauled a boot from the stirrup. A wicked sound came up off the ground as Heidi stepped from her saddle. Her cheeks went gray—I reckon mine did too. Scarcely three foot away from her a green-and yellow tiger snake writhed into a bundle of coils, th staccato ching of its rattles holding me rooted.

Not packing no hand gun she reached for the Win chester.

"Be still!" Jeff said sharply.

The rattler's beady eyes were like translucent bit of glass. The red forked lightning of its flashin; tongue went finally quiet. The snake unwound an went slithering off.

I begun to shake. Jeff was the only one with spi enough to speak. "That's the kind the Hopis use ii their dances." He considered us sourly. "If you ha fired that gun we might as well have gone home!"

I reached down when she come over and brough her up behind the cantle, half expecting Aguila t try and get his head down, but he behaved all right only dancing around a little, more nervous over th snake than he was of her. Someway it put me ii mind of Verdugo; an odd choice of mount he wa for a woman, a big strapping stallion and a spee horse besides.

He wouldn't be doing much speeding now.

We moved out at a walk, Heidi hauling her mar by the reins. We were getting into pretty rough cour try, about as hard to take as any I'd seen. Cracke slabs of baked granite thrust out of the earth's thi hide like bones. The pines were gone. Mazanita gre

ere, maguay and Spanish dagger, and the sun beat
own like a brass-plated fist.

Jeff was out front now, breaking trail through this
ell of rock, forced by drops to twist this way and
hat and sometimes, crossing places a goat would
ave shied at, we had to get down, blindfold the
orses and walk. I guessed he knew his way around
his country; if he didn't it was hard to see how we'd
ome out of it, such a chopped-up maze it looked to
ne, all cactus and stone and an occasional solitary
ray-horned ocotillo lifting its naked red-tipped
vands against the writhing glare of sky.

"You reckon we're lost?" I present muttered. Heidi
hook her head. "I think he's trying to find a short
ut."

I didn't tell her, but a lot of queer thoughts was
lopping in my head. That chase she had mentioned
ept chewing on me, and Geet harping about my
oing to the Boll Weevil, determined it seemed to
nake me own up to it.

Had Longly honestly thought I'd killed Farley or
vas this something that had come to him secondhand
rom Geet? It was after the marshal had been in there
apping that Harra had told me he'd hired someone
lse. Yet when I'd found them together behind drawn
hades there was nothing in Harra's scowling atten-
ion to suggest I'd come on things he didn't want
old. I begun to wonder if I'd misjudged the man.
t was Longly who'd ached to go for his shooter; and

Geet, by Jeff's tell of it, was only a straw man. Charley was the killer.

Piece by piece I went over the lot, stacking things I knew against what I'd been told, trying their shapes different ways for fit, growing more and more certain there was something I'd missed. *Was it tied in some way with the marshal's brother?* Was that where the truth lay?

Something begun to move through me darkly. I'd seen nothing to prove that gangling hatchet-faced gunhawk was jumping through hoops for the camp's biggest mogul. Most of the arguments used against Harra could be applied just as forcefully to somebody else.

What if Grant's Pass Charley was doing his stuff with mirrors? Supposin' there wasn't no 'bunch' involved in these stickups; what if the marshal's brother was playing it solo!

But where would this leave Farley?

It had me sure enough larruping in circles. I could wish I never had heard of him even. In life he had been a cardplaying shyster, dead he might be only a red herring—but he hadn't been croaked by no rattlebrained tramp. He had been done away with to shut his mouth.

I was more sure of that than I was of anything, yet it was three by Jeff's watch before the damned way of it slicked into place and left me, aghast, staring down through the windless silence into the yard of Red Rock Station.

The awful heat boiling out of that rim-locked pocket hardly touched me. The pole corrals, the paintless sand-scoured buildings starkly squatted without cover scantly two hundred yards out and down from where we stood among the gin-like smell of junipers, stacked up as less than nothing against the shock of my discovery. To put in bald words that rambling chaos of flying thoughts requires a mind much sharper than mine. Staggered and set back I stared askance at the truth, scarce wanting to believe I could have been so blind.

"Well," Jeff said, "they haven't come yet," and, now that he'd put plain words to the picture, I could see as much for myself.

Though there was no one in sight the fresh teams were patiently standing in their harness just behind the closed gate of the day pen. And, even as I looked, Heidi urgently whispered, taking hold of my arm, "There it is!"

Where the ribbon of road came down through the bluffs a boil of dust stood against the red stone. And presently we saw the top of the stage, an Abbott-Downing mudwagon, the hatted head and hunched shoulders of the man on the box. The whip, this was. He had the seat to himself, and I wondered again if Phipstadt had kept his reported promise.

I saw Jeff's glance turn to search Heidi's face. "Somethin's wrong!" he growled. "Where's the guard?"

"Inside?" Heidi guessed. She didn't look at me at all but went darting off toward where the horses were tied. A moment later she was back with the Winchester. "See anything yet?" she asked, breathless, of Jeff. "We better spread out a little."

He kept his eyes on the stage which now was in plain sight. "I warned you," he said. "They probably hit it at Burnt Woman."

I said, "There comes your hostler."

A feller in sun-faded jeans had stepped out of the station; at an old man's pokey saddle-cramped gait he set off to fetch up the teams from the pen. Heidi suddenly said, "That's not Fred!"

The stage was braking to swing into the yard when the man she said wasn't Fred, shoving open the gate, led out his replacements. "By God, you're right!" Jeff cried, lifting his rifle.

"Wait!" I said. "We better make sure."

But he wasn't going to wait; I could see it in his eyes.

I done the only thing I could do, whacked out with the barrel of Quail's .45-90. It took him in the muscle of that outstretched left arm. His gun went off but the shot went wild and he staggered back off balance, so furious mad he could scarcely speak. "What's the matter with you?"

"Look—" Heidi grabbed me. I could see her mouth moving but the rest was lost in the blast of a double explosion whooming up from the yard of the station. The still-smoking tubes of a Greener were oked from a curtain of the now stopped coach and beyond it, looking more than anything like a blown-over scarecrow, was the sprawled motionless shape of the feller who wasn't Fred. "He was fixing to stick up the stage," Heidi said. "See, there's his pistol!"

Feeling kind of hung-over I sloshed my stare back at Jeff. He had his gun up again. Only now, down here, there was nobody showing for him to drive his lead at. "Where in hell is the rest of them varmints!" He sure looked confused, out of sorts and half ugly.

"Where they always been," I said, sounding bitter. "With the rest of the loose talk that's been heaved around Post Oak. You still think they stopped that coach at Burnt Woman?"

"Anyone can make a mistake," he growled, sheepish.

"You made several," I said. "Now let go of that rifle before you make another."

He gaped at me like I'd tried to kick him in the belly. "Drop it," I snarled, shaking off Heidi's arm. "I ain't funnin' with you!"

Blowing out a great breath he let go of his shooter.

"Step outa that belt."

Like he was humoring a child the fat man done it.

"Git back away from them."

Dayne backed off, eyes rolling at Heidi. "You make any sense out of this?"

"She will," I said, "when she's had time to think a bit. And so will Mark Harra and the rest of them owners you been pointin' Charley's gun at."

"Harra," Jeff sighed. "I'm glad you dug his name from the pot—ought to show how crazy mixed-up you've got. If it's me you've picked for the brains of this outfit, how you goin' to explain *him* to Heidi? Grabbin' those claims an' bushwhackin' her daddy!"

"I been waitin' for you to get around to that. Heidi," I said, "get them stage fellas up here."

She looked from him to me. But not being one to swap broncs in midstream she set reluctantly off, pushing into the junipers, still toting the Winchester this fat crook had loaned me.

"I guess," he sneered, "you *have* come unstuck if you figure they'll walk off an' leave that specie."

Heidi heard him and paused. "Surely you didn't really think he'd send for it." She loosed a shaky laugh. "You must be even more gullible than me!"

She went on.

Dayne looked stunned. His mouth begun to tremble. "Be careful!" I said, stepping in toward him quickly. "You don't want to wind up like Charley down there!"

But he had nothing left to lose except his life; he was caught, and knew it. His arm flashed up, white hand blurring back. I hit him hard as I could with the barrel of Quail's big game gun. The knife fell out of his fist as he went down in a slanchways heap, squealing like a goddamn pig.

I said, "There ain't much doubt about where you stand *now*," and kicked all the weapons out of his reach. I stepped away from him.

Heidi came hurrying up with the driver and a rough looking oldish gent with a shotgun. Which last, with a hard sounding grunt of satisfaction, fetched his stare from the whimpering Dayne to growl, "Phipstadt here." He grabbed my paw and pumped it. "Reckon you're Farris. That varmint fit to travel?"

Jeff, moaning pitiful, dragged himself up. "Why, you've broke his arm." Heidi said, and I nodded.

"He tries any more tricks I'll break somethin' else. Now I'll tell you about Harra. It stands to reason he *ought* them claims. It's my idea he paid over that money and Farley, who witnessed it, tipped off Jeff. Jeff sent Grant's Pass to grab the loot and get rid of Heidi's dad. We'll prob'ly never prove it but it's the only thing that fits.

"Having got away with that, Jeff decided to throw he hooks into the rest of you big owners, and hatched up with Charley these payroll stickups. That saloon of his was the finest kind of place to start rumors. Then Farley got to nosin' around; mebbe he put the bite on Jeff. They had to get rid of him.

"Which is where I come in. Longly an' Geet tried to pin it on me. I'd broke a chair over Geet an' made him look silly. I'd knocked the marshall flat on his butt an' called his brother a horse thief in public. Both of them wanted me outa their hair. I don't think Geet had anything to do with this but Longly was tryin' to cover up for Grant's Pass. I think he must have known Charley was up to his ears in this business; he may even of known Jeff was roddin' the deal.

When Geet told him I'd been over to the Boll Weevil they tried to pound a confession out of me. Longly, when that didn't work, went to Harra. Harra had hired me to fetch in a payroll.

"When I went over yesterday the marshal was with him, guess he made me out a pretty desperate character. Harra made out he'd filled the job. Longly," I scowled, swabbing sweat off my jaw, "was all wound up to take a pot at me. Just as he got himself braced to do it Verdugo walked in—girl that sings at the Weevil. Jeff had spread it around she was gone on Charley; I reckon what she was is their go-between. When she come in I busted outa there."

"How'd you come to suspect him?" asked Phipstadt.

"Passel of little things begun to add up. Remember that snake?" I said to Heidi. "You had his rifle, that Winchester he'd loaned me. 'Be still!' he yelled when you started to reach for it. He'd already mentioned your havin' the gun—seemed to want it in *my* hands. And then he didn't want to come here, kept hollerin' Burnt Woman." I said to her, grinning, "Point that gun at him now an' pull the trigger."

She looked shocked. "He's no better than Charley," I said. "Go ahead."

Phipstadt nodded. With considerable reluctance she lifted the rifle. Pointing the barrel at the sky she pulled the trigger. Nothing happened, of course. She squeezed the trigger several times. The gun wouldn't fire.

Phipstadt said, "Guess that settles it. Ought to
.oot him out of hand, but he'll have his trial. A
iner's court oughtn't to take much longer. You just
ave him to us." He nodded to the driver, then con-
dered me and Heidi. "No sense you two havin' to
rushing back—prob'ly got things you want to talk
/er." He said, kind of grinning, "There's a preacher,
heard, puttin' up at Three Pines. Just write out
ur depositions an' I'll take 'em on back with Dayne
the stage."

That's exactly what we done.

Don't miss *Cheyenne #2: Death Chant!*
Available in November
at bookstores and newsstands
everywhere.

SPECIAL BONUS PREVIEW
FOLLOWS!

Although still not accepted by Chief Yellow Bear's tribe, Touch the Sky continues his warrior training. But while off in the wilderness learning new skills, he and the other Indian youths stumble across a new threat to their people—and if they cannot stop it, innocent Cheyenne blood will turn the grassy plains red!

CHEYENNE #2:
DEATH CHANT

Black Elk spotted something and knelt to examine the grassy bank of the river. Then he gathered the others around him and pointed to the tracks. "Iron hooves," he said. "White men's horses."

Black Elk showed them how to read the bend of the grass to tell how recent the tracks were. These were very fresh—the lush grass was still nearly pressed flat. A short distance along the bank, Touch the Sky and the others gaped in astonishment—the single set of tracks was joined by at least a dozen others!

They reached a huge dogleg bend in the river and worked their way through the thorny thickets in single file. The steady chuckle of the river helped to cover the sound of their passage. Touch the Sky emerged from the bend, following Little Horse, and cautiously poked his head around a hawthorn bush.

It took several long moments to understand what he was seeing. When the enormity of it finally sank in, he felt hot bile rise in his throat. Only a supreme effort kept him from retching.

The scene was a comfortable river camp. There were several pack mules, one of them asleep over its picket. The hindquarters of an elk bull hung high in a tree to protect it from predators. Buffalo robes and beaver pelts were heaped

everywhere, pressed into flat packs for transporting. The a
was sharp with the pungent smell of castoreum, the orang
brown secretion of the beaver. Touch the Sky knew it ga
off a strong, wild odor and was used by trappers as a lu
to set their traps.

But what made his gorge rise was the three naked, hideou
ly slaughtered white men in the middle of the camp.

All three had been scalped. They had also been castrat
and their genitals stuffed into their mouths. Their eyes h
been gouged out and placed on nearby rocks, where th
seemed to stare longingly at the bodies they had once belon
ed to.

The camp was crawling with living white men, who we
heavily armed. The strings of their fringed buckskins h
been blackened by constant exposure to the blood of de
animals. And while Touch the Sky watched, one of the
knelt beside a fourth dead man. Expertly, he made a c
around the top of the dead man's head. Then he rose, o
foot on his victim's neck, and violently jerked the bloo
scalp loose.

Touch the Sky looked away when the man castrated t
corpse and gouged his eyes out with the point of his kni
The buckskin-clad man worked casually, as if he were di
ging grubs out of old wood.

The man turned toward him and Touch the Sky took a go
look. Some instinct warned him this was a face he shou
know. The man was tall and thickset, he wore his lon
greasy hair tied in a knot. When he turned, Touch the S
saw a deep, livid gash running from the corner of his l
eye well past the corner of his mouth.

The huge man with the scar appeared to be in charg
Occasionally he barked an order that Touch the Sky cou
not hear from that range. Whoever and whatever these m
were, this slaughter appeared to be all in a day's work
them. One of the men was calmly boiling a can of coff
and mixing meal with water to form little balls. He toss

them into the ashes to cook. The leader casually scooped a handful out of the ashes and munched on them while his other hand still held the dripping scalp.

He barked out another command, and another of his men began folding beaver traps and lashing them to a pack mule. Only then did Touch the Sky become aware of all the whiskey bottles scattered throughout camp. Spotting more unopened bottles in cases lashed to the mules, the youth realized what had probably happened. The murderers had made their victims stuporous with spirits, then killed them in their sleep.

The scene was so horrible that Touch the Sky nearly cried out when a hand fell on his shoulder. But it was only Little Horse, showing him that Black Elk was signalling the retreat.

"There are too many and they are well armed. We must return to Yellow Bear's camp at once and report this in council!" Black Elk said as soon as they were out of earshot. "I care nothing if the paleface devils slaughter one another. But I fear a great storm of trouble will come—these killings were done so as to seem that red men did them!"

CHEYENNE

**Born Indian, raised white,
he'd die a free man!**

#2: DEATH CHANT
by Judd Cole

When he left the home of his adopted parents and returned
to his people, young Matthew Hanchon found that the
Cheyenne could not fully trust anyone raised in the ways of
the white man. Forced to prove his loyalty, Matthew faced
the greatest challenge he had ever known. And when the
death chant arose, Hanchon knew if he failed he would not
die alone.

WATCH FOR OTHER ACTION-PACKED
CHEYENNE NOVELS—
COMING SOON TO BOOKSTORES AND
NEWSSTANDS EVERYWHERE.

_3337-2 $3.50 US/$4.50 CAN

Young guns, old-time action!

CHET CUNNINGHAM

The Willy Boy Gang was made up of the youngest lawbreakers on the frontier, but each was ten times as deadly as any man twice his age. All six had a vendetta to settle, and they vowed to ride until every one of them had tasted revenge.

#4: AVENGERS. Headed for Denver, where the Professor had more than one score to even, the Willy Boy Gang planned to drain every cent from the Denver First Colorado Bank and murder any one who stood in their way.

___2896-4 $2.95

#5: RIO GRANDE REVENGE. Deadly *federales* had taken Juan Romero's wife and son hostage. But Romero and the gang would free them — even if they had to drown the corrupt officers in pools of their own blood.

___2967-7 $2.95

#6: FLAGSTAFF SHOWDOWN. In Arizona to save Gunner Johnson's mother from an embezzler, the gang had more than their share of trouble. For the swindler was desperate enough to kill them all — and crazy enough to succeed.

___3154-X $2.95 US/$3.95 CAN

LEISURE BOOKS
ATTN: Order Department
276 5th Avenue, New York, NY 10001

Please add $1.50 for shipping and handling for the first book and $.35 for each book thereafter. N.Y.S. and N.Y.C. residents, please add appropriate sales tax. No cash, stamps, or C.O.D.s. All orders shipped within 6 weeks via postal service book rate. Canadian orders require $2.00 extra postage. It must also be paid in U.S. dollars through a U.S. banking facility.

Name_____
Address_____
City _____ State _____ Zip _____
I have enclosed $_____in payment for the checked book(s).
Payment **must** accompany all orders.☐ Please send a free catalog.